MW01356346

Not since Marc[illegible]
there been a word on the whereabouts of the huge treasure in gold and precious gems that he brought back home with him.

The world is in for a shock . . .

In the far reaches of western China a psychopathic ex-Soviet mercenary plots the restoration of Genghis Khan's empire.

A Harvard professor knows too much and disappears . . .

Dr. Marya Bradwell and antiquities dealer Liam Di Angelo clash instantly at first sight as rivals for historic gold artifacts. They are about to learn that they both face a shadowy, common enemy and that they are on to a high-stakes secret effort to carve out an empire that will rock China and Russia to their foundations!

GOLD OF THE KHAN

BY BRANDON PHILIPS

A compelling historical adventure!

Gold of the Khan

BRANDON PHILIPS

In Memory of Genie

This story is a work of fiction. Names, characters, places and events are either products of the author's imagination or used fictitiously. Any resemblance to real settings, events and persons, living or dead, is purely coincidental.

ISBN 978-0-9857230-0-2 e-book
ISBN 978-0-9857230-1-9 pbk

Cover design by Barbara Pope Book Designs
Text design by Wanda China

CONTENTS

Prologue
1

Gold of the Khan
7

Afterword
509

PROLOGUE

A remote region of the Donets Basin, Ukraine, May 14, 1993

Five Tajik tomb raiders worked feverishly, scraping away the last few shovels of soil covering broad wooden planks. The ancient planks were part of the ceiling of a Scythian royal tomb that had lain buried under a thirty-five foot high mound for over two millenia. Three days of sweaty, grinding labor was about to pay off, like their other digs across the Asian steppe. The leader of the team grabbed a long-handled lever and ordered the others to stand off to the side.

Looking down at them from the rim of the excavation was their collaborator, Gregor Shevchenko, a white-haired official of the Ministerstvo Vutrishnikh Sprav Ukrayiny, the Ukrainian Ministry of the Interior. He wore a padded blue jacket with a fur collar and the sleeve patch of the Ukraine's anti-terrorist unit, King Eagle. As he circled the pit, his left hand tightened its grip on the handle of the Glock hidden in his pocket. Through his connections with the state oil monopoly he had been able to secretly divert a 178 horse-power Chetra 40 bulldozer and an MKSM 800 excavator to the site.

The Tajiks had located the burial mound, contacted him and struck a deal. They were obviously skilled and disciplined, he had to admit. But without saying as much, Shevchenko regarded them as foreigners on Ukrainian soil and, by his reckoning, the Ukraine was entitled to the lion's share of whatever they dug up.

For two days, the large yellow bulldozer had torn into

the south flank of the broad, circular mound and carved out a gaping wedge. Occasionally the bulldozer heaved violently as it struck buried slabs of rock but the operator skillfully worked them off to the side and piled tons of earth a short distance from the pit.

The Tajik leader of the team was a snaggle-toothed man with spectacles who called himself Shahryar. He had closely supervised his men on the project for three days. He sensed exactly when to call off the bulldozer and call in the excavator and exactly when to order his men into the pit with picks and shovels. At dusk of the third day, he had sets of floodlights turned on around the rim and one set mounted on a tripod planted in the soft earth down in the pit. Within minutes after nightfall, the men finished clearing away the soil and stood back when Shahryar took over with his lever. He loosened the rough-hewn planks and then got down on his knees with a pry-bar. In no time he was able to lift two of the wide planks with his bare hands and pull them off to the side. He got down on his knees again, peered into the gloom of the chamber, waving his flashlight from side to side and let out a gasp. "Hurry, get some lights down here," he ordered, before slipping into the musty tomb.

The chamber contained a plain wooden sarcophagus. He ripped its top off with his pry-bar. Inside he found the skeletal remains of a couple lying with their heads oriented to the west. The female lay behind the male, embracing him with her right arm. Enormous quantities of gold jewelry and other artifacts covered their remains and littered the ground around the sarcophagus. He called three men in. Working with speed, the team gathered up gold battleaxes, clasps and pendants in the forms of panthers, tigers, stags, goats and horses. They also collected model chariots, helmets, sword hilts, two death masks, combs embellished with humans in battle as well as thick, twisted necklaces and bracelets with the motif of mythical animals—all of gold—and loaded them into the crate. When the crate was full, Shahryar had it hauled up to a nearby truck and loaded onto the truck bed with a hydraulic lift.

Working by himself on the treasure-laden skeleton of the female, he focused on what looked like a crown. He leaned into the sarcophagus and carefully worked his fingers underneath its beautiful leaves to disentangle it from the skull. With the slight motion that he made to lift the ornament, the cranium fell apart, but the gold ornament remained in his hands completely intact. Slowly, gently, he lifted it away from the sarcophagus and held it overhead. It was a diadem of surpassing beauty. Its parts gleamed brightly in the harsh light of the electric lamps. With its elegant ring of laurel leaves and glittering spangles, it looked startlingly modern. The workers in the chamber stopped what they were doing and looked up in awe. Up above, on the rim of the excavation, Shevchenko noticed a curious silence. He called down to Shahryar and asked what was happening. Shahryar moved to the opening and held the diadem up to give Shevchenko a look. Then he put it into a small chest and passed it up to him.

The men got back to work filling a second crate. Among the most valuable items going into it were goblets, a heavy pectoral, a rounded clasp in the shape of a lioness, a dagger pommel and a stag with oversized horns. Leaving the three men on their own, Shahryar crawled out of the tomb to inspect the work done by a lone worker outside the burial chamber. He knew that typically, Scythian royalty went down to the underworld with many human and animal sacrifices that remained outside the burial chamber in a "death pit." This burial was no different. The worker had found the remains of nine human victims and five thick-necked horses. As experienced as Shahryar was with such digs, his stomach turned at the grisly sight.

He saw right away that the items from the death pit

lacked the quality of those found in the burial chamber. There were some ceremonial horse bits, several bracelets and dozens of small, thinly-hammered gold sheets that were used to decorate clothes and horse equipment. But he was disappointed that many of the items had been crushed, either from clumsy trampling or from the weight of tons of earth sitting on them for over two-thousand years.

Still, he was pleased with the total haul, knowing that several of the pieces, especially the diadem, would find a prime place in the personal collection of the Khan. He climbed to the surface, letting his men finish up and remove the last of the treasure. He took a cigarette out, lit up and gazed at the inky black sky. He exhaled slowly. It was now time to neutralize Shevchenko.

As he moved toward Shevchenko, a helicopter suddenly appeared and passed overhead. Shahryar, suspicious, followed its path to the east. "What was that?"

"An oil company helicopter out surveying the basin."

"On a Saturday night?"

"Why not? Money knows no limits."

Shahryar was not happy with the answer. "It had better be what you say it is… I'll take that, thank you," he said, reaching out for the chest that held the diadem.

"Afraid not."

"What? Hand it over. We have a deal. We're keeping that for our Khan. You've already been well paid."

"To hell with your Khan. This is Ukrainian soil and this treasure is ours."

"The Khan has already been fully informed of this excavation. He expects results from it and when he hears of this, he will have you killed."

"You are threatening *me?* Do you realize how stupid you sound? This is not Tajikistan or wherever you say you're from. This is the Ukraine and what is unearthed here is ours." Shevchenko drew the Glock from his pocket.

Shahryar backed up and raised his hands in surrender. "All right. We'll be generous. You can have half of the treasure." He looked over his shoulder, giving a nod to his workers. They quickly scrambled out of the grave behind him, each holding a gun. There was a momentary lull as Shahryar smirked at Shevchenko.

A burst of submachine fire broke the silence. The Tajiks looked up in terror, past Shevchenko, and saw two men advancing towards the pit, their AK-47s at the ready. Shevchenko grinned. "Tell your men to toss their weapons."

Shahryar complied and gave the order. His men dropped their guns in the dirt.

"That's good. Now, pick one of these four men and have him sit down over there in front of the Chetra."

Shahryar pointed to one of them and ordered him to sit in front of the yellow monster.

Shevchenko wagged his gun under Sharyar's nose. "I am a merciful man. I am going to spare your lives and let you leave the Ukraine by any means you can. We're taking the truck."

Shahryar was furious. "How will we get out of here? The road is miles from here."

"You'll find a way to get back to your Khan, I'm sure."

"What about him?" Shahryar asked, pointing at the pitiful man rocking in abject terror in front of the bulldozer.

"Well, my friend, I counted only nine sacrificial victims in the death pit. One short in my estimation... I'm throwing him in for good measure. Now, get the hell out of here if you don't want to spend eternity with the king and the queen down there."

Shahryar spoke urgently to his men. The three ran off into the hills even before he had finished translating. Then he tossed his cigarette and faced Shevchenko. "The Khan will learn of this, you infidel bastard, and he will track you down. You won't live to enjoy one ounce of this treasure." He turned and walked off into the darkness but stopped around the bend of a hill when he heard inhuman screaming that sent a shudder through his body. He heard a gunshot and the sound of the heavy engine of the Chetra being fired up. Shrieking, terror-filled screams rose over the noise of the bulldozer as it roared into action. One last heart-rending cry for help rang out. Shahryar cursed at the vast star-lit sky of the Ukraine and set off into the night, certain that the Khan would deal quickly with Shevchenko.

CHAPTER 1

Cambridge, Massachusetts, May 21, 1993

Marya Bradwell was about to leave her apartment for her morning undergraduate class in Western Civilization when the phone in the foyer of her Cambridge apartment rang.

"Hello? Dr. Bradwell?"

"Oh, Vittoria. You caught me…"

It was Vittoria Rodoni, her petite, blonde research assistant in Venice, calling about her pay or, rather, the lack of it. Marya had been expecting the worst—that Vittoria was calling to announce she was quitting after two years of hard, but promising research. There was an awkward pause. "Dr. Bradwell, I hate to bring this up with you. It's embarrassing, but I have to. I just can't continue working for you unless I'm paid this week. I have nothing to live on. I'm literally starving. If it weren't for my parents…"

Marya could not put her off again as she had so often done recently and she knew it. Vittoria, a higly intelligent girl, had been committed to the project all along; but now, Marya could sense nervousness in her rapid-fire Italian. The girl has definitely reached her limit, she thought. *Like me.* Realizing it might take a while and a lot of persuasion to keep her from bailing out, she put down her briefcase.

From the hallway credenza beneath an oval mirror, she picked up a framed sepia photo of her grandmother and studied it as she listened to Vittoria. She glanced at her watch. During the last spring break, she and the twenty-three year old assistant had spent two whole weeks, poring over collections of ancient documents in the Venetian

State Archives, in libraries and in private collections—all of which dated back to the 13th century. Vittoria was brilliant, dedicated and indispensable. Their work in highly restricted research environments had yielded some tantalizing discoveries about Marco Polo's personal estate and its disposition. It had been, at times, brutal, mind-numbing tedium, but Vittoria had never slackened or wavered in her commitment to the project.

During her stay in Venice, she and Vittoria had found a few leads. In several ancient petitions filed before the Maggior Consiglio, the City Council of Venice, they had found mention of certain famous solid gold artifacts described by Polo as gifts from Kublai Khan to aid them in their voyage back to Italy. Marya knew that the gold artifacts were rare Golden Tablets of Command, about a half inch thick, as wide as a human hand and a cubit in length, or, about as long as the average human forearm. Kublai had them engraved with a dire warning to all the people of his vast empire to assist the Polos in their travels westward or face execution.

But Marya and Vittoria's research had so far found no hint of the fate of the tablets, nor of the fabled hoard of jewels that Marco, his father Nicolo and his uncle Maffeo had amassed in their long, amazing years of residence at the court of the Mongol Khan.

When spring break had ended, she had retained Vittoria to continue following the interesting leads. She told her that she would keep in touch with her by email and send her bi-monthly payments for her work and expenses. Marya returned to Boston to teach several sections of Western Civilization and had kept up the payments through April, when her finances tanked and she stopped sending Vittoria her payments. She had appealed to Dr. Samuel Lafferty, Chairman of the Department of History, for funds for the ongoing research, but he had turned her down. Since then, she had given Vittoria nothing but excuses.

"I hear what you're saying, Vittoria, and I wish I could say the check is in the mail but frankly, I have to tell you, I'm broke. Can you hold out a little longer?

"There's no way, Dr. Bradwell. My parents..."

"I'll tell you what. If you can hold on for one more week, when I get paid, I can wire you some money. How about that? Please don't quit now."

"But, Doctor Bradwell, my father is angry. He wants me to find another job."

Marya scrutinized her grandmother's face in the old photograph. She raised the picture and touched her forehead with it. "No, no, no. Please. Hang in there, Vittoria. Wait. I'll tell you what. I'll wire you some funds this evening after work. You'll have something at least to show for all your work. Three-hundred dollars. Will that be okay for now?

"Thank you, Dr. Bradwell. I really hated to call you about this."

Marya closed her eyes in silent relief. *Will my bank balance cover the check?* "It's all right, Vittoria. You've earned it, and I've been tardy with your pay, I have to admit. By the way, have you found anything new in the records of the Maggior Consiglio?"

"Yes, I have. As a matter of fact I found something that was very strange. It might not be important, but I should mention it. It's a document written by Padre Giustiniani that was intended for the Council."

Giustiniani! Marco Polo's confessor and notary. In the mirror, Marya saw her own eyes reflect alertness. "Giustiniani? Are you sure?"

"Yes. I found it just sitting in the middle of volume seven, loose."

"We haven't seen this one before?"

"Correct."

"Can you sum it up fast? I've got to leave for class in

a minute." She knew that little Lafferty, the bantam rooster department chair, would squawk if she showed up late for class again. There was a pause during which she heard Vittoria shuffling some papers.

"Okay. Wait. I have a photocopy of it. Here it is. The padre tells the Council that he was in Marco Polo's bedroom with him moments before his death. Polo asked him to get his private journal from a chest next to his bed for him, but the instant Giustiniani turned around to do that, Polo died. Polo had told him that he wanted him to deliver the journal to one of his daughters."

When Marya heard this she fumbled with the picture of her grandmother. It fell from her hands onto the edge of the table and crashed onto the floor. Glass shards flew across the hallway floor. She jumped to avoid the spray of flying glass. "Oh, no! Dear God."

"What's the matter, Dr. Bradwell?"

"Nothing, nothing. I just dropped something and it broke." She moved away from the glass splinters on the floor and drew in a deep breath. *Wait just one minute. A journal? What journal?* "What did you just say, Vittoria? A journal written by Marco Polo?"

"That's what the document seems to say, if my translation is correct. My medieval Italian is not what it should be, but, yes, I'm almost certain that Giustiniani refers to a personal journal of Polo's."

"I'm not aware…wait…there's been speculation about such a journal but there's never been a trace of one. As far as I know, he only wrote one thing that has survived, and that was his book of travels. Is the letter authentic? You said it was a loose page. Is there a signature on it?"

"Yes, it was signed by Giovanni Giustiniani, priest of San Proculo and Notary. And yes, it is authentic. I've seen samples of his signature on other wills, believe me."

"Which daughter did he want to give the journal to?"

"To Moreta, the one who entered the Convent of San Lorenzo."

"My goodness! That's amazing. Look, Vittoria, I have to hurry now; but I have an idea. Could you do something for me right away? It's mid-afternoon in Venice, right? So, I think that you still have time to do it. Get yourself over to the convent library and see if you can find any trace of such a journal. I mean, any mention of it whatsoever. Will you do that? I know it's a long shot, but it's important."

"The convent is not far. I can do it."

Marya wanted to scream halleluiah but she managed a calm reply. "If you find anything at all on Polo, get back to me by phone or email, will you? This is exciting, Vittoria. I've got to run. Call me tonight, Okay? Ciao."

"Ciao."

She took a long look into the sapphire blue eyes in her mirror and straightened her shoulders, asking herself why she should really worry about that petulant, whiny Lafferty and his anal compulsions. She quickly fluffed her long, chestnut hair and picked up her briefcase. Tiptoeing around the broken glass, she headed for the door, cheered by the prospect of actually finding the journal of Marco Polo, the world's most renowned adventurer.

* * * * *

Marya pulled into the parking lot and hurried across campus to the old, red brick classroom building. Her mind was already scripting itself for the lecture she was about to give, but at times, her thoughts circled back to the insanely wonderful news that Vittoria had just given her. Sighting Dr. Lafferty, the chairman of the History Department, however, was like a dunk in a pool of ice-cold water. The last time she had approached him on more funding for her research on Polo, he had refused without hesitation, telling her that her project was foolish nonsense. He had also warned her in his near-falsetto voice that without a new, respectable publication, her chances of winning tenure would be in jeopardy. *Blah blah blah and blah blah blah. I'm so tired of hearing that.* She dashed up the stone staircase to the entrance of the ivy-covered classroom building, arriving for her nine o'clock class out of breath. A young fellow, one of her students in a Western Civ section, greeted her on the stairs, but just behind him, at the top, stood Lafferty, holding a packet for her. He ogled his wristwatch and furrowed his brow. "Good morning, Marya. Late again."

She climbed the last two stairs and stood in front of him, looking down at his gleaming scalp. She ignored his sarcasm. "Good morning, Sam."

He thrust a bundle of papers at her. "Here are the evaluation forms you need to hand out this morning. Have the students fill them out and leave them with the monitor. Tell him to bring them directly up to my office. We also need to go over your grant proposal and a few other things. We'll see you promptly at 10:10 upstairs in my office." He turned and headed down the hallway, leaving her lip-syncing his namby pamby style.

She took the packet of evaluation forms, entered class, and laid it on her desk. She always felt in her element with her students. The students in the large lecture hall were mostly seated and talking with one another while she went about preparing her slideshow and arranging her lecture notes at the podium. For her final lecture of the semester, she had decided to use the case of the amateur German archaeologist, Heinrich Schliemann, as her focal point. She thought that Schliemann's notorious excavations at the mound of Hissarlik in modern Turkey and his extraordinary claim to have unearthed "The Treasure of Priam" of the lost city of Troy would be a fun way to wrap up the semester.

Without any overt signal from her, it seemed, the

entire hall came to attention. She adjusted a little microphone device, picked up her laser pointer, and launched immediately into her lecture and slide show. She skilllfully wove the story of Schliemann's life, his travels, financial success and his highly controversial excavations at Hissarlik. What she found most interesting about the man, she said, was that few of his contemporaries even believed in the real existence of Troy. Not only did Schliemann believe that it had really existed, but also, the Greek classics he so loved would point the way to it. Excavating the eastern half of the hill of Hissarlik, he exposed one layer after another of a very ancient city that had at times seen the ravages of war. Marya was well aware that academics questioned his findings but there was little doubt that he did discover a large treasure trove of gold objects, establishing his name in archaeology for better or for worse. *And I wouldn't mind making an earth-shattering discovery like that myself* she mused.

Towards the close of the lecture, Marya placed the red laser dot on the photographic image of Schliemann's beautiful Greek wife, Sophia. Working side by side with her, as he later claimed, he found the trove while the Turkish laborers he employed slept nearby. Marya explained how later, in the privacy of their quarters, his wife pleaded with him to let her place a shimmering diadem from the dig on her own head. She brought a photo of the dark-eyed beauty wearing the gold crown up on the screen. The elaborate headdress drew admiring ooohs and aaahs from the students.

"It's a masterpiece, isn't it? Schliemann should not have let her wear such a precious artifact, but he did because he loved her. He was not a trained archaeologist. Still, not bad for an amateur, don't you agree?" The students responded with nods and laughs.

She brought up more slides of the "Treasure of Priam" for the wide-eyed audience and ended with the story of how the Schliemanns fled Turkey with the treasure, much to the anger of the Turkish government. "This would be a big no-no today, of course, when you consider the laws pertaining to cultural art and all the organizations that exist today to protect against such theft. The Schliemanns might not have gotten away with this loot in this century." She scanned the lecture hall. "Any questions before we take up housekeeping matters?"

One of the young men raised a hand. She recognized Brendan McGuigan. "Yes, Brendan?"

"Are there any chances of finding a big treasure like that today? That would be so cool."

"Well, I'd say 'yes' without a doubt. You saw how Schliemann didn't let the naysayers and the critics stop him. Sure, his work was controversial, but the point is that you have to believe in yourself, trust your instincts and look for the grain of truth in the written legends." She wondered if she should be more explicit and tell the students that that was precisely what she was doing in her own search for proof of Polo's travels to Asia. She decided not to go there except to throw out a hint, "Marco Polo is someone who comes to mind. The world called him a liar and a story-teller. I happen to think there is something of substance there, but so far no one has come across one single precious stone or gold bar from the treasure that he and the elder Polos bragged about."

Patty Miller, a thin, mousy-haired graduate student in the second row, raised the question of Polo's trustworthiness, however. "Dr. Bradwell, what do you think about the book by the Chinese expert at the British Museum, Elizabeth McManus? She claims that Polo did nothing more than pick up stories he heard from Arab traders around the Black Sea who had been to China. She says that all he did was paste all their tales together in his book of travels to create the illusion that he had really been there. She claims that his book was a fictional adventure, just a myth that has grown and grown over the last seven centuries."

Marya rolled her eyes. "Elizabeth McManus. Well, that sounds just like her. I've seen her at lots of conferences and it's always the same old tune. I don't think she's updated those old yellow notes of hers from forty years ago since she got her Ph. D. in 1970. I know what she thinks of Polo's Description of the World. But there has been a lot of new scholarship on this subject since her day, including my own." Marya inwardly recalled a bruising debate she had at Oxford's Trinity College with McManus. The old gal pulled no punches and threw Polo out as a faker along with anyone who defended the factuality of his story. "I'm sorry. Let's just say that modern scholarship has simply passed Elizabeth McManus by. I could answer your question in detail, but I'm afraid it would take some time."

The young lady persisted. "Just a quick overview, if you can."

Marya hesitated to waste time for the other students but they looked interested in how she would answer. She retrieved a file from her briefcase and cited a recent article based on Persian records that definitely mentioned all three Polos in Persia on the return voyage from Beijing in 1295. She also cited an article of her own based on material from the Secret History of the Yuan Dynasty. That source gave transliterations of foreign names that were none other than those of Nicolo, Maffeo and Marco Polo. Both of those sources describe the foreigners as very wealthy foreign merchants hired by Kublai Khan personally. How's that, Patty?" *If I ever had a chance for a showdown with that McManus again, I'd mop the floor with her.*

"Any other kind of evidence?" the young lady asked dryly.

"Yes, of an indirect nature. I've found an intriguing report done by the Institute of Anthropology at the University in Croatia, the Dubrovnik campus. Croatia is Italy's neighbor to the east. It tells of DNA tests done in Croatia in the wake of the terrible ethnic cleansings carried out by the Serbian president Milosevich. Listen to this. They have found evidence of Chinese genes entering several family lines in the region near Dubrovnik. The population is predominantly Slavic there. The tests estimate that the genes entered the pool anywhere between seven and nine hundred years ago."

"How do you interpret that? What are you saying?" the young lady asked.

"I don't see proof of a direct tie-in with Marco Polo or his family in this data at this time. DNA doesn't come with family names attached, but isn't it interesting that microbiology has proven connections between the Far East and Europe, even though recorded history makes no mention of them? And the time frame is about right. It is at least possible that the Polos returned from China to the Adriatic with some Chinese travelers in their party and stopped along the coast before arriving in Venice a few days later."

"And you're suggesting that this Chinese person or these Chinese people intermarried with a Slavic tribe near Dubrovnik?"

"Correct. That's a possibility that's within the scope of the report. Historically, there were only a few Europeans who went to China across the Eurasian continent during the 13th century of Mongol rule and returned to tell of it. The Polos were among that rarified circle of adventurers. And they were the only ones we know of who took this route along the Adriatic coast."

"Wow. But why would any Chinese person come all that distance when they believed that their empire was the center of the world?"

"I'm sorry. That's a mystery. We only have the biological evidence that we can cite from this study. We have no idea what was going on in their minds to take up such an arduous trek to the West."

"Doctor Bradwell," said another student, "It looks like you've done your homework on the subject. Why don't you go out and hunt for the Polo treasure yourself?"

"That would be fun," she said, glad that she hadn't gone much further in her Polo example. "Who knows?"

She looked around the hall once more. "Is that it? Then let's take up our last chore today, the evaluations. The administration will use them in evaluating my performance, so be merciful." With the help of two volunteers, she passed out the forms and the students immediately set to work on them. "Good luck on the final exam tomorrow and don't forget to leave your glowing evaluations with the monitor as you leave."

The class had gone well and she knew she would have no problems with negative evaluations. During the lull she busied herself with packing away her slide collection and her notes. She daydreamed for a few moments about an encounter with Elizabeth McManus and seeing her go down like the Maine under a barrage of unshakeable evidence. She even imagined striding into a debate on stage at Trinity College, in a kind of sequel to the debate, dramatically opening a finely worked wooden chest containing one of the great Golden Tablets of Command. That would cinch it. Such a coup would at once guarantee her a fully tenured professorship in History at Harvard or any one of America's most prestigious universities and make her the world-class authority on Polo in her own right. Relishing the thought before leaving for her appointment upstairs, she smoothed her hair back into a pony-tail.

* * * * *

Marya turned left into the hallway outside the lecture hall and almost bumped into Dr. Khalid Agarwal, the department's expert on South and Central Asia. He was a supportive colleague, and one of the few in the department that she personally liked. She had long had a tender spot in her heart for him and it seemed to be growing in recent months, though she was still not sure he had a serious relationship with her in mind. On occasion she enjoyed fine dinners in Boston with him and a few after-work drinks in Harvard Square but she thought she was ready for more. She found him darkly handsome and his graying beard distinguished. He reminded her of Omar Sharif. Very sexy. In fact, she felt herself blush when she remembered a passionate dream that she had about him the week before. When would he see the signs of a deeper interest in her eyes and take their relationship to another level? Had he been standing very long outside her open classroom door observing her, she wondered?

"Those were certainly the most stirring comments I've ever heard in praise of Schliemann."

"Don't start in on me, Khalid. You're just as bad with your hero-worship of the Moghal rulers of India."

"Hero worship? Oh, come on. I'm not that bad, am I?"

"Not that bad? Hellooo. You're a wild-eyed fanatic." She laughed and reached for his hand.

He clasped hers and held it tenderly. "So, are you ready for Lafferty this morning?"

"I'm really dreading it. It's not just Lafferty. It's Chen and Roache, too. Ugh. Lafferty has been yackety yacking with me about not publishing enough articles and he's holding it over my head. And, of course, the old boys have been sitting tight on the department's budget. I'm getting no support for my research on Polo. I just don't get it. Why do I have to fight so hard to get anything from them? Why do they ridicule my work?"

He gave her hand a light squeeze. "I think they're just jealous of your popularity with the students. I'll see what I can do for you at the meeting."

"I appreciate that. But still, why can't they see the urgency and the relevance of my research, Khalid? If I find concrete proof of the Polos' visits to China, it would be like a bomb going off in historical circles."

"Where are you right now with the project? Any progress in tracking down that Polo fortune?" Khalid Agarwal had listened to her many times talk about her pet project, applauding her little successes and constantly cheering her on.

They turned a corner at the end of the hallway and started up a flight of stairs. "I think I'm getting close to something. I really do. Did you hear my answer to Patty's question this morning?"

"Yes, I did. That's all new stuff—the secret Chinese history, the DNA, and all that. I'd like to hear more. Want to get together tonight? How about dinner with me in town this evening?"

"Sounds good." Marya turned slightly to look down the stairs. "I've got something amazing to tell you but you've got to keep it under your hat," she whispered.

Khalid leaned closer to hear her.

"I just got a call from my research assistant this morning."

"The Rodoni girl?"

"Yes. She was on the verge of quitting. No pay in weeks and weeks, you know. Frankly, I can't blame her. But, she told me something that really has me totally stoked. She said that she found a document in the Venetian archives that made reference to a journal written by Marco Polo."

"Wow. No kidding."

"I was blown away, because a Polo journal has been hypothesized forever but there's never been any contemporary reference to one. Vittoria said that from what she could determine it concerned a journal that Polo kept until his dying days. I'm waiting for further word on it, but I'm so excited right now you can't believe it." She stopped and gripped Khalid's forearm. "If this journal really exists, what a block-buster that will be, not to mention the clues it might contain. One thing I know, is that if Vittoria and I manage somehow to find it, it would change my whole situation."

Khalid agreed. "Yes, it would be big. Damn big. But don't get ahead of yourself just yet. Just sit tight until you get more word from Ms. Rodoni."

That's what she liked about Khalid Agarwal. His good common sense and advice. He never scorned or mocked her theories and speculation. When all the other male colleagues in the department laughed or threw up road-blocks, Khalid would lend an ear and encouragement. She would have felt totally alone the last three years without his support.

"I've already directed Vittoria where to begin a search for the journal and I'm keeping my fingers crossed."

"You think you know where it might be?"

"It's only an idea."

"Let's hope it's where you think it might be. I'll be anxious for you until I know, too."

"I've got to find it, Khalid. It's all I'm hanging onto right now. It could mean tangible proof of Polo's travels in the realms of Kublai Khan. I want to find the treasure, Khalid, more than the journal. Tangible, solid, irrefutable proof. Something to make the doubters believe. Vittoria is supposed to get back to me tonight. I'll let you know if she finds anything. In the meantime, please don't mention this to anyone. Please."

"I promise."

At the top of the staircase, Khalid gave her hand a reassuring pat and he told her that he had every confidence in her and her able assistant. He was confident that she would find both the journal and the treasure and put the doubters and mockers to shame. Before entering Lafferty's office, she disclosed how strapped she was for money at the moment and how important it was that she get Lafferty to loosen the purse strings. "I've got to tell you, Khalid, financially I'm on the ropes right now. I'd like to go back to Venice this summer. In fact, I'd like to leave in a couple of days if possible. But, the National Endowment for the Humanities returned my application without approval, and I haven't heard yet from the Fulbright people. My credit card is tapped out. It's vital that I get some grant money from the department if I'm to have any chance at all of going after Polo. If Lafferty says no again, I'm likely to go stark raving bananas in his office, believe me."

"I'm definitely going to speak up for you at the meeting. And if Lafferty still says no, I'll see what I can do personally to help. Count on it. So try and keep cool. Don't let your temper get the best of you."

"Thanks so much, Khalid. That's kind of you, but I won't impose on your generosity."

"My help is there when you need it, Marya. I want you to know that. And besides, I'm free this summer, if you should ever want to collaborate on this project . . . "

She read the sincerity on his face and felt like an ingrate but this project was hers and hers alone. She would rather end the quest than share it with a colleague, even someone as close as Khalid Agarwal. She owned the idea and she had cherished it since her childhood—since the first time her grandmother had told her that Marco Polo was their ancestor. "Again, that's very kind. But it's all so tentative. I can't say right now."

* * * * *

She was surprised to walk into Lafferty's office and find no one there. Lafferty was always so insistent on punctuality. She took a seat on Agarwal's left. Marya scanned the shelves of books reaching to the ceiling and realized that she had read all of them, and more, during the last five years. Lafferty had also crammed files and old issues of historical journals into every available space on the bookshelves. His desk was awash with monographs, announcements of conferences of the previous fall, students' papers that he failed to return, and masses of pink telephone memos. All this paperwork scrambled to maintain a foothold on his desk. She realized that a brisk wind would wreak havoc on the mess. She admitted to herself how tempting it would be to open the window behind his desk just to see what would happen.

While she waited, she fastened her hair in an up-do with an antique gold comb. Her eyes wandered to the campus commons that she could see outside the window beyond Lafferty's desk. A young man in his twenties tugged at a line, making a kite swoop and dive like a peregrine falcon above the buildings. Suddenly it was twenty years ago in northern California. She saw herself playing in the backyard of her grandmother's home, splashing in a three-foot deep doughboy pool, bobbing and crying out, 'Marco', 'Polo' repeatedly with the other children. After the game, her grandmother helped her out of the pool and wrapped her in a large fluffy towel. She threw her arms around her grandmother's neck and stroked her silky white hair. In her native Croatian, her grandmother called her a little princess and reminded her of their little secret. "Marco Polo was our ancestor and his wife was a queen. That's why you are my little princess. Some day you will visit their lands."

Lafferty's voice ended her reverie. "Marya, sorry to keep you waiting." She turned in her chair to see him enter the office followed by Dr. Theodore Roache, a noted authority on Russia. She saw a speck of saliva in the corner of Roache's mouth and a neck straining to burst his collar asunder. Lafferty took his seat, apologizing that Dr. Chen could not attend but said that he had conferred with him earlier about the extension of her grant. Lafferty seemed to gloat inwardly.

Marya was pleased that Chen had chosen to avoid the meeting. What a traitor, she thought. She recalled his disparaging remarks about her proposal being "rubbish" and "a waste of the department's scarce funds." They had hurt her badly.

Roache took the chair on Marya's right and immediately fastened his eyes on her long, lithe legs, not trying in the least to hide his hots for her. She detested the lascivious oaf. As she stood up to straighten her plaid skirt, he kept his eyes on her but shifted his stare to her blouse. She just wanted to haul off and smack him back to the Stone Age. As she checked the buttons on her blouse, she pointedly sighed in frustration. "Sam, could you send Roache out of the meeting? What do we need him here for? And more to the point, I'm teed off with his ogling. If he keeps this behavior up, I'll report him to Administration."

"Ted, knock it off," he simply said and then turned to Marya. "I need to get right to the point. The fellows and I have considered your request carefully and have come to the conclusion that we cannot approve an extension."

"But, Sam..." Khalid said, half rising from his chair.

Lafferty silenced him. "Our decision is final. It's none of your business."

Marya stared at Lafferty and refused to suffer the same fate. "Sam, you know that I haven't asked for much from the department. This time, I really need for you to release the funds I requested."

"For God's sake, Marya, let's not keep going over this. The idea of chasing after the Polo treasure and these goddam jewels and Golden Tablets of Command or whatever is simply ridiculous. There has been no trace of them anywhere since the time of Polo's death. You know what the experts and commentators have been saying for centuries.

The bars were, in all likelihood, melted down and made into rings. Same with the jewels. They chopped 'em up and made necklaces with them. End of story. Why can't you get that into your head?" He laid his right arm on his desk, knocking a few student term papers into the wastebasket.

"What are you talking about, 'ridiculous'? This is so unfair. You guys won't even throw me a bone." In sheer frustration, she stood up. "I know what you and the boys have been doing with the department's budget and it's not so god-awful inspiring."

"Sit down, now, Marya. You have no right to make insinuatons."

"You want to know what's ridiculous? I'll tell you what's ridiculous. How about your research into Ming Dynasty Confucian scholars? Give me a break! Who will ever read that arcane junk? Talk about wasting scarce departmental resources," she said, raising her voice.

Lafferty reddened. "My monographs have been read around the world."

Marya could not contain her frustration any longer. She rose and walked around his desk, her whole being expressing indignation and frustration with departmental politics. Lafferty sat up straight with a real look of worry.

"Marya, what the...? What's wrong with you?"

Roache took up where Lafferty left off. "Marya, I agree with Sam completely. Polo's story is nothing but a legend. People have debated whether it's fact or fiction for centuries and you expect to answer the question once and for all? Now, you may think it's worthy and interesting but no one in respectable academic circles is interested in Polo today. Personally, the subject just makes my eyeballs glaze over."

Marya had a swift reply. "If my research could make your eyes glaze over just a little more, that alone would make it all worthwhile. And by the way, your treatise on the sex life of Ivan the Terrible was just that: terrible. So, why don't you just zip it?" She looked down on him like a bug that she wanted to step on and grind underfoot.

Turning back to Lafferty, she felt she would give it another try, "Look, Sam, I know how much of the department's funds you three gentlemen get to spend, while the rest of us get only pittances. I'm not asking for much in this case. Just give me enough to cover a few weeks this summer. I'm completely convinced that the Polos brought home large tablets of gold and a huge quantity of precious gems. I will find them."

"Sorry, Marya. The answer is no. Now please sit down. I need to move on to the matter of your tenure. And let's discuss things with more civility, all right?"

"Wrong," she replied, moving quickly to the window behind his swivel chair. Lafferty fumbled with a sheaf of papers and swung around to follow her movements. "Marya, come on, what's come over you? Forget Polo. Hey, what the hell are you doing back there? Sit down, I said!"

"Sam," she said, pausing, "I'm going to give you one more chance to reconsider your position."

"And then what? Remember what you have at stake here. You better listen to me. Where is your gratitude for the fact that it was I who hired you?" His right arm shifted and pushed another pile of student papers into the wastebasket.

She felt her anger rising like molten lava in the throat of a volcano. "You boys are asking for it. Especially you, Roache," she said, throwing him a withering look.

Khalid gripped the armrests of his seat and rose. "Sam, let me have a word. Marya is on the verge of a breakthrough in her research. You have to give her a chance to…"

Lafferty cut him off, "What the hell do you know about her work? I told you before, Khalid, stay out of this. I don't want to hear anything more from either of you about Polo and this golden tablet stuff." Despite his threatening tone, there was a glint of fear in his eyes. "We better just end this meeting. I see no need to prolong the agony. Marya, any further communications with me will be in writing. Meeting's over."

Lafferty's last words angered her. She realized that her relationship with this bunch was over. Not that there was much of a relationship to begin with. For the last few years she had witnessed the gang of three choking and stifling her ambitions and sapping the patience of other good scholars in the department. It was time for a change of atmosphere in every sense, she decided. "You know what, Sam?"

"What?"

"It really stinks in here. You stink, Roache stinks. And Chen down the hall stinks. You all stink. What this department needs is a breath of fresh air." He didn't have a second to reply before she unlatched the window and raised it wide open. Great batches of papers took flight from Lafferty's desk as a powerful gust of air burst through the window. Lafferty scrambled to catch some of the papers. Roache looked paralyzed, sitting there with his mouth wide open.

She came back around to the front of Lafferty's desk, rested both hands flat on top of some papers remaining on the desk and brought her face within four inches of his. "Sam, I will find the Polo treasure. With or without you. Guaranteed." Then, she scooped up a batch of the papers and let them tumble on his head and lap.

Lafferty was speechless. Even Khalid, her comrade-in-arms, could not believe the sight. He got up and followed her out the door. Within seconds another strong gust of wind blew through the office and slammed the door shut with a resounding bang.

CHAPTER 2

Agarwal suggested that she take a little time to gather her wits in the cafeteria and she gladly went along with the idea. They chose a table in a corner. She took a seat and worked at getting her emotions under control while he got a pot of tea and two blueberry scones. When he came back, she told him how really sick and tired of the old boys she had been. "It was a long time coming but it felt good to get it off my chest."

"They deserved it. Both barrels," he said.

In her heart, she knew, however, that she had just torpedoed her chances of ever getting another nickel from the department, let alone win tenure on the Harvard faculty. Strangely enough, she felt liberated from the tension that she had been under.

After an hour of his hand-holding and commiseration, she felt calm enough to leave and go back to her office. Agarwal escorted her part of the way and then disappeared around a corner, leaving her to face a long line of students waiting for her.

She spent the afternoon meeting with more than a dozen of them. By four-thirty she was done. She packed a load of student papers in a satchel and locked her door. From the university, she drove to her bank to plead with a loan officer, but to no avail. He rebuffed her loan application. It was not unexpected.

On the way to her apartment she heard a frightening rattle under the hood of her aging Honda Civic and had to leave it at the garage. A pimply teenager drove her home in a shuttle van and took off. Upon arrival at the door of her apartment, it dawned on her that she had not separated her apartment keys from the car keys and would need to get a ride back to the garage or somehow find the surly building manager wherever he was and get him to let her into her apartment. She went off looking for the building manager and an hour later located him in one of the vacant apartments, sitting on a soiled carpet, finishing off a pepperoni pizza. “I’m having my dinner, ma’am. Take a seat. Whaddya want?”

“I’m locked out. My key is with my car at the garage.”

“Locked out? Again? This is getting to be a bad habit with you.”

She felt she could go ballistic with him after the day she had been through but just suppressed the urge. She stood outside on the landing and waited, watching the surly fellow for ten minutes until he scraped the last gob of cheese from the pizza box.

“Okay, let’s go, ma’am.”

When he let her into her apartment with his master key, he immediately noticed the broken glass on the floor. “What’s all this?” he demanded to know.

“What?”

“All this damn glass. What else do you think I’m talking about? Do you always leave broken glass lying around?”

“I had an accident this morning and didn’t have time to clean it up. I had a class to . . . ”

“That’s dangerous. Clean it up. And can I suggest something, dear? Get a duplicate key made.”

If she had a free hand, she would have slugged him. She stepped inside and slammed the door shut with her right foot. Once inside, she saw that the glass had literally exploded into small pieces covering the tiled entry way and even some of the carpet. She circled around the shards of glass and went straight to the phone. It signaled two messages waiting: one turned out to be the garage mechanic telling her that they would have to replace the fan belt and also replace some gaskets at an estimated four hundred ninety-three dollars. *What else can go wrong today?*

The other was a call telling her that she had been "selected" to participate in a grand offer, a chance for a free Caribbean cruise in exchange for an hour of her time at a "free seminar" on new condos in Wellesley. She erased both messages with a sigh. Vittoria had not called. *What could she be doing? She should have called in by now. Maybe there's an email.* Forgetting about her dinner date with Khalid and before checking her email, she went to the kitchen, got a jar of Barilla marinara sauce down from the cabinet and poured it into a saucepan. She put a pot of water on for fettuccine and dropped a few pinches of salt and a teaspoon of olive oil into it. "Crapola, what a day," she muttered, heading down the hallway to her home office.

* * * * *

It was a little after 3:00 P.M. when Vittoria stepped out of the taxi boat in a narrow canal, wondering if there was anything to her odd feeling that she had been followed. She dismissed the thought as foolish, climbed four marble steps and strode down a stone walkway leading to the main door of the Convent of San Lorenzo. She thought about her telephone conversation two hours earlier with Dr. Bradwell as she came to the recessed doorway of the convent and rang the bell. How kind the American professor had always been to her.

The exterior of the 10th century convent was full of cracks and bared patches of underlying brick. Its façade, especially near water level, was in extreme need of repair. The twice-daily inflow and outflow of the salty tides ate at the plaster up to the high-water mark. A thick mat of dark green algae clung to the walls, its enzymes further eating away at the façade. It irritated Vittoria to think that the process repeated itself all over Venice and that her beloved city was slowly losing its battle with an epochal rise in the level of the sea. She rang again and this time the small panel in the heavy wooden door swung open. She saw the face of a nun in veiled black garb.

"Yes?"

"I'm Vittoria Rodoni. I called a little while ago about coming to do some research today."

"Just a second." The nun slid a bolt and tugged strenuously at the enormous oaken door. "Come in. I am Sister Villana."

Stepping inside, she noticed an absolute, almost oppressive silence within as opposed to the bustle of everyday life on the canals. She felt the need for a little cheerful patter. "What a lovely convent, Sister. Thank you for letting me come this afternoon. I know it was short notice, but I am so pleased to be able to use the library. My American colleague..."

"Miss Rodoni. There is no need to go on like that. Let's get started because I need to prepare for the evening meal and prayers. I'll take you to the library shortly but, first, will you tell me what exactly you are here for?"

"I'm looking for original records dating from the first quarter of the 14th century."

"We have plenty of those," she said tartly. "Within that period, what are you looking for? Please be more precise."

"Social conditions following the naval battle between Venice and Genoa," she said, uneasy with this lie and trying to avoid looking into Villana's eyes. She looked at the wall behind the nun, focusing on a crucifix. She knew that if she stated her real mission at the convent library, Villana would have led her straight out the door.

"I'm afraid you'll be disappointed. Our collection is very limited and due to our prayer schedule, you won't be able to stay more than two hours. It's not widely known that we have a library. And we prefer to keep it that way.

We admit only serious scholars and clergy, with clearly defined research needs. We do not admit the general public anymore," she said, folding her hands in the sleeves of her habit. "I will take you to the library but you'll have to follow our procedures to the letter. Do you understand?"

"I do, Sister. I understand perfectly." Vittoria could not mistake the purposely frosty tone.

"Follow me, then." Sister Villana led her down a long, dimly-lit corridor. They turned through an arched doorway and into the library where Sister Villana introduced her to yet another scowling nun, Sister Fortunata, the library attendant. She could have been anywhere between fifty and eighty years of age. Vittoria could never accurately guess the age of most nuns she had known.

"I'll leave you with Sister Fortunata," Villana said before suddenly whirling around and disappearing out the door.

"Am I allowed to photocopy any of the library's papers?" Vittoria asked Fortunata.

"Absolutely not. Our books are in extremely fragile condition. We have no photocopy equipment here nor do we allow any such equipment in the library. Is that clear?"

"Perfectly." She wondered why the sisters were so on edge, so suspicious.

Sister Fortunata handed Vittoria a pair of white cotton gloves to wear while handling the ancient tomes and pointed to the table where she was to do her work. She then pointed out the rows where she might find the volumes of the period that interested her.

"Sister, is it true that one of the daughters of Marco Polo took her final vows at this convent?"

"Yes, that was Moreta," said the librarian. "She was very generous to our Order and provided funds for building this very hall. Her sarcophagus is beneath the floor of the chapel."

She nodded. “Thank you for your help, Sister.” She couldn’t help but wish that Fortunata was beneath the floor of the chapel, too. She looked around and saw in the dim light filtering down from the clerestory windows high on one wall that she was the only visitor to the library. She was glad that Villana had taken off and that Fortunata would be absorbed reading the Bible or saying the rosary to herself at her desk. She could not understand why the nuns were so defensive and unwelcoming. It was as if they were determined to keep the convent as off limits as possible, even to legitimate researchers.

She inhaled deeply. A faint scent of beeswax candles wafted in from the nearby chapel. A statue of Saint Lawrence sculpted in white marble stood on a pedestal in a corner with a flickering votive candle at his feet. The vaulted ceiling was plain and unadorned, as were the pillars and the marble floor. On both sides of a central aisle there were twelve tall sets of oak bookshelves loaded with leather-bound volumes, with ladders on wheels for access to the high shelves. Solid and in pristine condition, they held a huge number of volumes dating back to the 9th century. There must be over ten thousand volumes here, she reckoned.

She placed her notebook on the table Fortunata had designated. After putting on the white cotton gloves, she went to one of the tall stacks to begin her search. Up close, she saw that the oak planks that were used to build the bookshelves were of a quality that could not be duplicated in modern times. She spent a whole hour examining one side of one row, carefully examining each of the over-sized volumes. It did not help that she was only five feet four inches tall. The reaching, straining and bending required of her to read the title on the spine of each book was grueling work. Part of the time she spent on the rolling ladder to see what the topmost shelves held. Part of the time she spent crouched with her head close to the parquet floor. But she saw no sign of what would be a personal journal. Her arms, legs and neck were aching badly and her search seemed to be reaching a dead end. She stopped for a moment to brush the dust off her clothes but it only made matters worse. Her hands seemed to be smeared with the dust of centuries.

Sister Fortunata ambled over to the central aisle and called down to her, asking if she had found what she was looking for. She obviously noted that Vittoria had not yet spent one minute of her time at the table and closing time was in one hour.

"Not yet, Sister, and if I don't find it today, I may have to come back tomorrow."

"We shall see," Fortunata replied.

Vittoria rolled her shoulders and upper arms to relax her muscles and to relieve her neck ache. *Let's get back to work.* The thought of having to report total failure to Dr. Bradwell, was unacceptable, so she threw herself into the search again. She began with the lowest shelf on the opposite side, tackling the dirtiest work first. But discouragement and doubt began to seep into her thinking. What if she didn't find a journal? She realized that in that case, she would never raise the issue of salary again with Dr. Bradwell. It simply wouldn't be necessary. Perhaps her work with Dr. Bradwell would end today or, at best, tomorrow. That thought saddened her deeply.

Then, on the next shelf up from the bottom, in a dark corner that seemed not to have been touched since time began, she glimpsed a slender, inconspicuous volume jammed between two much larger ones bound in reddish leather. It was almost completely concealed from view. She knelt down, struggled to part the larger volumes and insert her hand. She gingerly eased the little volume out. Her efforts raised clouds of dust about her and she began to sneeze. Behind her, suddenly, she felt the looming presence of Sister Fortunata.

"Are you all right, Miss Rodoni? What are you trying to do?"

She rose and stood in front of the shelf she had been working on, holding the large volume for Fortunata to see. She read the engraved title to her and told her that she thought this was exactly what she was looking for. She brought it back to the table and made a pretense of taking notes from it while Fortunata resumed her pious reading. With fifteen minutes to go before she would be forced to leave, she returned to the stacks and found the little volume that she had targeted for closer inspection. She found it easy to slip it out and lay it on the floor. Slowly and gingerly she opened the cover. Adjusting her glasses, she looked closely at the faded, cursive script on the first page. "Dear sweet Mother of God," she gasped, and crossed herself with trembling hands.

* * * * *

Marya dragged herself to the spare bedroom that she used as an office and kicked her shoes off before sitting down at her computer. She wiggled her toes in the carpet as the computer went through its opening routines. At last, a congenial female voice cheerfully greeted her, "You have mail." Please let there be a message from Vittoria, she thought.

A list of over a dozen messages appeared, but one quick look told her that there was nothing from Vittoria. She snatched a Kleenex from the box to wipe some dust off the screen and around the keyboard. Instead, she began to cry. The phone rang. Wiping her eyes with the Kleenex and blowing her nose, she reached for the receiver.

"Hello, Marya? It's Khalid. I'll be over in half an hour. Meet me out front, would you?"

"Oh, Khalid. It's you."

"Well, who did you think it was? Remember? We have a date tonight. Are you ready?"

"I'm sorry. I didn't mean to sound rude. I was expecting a call from Vittoria," she said, clearing her throat.

"What's the matter, Marya? Your voice sounds . . . funny. Have you been crying?"

The very question brought on a bout of sobbing. "Oh, Khalid, things have been just going wrong all day."

"You have been crying. What's the matter?"

"I can't help it. It's been such a lousy day. I just got home. Things are a wreck, and that scene I made in Lafferty's office is only part of it." She grabbed another Kleenex.

"All the more reason to get together tonight and try to get past all that."

Though she normally looked forward to a night out with Khalid, this time, she felt she just needed some good downtime. Her sobbing made her sound like she had a stuffy nose. "That's really nice of you, but you don't want to be around me right now. How about another time?"

"No, Marya. Look, just wipe away those tears and get ready to step out with me. I'll be around to get you at seven, O.K? We'll have a great time, I promise. It'll be good for you." She tried two more times to dodge him, but he persisted and she ended up accepting his invitation to dinner in the North End of Boston for 7:30 instead.

As she hung up, the computer signaled the arrival of one new email. "You have mail," said the soothing voice once more. It was from Vittoria and she had entitled the message, "Eureka!" She watched tensely, as with one click, Vittoria's message appeared:

Dr. Bradwell:

I've been working late on translating something I found at the convent library on a low shelf in the first row on the right. You are going to be very happy with me when you read this. You were right! I found what appears to be a personal journal in Marco Polo's own handwriting! If it really is his very own journal, then we have discovered a national treasure, unknown all these years. Can you imagine? And the sisters at the convent seem completely unaware of its existence! I cannot tell you much about the contents of the journal because I had so little time, but I skimmed several pages and took notes. I found mention of a large donation of some kind that Marco Polo made to a church on the island of Korcula. That island, you may already know, is along the Dalmatian Coast of Croatia and is just north of Dubrovnik in Croatia. Who can say? This may be the very clue you need to unlock the secret of the Polo fortune!

Marya leaned back slowly in her chair, holding both hands over her mouth. "Oh, my God." She fanned her face quickly with her right hand. "Oh, my God." Suddenly she smelled something burning. *Oh, no! The sauce!* She ran to the kitchen, now filled with smoke rising from the saucepan, and turned off the flames under the sauce and the boiling water. She dashed back to the computer screen to read the rest, her heart beating wildly.

I hope this news will help you win support from your department. You should have little trouble convincing them of the worth of this project. Also, please study the attachment to this message. It's my translation of Padre Giustiniani's letter, the one I summarized for you already. You'll find that very informative, too. I am sure that this letter has never been published in any source. I do not want to spoil the good news, but I have to tell you that I had a strange experience this morning, one that may or may not be connected to our research. I think someone followed me today to the convent. Except for that, I feel so much better about our project today. And I hope that I will be hearing from you or, even better, seeing you here in Venice very soon.

Ciao,
Vittoria

The email left Marya momentarily paralyzed. She settled back in the chair. Her first reaction was that the discovery of Polo's journal was too good to be true. Her native skepticism warned her not to let her excitement blind her to the need for verification. *I have to get to Venice to check it out. But how? That's the problem. No money.* She rolled her chair away from the desk, got up, and paced around the cramped office. *Wow. Oh my God, a journal possibly written by Il Milione himself. And the report of a large donation on Korcula? Korcula! Yes! Of course. Nana always insisted that Marco Polo was not a Venetian, but was born on Korcula.* For her, the mention of Korcula lent more credibility to what Vittoria had told her.

Her mind soared in triumph over the magnitude of Vittoria's find. Then it plunged when she again considered her financial predicament. And that odd statement about being followed. Was Vittoria serious? How could anyone connect her with the research on Polo? She banished the worrisome thoughts and decided she must concentrate on the positives. With Vittoria's discovery, she felt she would find a way to push the project forward, regardless of Lafferty and the others. Besides that, Khalid was coming to pick her up for dinner. Maybe the night out with him was meant to be. She couldn't wait to share the news with him.

After a long, soothing shower, she chose a Thai silk knee-length dress for the evening. She did her hair up in a chignon and put a fine gold chain with a simple heart-shaped locket around her neck. She sat and checked her hair and makeup in her vanity mirror and just knew that she would capture Khalid's attention.

* * * * *

The moment that Marya sank into the plush seat of Khalid's Jaguar XJ she wanted to blurt out the news of Vittoria's discovery in the convent library, but she decided to wait for the proper moment at dinner. Within half an hour, he had whisked her through the narrow back streets of the

North End to what he claimed was the best Italian restaurant on the whole East Coast. He skillfully maneuvered the car into a tight parking space in front of Carlo's Caffé just as a couple in a Porsche pulled out.

"You'll love this place, Marya." Agarwal took his hand off the wheel and patted her knee. "I know Carlo well and his cooking is outstanding. He does the best Venetian food you'll ever taste."

As he came around and opened the door for her, she knew he was right. Delectable, spicy aromas permeated the whole neighborhood. The entrance to the restaurant struck her as a little tacky with its faux-marble pillars and the interior was a hodge-podge of fake-wooden tables, red plastic upholstered booths and faded murals. But Khalid was right. The place was full and the customers were eating with gusto. She knew the food would be great. Once they were seated and a silver-haired waitress had taken their orders, Khalid took both of Marya's hands securely in his. "Feeling better now? Aren't you glad you changed your mind?"

"Yes, I am. Thank you for bearing with me. I was at the end of my rope when you called."

"I could tell. By the way, I'm here to say that I really enjoyed the fireworks today in Lafferty's office. Serves them right, if I say so myself. I'm only sorry I didn't get a word in on your behalf."

"There was nothing you could say or do to change them anyway."

"I've never seen you show your temper like that before. You were adorable," he said, smiling in a way that showed every tooth to full advantage. It again made her think of Omar Sharif in *Doctor Zhivago*.

"I don't know what came over me. I'm almost ashamed that I let my temper get the better of me. I don't like making a scene—usually."

"Well, don't be ashamed. They deserved what they got and more."

"They've been getting through to me more and more, lately. The way they always hog the department funds for their own ridiculous junkets all over Asia. The way they treat others, including you. The way they just laugh at the rest of us and our work. I couldn't take it any more. I've had it with those two, you know. If Chen were there, I would have behaved even worse." She nibbled on her index fingernail. She decided it was the moment to open up to Khalid. Her eyes locked onto his. "I'm glad I did it but in a way, I regret it, too. Because now I'm in a real pickle. Worse off than before."

"Oh?'

"Well, sure. My research is now stalled. My grant proposal for the National Endowment for the Humanities was not approved, as you know. And a loan officer at the bank almost laughed me out the door just this afternoon. My car is on its last legs. It's just my luck. The moment my ship comes in, I can't afford the price of a ticket."

The waitress brought a small bottle of Gingerino, a platter of olives with bread and a small bowl of dipping oil. Khalid poured Marya a glass, looking at her quizzically, and then poured one for himself. "What do you mean about your ship coming in?"

"Mmm, good," she said, sipping the non-alcoholic aperitif. "What is this? Is it a liqueur?"

"No, it's something new from Italy," he said dismissively. "What about this ship of yours that's come in? What's up?"

"Khalid, I've got exciting news from Vittoria. She emailed me after you called. You've got to promise me that you will keep this a secret," she whispered. "Cross your heart."

"I don't do the cross, dear. I do the crescent moon, but you can still trust me. I'll keep your precious little secret, whatever it is," he said in a conspiratorial hush. "Promise. So, what did she tell you?"

She took another sip, looking at Khalid with sparkling blue eyes. "You'll never guess!"

"Come on, Marya. Stop playing with me. Out with it."

"Vittoria has found an original journal."

"An original document. Big deal. That's what you're supposed to find in an archive."

She lowered her glass of Gingerino. "It could be Marco Polo's journal."

Khalid sat up straight, making a low whistling sound. "Christ, are you serious, Marya? Polo's journal. That's just... I'm flabbergasted."

"People have speculated about a journal forever but nothing has ever turned up. Until now." She broke out in a wide smile. "I'm going to Venice, Khalid. I swear I'm going if I have to get there by kayak."

"You really think she found the journal mentioned in that other document? Are you sure about this?"

"Vittoria has been working for me going on two and a half years and she has been brilliant. I know I need to evaluate this journal before I can say for certain, but right now I'd lay my bets on Vittoria's word. This stands a very good chance of being the real thing. What's even better is that a part of the journal mentioned a large gift that Polo made to a church on the island of Korcula—totally consistent with his true origins, the way I see it. Incidentally, my grandmother came from that island, or somewhere near there. Have you ever heard of Korcula?"

"No, never." He raised his glass and clinked it against hers. "But, back to the discovery! Congratulations! Now that is something to celebrate. If the journal turns out to be authentic, it would be a major discovery in itself! Christ! This is going to be big! It's... It's... my God,... do you realize how big this could be? This is terrific news. You deserve this, Marya. You know, I've always had this feeling that you would be the one to unlock the mystery of the Polo treasure."

"I can't tell you. I've been at a fever pitch since I got the email. I wanted you to be the first one to know—and the only one to know."

The silver-haired waitress cleared the remains of the antipasto from the table and set down a piping hot dish of baked manicotti for Khalid and an inky squid risotto for Marya, along with a basket of warm, crusty Italian bread. She refilled his water glass and set a glass of white chardonnay before Marya. "Enjoy," she said and left.

Marya and Khalid had confided with each other often over the last three years about his work on Central Asian politics and her research into the history of the Silk Road and Marco Polo but she had never told him how she had first become interested in Polo in the first place. She began by opening the heart-shaped locket she was wearing and showed him two small black and white photos, one of her mother and the other of her grandmother. "This is my grandmother, the biggest influence in my life. Without her, I would not be here at Harvard today and I wouldn't be here with you sharing this news about Polo's diary. You see, Polo is more than just a historical figure to me. He's also an ancestor, according to my grandmother."

"Wow. Now I understand." Khalid scrutinized the picture of the beautiful woman in the locket and noted that Marya had her high cheekbones. Marya told him that her grandmother had come to the United States from Croatia when it was still part of the Austro-Hungarian Empire and settled in California.

Khalid questioned her on the point of Polo's place of birth and Marya cleared up a common misconception. Contrary to the usual historical wisdom, she said, Polo was not Venetian, but Croatian. To be precise, he was born in

Korcula and he went up to Venice with his father and his uncle only to find work. She cited a few works that supported this point.

Khalid asked her how she handled Polo's reputation as a liar, or at least a great story-teller, as was so evident from the fanciful tales found in his book of travels. She reiterated to Khalid in greater detail than she had explained in class that her own work in Persian records and Yuan Dynasty secret histories had definitely confirmed the presence of the Polos in China, their years of work under the great Kublai Khan's protection, and the untold wealth they had amassed in those years of service prior to returning to Italy.

The waitress reappeared to clear the table for a dessert: a rum-raisin gelato, anise-flavored biscotti and two cappuccinos. Khalid wanted to know more about the DNA evidence she had spoken about in her last session of class. She explained that shortly after the atrocities and the brutal ethnic cleansings during the recent Serbo-Croatian clashes, DNA tests were needed as evidence for war crimes trials. The tests revealed something quite unexpected by the forensic experts. Genes that were typical of the population of southern China had entered the Croatian gene pool in the south around the late 13th or early 14th century. When she had seen the results she found them far from surprising and she surmised that it happened just about the time when Polo had returned from the Far East. She theorized that the Polos had brought one or several Chinese with them and that they had married into the local population. "At least it confirms a physical connection, excuse the pun, between East Asia and the Adriatic in those times. Who knows?" she laughed. "Maybe old Marco brought a young Chinese bride home with him? I wouldn't put it past him." She decided not to share her grandmother's claim of Polo's relations with a Chinese queen he had brought home to Italy. Khalid would just flip out, she thought.

Khalid shook his head. "Just amazing. It's all falling into place!"

"You can say that again. But, unfortunately I don't have lots of money. Not to worry, though. I'll figure something out. I just have to."

"Marya, listen. You're not going to miss this opportunity, not if I have anything to say about it. You need some money? I'll lend it to you. In fact, I'd like to have a chance to collaborate." He placed his warm right hand over Marya's on the table for the second time in one evening. "Would you consider that? I'm free this summer. Between your expertise on Yuan China and mine on Central Asia and the old Silk Road that Polo traveled, it would be perfect! I'd follow you to Venice, Baluchistan, Upper Ossetia, the ends of the earth if you asked me."

Marya looked at his imploring, dark eyes: *Omar Sharif in Doctor Zhivago. That look!* She felt the warmth of his hand on hers and remembered all his kindnesses. But unraveling the Polo mystery was her life's calling. Something her grandmother had practically imposed on her. Something she must accomplish by herself. Something she could not share. She knew she would appear to be the proverbial dog biting the master's hand if she refused Khalid's request, but he needed to understand. "Khalid, if there was anyone I would ask to work with me on this project, you know it would be you, and no one else. But I must do this myself. I'm sorry. You've always been so generous with your support. I hate not being able to bring you into this research."

Khalid looked crestfallen and withdrew his hand from hers. "That's all right, Marya. I understand. I'm still willing to help, though. Look, let me at least lend you some funds to get you back to Venice this summer. It would make me happy and, in return, I only ask that you keep me posted from time to time on developments over there, for the thrill of it. How's that?"

She was happy that he took it so well and was still willing to help. It was her turn to reach out and take his hand. "Thank you, Khalid. I'm already so indebted to you. If there is any way I can reciprocate, I will. I promise to keep you thoroughly informed all the way and I'll pay you back as soon as I can."

"We'll take care of that in due time. There's no hurry."

Chef Carlo came over to their table, his chef's toque at a slight angle and the front of his white chef's uniform flecked with tomato sauce. "How did you like-a the manicotti, Mr. Agarwal? I see you've a-cleaned-a your plate."

"Great. *Multo bene*, as always."

"And who is this-a beautiful young-a lady, may I ask?"

"Excuse me. This is Dr. Marya Bradwell, professor of East Asian History at Harvard. We're celebrating a terrific discovery and maybe an incredible new chapter in Italian history."

Marya threw a mock look of offense at him. "Why Khalid, you haven't been listening carefully. We've been talking all evening about Croatian history and a Slavic gentleman." She gave an apologetic look at the chef and shrugged. "I happen to believe that Marco Polo is not Italian."

"It makes-a no difference to me. I just-a want to know if you enjoyed-a the meal."

"The best Italian food I've ever tasted." Marya put her napkin on the table admiring the chef's dark eyes rimmed with black eyelashes. He appeared to be a vigorous man in his late forties.

Khalid informed him that Marya would be spending some time in Venice. Carlo was pleased at that and wiped his hands on a clean dishtowel to shake her hand. He wished her a pleasant stay in his hometown and hoped she'd come back for another dinner at his restaurant. "I very definitely will," she promised

Carlo left with a *ciao* and moved on to another table of guests.

* * * * *

After dinner, Marya and Khalid took a leisurely route back to her apartment so they could discuss their next moves. Marya wanted to get off to Venice at the earliest opportunity. With tests scheduled for tomorrow and grades and other paperwork due on Thursday, she figured the earliest she could leave would be three or four days from now, if she could get a reasonably priced ticket. In the meantime she would need to pack her clothes, computer, CDs and reading and take care of her bills and a myriad other matters for what might be a month's stay in the Adriatic region. For the time being she left open the idea of the return trip. Considering her clash with Lafferty this morning, she might not have a job to come back to. Besides, there was no telling how long it would take her to find what she was looking for. Khalid listened, offering to help her with a few chores, and suggested that he transfer about ten thousand dollars into her account. He told her that he knew a great hotel in Venice, the Gabrielli Sandwirth, and that three nights there would be on him. Marya was staggered by his generosity, but didn't refuse. Before she was finished in Venice, she thought, she might be asking him for another infusion of cash, God forbid. Khalid pulled into an empty space at the curb in front of her apartment building, leaned across the seat and gave her a rapturous, breathtaking kiss. Never before had he kissed her like that.

"You pick a fine time to kiss me like that," she said, opening the car door. "I'm going to have to speed things up in Venice if that's a preview of coming attractions." He gave her his dazzling smile and a torrid, lingering look. "Yes, I'm sure we can collaborate in other ways," he said with a sly smile. "Look, I'll take care of the banking tomorrow and come over to take you to the airport whenever you have it all arranged."

The following days were an exhausting slog, a whirlwind, as she accomplished everything on her checklist. The best deal that she could get was a flight out of Logan Airport on Friday night at 8:20 P.M., arriving at Heathrow, England the next morning. She would have a long layover until she could board a British Airways flight to Venice in the evening that would get her in around 10:30 P.M. Venice time. With the time she needed to get her baggage and take a *vaporetto* from Marco Polo Airport to her hotel it could easily be midnight before she checked in. After making her flight reservations, she called Vittoria Thursday evening but couldn't reach her.

Friday evening Khalid took her to Logan and unloaded her bags at the curb as dozens of cars and taxis came and went. He was disappointed for her that she could not get better connections but he was happy that she was able to get to Venice hot on the trail of Polo. He held her tightly in his arms and gave her another amazing kiss. Travelers came and went all around them, standing on the sidewalk. She was stuck for words. She simply touched two fingers of her right hand to his lips and looked into his adorable eyes. She really was beginning to regret that she had to leave for Italy so quickly and wished they could have had some time alone together before her departure on their own. *A bed and breakfast in Maine or Vermont for the weekend maybe.*

"If you need anything, just call, Marya."

"Thanks so much, Khalid. You're the best. I owe you big time. Someday, I'll find a way to repay all you've done for me, with interest."

"Just go get 'em. Find that Polo treasure. Then we'll take it from there. Bye, love."

CHAPTER 3

Vittoria waited patiently for the arrival of Professor Nicolo Baldi in the ornate first-floor reading room of the Biblioteca Nazionale Marciana, built in the 16th century as one of the world's first public repositories of books and manuscripts. It was bedecked with every imaginable Renaissance bell and whistle, from frescoes on the ceiling to complex designs on marble floors. She had had several opportunities to work with the famed scholar already through her connection with Dr. Bradwell. She thought highly of him, but was irritated by his tardiness, especially this evening, when she wanted to capitalize on her momentous discovery at breakneck speed.

There he is. She stood up and raised her hand discreetly to get his attention. The old gent was a tweedy sort, wearing a maroon-colored cardigan sweater under his suit jacket and a pair of rimless eyeglasses. Baldi was good. Not only was he trained in ancient Greek and Latin, he was also the paramount scholar in medieval Italian language and literature. He greeted her and blamed his delay on heavy traffic on the canal. She invited him to sit next to her at an oak desk near a collection of reference materials on medieval and Renaissance Italian dialects. As she slid a bunch of photos from her satchel she wondered whether she was doing the right thing. She had hired Dr. Baldi on her own initiative, without clearing it with Dr. Bradwell, since she needed help translating these pages into modern Italian. How much would he charge her for the two or three hours of work she estimated it might take? Would he ask for payment this evening? He hadn't made the terms of his work clear yet.

But what really made her nervous was what he might

do with the information she was about to share with him. What would Dr. Bradwell think if she made a fatal error in letting Baldi know of the existence of a Polo journal? There was no way she could hide the nature of the material from the shrewd scholar. She decided to proceed anyhow.

The photographs that she placed on the table before them were blown-up images of pages she had copied from Polo's journal, during her second visit to the convent library the day before. On that visit, she could tell from the deepening scowl on Sister Fortunata's face that she was even less happy to see her again, if that were possible. She almost expected Fortunata to ask her to hand over the journal and hustle her out the door immediately.

Instead, Vittoria got lucky. Fortunata fell asleep holding a pious tract in her hands, snoring so loudly that Vittoria got the chance she was waiting for to use a small camera. Vittoria soon got into a rhythm of taking a picture with each snort the nun made. She took nearly forty photos before the nun, startled by her own snoring, woke up. She quickly packed up and returned the journal to its usual place on the shelf. From home, Vittoria had phoned Baldi and arranged for his translation and opinions on the material she had gathered.

Vittoria wanted Baldi to translate selected parts of the photographed material from medieval Italian into modern Italian, passages that she suspected were critically important. She was proficient in English, German and French in addition to her native tongue, Italian. She had also taken classes in Italian Renaissance literature and was able to decipher some of the material on her own. However, Baldi, like Dr. Bradwell, knew medieval Italian much better than she did. Before sending any more material to Dr. Bradwell she wanted to be certain that it was worthwhile to proceed. Vittoria prioritized the most important passages, focusing on Polo's appearances on the island of Korcula and what she thought was mention of a gift to a church there. She was also curious about the identity of a woman of noble rank traveling with the Polo party, a woman referred to in the photocopied pages as 'la Tatarica.'

He got to work immediately, writing his translations by hand, working without interruption for about one hour. He already had a small pile of nine or ten pages of translation completed when fatigue set in and he had to get up and stretch. He also needed a special dictionary from the reference section.

Returning to his seat he turned to Vittoria abruptly. "You know, Vittoria, I don't believe you've been completely honest with me here. You haven't given me any background on the source of these pages, who wrote them or when and how you came upon them. It appears to be a journal. Whose journal it's supposed to be, I think I know. You are still working with that American, Dr. Branwell, aren't you? This is part of her project on Polo, I suspect."

His guess frightened her. "Yes, Dr. Baldi. I apologize. By the way, her name is Bradwell. But what is your impression of this material? I need to know. It's urgent. I have already told her about it and I have urged her to come to Venice to see it for herself."

"So, you think this is something that Marco Polo himself wrote?"

"Yes, I do."

"I'm sorry to disappoint you, then. Whatever the source of these pages, they will not live up to your expectations. This cannot be Marco Polo's journal."

"Why not? Isn't this material authentic?"

"Well, there are different levels of authenticity. Different ways of looking at it. The writing is indeed authentic, that is, it was written in the 13th century. It is not a hoax or a forgery done in a later period. The question really is, did Marco Polo himself write it? I conclude he did not."

"Please, continue." Vittoria's stomach churned.

"First of all, we know that Polo was known in his day as 'Il Milione' because people thought that everything that came out of his mouth was a grand exaggeration, if not a great big lie. His reputation on that score... well, I don't have to tell you or Dr. Bradwell anything. You already know that. But what I've been reading in these passages that you've selected is just too incredible. It goes far beyond the level of exaggeration that even Polo was well known for. I mean... It's just hilarious."

"Like..."

"Like these jewels that were donated to some church. The author claims that they were as big as a man's fist. Emeralds, diamonds and rubies. Big as a man's fist! Come on, now! And dozens of them!" Baldi started to laugh. He took a handkerchief from his pocket and wiped his eyes. That's a good one. And the plan that the Khan had for uniting China with Christendom. And sending a concubine back to Europe with the Polos for betrothal to a European monarch? I'm sorry, dear, but some of this stuff is completely over the top."

Vittoria cringed but prodded him for some more examples. Baldi cited another issue, the fact that Polo never referred to himself at all in his book of travels, but in this document, he referred to himself often and shamelessly and went into depth about his relationship with the Chinese concubine. "A woman from Asia, for God's sake. And children by her, no less. Well, this is totally out of character on all counts. Polo would never have committed such things about himself to writing. What's more, the author of these passages keeps referring to his home in... what is that place... oh, yes, this island of Korcula. I've never heard of that until I read this. We all know that Marco Polo was a Venetian, born and raised here. He's an Italian hero. It's a well-known fact. We have the airport and thousands of place names to back it all up."

Vittoria wondered who, then, did write the journal, if not Polo, and why someone would want do such a thing. Something didn't ring true in Baldi's analysis. She asked him and he confessed to not having any idea about who would produce a fake journal and what was to be gained by it, but he conjectured that with such preposterous content, it could only have been an enemy of Polo who wanted to discredit him and make him look more ridiculous to his countrymen than he already did.

At first, when Baldi began giving his opinion, her stomach had knotted up. But after hearing him out, she began to take heart. He had not dismissed the age of the writing. He only disputed that it had been by Polo's own hand. So, the age of the book was consistent with the possibility of Polo being its author. Furthermore, he knew nothing of the provenance of the material and how she had come upon it in the convent library—the very convent where Polo's daughter had been a nun. And Vittoria was not about to share that with him. So his arguments against a Polo authorship of the volume were shaky. She was also relieved because Baldi would probably have little interest in going any further than this with it because he believed it was written by someone other than Polo.

"Where did you find this book," he asked. "It's unique in its own way and interesting, but as I said, it's not what it purports to be."

"I found it in a flea market," she said. "It looked old. I guess I jumped too quickly to a conclusion I wanted to see. I'm afraid I better get in touch with Dr. Bradwell and tell her about this. Oh, this is a mess. You've saved me from terrible embarrassment, Dr. Baldi. *Grazie*." She lied with such facility that it surprised her. "Don't feel so bad, Vittoria. I still think you have something valuable."

"By the way, how much do I owe you for all this inconvenience?"

"Let's call it even. I had a few chuckles over this. Call me if you ever want to follow up with it and then I'll bill you."

Vittoria was privately thrilled with the results of the session. Baldi's translation had confirmed her suspicions that an immense fortune on the island of Korcula was concerned. She also knew that word of a Marco Polo journal probably would not be leaked. She just hoped that Dr. Bradwell would get to Venice fast and get going with this lead.

* * * * *

The translated pages were tucked away safely in the satchel that Vittoria carried under her arm as she made her way home, deep in thought, along the narrow walkway skirting the canal. She planned to stay up again all night until she had finished transcribing the translations to email to Dr. Bradwell. These revelations would light a fire under her, for sure, she thought.

She was so proud of her achievements. It had just taken a chance discovery of a letter by the priest, Giustiniani, and sharing that with Dr. Bradwell. It was very astute of Bradwell to send her snooping around the convent library. But it was her own tiring search among the ancient tomes at the convent that had brought the journal to light. It was her own initiative in contacting Baldi that confirmed an exciting clue about a treasure stashed somewhere on the island of Korcula. No, without her going the extra mile these past two days, it would never have happened. Would Dr. Bradwell be as grateful and generous to her as she deserved? Or would she be let go? She hoped that the American professor would invite her to continue to participate in the tasks that lay ahead. It was imperative that they somehow get a complete copy of all the pages in the journal, another fifty pages by her estimate, and get a reliable translation of the whole book done. Bradwell and she were on the verge of something very exciting.

It was starting to dawn on her that her discovery would propel her into the limelight with Dr. Bradwell. Her discovery was likely to rock the world of professional historians, make big news on television, and have incredible consequences if the clues led to a treasure on the coast of Croatia. Her mind raced dizzily ahead to the possibilities for her career. Her father and mother would be proud of her, she was sure of that. Her future definitely seemed much brighter today.

She looked forward to Dr. Bradwell's arrival so they could get photos of the entire text and forge ahead quickly to find what they had been looking for over the course of the last two years. They would need to work out a plan to access the journal at the convent without arousing suspicion and that would certainly be difficult because Villana and Fortunata were, for some reason, extremely nervous about their library collection.

Eager to get on with the transcription and send an email to Dr. Bradwell, she hurried her steps in the fading light along the canal. She glanced at the rippled reflections of three-storied apartment buildings in the blue-green waters of the canal. She could hear the dim noise of TV programs and an occasional voice or loud laugh from behind shuttered windows. It was a fair guess that the occupants were preparing dinner or just sitting down to eat. Approaching the entrance to her apartment building she heard the voice of her downstairs neighbor, Franco, evidently talking with his wife Josefina. She wished that she could share her good news with them but didn't dare. Not yet. There would be time for that later.

She slowed her pace as she fumbled around in her satchel for the keys to the front door. She looked up and was startled to see a dark-haired, slightly-built fellow, in his thirties, emerge from the recessed front entrance and confront her. The suddenness of his appearance and his threatening manner put her on alert and she wavered between screaming for help and turning to run. He had his eyes on her satchel, she could see, and her fear of losing it horrified her. As she turned to run, another large man appeared behind her and flung a muscular arm around her abdomen. At the same time, his huge right hand clamped down tightly on her mouth. Her eyes shot wide-open in terror and she tried to wriggle out of his grip.

He tightened his grip on her and raised her several inches off the stone pavement, forcing her to release her satchel and let it drop. She felt both shoes fall off her feet. The smaller thug bent to pick up the satchel and she instinctively kicked him in the face with the heel of her right foot, sending him reeling backwards. He scrambled to his feet and came storming back for the satchel. He opened it, slid out the batch of photos and looked satisfied. Vittoria was puzzled, thinking that they were common crooks looking for cash. What could they want with the photos?

Then still holding her like a rag doll, crushing her against his rock-hard chest, the bearish oaf began to argue with the smaller one in a strange, guttural gibberish that she had never heard before. It wasn't difficult for her to figure out that the small guy wanted her dead. He whipped out a knife and let out a vicious stream of curses. She writhed and twisted but her feeble attempts had no effect at all.

The large thug backed up a step and stumbled on an uneven paver, losing his tight grip on her mouth for a moment. In that second she let out a scream for help and bit down on her captor's small finger. She tasted his blood and spit it out after he yanked his injured finger from her mouth. She twisted her body, making another attempt to free herself and saw a monstrous, pock-marked face above her. The very last thing she saw was the huge thug's balled fist come slamming down on her right temple and in total darkness she felt herself falling, falling, falling until cold water slipped about her and enveloped her like a shroud.

CHAPTER 4

In her windbreaker, sneakers and jeans Marya trotted down the enclosed boarding ramp to her plane. In spite of her recent clash with Lafferty, her mood was buoyant. In fact, she was almost euphoric. She knew she was about to take a dramatic step toward fulfillment of a life-long dream. She remembered the failed attempts to contact Vittoria and the disturbing message she had received from her about possibly being followed. She looked forward to getting in touch with her right away upon arrival in Venice.

In the meantime, she had to concentrate on her reading. She settled into her seat by the window. The plane was half-empty and many of the passengers luxuriated in the extra space. She drew out her copy of Marco Polo's travels and prepared to make the best of the flight time to review the whole account of the Polos' return voyage from China that began in the year 1292. She wanted to read through it with a fine-toothed comb to see if there were any clues as to what might have happened to the vast Polo treasure.

Marco Polo's book told of seven golden tablets that they had been given to be used as passports through dangerous parts of the Mongol Empire. His book also reported a large stash of precious gems. Upon return to Venice in 1295 A.D., they displayed some of the jewels to family members. But what had happened to those jewels and tablets? It always struck her as an amazing discrepancy that the Polos boasted of a huge fortune hauled home from Beijing, but they left only meager estates in their wills. When Polo died in 1324, he left nothing of importance to his family. The papers filed at a court in Venice spoke of some money, some bedroom furniture, a house and some jewelry that came to a mere $15,000 in current value. Something definitely seemed to have gone astray, maybe en route, and she needed to figure out what and where. Korcula came to mind as a prime target, thanks to Vittoria's last email.

The airplane skimmed off the runway at Logan Airport and in minutes Marya saw nothing below but the vast dark blue expanse of the Atlantic. She propped a little pillow behind her back, pulled her feet up on the next seat and opened her well-worn copy of the travels of Marco Polo. She preferred the original French version, *Le Devisement dou Monde*, penned by a writer named Rustichello when he and Marco were being held prisoner in Genoa. Wanting to reach a wider audience, Rustichello wrote Marco Polo's story in French rather than in some Italian dialect. For Marya's purposes, there were two crucial parts to examine, the Prologue and Chapter XVIII, entitled "How the Two Brothers and Messer Marco Took Leave of the Great Khan and Returned to their own Country."

She reached up and adjusted the nozzle to let cool air play lightly across her face. The book, opened to the Prologue, lay on her lap. A vision of the vast empire of the Mongols unfolded in her mind. The words of the Prologue faded from the page and she saw the three Polos—Nicolo, his son Marco, and his brother Maffeo—emerging from their long trek across the Gobi Desert in Asia. They entered Beijing in tatters and under escort to the palace of Kublai Khan. It was as if Marco Polo were telling her the story himself.

I was 17 years old when I came to the Court of Kublai Khan first in Shangdu, the summer residence, and then at Cambaluc. It was the second trip to the Khan's court for my father Nicolo and my uncle Maffeo. I immediately became a favorite of the Emperor. He ordered that I be trained and groomed for high responsibilities in his government. The

Khan preferred foreigners from distant lands to help control their teeming Han subjects. For seventeen years, he sent me out to gather information about the distant provinces and to administer tax levies. Not once did I disappoint him, because, whenever I returned to the court in Cambaluc, I always gave him a complete and faithful description of all that I had seen in the faraway provinces. He often summoned me immediately to his presence, eager to hear my news.

Upon returning from my last trip to India by sea, I found the situation in the palace nearing a crisis for the three of us. Years of shrewd trading by the grace of Kublai Khan made Nicolo and Maffeo very rich. I, too, enjoyed privileged access to inner circles and to the emperor himself. Now the emperor was 70 years old and no longer the vigorous man he was when I first arrived in the City of the Khan.

Our enemies were gathering and when the Khan died, we were sure to forfeit both our accumulated wealth and our lives. The Khan soon would "mount on high on the dragon" as our Mongol friends referred to death. The three of us had to find a way to excuse ourselves from his court before that day came.

One day my father saw the emperor arrive in the throne room and believing him to be in an affable mood, went to him immediately to ask permission for us to leave. That day I will never forget. The old Khan leaned on the arm of a eunuch as he tottered to the Dragon Throne in the great hall. His usual sallow countenance was now flushed and when he spoke, he bared only a few teeth. He faced a vast audience of Mongol royalty as he dropped his slight body onto the throne. He stroked his wispy beard and called for my father. When my father turned to look at me for encouragement, I saw sweat beading on his forehead. He rose and approached the throne, going through the traditional three kneelings and nine knockings of the head on the floor. Then he asked the emperor the question uppermost on our minds.

I heard the enraged tone in the Khan's quavering, reedy voice, "It is Our Will that you remain with Us and continue to receive the generous benefits of appointment to Our service. What has happened that you should desire to leave Us? Have you not grown wealthy and secure in your position in Our household? If it is because of wealth that you seek to leave, We will give you twice what you now possess. Under no condition at all will We grant you permission to leave Our Central Kingdom, though We will gladly permit you to travel within it wherever you please. Why do you want to attempt such a perilous journey? Beyond Our borders are the realms of barbarians. Your families have long ago forgotten you. Return to your residence here in happiness and gratitude. There will be no further petitions of this kind or Our displeasure will be boundless."

"But, Excellency," my father said with fear in every word, "I beg of you to let us return. It is not that we ignore the greatness of your empire, or are wanting in any respect or love for you, but it is for the laws of our Christian faith that I beg permission to return to Italy. By those sacred laws, I may not renounce my beloved wife while she is yet alive."

Kublai's face reddened and he tried to rise from the throne, but fell back upon his seat. "You will not leave Our realm, both for the profound love which We have for you and for your usefulness to Our reign. You will not ask again. We have decided."

We left the audience hall believing that we were doomed to die at the hands of our enemies the moment the Khan should die, and by all appearances, that would not be long. In our chambers, my father shook his head and told me, "That was our last opportunity. We cannot petition the Khan again, no matter how great your influence with him, Marco. Surely such a petition would be our death warrant."

"Father," I told him, "there is another way. Several weeks ago, a bridal party bound for Persia by the Old Silk Road was

forced to return to the capital. Three Persian envoys escorting the party judged it too dangerous. Rebels and bandits plague the road. I spoke to these men. They are now looking for a safer way to transport the Princess Kukachin to Kublai's nephew Argun."

Who are these three?"

"Uladai, Apusca, and Coja. They all came to me, thinking that we can help them."

"What do they want with us? How can we help them?"

"We can help them and help ourselves at the same time, Father. They know of our experience in traveling by sea and want to convince the Emperor that it would be safer and faster for the Princess and her retinue to go to Persia by sea. The envoys are also tired of being away from home. It has been three years since they have seen their land."

My father could not conceal his pleasure. "This is a plan that could work. Go at once to them and give my approval. Ask them to petition the emperor themselves so that if there is any blame, it would fall on them, not us."

So, I went immediately to the rooms of the Persian envoys.

"What does your father say, Marco?" Uladai asked.

"He tells you to submit a petition immediately requesting our guidance to Persia by sea. Tell the Emperor what we will need for the expedition—thirteen large ships for the retinue, the crew and the soldiers. We will need much food, means to store a large supply of fresh water and presents to offer to rulers in the lands we will visit in the southern seas. Ask him to grant us two great golden tablets of command that we may safely travel through all parts of the empire."

Uladai nodded in agreement. "Yes, we shall. We shall ask for all these things and convince him that a return by sea is the safest and fastest way for Princess Kukachin to go to her betrothed. Pray that Kublai is a man of reason."

I told him, "We too pray that he will be reasonable,

for this is our last chance. Our enemies have marked us for execution when Kublai meets with Eternal Heaven."

Uladai drew up the petition to the Khan, pointing out the advantages of a sea voyage over a journey through dangerous western lands. He pointed out that we were experts at travel by sea and would guarantee the safe passage of the Princess to Argun's realm.

Kublai again summoned us to his presence in the great audience hall. "You shall have your way, Marco. We have favored you over all Our advisors these many years and you have been worthy of Our confidence in you. Who will be Our eyes and ears as you have been in every province of China? But there is no argument. Princess Kukachin must be delivered safely to Argun. Only you can be trusted for this important mission." He looked pitiful. He spoke in short sentences, gasping for air, slumped in the throne.

"Thank you, Excellency. We shall regret our need to depart from your realm."

"Be assured, you will not want for provisions. Ships will be made ready and you shall depart from Quanzhou." With a wave of his hand, he summoned forth a servant who held a heavy weight concealed in embroidered silk wrappings. "We have prepared for you these emblems of our authority. Our subjects everywhere will assist and protect you along your journey to the West."

The servant laid down the burden on a carved table and drew back the silk coverings for the Persian envoys and us to see. I heard my uncle Maffeo say in Italian, "Holy Mother of God and all the Saints." Two large tablets of pure gold radiated a light of their own in the hall. They were very thick, as long as a man's forearm from elbow to fingertips and as wide as a big hand. An engraved warning in Mongolian script ran the length of the tablets. The same message appeared in Chinese on the other side. The message ordered all subjects of the Khan to hold his name in respect and to provide us assistance throughout the realm or die. I knew that even illiterate peasants would respect us just by looking upon these tablets. Our safe passage to Venice was assured.

The wedding party left the northern capital of Cambaluc taking the road along the Great Canal through regions west of Shandung where I was once the chief tax collector for the Khan. From there our large group went to Nanjing and Hangzhou. Hangzhou is the city of China that most reminded me of Venice—it had many canals and beautiful lakes. It was also once the capital of the Sung dynasty, now in retreat before the Mongolian armies. From Hangzhou farther south, we went until we reached Quanzhou on the coast. Beyond the coast, in the Great Peaceful Ocean, lies the island of Taiwan—an island of rebels that resisted the Khan's conquest. Into Quanzhou come envoys from nations of the southern seas, bringing tribute to the Khan. When we departed from Quanzhou, we saw a large fleet being readied for an assault on Java. We cared not to observe this but, instead, put all our efforts into installing the imperial wedding entourage and packing our wealth of gold and jewels aboard our ship.

The flow of air from the nozzle overhead had gone from refreshing to frigid. As Marya reached to close it, the vision dissolved and she knew that the Polos were en route to Venice. They had packed their wealth, exotic stuffs, jewels and heavy gold tablets aboard one of the thirteen ships leaving from the southern port of China. She felt a gnawing pain in her neck as she put her book down. She rubbed it and stretched her feet out as far in front of her as she could. She sat up, peered over the headrest in front of her and saw a crop of dark hair and neatly trimmed sideburns belonging to a man probably in his late twenties. He alternated between examining several glossy photos of golden artifacts and tapping numbers into his HP calculator. What a coincidence, she thought.

She decided to stand up, stretch her long legs, and go to the restroom at the rear of the plane. She grabbed the headrest and lugged herself into a standing position, rocking the seat and getting a loud complaint from the young man.

"Hey, can't you take it easy back there? What's going on, some kind of wrestling match?" He turned around with a glare that melted away as his eyes met hers. A handsome man in his late twenties, with dark brown eyes and curly black hair looked up and stared at her for a long moment before looking away. She liked his looks, but not his manners.

"I just want to get up and stretch a little. What's wrong with that? Is that some kind of crime?" She had seen him before, she thought. *Oh, yes. In line at the ticket desk at Logan.*

She had to get to the restroom fast and practically trotted to the rear of the plane. Nearly everyone was asleep, lying at odd angles, some with their mouths agape. Others sat upright but with their eyes closed and their chins down on their chests. The aroma of coffee grew stronger the closer she got to the rear of the plane.

The plane rose on a swell of air, giving her the feeling that she was in an elevator. The stewardess stationed in the alcove near the lavatories was pouring some orange juice. Suddenly the plane shuddered and shook and Marya fell backwards, instinctively throwing her arms out and back. Then, from behind, she felt strong arms under each of hers stopping her fall in mid-air. She scrambled to gain her footing and came back to a vertical position, though the man helping her did not immediately release his hands from the sides of her breasts.

"Let go of me, I'm okay. Thanks." She felt the stranger's arms suddenly drop away from her. She sensed that the man had held on to her perhaps a little longer than necessary for her to regain her balance. Deciding to be as low-key as she could be, she turned and found a familiar face, that of the guy who was seated in front of her. "Oh, it's you, again."

"You, you... I thought you were going to fall and..." He looked as embarrassed as she felt.

The stewardess came towards her with a white cloth to sop up some of the orange juice that spilled on Marya during the turbulence. "I'm so sorry."

"It's nothing, really. I can clean up in the lavatory. It's only a pair of jeans." Just as she turned to go into the lavatory, a fat man exited and the fellow with the sideburns quickly entered and slid the lock before she had a chance.

When she finally returned to her seat a few minutes later, the guy was back in his seat, absorbed in his own work. She deliberately bumped his seat before she sat down but drew no response from him this time.

She picked up her book and stretched her legs across the adjacent seats, tossing a blanket over them. She reflected on the incident outside the lavatory. *I'm glad he spared me a fall, but he was a little too helpful with those hands. And he got into the lavatory before me. How rude. I was next in line. Is he dark Irish or Jewish?*

She adjusted the flow of air once more and took up her reading. She realized she still had hours before arriving at Heathrow, so she relaxed once again with Marco Polo's unrivaled tale. After her break, she felt her imaginative powers enhanced. She resumed tracking the imperial wedding party where she had left off—at Quanzhou, the coastal city on the south coast of China across from the island of Taiwan.

The Polos boarded their ship, seeing to the safe storage of their enormous treasure. The Persian envoys escorted Princess Kukachin and her ladies aboard the same colossal ship. Again, eerily, Marya felt as if Marco were speaking to her personally, as a father would to a daughter, privately conveying important family secrets.

We left Quanzhou, China in *anno domini one thousand two hundred ninety-two. I must admit that our departure from Beijing was none too soon. At our very last audience, the Khan appeared most frail and destined soon for his reunion with Shang Ti, the Celestial Father.*

The twelve ships in addition to our own that were outfitted for this great voyage were of great capacity. None like them has ever been seen in the waters of our Mediterranean Sea. They were of fir and pine of such dimensions that each ship contained up to sixty cabins. These cabins comfortably accommodated the princess, her retinue, officers, merchants traveling with their families and us.

Facilities existed not only to cook for up to three hundred sailors and passengers aboard each ship, but also to grow certain kitchen herbs of great delight to the palate, but which are unknown in our poor Venice. The captains of the ships were highly esteemed and each boarded his ship with great fanfare of horns and drums and flourishes of swords. My father, my uncle and I commanded a following of twenty slaves and servants. All the quarters on each ship were water tight and adequately furnished. We stored the golden Tablets of Command safely in our cabin along with chests of fine jewels acquired from years of service in the household of the Great Khan.

The apartments of the Princess Kukachin and her entourage whom we escorted were even more spacious and well furnished than ours. Our ship was the largest in the fleet, though each had four masts and a spread of sails that would astonish our countrymen, were they ever to see them. We prayed that Almighty God was willing to see us complete our mission of delivering the Princess to the King of Persia and see us safely over both sea and land to our destination! We made our first landfall in the land of Champa to the south of China in order to replenish our supplies, and, from there, we went to Sumatra, a land of great peril.

In Sumatra, we spent five whole months. We made a camp on the shore using the labor of two thousand men. It required weeks to build a palisade of trees from the forest and to dig a deep ditch around it, such was the hostility towards us of the people who lived here. The savages stalked the unwary and any who strayed beyond the safety of our compound. In the night, we heard their screams for mercy and for help, but there was nothing we could do for them. Only after four months of maintaining a strict vigilance amongst ourselves and a cruel discipline with the savages, did they change their vicious disposition towards us. In the last month, we traded our articles for food and other necessaries without trouble.

After leaving Sumatra, we sailed west and north in turbulent seas until we came to the middle Andaman island. Here the people were of a most repulsive character. We stayed only by necessity, to acquire fresh food and water, and to make some repairs to our ships, now reduced in number. I tell you that hundreds of voyagers died before reaching these islands and fortunately for them. The people of these islands, both men and women, went about naked, making no attempt to cover any part of their bodies. They were savage and low, their faces betray an animal nature. For here, if any of our party were to stray beyond the group, whether out of curiosity to see the interior of the country or by accident, then his life was forfeit. This brutish race of people, finding someone not of their nation, fell immediately upon him to kill and devour. In this manner, our group lost forty souls. We thanked God that of all the young women in the wedding party, not one of them has perished, so cautious are the guards and the envoys for their safety. One of the envoys has died, leaving Uladai and Coja. We were happy to leave this cursed land.

A heavy thump of wheels being lowered in preparation for the landing drew Marya from her dream-like state. She stretched her arms and set aside her reading. Her body felt cramped. Her neck ached again. She swayed her head left and right to relieve the tension. From Polo's tale vivid images of savagery and death lingered on her consciousness. Her careful reading assured her that the Polos were still in full possession of their treasure as they headed on to India, though many lives had been lost along the way. She packed her book in her carry-on bag, checked her make-up and brushed her hair.

CHAPTER 5

Liam Di Angelo was the product of an Irish-Italian family from the North End of Boston. His father, an Italian immigrant, had lived in the neighborhood for over two decades and operated a combination Italian restaurant and deli there. His mother from Irish South Boston worked there alongside him every day since they opened the business together.

Liam showed no special brilliance in his high school studies, but somehow drifted into admission to Boston College where he majored in business. Surprisingly, he graduated cum laude. He developed a taste for the fine things in life and parlayed that taste, within three years, into a growing business of his own as a middle man dealer in antiquities. Most of his clients lived in the wealthier communities of the North Shore and his clientele there had doubled in the past year. He was in the right place at the right time with the right people.

The Di Angelos were regulars at Saint Joseph's Church every Sunday. They called Liam a pagan because he just slept in on Sundays. His parents rode the MTA. Liam owned a Lexus. The Di Angelos lived around the corner from their restaurant, but Liam had moved to Newton and bought a sprawling three-story mansion. They read the *Globe*. Liam subscribed to the *Wall Street Journal* and *Barron's*. "When are you coming over to have lunch with the family for a change?" his mother often asked. He usually had an answer like, "I can't, Ma. I'm heading up to Newburyport for lunch with Melissa's folks." Melissa's father was an assistant secretary in the Commerce Department in Washington.

Liam traveled frequently to Europe and cultivated a

network of suppliers who, like himself, were not always scrupulous in determining the source of the goods they traded in. He knew, in fact, that one of his suppliers, the house of Bellardo in Venice, regularly violated international laws against the exportation of cultural treasures. That was almost to be expected in the business, he told himself.

Aboard the flight to London he prepared for an upcoming deal with Bellardo who had alerted him to the arrival of a special cache of Scythian treasure from a burial mound in the Ukraine. He would push hard for prices that would guarantee him fat profits when he sold the pieces to his New England clientele. He would also keep his eyes open for a bauble for Melissa, a peace offering to make up for their latest argument over a prenuptial contract.

He estimated his profit from this expedition would be in six figures. Photos of Bellardo's new collection of artifacts told him that their quality was on par with the finest he had seen at museums in the northeast and in the oil-rich southwest. Bellardo told him that his personal relations with a Ukrainian official in the Ministry of the Interior itself had made the deal possible.

Aboard this flight to London, Liam was leaving nothing to chance. He was checking photos Bellardo had sent him and making calculations he would use in his bargaining. Once he landed in London, he would take time to size up the important collection of Scythian gold objects in the British Museum in London. He wanted to prepare thoroughly for the meeting with Bellardo and he needed to focus on all aspects of the deal. But the level of concentration he needed for this was impossible to achieve, thanks to the passenger seated behind him. He first saw her in line at the ticket desk at Boston's Logan airport. Her luxuriant hair, the nice fit of her jeans, the delicate scent of a fine perfume. *She's probably in fashion.* She held up the whole line at the ticket counter at Logan, flapping those lips endlessly. As he stored a carry-on bag aboard the plane and took his seat, he saw her take a seat in the row right behind him. After take-off, when he tried to get some work done, she kept bumping the back of his seat, demolishing his concentration. And then the most annoying thing occurred outside the lavatory at the back of the plane. Just as he got there, air turbulence threw this woman off balance and into his arms, giving him more than he bargained for. After helping her to her feet, he had not been quick enough to loosen his hold from her and her squawking embarrassed him. His heart beat furiously as he ducked into the lavatory. Before getting seated again, he managed to bump his head on the overhead storage bin.

When she returned to her seat a few minutes after he did, he studiously avoided looking back at her. He tried to get back to work and to thoughts of what else he could do to repair his relationship with Melissa but his mind returned to the incident at the back of the plane. She spelled nothing but trouble for him on this flight and he would do all he could to keep from bumping into her again as they exited.

CHAPTER 6

The British Museum, London

Marya took a shuttle to the Tube for a day in London. It was 10:30 A.M. and she was still feeling quite awake. What a relief to get out and stretch her legs, see some sights, and get away from that pain in the butt who sat in the row in front of her. She had calculated that she had about six hours to visit her favorite place in London, the British Museum, before she had to get back to the airport. Her flight on British Airways from Heathrow to Venice was scheduled for takeoff at 9:15 P.M.

En route, she surfaced from the subway at Harrods, knowing that there would be a vast array of things to choose from for a take-out lunch. One look at the incredible displays and she quickly spotted a pork and porcino mushroom terrine on a baguette. She paid for it and rushed back to the Tube. She arrived at the Museum after a brisk ten-minute walk from the Tube station to the tall wrought iron gates before the main entrance on Great Russell Street. She passed between tall classical columns and shoved five American dollars through the slot of a cube-shaped plexiglass donation box, heading for the vast reception area called the Great Court. She sat munching on her sandwich, admiring a cross-hatched, sweeping ceiling of glass that illuminated the interior space, bathing it with natural daylight that reflected off cream-white marble walls and floors. In a few minutes she was up and on her feet.

Intellectually, Marya was at home with the lands that stretched from Islamic Western Asia to China, a vast continent conquered for the first time in history by the Mongols.

It had been thanks to the Mongols who encouraged trade that the Polos were able to travel from Italy to China and back. She was a recognized scholar not only of the Mongol Yuan Dynasty in China, but also of contemporary inner Asia. She always admired how cultural traits diffused across this enormous space in spite of barriers such as the Gobi Desert, raging rivers and the tallest mountains on earth. And she greatly admired the superb collections and displays of the region found in the British Museum.

She had read about the major renovations to the Museum that had taken place two years earlier and especially wanted to see the exhibits in the Raymond and Beverly Sackler Gallery on the third level. First, however, she would take a look at the exhibits on the Silk Road and the Caves of the Thousand Buddhas at Dunhuang. The Museum was so vast and had so many famous pieces that she would have to confine her attention to a few select exhibits.

On the first level, in Room 33, she passed by a tall, see-through case in the center of the room featuring two large Yuan Dynasty glazed ceramics depicting a pair of stubborn Bactrian camels. They were done in a totally naturalistic style in tan, off-white and green, rearing their homely faces and showing their hideous mouths open in protest against the human figure leading them. Ahead of the pair of camels was a pair of large-rumped horses in the same style. These were animals that Marco, his father and his uncle would have seen on their trek across the western reaches of China on their way to Beijing, she thought.

After a couple of hours on the first level exploring the rest of the Asia collection, she took the stairs to the third level, turning at right angles a number of times around a huge Egyptian statue three stories tall standing rigidly erect in the stairwell. As she glanced upward, she caught the profile of a handsome man who had the same haircut as the obnoxious man on the plane. It was only a momentary impression, however, because he quickly turned at a right angle in the staircase and he was soon hidden from view by the massive statue. She hurried up a few steps to get another look but her way was blocked by two public school teachers out for the day with their flocks of rowdy fifth graders freshly excited by the Egyptian mummy exhibit. Once she had reached the third level, she looked around but saw no sign of the young man. Somewhat disappointed at not locating him, she headed off to see the Mesopotamia Collection in the newly-done Sackler Gallery.

The exhibit that most caught her eye was the tomb of Puabi of the Early Dynastic III Period from 2600 to 2300 B. C. Hers was one of the many royal tombs of the ancient city of Ur in Iraq. The Royal Cemetery of Ur, discovered in the 1920s, thrilled the public with the high quality of its well-preserved grave goods. Her tomb was unique in being untouched by looters through the millennia and had been filled with remarkable artifacts. On display was an incredible headdress found in her tomb, set upon the stylized head of a woman with a bouffant hairdo. The crown was made of many hammered gold leaves, loops and a top piece of rosettes that reminded her of a fireworks starburst.

It was magnificent, though she read on the signage that it was a reproduction, the original now kept at the Iraqi National Museum in Baghdad. That's where it belongs, she thought. She had heard of Puabi's tomb before but had forgotten its details. The woman was buried in a stone and brick chamber with a ramp leading down to it. On the ramp lay the bodies of five men with weapons and ten women, laid out in rows, wearing elaborate headdresses. The signage in the exhibit told her that the death pit was 12 feet by 36 feet. It was once thought that the sacrificial victims had been poisoned or had poisoned themselves and went gladly into the afterlife with their mistress. A more recent examination of the skulls of two of the soldiers revealed serious perimortem cracks with circular holes, indicating that their deaths were by blunt force trauma to the back of the head, probably with a heavy, pointed instrument. So much for their merry, happy march to their deaths, she thought.

She moved on to the nearby Rahim Irvani Gallery for the Middle East from 3000 B.C. to 651 A.D. The map of the museum she was holding in her hand mentioned an exhibit of the Oxus Treasure in Room 52. From her own recollection, this rich treasure of gold artifacts was the subject of a dispute between Tajikistan and the British Museum. In the midst of a vicious civil war, the President of Tajikistan called for the collection to be placed on display in his country and to be repatriated afterwards. The British replied that repatriation was not likely to happen, not the least because of the turbulence the country was going through. She empathized with Tajikistan but was also as concerned as the British about protection of these riches from theft and sale on the international market. The problem was not unique to this treasure. She only had to remind herself of Aurel Stein's clever purchase of thousands of Buddhist manuscripts at the Caves of the Thousand Buddhas at Dunhuang, China and their placement at the British Museum.

As she entered the vaulted Irvani gallery, she toyed with the idea of paying a courtesy call on Elizabeth McManus on her way home from Europe. Suddenly, though, she spotted him again, Mr. Sideburns, aiming his camera into a tall, rectangular Plexiglas case. He took two photos and then drew out a small notebook to jot something down. He seemed totally absorbed in what he was doing. Like her, he seemed to be there for professional reasons.

She moved forward, pretending that she had not noticed him and stood looking right at the lower part of the exhibit as if enthralled by a fine golden model of a chariot from Iran. She hesitated before raising her eyes to look straight at Sideburns. He had placed his notebook back in his pocket and was staring back at her!

Staring or glaring? She couldn't tell by his poker-faced expression. She looked away and sauntered to a case against the wall to her right, giving her a chance to turn her back on him. She spent a few more minutes meandering around the gallery, hoping she would not have to face him again and then slipped out the door on the far end of the gallery.

On the same level there was a court restaurant open for afternoon tea. A break was overdue, so she stopped and had an Earl Grey. She thought over the near-miss she just had with that obnoxious man. Still, she wondered what he had been studying with such intensity and thought it worth taking a look. She finished her tea and went back to the gallery to satisfy her curiosity. After seeing that he was nowhere in sight, she went to the case and discovered that he had been studying and photographing artifacts from the Caucasus region and the steppes all around the northern end of the Caspian Sea. The collection included some beautiful gold pieces of the Scythian type, dating back hundreds of years B.C. Among them were horse pieces found in Iran in the 7th century B.C. that were used to hold a horse bit and straps. She thought it amazing that whatever his purpose was in photographing this exhibit, he shared one of her interests. She wondered if he might be a curator or assistant administrator at a major American museum. *But why was he using that calculator on the plane?* As she gazed at the gold pieces decorated with animal heads she caught the reflection of a person standing very close behind her. She turned. It was Sideburns. "What are you doing here?" he snapped at her.

CHAPTER 7

She boarded British Airways 206 to Venice at 9:00 P.M. and stored a bag in the overhead after taking out her copy of Polo's travels. With a sigh, she plopped into her seat and looked out the window onto the tarmac, recalling the sharp words she had with that boor at the British Museum. He had raised his voice at her and she responded in kind, their loud bickering drawing a guard over to shush them and get them moving along. It was lucky for him, she thought, that there was a guard standing nearby who intervened. She resented the way he had laid the guilt on her for "three very unpleasant encounters," as he had put it.

She opened her book as dozens more passengers continued boarding and buried herself in her reading. Suddenly the backrest of her seat was wrenched backwards several inches as a passenger piled into the seat in back of her.

"Hello there. It's me. I just wanted to let you know I'm in the seat behind you," she heard someone say in a hushed voice through the gap between her seat and the one next to her. She ignored the voice, thinking the gentleman was talking on one of those new cell phones.

"Dear, I'm talking to *you*."

This can't be happening, she thought, as she recognized the man's voice. She turned her head to the right and peered between the gap. Sideburns was looking back at her. "Don't call me 'Dear.' I'm not your dear," she angrily whispered.

"Hey, whatever. I'm fine with that, lady. I just didn't want you to go ballistic again. Sorry, I was just thinking of a truce but I'm afraid you're still on the warpath."

"Oh, my Lord." She tossed her book aside, loosened

her seat belt and stormed up to the forward galley to find a stewardess. Several minutes later, the stewardess had found a seat for her twelve rows back from him.

* * * * *

Marya's passage through customs at the small Marco Polo Airport was quick and uncomplicated. She hauled her bag to a bank of phones and even though it was nearly 11:00 P.M., she called Vittoria but still only got a voice message machine. She was puzzled at still not being able to reach her. She vowed to try again in the morning. She saw a sign reading "trasporto acqueo publico" and followed the arrow on it to the transportation desk where she purchased a ticket for a *vaporetto* ride across Venice's lagoon to Arsenale Station, a crossing that would take under an hour. From the desk, she caught sight of Sideburns, already heading out across the lobby to a set of automatic doors. She couldn't believe it, but it appeared that he was heading for the same place.

Most of those who had arrived on her flight had left the main concourse by shuttle buses and taxis or went out from the baggage claim area to the parking lot. A clutch of passengers were wheeling their luggage out to the quay behind Sideburns. She gathered her luggage, her purse and briefcase and wheeled it all out through the sliding doors. There was at least a five-minute walk along the quay to the *vaporetto*. Halfway there, she saw an attendant at the foot of the metal ramp leading down to the boat helping an elderly couple with their large bag and heard him calling to the pilot to get ready to take off.

Marya screamed in Italian, "Wait. Please. I'm coming."

The attendant yelled to her, "Hurry, signorina."

She flew to the ramp and descended the gangplank to the *vaporetto*, completely winded. Stepping onto the boat, she lurched as the boat backed up and swung around for the choppy ride across the lagoon. She thanked the attendant profusely in Italian as she left her bulky suitcase with the other passengers' bags. She slung the carry-on over her shoulder, grabbed her purse and briefcase and proceeded to the back part of the vessel.

There was not a seat to be had. More than thirty travelers were crowded in rows of seats, along with their light bags and parcels. They stared at her vacantly as she staggered with the rocking of the boat.

"Over here," she heard someone calling from the rear.

She looked around and saw a waving hand.

Oh no. Not him again.

Rather than stand for a half hour, rolling with the *vaporetto* she gave up and threaded her way towards Sideburns, irritating a few passengers as her bag bumped their heads and shoulders.

"Here, have a seat," he said, patting the wooden bench.

"Please. Don't say another thing. It's better that way." *I can't believe this. He's there at every turn, from Boston to the lagoon of Venice.* She remembered a French play, *The Bald Soprano,* by Ionesco that featured a scene with one amazing coincidence after another. She thought at the time that it was hilarious, but these coincidences with this gentleman on this trip were anything but funny.

"I'm Liam Di Angelo," he said putting out his hand.

She didn't take it. She looked at him dispassionately, the way a scientist looks at a specimen in a jar. He had fair skin and a kind of Celtic cast to his eyes. He was well-dressed and wearing a very expensive gold watch. What makes this guy tick, she wondered? She thought he had had enough of her at the British Museum. Hadn't he heard what she just said? She sat stiffly and folded her hands over her purse.

"Is this your first trip to Venice?" he asked.

"No, my third," she said, looking away from him towards the lights along the shore.

"My sixth. Do you want to know what I do?"

"Not really, Mr. Di Angelo."

"Well, I'm into art, gold and antiquities. For collectors. Sometimes museums. It's good work and it's rewarding. Lucrative, in fact."

"Nice vocabulary you have."

"Want to tell me what you do?" he asked, brushing off her dig.

"No."

"I'm from Newton. I used to live in Boston, but I moved out and just bought a nice house up there. Six-thousand square feet and I'm filling it with some stuff I pick up over here when I'm on business. Let me guess what you do. You're a buyer. You're into fashion. Right? Teen fashions."

"Fashion? A buyer? Me? Certainly not. I teach. In Cambridge."

"Oh, a school teacher. I would never have guessed. That's a very noble profession. Takes a special kind of person. Handling those teenagers, I don't know how you folks do it. My hat's off to you. I'd never be a teacher. It's not only the crap you have to put up with, but the salaries aren't anything to crow about."

"I'm not a high school teacher. I'm a professor. I teach history at Harvard." She wanted to end the conversation with him right there.

But Di Angelo was unrelenting. "Whoa. I'm impressed. You speak Italian, too, I see. I heard you calling to the attendant. I wish I had your command of Italian. I'm afraid the only Italian I can speak is the street variety. Want to hear a sample?"

"No, spare me, please." Was this guy for real or was he just trying to get on her nerves, she wondered.

As the *vaporetto* sped south across the lagoon towards the Grand Canal, Marya figured she had nothing to lose. The Irish-Italian bozo would soon be getting off the boat and she would be rid of him. So, she asked him about his odd name. He explained that it was a compromise that his Irish mother from Waterford and his Italian dad from Venice had settled upon, the same as they did with all his other brothers and sisters.

The boat veered into the Grand Canal, pointing its bow towards Arsenale Station. The passengers shifted around in their seats, gathering up their belongings, making the usual, useless preliminaries for a hasty exit.

"So, where are you staying?"

"The Gabrielli Sandwirth."

He laughed. "You're not going to believe this."

CHAPTER 8

She wheeled around, "You're getting off at my hotel, too?" She was aghast. The horrible, impossible, insufferable thought crept into her thinking that they would now be having an endless number of encounters. When would it end? His rudeness, his disrespect, his crass materialism. It had to be an act, she thought.

The motor slowed and the boat glided towards a long pier.

"Listen, I wonder if you'd like to get together this evening for a few drinks." "I'm afraid not, Mr. Di Angelo. I've got a lot of work to do tomorrow and I'm just dropping on my feet. I need to get some sleep real soon."

The boat further slowed with a reverse motion of its propeller. The attendant threw out a bowline and then let out a stern line. The pilot maneuvered the boat and brought it alongside the quay with a gentle thud.

"Do you need any help with your things?"

She knew that she had to haul her load from the station across the Ponti Ca di Dio, but she would much rather tangle with the steps and the footbridge alone without his help. "Thanks, but I can handle it. Lots of luck with your business here, Mr. Di Angelo," she said, and immediately realized that this was the absolute wrong thing to say. Her feelings and respect for antiquities must be the exact opposite of his.

"Good luck to you, too."

Marya was on her feet with her carry-on and only a few paces away when he called her back. "Hey, lady, you forgot something."

Looking back, her heart sank. He dangled her briefcase aloft. *My God, all my research.*

It irked her that they got off the boat together and that her fatigue was getting the better of her. Reluctantly, she let him take the large suitcase from her at the station. They crossed the bridge together and turned an immediate right across a broad terrace that flanked the canal, arriving at the Gabrielli Sandwirth. The reception area was elegantly decorated with exquisite Murano glass chandeliers and furnished in tasteful, Venetian-style chairs and sofas. The reception desk was staffed by a dark-haired woman wearing orange horn-rimmed glasses and a necklace of large red beads. She beamed at Marya as if she recognized her. "Mrs. Di Angelo? Benvenuto. What a pleasure to meet you at last. Hello, Mr. Di Angelo. It's so good to see you again. Everything is ready for the both of you."

Marya slapped her purse on the marble-topped desk and glared. "What did you just say?" She looked at the woman, trying to make sense of what she had just heard.

"Mrs. Di Angelo, no?"

"You better believe it's no. You've made a mistake, Signorina." She looked at Liam, now standing beside her. "I'm not with him."

Liam put both hands on the desk. "She's right, Teresa. We're not together."

"You two have divorced?"

"No, we've never been married and we sure as heck don't intend to get married," she said, placing her hands on her hips.

Teresa looked completely baffled. "I'm sorry, Mr. Di Angelo. Excuse me, Signora…"

"Dr. Bradwell. Marya Bradwell."

"Oh, this is really strange," she murmured, studying the list of reservations on her computer. "Whoever took your reservations booked the two of you into the same room, unit 330. That's why I thought…"

Marya opened her mouth to protest, but words did

not come to her. She made a number of wha...wha...wha sounds before she could manage a sentence. "Well, that can't be. There's no way that's going to work." She shook her head. "You've got to straighten that out right away."

"Of course, Dr. Bradwell. We'll take care of it. Just a minute." She spent a moment looking at the computer screen, anxiously tapping away on the keyboard. "But, I can't...it seems..." She looked at Marya very apologetically, fingering her necklace. "It looks like we don't have any other rooms available. Would you consider an arrangement, Dr. Bradwell?"

Marya's lower jaw went slack. "An arrangement? This is just unbelievable. Would you please just call the manager? I want to speak to him personally." She turned to Liam and detected a grin. "What's so funny? I don't think this is one bit amusing. It's ridiculous. All day, on airplanes, and now this. If I weren't so tired, I'd go find another hotel this instant."

"It's too late for that," he said, looking at the clock on the wall behind the receptionist. "It's almost midnight. You couldn't get a taxi boat, let alone a room at another hotel at this hour."

The manager arrived, a short man, whose cologne preceded him to the desk. He twiddled a set of keys as Teresa explained the whole situation to him. Marya's nerves jangled as she sized up the manager. He and Teresa turned their backs to Marya and Liam to confer. In a minute, they had a solution. The little manager broke off talk with Teresa and turned to her. "Our deepest apologies for this inconvenience. I think I have an agreeable solution for you, though. You see, suite 330 happens to have a small adjoining chamber. If you agree, Dr. Bradwell, we can move a bed in there for the night, which will give Mr. Di Angelo a place to sleep."

"An adjoining chamber? Is there a lock on the door between the rooms?"

"Yes, but you must work out an agreement with Mr. Di Angelo on using the bathroom, which is on your side."

She was stupefied. "No. Absolutely not."

Liam looked down at her. "Dr. Bradwell. I *can* be a gentleman. It will only be for one night. It's a bad hour to think about checking out other hotels. You've got to take what you can get."

"No, I'm not at all happy with that idea. If you were a gentleman, you would go find another hotel, Mr. Di Angelo, and let me take that room."

A frown appeared on his face. "Look, Lady Jane, this is where I always stay on my visits to Venice. The room's in *my* name, and you can sleep on a sofa in the lobby if you don't like the solution, for all I care." He gestured grandly to a black and gold satiny sofa against an opposite wall. "There, that one over there looks comfy."

"No. I need a room and I need peace and quiet."

"Ms. Bradwell. Be reasonable The staff here can vouch for me. I come here all the time on business. I suggest you go along with the manager's idea. It's been a long day for both of us."

"Early tomorrow morning we can have Mr. Di Angelo installed in his own unit," the manager chimed in, twirling his keys and waiting for Marya's decision.

Marya considered the dead end she was in and resigned herself to the plan. The manager unhooked a key from the wall behind him and handed it to Di Angelo. Teresa gave them both a syrupy smile. "Sleep well," she said. "And sweet dreams. We'll straighten things out in the morning. Have a good night."

* * * * *

Mr. Di Angelo's word was good. He knocked on his side of the door before coming into her room. He strode past her bed clad in a towel on his way to their common shower. She tried not to gape when she saw his lean, chiseled torso. From inside the bathroom, he hollered, "I'll be in and out in a minute, not to worry."

CHAPTER 9

Marya paced around her room for a while listening to the sounds of Di Angelo, singing and splashing in the shower. She was incredibly weary from the long trip across the Atlantic, the full day at the British Museum, Mr. Di Angelo's jabbering on the ride across the lagoon and the hassle she had just been through at the reception desk downstairs. Until he got out of the shower and returned to his room, she resolved to pass the time reading Polo's travel adventure. She undressed behind a room divider and got into her pajamas. Then she propped up a few pillows to read it in blessed comfort. Her bed was luxuriously wide, like two full beds joined together.

As she took up her reading, she found the Polos and their fellow travelers leaving the Andaman Islands for Persia. The flotilla of ships moved on to Ceylon and to the west coast of India. What had the Polos done with the gems, the golden passports and other trade goods they had stowed on board in China? While Liam showered, she read on, letting the words on the page dissolve into the scene of a lavish banquet and a half-naked, bejeweled king sitting at the head of a low table.

Before we left Ceylon, we visited the King and dined at his table. He was dressed most simply, like his subjects, with one difference: he wore an immense quantity of jewels in the form of long strings of pearls about his neck and waist, gold bands around his arms and legs and two large rubies around his neck. He also carried a ruby so large that when he held it, it stuck out from both sides of his hand nearly an inch. With this ruby, he wiped his lips and his beard. The noble Khan had once heard of this jewel and offered to buy it, but the king of Ceylon refused to part with it.

When we left Ceylon, heavy seas caused us to be separated from four of the ships in our convoy. They were not to be seen again by us. We pray that they did not fall into the hands of the savage creatures such as those who inhabit Sumatra, nor into the hands of the Andamans who go all day stark naked and who are known to partake of human flesh. We have been fortunate because the wedding party, the envoys and we ourselves fared well. For I tell you, that in crossing from Ceylon to Malabar, we encountered storms, adverse winds, illness and many other trials that caused loss of life among the sailor crews and passengers alike.

We passed many months among the people of the coast of western India. I can tell you much about the strange customs of the people of these lands, but fear to wear your patience away. Therefore, I merely mention that we visited the pearl fisheries. We participated in the wedding festivities of the Hindus. We saw the spectacle of what is called suttee, whereby the beloved wife of a deceased husband mounts a pyre and is consumed alive in flames to show her devotion and fidelity to her husband. Such women are greatly admired in those parts.

Our dear Princess Kukachin grew fearful when she observed such customs, but another princess in her retinue consoled and comforted her, for Princess Kukachin was yet a child. The other princess was not of the Khan's people, but of the imperial house defeated by Kublai Khan.

We used our stay of four months among the people of India to conduct much profitable trade. We exchanged silks, porcelain, and tea for emeralds, topazes, sapphires, rubies, lapis lazuli, and gold.

Our departure from Malabar was marked with bloodshed and the loss of three more ships of the royal wedding expedition. Three miles off the coast, there lay waiting many ships of pirates, all in a line, a distance of one mile between each. It was necessary for us to breach that barrier to escape to the open ocean. In spite of the bravery of our sailors, our losses were heavy.

I tell you that we sailed the sea of India a full eighteen months before we arrived at the port of Hormuz in Persia. When we had begun our voyage in Quanzhou, we had altogether more than six hundred passengers, but I assure you that when we reached the shores of Persia and counted, all had died except eighteen, not counting the crews of the ships. Only one of the three Persian envoys, Coja, remained. Besides Nicolo, Maffeo and me, the rest were women of the bridal party....

Marya felt her eyes growing heavy and her concentration hard to sustain any longer. She resisted the signs of sleep because she wanted to know more about Hormuz and she wanted to remain awake until Mr. Di Angelo closed the door to his room. In her reading it appeared that the Polos had not lost any of the treasure that they had transported as far as the Persian gulf. In fact, quite the opposite. In India they had added to their hoard. Her head rocked lightly and her eyes drooped. A strange numb feeling in her head made her quit reading and release her body and mind to blissful sleep.

The book slid from her hands and the vision of pearls, the rubies, porcelains, silk fabrics, gold—all evaporated. Only seven minutes had passed since she had come to bed. After his shower, on his way back to his room, Liam turned Marya's bedside lamp off.

CHAPTER 10

She awoke the next morning to find that the hotel staff had kept their word, too—Mr. Di Angelo had already moved out and evidently been given a different room. She reminded herself to do all she could to avoid him and to get on with her business without entangling herself with menfolk. She didn't need any complications. It was her first day back in Venice on a critical mission and her first order of business was to get in touch with Vittoria.

She tried calling again, but got the same recorded message. She was beginning to feel somewhat unnerved about Vittoria's absence. She decided to dial Vittoria's parents to see if they knew anything. Mrs. Rodoni answered on the first ring.

"Hello? Mrs. Rodoni? This is Dr. Bradwell calling."

"Hello, Dr. Bradwell."

There was an awkward pause. "I just got in last night. I've been trying to reach Vittoria; but so far, I haven't had any luck. Do you know where she is?"

"I'm sorry, but I have terrible news. Vittoria is in the hospital in intensive care. A neighbor of hers found her last night almost dead on the steps of the canal near her apartment. She was badly beaten."

My God. "Mrs. Rodoni, I am so sorry to hear this. Do you have any idea what happened? Is she going to be all right?"

"She has been unconscious most of the time since she was admitted. Her condition is serious, but we are hopeful. The doctors are concerned about a cerebral hemorrhage after running tests. The police are investigating, but they don't know why this happened. They told us her purse was not taken. Nothing of value is missing. It was just a vicious attack. Please say a prayer for her."

"I certainly will. Can she have visitors?"

"Yes, but you won't be able to talk to her."

"That's all right. I'd like to see her anyway. What hospital is she at?

"Ospedale Civile di Venezia. My husband and I are going there this morning. Maybe we will see you there?

"I would like that very much. I'll leave right now, Mrs. Rodoni. Ciao."

"Ciao."

The news of Vittoria's condition staggered Marya. She had her heart so set on viewing Polo's secret journal, that the possibility of violence affecting Vittoria had never seriously entered her mind. She recalled now what Vittoria had mentioned in her email. It seemed that someone had followed her to the convent library but it was just inexplicable. It could not have been connected with the research, she thought. Impossible. Except for Vittoria and herself no one in Venice knew of the journal. Marya cast aside her plans and do what mattered more—visiting Vittoria. The journal could wait.

CHAPTER 11

At 10:00 A.M. Marya stepped out of the elevator on the third floor of the Ospedale Civile di Venezia. A mixture of antiseptic odors in the hallway put her on edge. She found Vittoria's room in the intensive care unit and Mr. and Mrs. Rodoni already in her room, standing by her bed. She knocked on the open door and entered. The sight of Vittoria's face shocked her.

She came around to the side of the bed opposite the Rodonis. Severe bruising covered the right side of her face from the temple to her jaw. Her right eyelids were grossly thick with fluid and were swollen shut. An intravenous tube led to her right arm and a monitor beeped periodically at one side of her bed. The beeping instantly reminded her of her own mother's long hospitalization for a devastating cancer she did not survive. It was as if the sound had been engraved in her mind forever. She glanced up at Mrs. Rodoni and saw a face glistening with tears and her right hand clutching rosary beads—the image of the Sorrowful Madonna. It made her want to go around the bed and put her arm around her shoulders.

Outrage welled up in Marya. She wanted to know why this had happened. Who could have wanted to harm this girl? A tinge of hysteria gripped her as she pleaded, "Who did this to you? What happened, Vittoria?" She reached out to touch Vittoria's hand, but withdrew it before making contact.

Vittoria's left eye half opened and she strained to move her lips to say something, but her voice was so faint that nothing made sense to Marya.

Mrs. Rodoni whispered, "Vittoria is in no condition right now to…"

"Vittoria, can you tell me?" Marya pleaded. "I must know."

"Dr. Bradwell, she has had a severe concussion. The doctor told us not to..."

Marya wished that she had done something the instant that Vittoria mentioned in that email that she might have been followed. But what could she have done? Waves of guilt and helplessness washed over her and made her feel faint.

Mr. Rodoni stood mute, looking at his daughter. His face was flushed and his gray hair bristled. He bit his quivering lower lip. Then he spoke up with a tone of blame Marya could not miss. "She was returning from the Biblioteca Marciana when this happened to her. What a pity. Another day or two and she wouldn't have been involved in this damned foolish research any longer, Dr. Bradwell. Just another day or two. That's all. She was planning to look for another job," he said, pinning her with his glare. Mrs. Rodoni put her hand on his forearm and whispered something to him.

Marya was overcome and confused by his statement. Her mouth went dry and her legs weakened. She knew that if she did not sit down right away, she would faint on the floor. She left Vittoria's bedside and took a seat by the door, fanning herself with her hand. How exactly was this her fault? What had she done that would have landed Vittoria in this hospital ward?

Mrs. Rodoni went over to Marya and with her free hand patted her on the head. A troubled look crossed her face. "Dr. Bradwell, I must tell you something. When they brought Vittoria in last night, she kept repeating your name. The emergency room workers didn't know who she was talking about. I straightened it out with them and the police that she was your assistant. But I have a bad feeling that she was calling your name out for a reason. And now,

I'm telling you that if you remain in Venice, please be careful, because I think Vittoria was trying to warn you."

There was a sudden choking sound coming from Vittoria's mouth. Her eyes were wide with terror and she seemed to be nodding at her mother's words. Mrs. Rodoni rushed to her side and held her hand. "What is it, Vittoria? Did you hear what I just said?"

Vittoria nodded again and closed her left eye tightly. A nurse entered the room and announced that it was time to take Vittoria for X-rays and further tests. The nurse asked Marya and Vittoria's parents to step aside to let her move the hospital bed from the room. As the bed rolled by, Vittoria stared at Marya with her left eye and strained to move her lips. Without stopping, the nurse rolled the gurney out into the hallway and disappeared with it into an elevator.

Marya did her best to stand and say good-bye to the Rodonis, her emotions in a tangle. Once she had left them and the elevator doors had closed, a wave of pity for Vittoria and her parents overcame her and she began to weep. She left the hospital and boarded a water taxi to return to the Gabrielli Sandwirth, vowing to find the thug who had beaten Vittoria so savagely. She had no answer as to what she would do about continuing with her research because she decided she simply could not ask the Rodonis' help in locating the records she so desperately needed.

* * * * *

A wave of remorse engulfed her once she reached her hotel room again. She could only pace and glance through her balcony window at the Grand Canal. She knew that her beloved Piazza San Marco was literally steps away, but she had no desire to go there, even for a walk to gather her thoughts. What had happened to Vittoria was emotionally crushing. Her mood halted her in her tracks. But she couldn't just hang out in her hotel room or, worse, turn tail and run home to Boston. She needed to do something. Anything. Khalid had told her at Logan that if she needed anything, to give him a call and he would be by her side in a flash.

She thought that if there was any time that she could use his consolation and his advice it was now. Should she call him to her side? She reflected on that as she looked down from her third floor window at the boats moored at their piers on the Riva degli Schiavone. She decided that she would call him, yes. But not to come to Venice to hold her hand. She was strong, like her mother and her grandmother, and like them she would get through it. She just needed Khalid to buck up her courage over the phone. Besides, she had promised him regular updates from overseas. He deserved to know the truth about how she was doing. She picked up the phone and dialed his number.

Once he heard her voice, he knew that something was wrong. She didn't want to let him know that she had been crying miserably but she was unable to hide it from him. She poured out her grief to him in one, long, uninterrupted tale, reciting the brutal attack on Vittoria, her diagnosis, the grief of her parents, the suspicious nature of the attack and the possibility that she herself might be in some kind of danger, judging from Vittoria's limited communications.

Khalid expressed his profound sorrow over what happened to Vittoria and how the attack affected Marya both personally and professionally. He said that he saw no possibility of a connection between the work she was doing and the business with Vittoria. He offered to come right over the minute she wanted him there, but Marya explained that she would have another cry or two then get her emotions in check and get straight to work. It was through her work that she would find her strength and possibly pick up any clue about the assault. She gently declined his offer to come over but was thankful for it nonetheless. He cautioned her that if she felt personally threatened to either go to the police or get out of town and under no condition to try to take on a potential killer or, God forbid, the Mafia.

He asked if she had had a chance to review any of the work that Vittoria had done recently and she replied that under the circumstances she felt she couldn't even broach the subject with the Rodonis but she planned to contact them again or go directly to the convent library herself to locate the journal using the few clues Vittoria had given her.

"All right, Marya. I know you're a big girl. I admire your spirit and all that, but I hope you don't take any risks. Just promise me that you'll exercise some caution and don't go off thinking you're some kind of Warrior Princess, all right?"

"Don't worry, Khalid, I won't. But you know something? I swear I'm going to find that low-life coward if it's the last thing I do."

"Marya, I love you and I don't want anything to happen to you. Just be careful. That's all I'm asking and call me again when you've got something or just feel like you need someone to talk to."

She hung up, happy knowing that Khalid was thinking of her. How many times Khalid Agarwal had been there for her over the past three years, she couldn't count. It was now the time to act. She picked up her gold locket from the mirrored dressing table by the balcony window. She opened it and looked at the two photos it contained, one of her grandmother and the other of her mother. She could almost hear the words her mother used so often with her in the last weeks of her life: "Don't ever quit, Marya. And don't be afraid of trying. You can do whatever you set your mind to accomplish." She put the locket around her neck and closed her briefcase. She locked the door and went to the elevator. Out in front of the hotel, she would get a taxi-boat to take her to the Convent of Saint Lawrence.

CHAPTER 12

As the burnished copper-colored doors of the elevator opened, Marya was disturbed to see Liam Di Angelo facing her. She entered, avoiding eye-contact with him. The doors slid shut quietly. With her face close to the reflective doors, she caught a distorted image of him behind her and to her right. She hoped he would not address her in any way whatsoever. The thought of Vittoria lying in her hospital bed left no tolerance in her for idle chit chat. Today, she was on a mission: to locate the journal that Vittoria had found at the convent.

He coughed. “What’s on your agenda, today? Hours of study in some musty library?”

Marya tightened her grip on her briefcase.

There was a long silence as the elevator approached the ground floor. She pursed her lips and said nothing. The man had a gift for provoking her; but, still, something inside of her responded to him physically.

“Look, I didn’t mean to offend you,” he said.

Without looking at him, she asked haughtily, “And how about you, Mr. Di Angelo? Heading off to meet some money-grubbing peddler of stolen antiquities?”

“I’m sorry. I shouldn’t have been so flippant. I didn’t mean it. I’d still like to have a truce. How about it?”

“You know, you were right in London when you called our encounters unpleasant. I’d go a step further. I’d characterize them as nasty. So why don’t you just give it a rest? Please. Just leave me alone.”

After what seemed an endless ten seconds, the elevator slid imperceptibly to rest. The doors glided open and she made her first step out onto the gorgeous marble floor of the lobby. The heel of her left shoe caught in the gap between the elevator and the lobby floor. She stumbled forward and dropped her briefcase. She caught herself from falling on her face by landing in a genuflection, with the right knee touching the floor, but her briefcase flew out of her hands and went sliding along the highly polished surface. It snapped open, throwing out dozens of pages in front of a group waiting for the next ride up. None of them made a move to assist her.

Di Angelo's voice right behind her irked her. "You all right?"

She felt him taking her by the arm with one hand while positioning the other lightly under her rear to help her to her feet. "Just get away from me," she said brushing his hand away from her rear. "There you go again with those Roman hands."

"I'll get those things for you." He rushed off to pick up the papers that lay scattered on the floor.

"Leave them alone! I can manage without any more of your help."

Ignoring her, he gathered up the stray papers and took them to an oversized glass-on-steel coffee-table. He sat down on a leather sofa and proceeded to inspect them while Marya got her briefcase.

"Whoa! This is very good," he said, admiring a drawing.

"Leave my things alone. Give me that." She tried to take the paper he was looking at but he held it out of reach.

"Give that to me, you… "

"This is just the kind of thing that I'm looking for. I could sell this stuff in a second in Boston or Dallas."

"Not if I can help it. Give me that, I said, or I'll call hotel security."

"What are these things?"

She was exasperated and wanted to get the paper back from him so she could leave. "All right, if you must absolutely know, those are the Golden Tablets of Command that Marco Polo and his family received from Kublai Khan. Super-passports of solid gold. Now give that to me."

"And you're looking for them?" he asked. "What are they worth?"

"More than their weight in gold. Way more. Probably tens of millions of dollars."

"Why so much? Gold is gold, isn't it?"

"These are not just so many kilos of gold. They represent a tale of two worlds and two civilizations, the connection between Asia and Europe, Marco Polo and Kublai Khan. They are priceless and they are the heritage of mankind. I don't expect you to care about any of that, though." She felt she was talking to a mere philistine who knew the price of everything but the value of nothing.

"Look, Ms. Bradwell, tell you what. I'll give it back if you have lunch with me out on the terrace where we can catch the breeze. On me. As long as you order for us in Italian." Di Angelo took another long look at the picture.

"You can't bribe me like that, Mr. Di Angelo. That drawing belongs to me, anyway."

He looked chagrined. "You're right. I'm sorry. Here it is," he said, handing it to her. "I was just angling for a truce between us."

"What good would that do? If you're thinking that we are going to meet again, let alone talk like bosom buddies, I have to tell you it ain't going to happen." She placed the picture in her briefcase and turned to go.

"Wait. Please. I've got a business proposal."

"What? Are you kidding? You are just maddening."

"No, I'm not kidding. I'm proposing a partnership. I specialize in art objects of historical importance for clients around the U.S. Some of it, is literally straight from the ground, I'll admit. But I can see that we—I mean you and I—we deal in the same merchandise."

"First of all, I don't deal in anything. Second, what you do is illegal in most countries and that is precisely why a partnership with you would be utter madness. I know what you do, Mr. Di Angelo. How can you engage in that kind of trafficking? And how dare you approach me with such an outrageous proposal? Your kind is responsible for the looting of important archeological sites, damage to the artifacts and the loss of crucial scientific data forever. And the public does not get to appreciate the beauty and the history of those treasures. Frankly, I'm shocked that you can sit there and matter-of-factly admit what you do for work. It's just…" She was so angry with him that she could not continue.

"It's a living and I do very well at it. I'm not going to spend my life slaving away like my parents still do. Besides, my clients appreciate the services I provide. The artifacts we pull from the ground go to loving families and sometimes these wealthy folks bequeath them to museums. In the end everyone is happy. I'll say it again, and proudly, that we should form a partnership, considering the quality of the objects you deal in, the status you have in the field, your curriculum vitae and so on. Those are real assets in this business. As for myself, I have important and useful connections both here in Venice and in a couple of other places. I'll introduce you to them. What do you say?"

"What did I just tell you? Didn't you hear a thing? We're poles apart. I'm a historian, not a gold digger and my research is not going to be turned into a grubby treasure hunt."

"Of course not. I wouldn't think of it. What I'm trying to emphasize is our great complementary skills. I operate down on the street level. You're an ivory tower type. It's a match made in heaven. We can work out our differences to mutual advantage."

"That, Mr. Di Angelo, would take a miracle. And I don't believe in miracles."

She snapped the catches on her briefcase and looked down at him. "It's plain to me that you want to get your hands on these Tablets of Command, but let me be perfectly clear. Stay away from me. I don't have anything further to say to you. And if you so much as come close to me again, I'll get the *carabinieri* to haul you off."

CHAPTER 13

As Marya stepped aboard the taxi-boat at the pier in front of the hotel, she was feeling a new-found courage and she was just plain glad for the first time in days. She had an appointment with the nuns at the convent in fifteen minutes and she was eager to plunge into the mystery of Polo's journal. At the same time, she pledged to herself to try to learn why Vittoria had become the victim of a vicious assault. She was glad that she had decided to leave her briefcase off at the reception desk to be stored in the hotel safe. It was more of a nuisance than it was worth. Most of all, she was glad at having put Di Angelo in his place. She detested his ilk and had seen more than once how men like him and his suppliers had brought scandal and ruin to the fields of art and archaeology. She had also seen the careers of some big museum directors go down in flames thanks to the same kind of shady dealing.

Following the trail that Vittoria had blazed for her, she told the pilot where to take her. He maneuvered the little craft skillfully down a series of narrow canals, passing under many little arched bridges. It drifted to a halt at a landing near the Convent of San Lorenzo fifteen minutes later. She paid the driver, stepped out and hurried along the same walkway she imagined Vittoria had taken until she came to the ancient main door of the convent with its intricately sculpted stone frame. She rang once and waited, sizing up the cracks and holes in the convent's façade that gave it the air of a derelict, storm-battered ship. She looked into the repulsive waters of the canal and felt a queasy roll of her stomach. It was plain to see that the city of Venice did not have a state-of-the-art municipal sewage system.

It often revolted her when she saw starry-eyed tourists in gondolas skimming those waters with their hands.

No one had come to the door, so she rang again, her thumb holding the button down for a half minute. She waited and still no one came. She wondered if the nun who took her call remembered the appointment. She heard the sound of a motor far down the canal. She looked to her left and saw a small craft slowly coming her way. As it passed from the shadows under a low arched bridge she saw that its only passenger was a rather large fellow. He appeared to be part Asian, part European, and of massive build. The boat stopped at the same place where she had disembarked and the hulking fellow stepped off.

He wore a western-style suit that seemed incongruous, as did his lumbering stride. This was not your average tourist in Venice, she decided, and rang the doorbell again, longer than before. Something had to happen soon or the brute would soon be upon her. Where is that nun, Sister Villana? When will someone open this door, for God's sake?

She had a fresh image of Vittoria in her hospital room, her hair fanning out on the pillow, a purplish-yellow swelling about her right eye, her inability to mutter an understandable word, the constant beep of the monitor and the antiseptic odor in the room. My God, she thought, if no one answered soon, she would scream. She rapped repeatedly on the door with the flat of her hand and on the fifth rap, a nun opened the small window in the door.

"Yes?"

"I'm here to do some research in the library. I called earlier for…"

"Oh, yes. You're Dr. Bradwell. Didn't Sister Villana tell you that we are closed at this time for two hours? You will need to come back later."

"I need…" She glanced to her left and the monster had disappeared from view into an alley. "I need to come inside. Sister, just open the door and let me in. Jesus, Mary and Joseph. There is someone just around the corner. I'm afraid he's going to attack me. Please. Open up." The panic she was feeling constricted her throat and made her voice strident.

"I'm sorry," said the nun peering sideways up the canal in the direction Marya had just looked, "There is no one out there. You'll be all right. These hours are reserved for our holy offices. It is policy. Please come back later." With a forced smile, she shut the window abruptly.

Marya pounded on the door. "No, please, just let me wait inside," she cried. It was useless.

She looked up and down the canal. There were no taxiboats anywhere except the boat that had dropped the man off a minute earlier and its motor was still idling. She was confused. Where had the giant gone? Was she mistaken? Maybe the nun was right after all. She waved to the pilot of the taxi boat, still in the same place, and was relieved as the pilot hit the throttle and brought it forward to pick her up.

It inched closer and stopped. The pilot was a cheery-faced young Italian, she thought. He saluted and asked her where she wanted to go. "To a café. I need a coffee. No, I think I need a good drink."

"Sure, just hop in. I know a good place, Signorina." For the second time, she was grateful for the haven of a simple taxi-boat. She got in, thinking how foolish she had just been, reacting to the seeming threat of a large man. It must have been all the insane activity and experiences of the past two or three days, she thought. Then she heard a deep base voice coming from the walkway.

"Move over."

She looked up to the walkway and almost jumped into the canal from the shock. The massive brute was back and he was talking to her!

"Who are you? Why are you following me?"

"We need to talk with you about the Tablets of Command."

"Who *are* you? What do you want?" In a flash, she recalled the scene she had made back at the Gabrielli and that ever-helpful Mr. Di Angelo. She remembered how he had so eagerly gathered up all the contents of her briefcase in the hotel lobby less than a half hour earlier and that he had zoomed in on the picture of the golden tablets like a guided missile. He had offered to introduce her to his local business partners. If this big oaf happened to be one of them, she would get the police after Di Angelo. But the thuggish lackey shocked her with his bluntness, "That's none of your business. You will just come with me for a talk about the Tablets of Command."

"You know what?" she said with her hands on her hips. "You people have a lot of nerve. I'm not going anywhere with you and you can tell Di Angelo that I'm reporting this incident to the police." She felt her gumption coming back as she spoke up.

The Italian-looking pilot egged her on. "That's right, miss. Tell him and that Di Angelo guy to take a hike."

She was thankful for that backing. How right he is, she thought and challenged the bully on the walkway. "Let Di Angelo know that I don't deal in stolen art, never have and never will. If he keeps on bugging me, I'll get in touch with Interpol and the Italian customs people to round up the whole darn bunch of you. Now get lost."

Her words appeared to have a sobering effect on the lout. He gave her a quizzical look and toned down his message. "You are invited to a meeting with my superior and you will show him respect. If you refuse to do so willingly, I will use other methods."

Then it struck her. This goon was not only one of Di Angelo's men, he was also the one who had clobbered Vittoria and nearly killed her. And all those chance encounters with Di Angelo? They were not by chance at all. He had been on her tail, literally, all the way from Boston to the Gabrielli Sandwirth. Good God, she thought. Aboard a taxi boat or not, she was still in grave danger. She feared that if she didn't high-tail it out of the isolated canal right away, she'd take a fatal beating. She turned to the boat pilot and ordered him loudly to take off.

"Yes, Madame," the pilot said.

Satisfied that she was in safe hands, she hurled an insult at the hoodlum on the quay. "I don't care how you threaten me, you goon. I'm not going anywhere with you."

She turned away from him and flicked her wrist at the pilot to get going. "I'm out of here," she said, taking a seat. Suddenly the taxi boat rocked violently. The would-be kidnapper had stepped aboard and made a lunge to seize her left arm. "Just shut up and move over. You're coming with me."

CHAPTER 14

Liam Di Angelo left the hotel shortly after Dr. Bradwell, smarting from the brush-off she had given him. She had a snooty, high-and-mighty attitude that a Harvard professor like her would have towards all mortal men. He had not anticipated the way she called him out for the kind of work he engaged in. Certainly, no one he had ever met had done that. He dismissed it as typical ivory-tower preachiness towards real-world people. But he meant what he told her about what a team they would make and he had not completely given up on pushing the idea even harder. Having her as a partner could double his income.

His taxi-boat brought him to the Riva de Blasio in the Santa Croce district and let him off at a pier in front of a Renaissance palazzo. It was the property of Giovanni Bellardo and Sons, dealers in antiquities for over seventy-five years. Its entire ground level served as its showroom and had a partitioned area set off for a private office and some private living space. The second level served as a warehouse and the top floor served as the main residence. The three levels were connected by a stairway and two elevators. The Bellardo name was well thought-of and the premises looked not just honest and respectable, but impressive.

But looks are deceptive and no one knew that better than Liam. From four years of behind-the-scenes dealings with Giovanni Bellardo, son of the founder and the present owner and manager, he understood well the reasons for the success of the business. Bellardo and Sons was not all that it appeared to be. Neither the core trade of the business nor the activities of his two grown sons were suspected by the outside world. And it was this hidden side of the business that made Bellardo exceptionally prosperous compared to similar establishments in Western Europe.

The door to the showroom was open and he entered and found a buzzer in an out-of-the-way place a few steps from the entry area. He pressed it and strolled down the central aisle of the cavernous display room. As always, he lingered here and there around sculptures, massive pieces of furniture that could only have come from other palazzos from the region, gorgeous bronze lamps and vases. It was all sumptuous, exquisite and ornate. Grand and breathtaking, too, but not to his own taste, with rare exception. Why would anyone want to own these over-sized dust-catchers?

He was inspecting a seven-foot tall rococo armoire studded with cherubs when Bellardo came out and greeted him, his arms outstretched for a hearty embrace. Liam thought that Giovanni looked a few years older than he did six months earlier. A few wisps of gray hair brushed back over his head did little but emphasize his baldness. Bellardo led him to his office behind the showroom, unlocked it and had him enter first. He asked Liam about his flight and whether he and Melissa were making wedding plans. Liam replied that the flight over the Atlantic had been rocky and so was his relationship with Melissa lately. He declined an offer of a glass of brandy because there might be purchases north of five or six million dollars as a result of this session, judging from the photos of the exciting collection of gold artifacts Bellardo had recently mailed him. He had to keep his head perfectly clear when negotiations got under way.

"I'll go get those articles in a little while. You're going to love them. And remember, Liam, you are like a son to me. A son. Do you hear? You will be the first one to see them and have a chance to buy them. But before I do that, I'd like to show you a few miscellaneous pieces. Do you mind?"

"No, certainly not." Liam was used to this delaying tactic that Bellardo used unfailingly, hoping to sell stuff he had not been able to unload on anyone else.

"You sure you don't mind?"

"No, fine, fine. Go right ahead."

He sat Liam down at a three-meter long table covered in black velvet where there was already a white cloth sack tied with a gold silk-braided cord. He loosened the cord and eased a triptych reliquary of Armenian origin out of the sack. Liam examined the human figures and the inscriptions on it and told him that it was very nice. Privately, he thought there was a client at a southwestern museum who would pay double what Bellardo was asking for it. "I'll think about it, Giovanni."

Liam would rather that Giovanni get on to the two Scythian collections but he let him try one more item on him. This time Bellardo gently slid a fine wooden chest across the table towards him. "Take a look, Liam. This is really unique. Go ahead." Liam opened it and carefully removed a unique gold horn—four repoussé Christian saints were portrayed standing between two bands of Arabic inscriptions. Giovanni pointed out its fine emerald insets and said that for a 14th century Syrian piece it was a true rarity. Liam agreed and said he had never seen anything like it. When Giovanni told him he was asking ninety-thousand dollars for it, he just nodded noncommittally.

Liam was impatient to see the Scythian collections and snapped when Bellardo reached for yet another artifact at hand. "Giovanni. Let's cut to the chase. You know what I'm here for. How about it? Where are those Scythian pieces?"

"Of course, of course. Didn't I tell you you're like my very own son? Wait here. I'll go get them." Bellardo went into an adjoining room and returned a minute later straining with the weight of a heavy chest. Liam leaped from his chair and helped the old man lay it down on the table.

"Christ, this is heavy. Why the hell didn't you ask for some help? You could have dropped it."

"That's my private room back there. I don't let anyone, even my sons and my daughter in there. You're privileged just to be admitted to this office. I'll lay the pieces out myself. Just sit down and enjoy. You will go crazy when you see this first set."

"Where does it come from?"

"Fresh from the grave, you might say. The second set, too. They're from a burial mound in the Ukraine. A royal grave west of the Caspian Sea, according to my supplier."

"Your supplier? Don't you mean some government official on the take?"

"Yeah, all right. A guy name Shevchenko. I don't exactly know what branch he works in and personally I don't care." One by one he laid out lustrous gold artifacts on the long table, handling them like newborn infants. "Lovely, aren't they?"

This is what Liam had made the journey for. The gold artifacts were far more splendid and radiant seen in person than they were in the photos. He felt goose bumps with each breathtaking artifact. "This is more like it." As the collection on the table grew, Liam tried to stifle any appearanace of enthusiasm. He realized that Bellardo was sizing him up and would ramp up his asking price for the collection if he sensed interest on Liam's part.

"You don't see treasures like these on the market every day, my son. You can bet your ass on that." Scythian, 8th century B.C. Superb design. Take a look at this." He hefted a gold pectoral decorated with a wounded stag. Its body was anatomically perfect, except for its highly exaggerated antlers.

Liam had become a little familiar with the motif that was found all over central Asia, thanks to his crash studies on the subject aboard the transatlantic flight and his visit to the British Museum. He had learned that the Scythians were a nomadic culture of horsemen who roamed the steppes north of the Caspian Sea. They were very important in the middle of the first millennium B.C. and had a major impact on the high civilizations of the Greeks and the Persians. He had also just studied and photographed the Oxus Treasure in the British Museum. Twisted gold bracelets on the table bore the same representations of wild animals from lions to griffins and goats. And he marveled at the quantity of gold sequin-like squares that Giovanni laid out for him. The persons that they had once adorned must have been of very high rank.

Liam's eyes roamed greedily over the collection and he wondered how the second set would affect him. The objects laid out on the table were the best he had ever seen when he compared their workmanship and condition to those of other cultures, bar none. Items such as these, though not of this high quality, had been snapped up at Christie's auction for small fortunes. "What are you asking for them, Giovanni?"

"Six million five, not a cent less. And remember, there's more to come."

Liam knew that this price was a starting point in the negotiations and that it was expected he would bargain him down. He also knew that objects such as these would command a decent premium over the purchase price because they were rare Scythian pieces and these were in growing demand from well-heeled clients and institutions. He thought of the modest display of Scythian art at the British Museum and figured that he could interest them in this set for a hefty price provided he had the technical support of a scholar of standing like Dr. Bradwell of Harvard. He could also sell them in Boston, New York and San Francisco easily with her fronting for him. She had the impeccable and impressive credentials that his clients demanded and that he lacked. Moreover, she knew the field probably far better than he did. What else could he do to draw her into an alliance? He had to get her on board.

After Bellardo's usual hype about the rarity of the gold objects and their indisputable provenance, Liam made an offer that Bellardo accepted. They shook on the deal and toasted with a fine liqueur. It took Bellardo almost half an hour to gather up the pieces from the table and store them away in the adjoining private room.

He emerged with yet another large chest. "And now for the crown jewels," he said with an air of triumph. "Wait until you see this. If you think you've seen Scythian treasure…" He didn't finish his sentence as he hefted the chest onto the table.

Liam was bug-eyed as the old salesman gingerly removed the artifacts from the chest. He explained that they had come from the same burial mound in the Ukraine as the first set but he had separated them for marketing purposes. These objects appeared to him so magnificent and stunning taken together that they would be the main draw at any world class museum for decades. Among the choicest items were a necklace of twisted gold portraying two lions feasting on a stag, a gold helmet and a glorious diadem of golden leaves.

Liam drew in his breath as Giovanni laid the last piece out on the table, careful to avoid damaging the delicate masterpiece. At the sight of it, any reserve he felt simply disappeared. "It's stunning. I'm amazed that a nomadic culture could do anything this refined. It must have been made for a queen, I mean, really. Reminds me of the diadem that the Schliemanns uncovered in Troy. You've seen that photo of Schliemann's wife wearing something like this, haven't you, Giovanni?

"Of course, I have."

"How much are you asking for the batch?"

"Twelve million. And I'm selling it as a collection."

"Dollars or pesos?"

"Ha ha ha."

"Sorry, Giovanni. I'm going to take a pass on this. I don't have the funds right now. Too bad. I could retire on the sale of this collection."

"You sure you don't want it? You won't have a second chance, believe me."

"I'm up to my armpits as it is. Besides, I'll have enough trouble getting the other stuff through U.S. Customs. I'm thinking of having it flown in by a Colombian cartel."

Bellardo laughed and began putting the pieces back in their container. "Another drink?" he asked, raising a crystal decanter.

Di Angelo raised his glass. With the day's business past them, Bellardo took an arm chair opposite him and told him some more about the Scythian treasure. "Like I said, it was a Ukrainian official who handled the delivery. That guy, Shevchenko. Nice guy. Seemed more than pleased with what I gave him for it. He said he and two other Ukrainians brought it up through Bulgaria, Montenegro and Croatia.

"That couldn't have been easy."

"He's mastered the art of payoff. He sat right there where you're sitting now and told me that he liberated—that was his expression—the goods from a bunch of Tajiks operating illegally in his country. He claimed they were working for some kind of mastermind who is coordinating a search for gold caches like this all across the Asian steppe. Shevchenko's not a stranger to this but it's not easy work. He said the Tajiks are ruthless and when you do a deal with them it's dog eat dog. I have no reason to doubt that there's blood on this treasure." Bellardo drained his glass in one slug.

"You said Tajiks. As in Tajikistan? Are you shitting me, Giovanni? I doubt there is one soul in the whole country who could scrape together enough money for this quality stuff."

"They're not buying the stuff, Liam. They're mining the tombs and they're keeping it."

"How long has this been going on?"

"A year? Two? Three? I don't know. But one thing is clear. If they have removed treasure from other burial mounds, none of it's reaching the world market. This is the first time that the contents of a rich Scythian burial have come to my attention in a very long time and I keep an eye on that. It makes you wonder, doesn't it? Who's the guy that's collecting all this shit? And why?"

"Well, I'm glad I got my share before your mastermind got it all. By the way, you won't see me trotting off to Tajikistan for my next buy. There's a brutal civil war going on over there. Lots of Islamic fundamentalists running amok. The place makes Afghanistan look like the land of milk and honey. Other than making war on each other there's not much else to do in that neck of the woods but sell opium and smuggle weapons."

Giovanni's tale about the plundering of Scythian treasure on the Asian steppe reminded him of the raking over the coals he got from Dr. Bradwell earlier. It was clear to him that the Ukrainians had battled the Tajiks and between them, they surely must have left a wreck of a prime archeological site behind them as they took out the loot. Her scolding about his part in the scheme of things had left a bad taste in his mouth and he knew that a little part of what she said was true.

He shifted in his chair uncomfortably and asked Bellardo if he had ever heard of gold tablets that Marco Polo had once owned. Bellardo told him that he had seen only one such artifact and it was at the Hermitage Museum in Russia. In his opinion, if Polo had ever owned one it would have been melted down long ago into earrings and pins.

"Are you sure?"

"Polo never really had much, despite his bragging and exaggeration. A small collection of his valuables went to the Doge and the rest went to his three daughters and his wife. Polo had no direct descendants after the third generation. Whatever so-called treasure he had was gone by then. Why do you ask?"

"I'm in touch with an American who's looking for Polo's gold right here in Venice. I saw some artist's conception of them and I wouldn't mind getting my hands on them, either." He omitted telling Bellardo that he had angled for a partnership with the woman.

"Your friend is nuts. It's as far-fetched as the claims for UFO's. Ridiculous. There aren't any of those around today except one on display at the Hermitage Museum in Russia."

"My acquaintance believes they could be worth hundreds of thousands of dollars, maybe millions."

"Bah! Forget it. Tell him to take his meds every day."

"It's an American woman who's looking for them."

"I see. Well, tell her to come over and look at what I've got for sale. I've got plenty of gold to look at. Ha! Why not bring her over today?"

"I don't think so." He looked at his watch. "Well, Giovanni, I've got to go." He shook hands with Bellardo across the table and stood up. "Give my regards to Francesca. Always a pleasure."

On his way back to the hotel, a blissful mood settled upon him as he tallied up the profits he would make off his genteel clients in the U. S. Overall, he felt good about the deal he reached with Bellardo and little, if any, remorse. He thought of Dr. Bradwell as an intelligent, if somewhat self-important and uppity academic. He wondered how she fared after she had left him. Certainly not as well as he made out, he was sure. He figured he would find out when he bumped into her again at the hotel.

CHAPTER 15

It didn't take Marya long to decide on her next move. In a split second she had bolted to the far side of the boat and got a foot up on the gunwale. She eyed the foul, blue-gray waters of the canal and figured it would be far better to take a dunking than to end up bound and gagged and god-knows-what-else in some damp palazzo down one of these dead-end canals.

The hooligan swiped at her with his thick, meaty hand but she ducked and evaded his grasp. Almost. With his other hand he grabbed for her neck, but only managed to hook two fingers around the chain of her gold locket. As she swung away from him, the delicate chain of her locket snapped and both the locket and the chain dropped into the murky waters. She quickly followed, mounting the side of the boat with her shoes still on her feet. She teetered on the brink for an instant, then thrust herself off. She swam ten yards under the surface of the putrid, brackish water, coming up near the opposite side of the canal just yards from a marble stairway. She shook her hair and wiped the stinking, briny water from her forehead and eyes, trying to gauge how far she was from the boat. She saw that it had backed up and turned and was now rumbling straight at her, the gleeful Italian at the controls.

She took a deep breath and with rapid strokes and furious kicking made a four-yard dash to the stone-lined side of the canal. As she tried hauling herself out, she struggled again and again to gain purchase with her fingers on the wall but a mossy growth caused her hands to slide off. She fell back into the water just as the boat closed in on her. She dove again beneath the surface, swimming it seemed like forever, her eyes tightly shut, her lungs aching for air. It must have been another whole minute under water and yards away from the boat before she broke the surface again. She looked around and spotted the stern of the taxi boat and the two men leaning over its sides trying to locate her. She was safely in the shadows of a bridge and looked up. Overhead, she saw its name in white lettering on a blue-glazed tile: Ponti Marco Polo. Perfect, she thought.

She slithered quietly out of the water onto a stone staircase. Trying hard to silence the squishy noises of her soggy shoes, she sidled up against a palazzo wall and around a corner into a dark alley. Only then did she burst into an all-out run. In her headlong rush to escape, she stumbled, losing one of her shoes. With no one now following her, she stopped, tore off the other shoe and carried it through twists and turns until she suddenly burst out upon a bright open space along a broader canal.

She didn't care that she looked and smelled as bad as a bucket of mud at low tide. She spotted several idle taxi boats bobbing at their moorings a few feet from the alleyway from which she had just emerged. She needed help, any help at all. Dripping wet, she ran to a startled pilot of one of them and begged him to take her to the Gabrielli Sandwirth fast. He looked her up and down with disgust, but agreed to take her aboard. He revved up the motor and handed her a grubby shawl. As they started to inch away from the pier, he told her to help herself to some hot coffee from a two-quart stainless steel thermos on the seat next to her.

She didn't feel like coffee after what she had been through. She looked at herself with revulsion. Her clothes were wet and sagging like rags. Her hair was knotted and stringy. A septic odor clung to her like Romanza di Venezia, the strong cheap perfume sold in the tourist boutiques. She shivered from the dampness but at least she felt safe.

The feeling did not last long. The taxi suddenly listed

heavily. With eyes wide with shock, she looked up to see the huge lout again, one leg on the landing, the other on the side of her boat. She searched for anything in the boat she could use in self-defense and suddenly found her hand resting on the stainless steel thermos. Her fingers instinctively hooked into its handle as she clenched her jaw and rose. In one wide, circular motion, she threw all she had into slamming the man's shaved head with the thermos. It was full of liquid and it hit its target broadside at the very moment when his balance was weakest. His waved his arms like rotors and threw one foot in the air. With a deafening roar, he tilted backwards and flopped into the growing gap between the boat and the landing. "Hold it a minute," she shouted to the pilot. The pilot dared not contradict her. He brought the boat alongside her would-be captor who was floundering in the water. She unscrewed the cap of the thermos, poured out a cup and tossed the scalding coffee in the lout's face. "Take a good long drink," she screamed. "Come on. Let's get out of here," she yelled at the pilot.

Exhausted, she slumped on the seat and struggled to come down from the adrenalin-pumping high. She took long, steady, slow drafts of air into her lungs. Who was behind this attack? Clearly, the big thug was taking orders from above and whoever that was also knew that she was hunting for the Polo treasure. She shuddered, seeing Vittoria's face and knowing she had escaped a similar brutal attack from this very same monster.

Her rude encounter with Di Angelo at the hotel this morning gave her something to think about. The way he had pawed around in her papers. His admitting that he had connections in Venice with shady dealers in antiquities. Above all, his attempt to rope her into a partnership to go after the golden tablets aroused her suspicion. There was no mistaking his goal, no matter how well-dressed and handsome he looked. When she got back to the hotel she planned to get in touch with the Italian police immediately and get him arrested. He would learn not to mess with her again!

The pilot got her to her destination in minutes. Only there did she realize that what she was holding in her hand was her one remaining shoe and had long since lost her purse as she fled from the attack. "Give me a minute and I'll go in and get your money," she said. She tossed him the shawl and stepped onto the platform in front of the hotel. "Thanks for the coffee. I'll be right out."

As she climbed the few stairs to the entrance, still holding her shoe in her hand, she took another look at her clothes. She almost gagged. A group of the hotel's well-heeled clientele passed her going down the steps, whispering and curling their lips at her. She must look like a forlorn, wretched cur, she guessed, but inside, she felt as mean as a junkyard dog, ready to go after her tormentors. She straightened up and held her head high, determined to get to her room immediately and call the police.

Suddenly, from the direction of the pier she heard Di Angelo call her name and she halted.

CHAPTER 16

Liam ran up the steps, taking two at a time, his face registering disbelief. "I almost didn't recognize you. You look like a drowned rat. What happened? Can I help you?"

His choice of words inflamed her already foul mood. "You lousy, rotten hypocrite!" she yelled. "You know damn well what happened to me and I'm going to make you pay for it." She half-raised her shoe in her right hand to strike him with it before he grabbed her wrist to stop her.

She tore loose from his grasp and wheeled around to enter the lobby of the hotel through a gleaming brass revolving door. The doorman tried to stop her, but she placed her hand flat on his chest and shoved him away. Liam caught up with her, baffled.

"What do you mean, hypocrite?" I'm not a hypocrite."

"Just get away from me and leave me alone. I'm calling the police on you. You have a lot to answer for." She left a steady trail of drops behind her as she walked across the luxurious marble and carpeted floor.

"What?" he shouted. "The police? You're crazy. You've gone bananas. What did I ever do to you?"

"Just look at me. This is what you did, you creep," she hollered, veering around. She took the hem of her dress in both hands and wrung out enough canal water to make a foot-wide puddle on the beautiful floor. "Look at that. See what you've done? You're not getting away with this. I promise you that."

"I still don't get it. How come I'm to blame for this?" he asked, gesturing at her dress and the water on the floor.

"All right, then. You didn't do it personally. Naturally, because you wouldn't want to risk mussing up that fancy suit and your awesome hair. You just got one of those nice friends of yours, that big goon, to come after me. I had to jump in the canal to get away from him. And two to one he's the same thug that attacked my assistant two days ago. He could have snapped my neck like a twig."

"I don't have friends like that here and I don't know a thing about your assistant."

"Oh, you don't have any big, huge friends, huh, like this big?" she asked, raising her hand over her head.

"Well, in fact, I do. My supplier's son is very big, but he's gentle as a lamb. He wouldn't do anything like this to anyone."

"And I suppose he wouldn't know about Polo's tablets of command, would he?"

"Well, as a matter of fact, I was just talking with his dad about those tablets. The ones you showed me this morning. But so what? I'm not connected in any way to what happened to you."

She gave him a knowing look. "The tablets that I *showed* you? I did no such thing. You went nosing around in my personal papers without my permission and got a good long look at them. Face it. Once you saw the picture of the tablets you had to have them and the rest of the Polo treasure and you wanted to snooker me into working with you, didn't you? Admit it. Look, Mr. Di Angelo, I didn't fall off the cabbage truck this morning. I'm no one's fool."

Clients at the desk turned and stared at the two of them arguing heatedly in the middle of the lobby. The receptionist pressed a buzzer underneath the counter to alert the manager.

"Look, Dr. Bradwell, we've got to get to the bottom of this, because there has to be some terrible mix-up here. I am not responsible for what happened to you today and you still haven't explained it to me."

"You're after Polo's gold. It's as simple as that. And one of your goons made an attempt on my life."

"Me? After Polo's gold? You keep saying that. No way. Well, yes. That drawing of the gold bars was interesting but..."

"Exactly. Excuse me, now. I'm heading for my room and I'll let you do the rest of your explaining to the Italian authorities. I'm going to tell them the whole story, what you did to me on the airplane, how you groped my butt here in the lobby this morning and all the rest, right down to..."

"Groped you? What the? In your dreams! I didn't grope you. I was *helping* you up. And if you weren't so damn clumsy getting off the elevator, I wouldn't even have known about your stupid Polo treasure. You know what else? It won't help your case at all to make those kinds of accusations about me because here in Italy they are not taken seriously. This is what Italian men just do. It's normal. So go ahead."

Marya fumed. Worse yet, she felt beyond ugly as she saw herself in a gilt-framed mirror. She could win a prize. She really hated that he looked dapper and debonair in a superbly tailored suit with a linen shirt and silk tie while she looked like she had been through nine rounds of mud wrestling in Little Rock, Arkansas. Like *Beauty and the Beast* and *she* was playing the Beast. And he was right about her clumsiness. She hadn't taken that into account. How could anyone have planned her dumb accident outside the elevator?

"Just go away and leave me alone," she said wearily.

"Please, what's the matter? What happened to you? Let me help."

"I don't need your help. Just go away." On her way past the reception desk she asked the clerk for her briefcase. The clerk got it for her and asked if there was anything else she could do.

"Yes, there is. Could you dispose of this for me, please?" She handed the soggy shoe to her and moved on past gawking tourists to the elevators. In her wake there were three men: Liam, a bell-hop boy and a manager with mops and pails.

She punched the button for an elevator and suddenly spied the taxi-boat pilot heading her way fast. *Shit, shit, shit.* He caught up with her and demanded his fare in rapid-fire Italian. She apologized that she had not yet had a chance to get to her room to get the money, but if he'd wait here in the lobby she'd be back down in an instant. She knew it was a brazen lie, because she had no money in her room. She had lost her purse, her cash and her credit cards when she dove into the canal. Liam instantly took out his wallet and paid the fellow what he was owed and sent him on his way.

"Dr. Bradwell, I swear. Honest. I would not do what you're accusing me of. I had nothing to do with this. Believe me. What can I do to prove it?"

She parted her bedraggled hair from her face and saw an earnest, sincere expression. "You didn't have to pay him. I have more than enough cash in my room."

"It's peanuts."

"I still don't trust you."

"And I'm more than upset with you. Those accusations you made. I think you owe me a better explanation than you've given me. I swear, whatever happened to you was not my doing. There's gotta be a way that I can convince you of that."

"If you aren't the one, then who is? You're the only one in Venice who knows about my research... and you've been practically tracking me without let-up all the way from Boston. Explain that. I mean, it's unbelievable how many times we've been just thrown together."

As they rode up together, he did explain. He gave her even more details of his handling of cultural art for personal gain than he really had to. She held him in even less esteem for that but she felt he had at least given an honest account of himself. He escorted her right to her door when she finally told him about Vittoria. He began to understand her viewpoint. What it meant, he told her, was that she, too, was in serious danger and really needed the help of the police, not protection from him. Her near-miss today was clearly connected with the sad situation of Vittoria and there was definitely a third party out there who was tracking her. He wished that he had understood all this sooner.

"Well all right, Mr. Di Angelo. I'll see. I'm not ready to forgive you completely but we may be back to the status quo ante. If you'll excuse me, I desperately need to get into my room and take a shower." She slid the electronic key into the lock and opened the door. "You can go. I'll be all right now."

Liam caught a glimpse of the inside of the room even before she did. And the look on his face made her wheel around. Her jaw dropped and Liam barged past her into the room to check out a nightmarish disaster scene.

CHAPTER 17

Marya followed him into the middle of the room where she stood gazing at the chaotic mess for a minute, totally transfixed. Desk drawers were left hanging open. Her large suitcase had been emptied and her clothes were strewn about. The mattress lay at a crazy tilted angle, half on and half off the bed. The sheets were pulled off and tossed aside. In the meantime, Liam had cautiously opened the bathroom door and turned on the light.

"You better come in here and take a look," he said somberly.

"What's wrong?" she asked in a timid voice.

"Just come in and look. Maybe you can figure it out."

From the doorway, she peeked in as Liam pointed to the large mirror that stretched across half the bathroom wall. He pointed at a symbol crudely drawn on the mirror.

"That's my lipstick," she said horrified.

"What do you make of it? It looks like a large letter or a variant form of a crucifix. It could be the letter 'T.'"

"I don't know. I..." She placed her hands on her cheeks. "It's creepy."

"Are you all right? Come on, let's get you a seat," he suggested with a motion to the bedroom. He raised the mattress and shoved it into place on the bed and pushed the suitcase to the far side. "Here, sit down for a minute. You look pale."

She sat in a stupor before mumbling, "This is bad."

"Real bad. I'd say you're in deep trouble with someone right here in Venice. Considering what has happened to you today and to your assistant a couple of days ago, I would seriously reconsider my plans if I were you. You've got to get out of here and go back to the U.S."

"No. I'm not leaving Venice," she said with her jaw set in grim determination.

"Are you nuts? Your life is in danger. That much is clear."

"I'm not leaving until I find what I came for. You hear me?"

Liam paced, ran his hand through his hair and tried to think of a solution, fast. "Okay. If you want to stay in Venice, you've got to find a place to stay where whoever did this can't find you. And I don't mean that you just move to another hotel. You have to go into hiding."

"But where can I go? The only people that I know here are Vittoria's parents and right now, the way things are between me and her dad, there's no way I could ask them for help."

As Liam set a toppled chair back on its four legs, he asked if she remembered that he had business connections.

"I do," she said warily. "What about them? You're not suggesting I go move in with strangers I don't know who, by the way, are involved in trading in cultural treasures, are you?"

"They can help. And you better face it. You are in deep kim chee."

"Yes, but can I trust them? I can't let word of my research spread any farther than it has already. And I don't want to wake up one morning finding them competing with me in the search for Polo's treasure."

"Hey, believe me. I know what you're thinking but I've been doing deals with them for three, four years and they've always been dependable."

"I'd rather hear you say that they're honest and legitimate."

He scratched his chin. "Yes. Well, no. Ah, let's just stick with dependable. And decent," he added encouragingly. "They may not do everything according to the letter of the law, but they'll give you the personal space you need. And above all, you'll be safe from whoever did this."

"Who are these friends of yours?"

"The name is Bellardo. It's a family that's been in the antiquity business for nearly a century. They're well-known here in Venice."

"I think I've heard of them before: the House of Bellardo. They own a big show-room, right?"

"Right. Their place is a former palazzo and they have loads of room upstairs. The old man has offered me a place to stay the next time I come to town."

"You think they'd take me in?" she ventured to ask. "I mean, it's weird, but I might be putting them in danger rather than the other way around."

"I'm sure they'd take you in. They'd probably take the two of us in. And in case you're worried, Bellardo's no stranger to trouble."

"Wait a minute. Why should you get drawn into this, too, Mr. Di Angelo?"

He smiled. "Try Liam."

"Okay, Liam it is. Call me Marya. So, why get involved?"

"Nothing better to do."

"Right."

He continued straightening the furniture in the room. "Actually, you want to know the truth? Before all this happened, I was planning to come down and invite you out to dinner; but that will have to wait, obviously."

She wavered. "Give me a little time to think everything over. I can't make a snap decision on this. My mind is still taking it all in. Besides, I feel downright toxic," she said, pinching her dress.

"Tell you what. I'll go upstairs, report this break-in to the desk and call Bellardo to sound him out. When you're ready, give me a call and tell me what you decide."

Half an hour later, feeling as though she had washed a

layer of deadly microbes off her body, she considered Liam's idea and came to her decision. The faint whiff of shadiness about the Bellardos disturbed her, but she felt she had to compromise—at least temporarily. She agreed that it was too dangerous to stay at the Gabrielli or to simply transfer to another hotel. What could be worse than remaining at the Gabrielli Sandwirth waiting for another assault that would surely come? Whoever was tracking her in Venice was bound to know of her moves and would make another attempt to kidnap her—or worse. However, she was determined to remain in Venice until she could put her hands on Marco Polo's secret journal and follow up on the quest, wherever it took her. To come this far and just quit was not an option. The Bellardos' standards were their own business. She slipped into a pale blue shift and got her things together.

When Liam got her call, he told her that Bellardo was looking forward to having them both come stay at his place. The turn-around in her thinking about Liam surprised her. Just an hour earlier she had returned to the hotel, screaming mad at him. Now, she was about to leave the place arm-in-arm with him in a state of truce, if not exactly adoration. Yes, the one hundred eighty degree turn in that short space of time was unprecedented for her but it was the right move, she told herself.

When she heard Liam knock at the door, she looked through the peephole, and let him in. "Are you cool with this?"

"Yes, I am. You're right. I have to do this. Quitting is not an option and I can't just go looking for another hotel to hide in. I've got nowhere else to go."

As Liam hauled her bag out the door, she asked him what he had shared with Bellardo about her emergency.

"I hinted at the trouble you've had, but I didn't give him all the specifics."

"Shouldn't you have been completely honest with him?"

Liam hurried past her towards the window. He looked down, scanning the area in front of the hotel from the window. "No, we can handle that part later. Come on, Marya, the sooner we get you out of here the better."

Teresa was sitting at the reception desk fiddling with a garish necklace of turquoise-blue beads as Liam and Marya approached. "Dr. Bradwell and I have changed our plans, Teresa. We'll both need to cancel our reservations." He passed her his credit card. "I'm taking care of the bill for Dr. Bradwell. She lost everything in that assault on her earlier. I'm sure you've heard."

"Oh, yes. My goodness. That was terrible." She took his credit card, handled the paperwork and handed two sets of receipts and his card back to him. Smiling sweetly, she thanked them for choosing the Gabrielli Sandwirth Hotel for their stay and apologized for the slip-up last night. "Please don't hold it against us. I'm so glad that it all worked out well between you two. I must say that you make a lovely couple."

"Why thank you, Teresa," Marya said archly. "We haven't yet set a date for our wedding. We just got engaged and need just a little more time to get to know each other better."

Liam saw how the joke had caught Teresa by surprise. "She's only kidding, Teresa," he said. "Isn't she funny?" He took Marya by the elbow and hustled her towards the entrance. The bellhop followed them out with their bags.

Teresa gazed at the couple as they headed for the taxi-boat awaiting them at the pier on Riva degli Schiavone. "Crazy Americans," she muttered as she stamped both accounts paid.

CHAPTER 18

When Liam came back and sat by her side after helping the pilot with their bags, he was wearing a broad grin. "So, what was that all about back there, you know, that stuff about our engagement and us needing a little more time to get to know each other. I'm all for it. I mean, the part about getting to know you better."

She was thinking the same thing about him, actually. She laughed. "I don't know. It just struck me funny that here we are together again and I really don't know all that much about you. We keep getting thrown together somehow. It would be hilarious, except for the danger I'm in." She rested her folded hands on her lap and looked at her shoes, thinking it was the only pair she had left and how trivial it was to think about her shoes at a time like this.

"Why don't we talk, then? Before we get to Bellardo's," he suggested.

She agreed and offered to go first. She told him about her childhood, growing up with her grandmother after her mother had died of cancer and how her grandmother had had a big influence on her education, right down to her life-long interest in Marco Polo. And then, she listed all the things in life that she personally loved. Horseback riding, flowers, good cooking, country life, strolls along the beaches, swimming in the fast-running rivers of Humboldt County.

Liam was more cut-and-dried. He spoke of his studies at Boston College, his major in business and minor in history, his frequent travels to Europe and his new home in Newton. She noticed the absolute lack of anything personally revealing so she probed, needing clues to his inner self. He told her that there wasn't much to tell. His parents owned a restaurant in Boston where they had slaved for thirty years. They raised a big family and put them all through college, still lived in the same run-down neighborhood in the North End, had no savings, took little time off—all the things that he wanted to avoid. "Is that personal enough for you?"

At his mention of his parents' restaurant in Boston, Marya had a flash recall of the excellent dinner she had had a week earlier in the North End. And the passionate kiss that Khalid had given her when he dropped her off at the airport. She blushed.

"What's the matter?" he asked.

"Oh, nothing. I guess neither of us is really telling very much. Do you have someone special?"

"You first."

"I think so."

"You think so?"

"A colleague. A little older than me. Teaches at Harvard. He's been a dear."

"Doesn't sound like he's swept you off your feet."

"What about you, then, Mr. Romeo?"

"I'm engaged."

"You say that like you're in bondage." She looked at him with smiling eyes. He seemed at a loss to respond. "I'm sorry, but you asked for it. So it's not working out, huh?"

"Can't we leave personal matters out of this?"

"Sure, if you you don't want to talk about it. It's just that you suggested this little tete-a-tete. But you're right about my beau. He and I, well...it's more platonic than I'd like. I wish it were different."

He remained silent, staring ahead at the canal.

"Fine. We can leave our personal stuff out of this. I'm sorry I embarrassed you."

"I'm not embarrassed. We just need to keep our minds focused, that's all."

She kept looking at him.

"All right. I'll tell you. It's not going all that well between us. We've hit a rocky patch. So, you happy with that?"

A little voice inside her said, "yes." The taxi-boat passed into the shadow of Marco Polo Bridge and when Marya recognized it, she shuddered. Liam noticed immediately and asked her what was wrong. She tried to make a joke of it by telling him it was her "Waterloo" and that it was in this very section of the canal that she had barely escaped the goons who were after her this morning. He took her hand in his.

"So, we'll be at the Bellardo's in a minute or two. It's right around the bend ahead."

As the taxi-boat puttered along slowly, she was starting to feel a glimmer of trust in him, but she agonized in silence, wondering how much she could tell him. She was fixated on finding the journal hidden at the convent library. She revisited Vittoria's nightmare. In the back of her mind, Lafferty loomed, threatening an end to her career at the university. And above all, she had a newfound fear of the dangerous, faceless force that threatened to terminate her quest. How long would Liam remain involved? Would it be better to call Khalid and ask him to come aboard the project?

She stole a glance at Liam and realized that he was innocent of the accusations she had made to his face. And, he had come to her rescue. In some respects he was an honest man, if blunt at times about his work and tight-lipped about his private life. Could she trust him? Should she take the chance?

Suddenly, she broke her silence. "Liam, I need advice. When we get to Bellardo's, I'm not just going to sit around, twiddling my thumbs. I've got to get my hands on something real fast before someone else does."

"What is it?"

"I have to get over to the Convent of San Lorenzo and follow up on Vittoria's work there."

"Are you serious? That's a pretty dangerous thing to do. What's so important that you'd risk your life going back there? I wouldn't if I were in your shoes."

She decided she would not hold back. She told him that Vittoria had found what appeared to be the journal of Marco Polo and that if it were authenticated, it would not only be a critically important historical document but would also contain vital clues to the location of the Polo treasure. "I've got to find it at all costs before someone else does, or I'll never be able to find the treasure."

"You want my advice?"

"Yes."

"Don't go there. They're watching you, obviously. They'll come after you, for sure."

"Then what do I do? I refuse to sit by and watch this chance slip away! I've got to get that journal. No ifs, ands or buts. I'm not moving to Bellardo's for nothing."

"Do the nuns know about the journal?"

"Vittoria seemed to think they didn't. I got an email from her that told me where it was hidden. On a lower shelf, among the 14th century volumes, in the second row on the right."

"Did she tell you what it looked like?"

"Yes, it's a small volume jammed between two large ones. Liam, if I could only get over there and copy what I need out of it or borrow it, even for a little while… "

"Borrow? Don't you mean take it without permission? I don't think the dear sisters would let you just *borrow* that little treasure."

"You know very well what I mean. I would certainly return it. I have no intention of keeping it, if you're implying anything like that. I've got to get my hands on it."

He suggested an idea. Go to the convent wearing a

nun's habit. The nuns would trust her based on her fluency in Italian and her impeccable scholarly credentials. The folds of the habit would provide plenty of room to conceal the journal when it came time to check out.

"I can't do that, Liam. I just can't. I'd be so nervous I'd . . . they'd catch me."

"Then let me do it."

"You? Go as a nun?"

"No, silly. I would go as a priest, maybe even as a monsignor."

"No, I don't see you as a priest. It wouldn't work." She held her hand to her mouth to hide a smile.

The taxi-boat turned a corner and plowed its way past gondolas and other taxi boats coming from the other direction. Just ahead on the right side was the Bellardo place. The driver slowed his craft and drifted towards a staircase rising from the waters.

Marya was mulling over what she should do when she looked up at the driver of the taxi boat and saw a look of terror on his face. He desperately turned the wheel, struggling to reverse the drift of the taxi boat to avert a disaster of some kind. When she looked towards the staircase, her stomach churned violently. She heard Liam groan, "Oh God, no."

A huge, barrel-chested man in his thirties charged down the staircase towards the taxi-boat, wielding a gleaming sword above his head and roaring, "Die, infidels! Allah Akhbar!" In an instant, Marya was on Liam's lap, her arms around his neck in a death grip. As she buried her head in his shoulder and kept her eyes shut, she felt him draw her in tightly.

The pilot continued grappling with the wheel but it was too late to correct the boat's course. It continued to drift helplessly until it reached the staircase in front of the House of Bellardo. She closed her eyes even more tightly as she felt a broad blade whir inches above her head.

CHAPTER 19

"Marya, Marya, it's okay. It's all right. Here. Take it easy. Look, it's only Ambrosio." She felt Liam gently take her by the shoulders and turn her around to face the mad Islamist with the sword. She opened her eyes and saw a man with a massive head and a tangle of dark, curly hair staring down at her from the stone embankment. He evoked the image of mighty Samson, but this giant was contrite, hiding his sword behind his thick trunk. Liam knew that Ambrosio could speak a little English and understood a lot more. But when Ambrosio apologized to Marya in Italian, he had to ask her for a translation. "He said he was sorry for clowning around and scaring me like that. He didn't mean it." Then Ambrosio set his broad sword by the entrance and got their suitcases from the taxi-boat, lifting them as if they were picnic baskets.

Liam scolded him. "I knew that you were just goofing off, Ambrosio. Trouble is, Marya here had no idea what you were doing. You scared her half to death." Ambrosio looked deflated as he hauled their bags into the showroom.

Marya stepped up onto the promenade in front of the House of Bellardo, a bit rattled by Ambrosio's antics and still holding Liam's hand. Liam led her through the front doors and buzzed for Giovanni. "I'm sorry that happened, Marya. This was just not the day for this kind of thing to happen. I know Ambrosio. He loves playing with swords. He's just an overgrown kid. He belongs on a movie set, or in his own personal, medieval castle."

Marya thought Liam was far too lenient with him. "No, he's not just an overgrown kid. He's one brick short of a load and he's a danger to anyone within reach of that sword." She just knew that something like this would happen when she agreed to Liam's idea.

"Are you okay, now? Come on. Let's go inside."

She wasn't okay. Once she entered Bellardo's showroom, the first thing Marya noticed was another man of powerful build. He was grappling with a tall, baroque armoire. "Another one. Keep him away from me."

The man's face lit up when he spotted Liam.

Liam waved to him. "Buon giorno, Pietro." He whispered to Marya that Pietro was Giovanni's other son.

She thought he looked like a hoodlum and totally out of place among the sumptuous furniture in the showroom. She subconsciously gripped her briefcase more firmly, her misgivings about coming to this strange place growing by the minute.

As Liam led her down the aisle, however, she was entranced by the most outstanding, high-quality antiques she had ever seen assembled in one place in her life. Massive pieces of furniture that only palatial chambers could accommodate crowded the showroom: four-posted beds of walnut polished to a high luster; wall-length, mirrored armoire sets; extraordinary tables with marquetry that reflected the highest degree of craftsmanship; solid, ornate chests—a profusion of superb pieces to decorate any room.

She placed her hand on Liam's left arm to stop him as they passed a pair of writhing, Renaissance marble figures wearing agonized expressions. "Got room for these at your palace in Newton?" she teased.

"Yeah, in fact I do. They might look good in the upstairs, east-wing ballroom. I'll ask Giovanni if he'll give me a deal on them."

"Right." Further on, she noted musical instruments, tapestries, huge gilded rococo frames for paintings and cabinets containing exquisite glassware and jewelry. It was all here, she thought: remnants of the glorious history of Venice, La Serenissima and Mistress of the Mediterranean.

Eight centuries of domination of the Adriatic and links to the Levant, the Black Sea, the Islamic world and the Orient.

By now, she was regaining her composure after the traumatic reception out front. "This is the most incredible collection, but where's the gold? I haven't seen any gold articles like the ones you're interested in."

Liam hushed her. "You're not supposed to know that. Bellardo doesn't put any of that merchandise on display. It's all traded *sub rosa*. So, keep that to yourself, please."

She was miffed. "Fine, if you want it that way. I'm not supposed to know. But what have you told him about me and what I'm doing here?"

"I just said that you were doing research into the history of the Polo estate and left it at that. He told me that he didn't think you'd find anything new on that subject."

"I disagree with him on that, but all right. You should have told him what happened to me and my assistant."

At that moment, a man in his late fifties or sixties stepped out from behind curtains at the end of the aisle. Marya noted the same heavy facial features that she had seen on Ambrosio. He came down the aisle extending both arms to greet them.

"Welcome back, Liam." He beamed at Marya. "And this lovely lady must be your Professor Bradwell. I am very pleased to meet you, Dr. Bradwell."

"Please, just call me Marya."

Bellardo took her hand and kissed it. "My friends call me Giovanni."

He turned to Liam, "I'm glad that you and Marya feel comfortable enough to accept my invitation, though I didn't realize that I would be enjoying your company so soon."

"Like I told you, Marya had an emergency situation this afternoon. Thanks for taking us in on such short notice."

"My thanks, too, Mr. Bellardo. I hope this doesn't put you out too much. I won't need to impose on you for more than two or three days, if that's okay with you." Marya took a small gift-wrapped box from her purse and handed it to him. "This is for you, Giovanni. I hope you like it."

Bellardo accepted it and thanked her. He told them both that they could stay as long as they needed to and that their rooms upstairs were ready for them. When he added that there would be a chance at dinner to discuss her quest for the Polo family's golden tablets, she was taken by surprise. Liam looked about the showroom to keep from facing her hard stare.

Giovanni left them momentarily to bellow out to his wife upstairs. "Francesca!"

Francesca came thumping down the stairs wearing an apron liberally dusted with flour. She was short and stout and looked as if she had been working in the kitchen for hours. She wiped her wet hands on her apron and pushed back a few strands of hair from her forehead with her wrist. Giovanni introduced her to Marya with a flurry of jumbled English and Italian.

Francesca nodded that she understood everything and said she was still preparing dinner. She smiled at Marya and took her hand. Then, she actually had Marya turn about so that she could look her up and down. She shook her head, as if disapproving of something. Marya heard her mention skeletal-looking Ethiopians. Without warning, she reached out and pinched Marya at the waist and waved both hands in the air, complaining to Giovanni. She was about to do the same to Liam when he stepped back and avoided the pinch.

"What did she say?" he asked Marya.

"She says that she thinks we make a lovely couple but we are underfed. I think she compared us to a pair of Ethiopians. She wants to fatten us up."

"Oh, that's just typical Bellardo hospitality. Don't think anything of it."

Francesca went back upstairs, looking delighted at the prospect of feeding two starving guests. After she had gone, Liam asked about the missing member of the family, Carlotta. Giovanni told him that she was at the firing range practicing. She'd be back in time for dinner, he added. Marya blinked and looked at Liam for an explanation. It seemed like an unusual hobby for a girl. She envisioned this Carlotta dressed in black khaki, festooned with ammunition.

Bellardo had to close up for the day so he ordered his two sons to take the bags and show the guests to their rooms in the living quarters upstairs. When Pietro and Ambrosio appeared, she took a second look at Pietro, the younger of the two. Up close, though shorter than Ambrosio, he looked as rugged as Godzilla and just about as muscled.

The boys went ahead with the bags, with Liam and Marya following a minute later. She took him by the arm of his shirt and tugged, "You didn't tell me that the whole family was a bunch of weirdoes."

"They're not weirdoes. Just a little bit different from most Italians."

"Liam, listen. They're certifiable. What have you gotten me into?" she whispered hoarsely. "I don't think I can stay here. Isn't there any other place in all of Venice we can find? Think!"

"Hey, just stay calm. They'll grow on you in a couple of days, I promise."

"It ain't gonna happen. I'll be out of here tomorrow, if not sooner. Just look at those boys. That Ambrosio almost lopped my head off. Pietro looks like the son of Al Capone. Mama Bellardo pinches my belly and wants to fatten us both up like Hansel and Gretel. Did you see her? Looks like a Neolithic fertility goddess. Papa G tells me my research is over before it has begun. And who's this Carlotta? Oh, don't tell me. I can just guess. She's a professional assassin." She paused and looked around as if the Bellardo tribe surrounded her. I don't need all this, Liam. Thank you for trying to help, but there is something definitely wrong with this place and I won't be sticking around to find out what it is."

CHAPTER 20

In one quick glance upon entering the dining room, Marya knew that the Bellardos were not into fast food. Mrs. Bellardo had prepared a glittering gala and it would be a while before they got up from the table. The three plates, three glasses and innumerable forks and knives at each place setting told her so. The sixteen-foot long dining table was spread with a fine Idrija lace tablecloth and sported three large, gilt-bronze candelabra like the kind she had seen in the Imperial Apartments of Franz Joseph of Austria.

She was wearing a chic black dress and a simple string of pearls when she took her seat at the head of the table on Bellardo's left. The table was a beautiful sight, stunning, in fact. But she had a continuing sense of foreboding about the house and she just knew something awful was going to happen, though she vowed to do all she could to dodge it.

At the start, all went well. She gave Mr. Bellardo a gushing compliment on the elaborate candle holders. Bellardo was delighted. "Thank you, Marya. I got them in a kind of fire sale from an estate in Lombardy. Their provenance is interesting. They're the only two that remained in Italy from the large collection of the Duke of Lombardy that was sold to the Hapsburgs of Austria. They have dozens of them in Vienna at the Hofburg palace that are still used for state dinners. I'm pleased that you like them."

He repositioned his eyeglasses over his arched nose and flattened a few defiant wisps of hair with the palm of his hand before sitting down with the whole family: Signora Bellardo who smiled, crinkling her eyes; Ambrosio who took her hand in his large mitt; Pietro and a beautiful young lady she had not yet met. "This is my daughter, Carlotta," he said to Marya's great astonishment. She was a beauty with her hair done in a chignon and ringlets that framed a delicate face with a creamy complexion. Carlotta inclined her head in Marya's direction. "So glad to meet you, Signorina," she said in a dulcet voice. Marya thought she could not be older than twenty-two years and must have been an adopted child. There was no family resemblance between her and her Neanderthal brothers.

Bellardo abruptly stood and raised his glass. "A toast," he announced. Everyone around the table stood and followed suit. "To my father, Michelangelo Bellardo. *Salute*," he said with a slight bow towards the mummy-like figure at the end of the table. All faces turned to the diminutive old man, dwarfed by the chair he sat in. With only a nod of the head, the old fellow acknowledged the toast. When everyone had sat down again, Bellardo pointed out two young people standing near the kitchen door, a shapely, teenage girl named Emilia, his niece, and a dark-haired nephew, Giuseppe, who resembled Liam enough to be his own brother. "They will be serving tonight."

Marya sipped her wine and looked around the table at all seven of the others and regretted two things. She was seated close to Giovanni who would likely bombard her with questions about the Polo research and she was on the opposite side of the table from Liam who sat next to that gorgeous Carlotta. So be it. Let the games begin, she thought.

Bellardo chose to address Marya first, "We welcome you and Liam this evening. We're honored to have an illustrious college professor such as yourself at our table. Do you realize that this is the first time that Liam has had dinner with us, too? It's a miracle. I've invited him so often, I can't remember."

Bellardo's niece and nephew brought out two steaming bowls of *broetto*, a Venetian fish soup, and ladled it into eight smaller bowls. She remembered the flavor instantly. Her grandmother had often made it. Baskets of *pandoro* were within easy reach while Signore Bellardo poured Soave, a white wine. The sip of wine she had taken earlier was now reaching her cheeks. A tingle of warmth stirred within and she felt surprisingly relaxed with this gathering around the table. These people reminded her of her own family's numerous holiday gatherings and outings along northern California's coastline and redwood parks. The elder members of her family were ghosts now, leaving only her, a sister who had moved to Tonga, a cousin and a father who, for all she knew, might be dead. She knew that things would never again be as they were in the early days of her youth. She had missed the feeling of being surrounded by a loving family.

The light mood that had marked the opening of the dinner did not last. The conversation took an ominous turn when Bellardo asked Marya to discuss her interest in the treasure of the Polos. She was not surprised, just irritated that the spell of the glittering evening was broken. She had not wanted to discuss this issue and she had only Liam to blame for sharing her secret with Giovanni.

"So, you think 'Il Milione' told the truth about coming home from China with a fortune?"

"I certainly do," she said, stealing a look at Liam. He averted his eyes and found something to talk about with Carlotta next to him. "I'm certain that Marco, his father, and his uncle all came home from their travels very wealthy men."

"How about the golden tablets? Liam tells me you believe those may still be around."

"I believe there's more than an even chance that they can be found, too."

"You're serious."

"Yes, I am."

"But history shows that he died with only a modest estate that he left to his wife and three daughters."

"Something tells me that's not the whole story, Signore Bellardo."

"Call me Giovanni, please," he reminded her, taking a piece of bread and dipping it in his soup. "All of Venice laughed at his claims and you know, of course, that there has been no trace of any of his treasure in the last seven hundred years. Why do you think that you will have any better luck than anyone else in locating it?"

"Luck, Giovanni? I've never counted on luck to get me anywhere in my life. My research is all about reason and perseverance." She had an impulse to tell him what had happened to her this morning as well as what had happened previously to Vittoria. Instead, she flashed a disarming smile and told him that tomorrow she would be following up on some very promising clues.

"I wish you the best in your endeavors. But, I hope you won't hold it against me if I tell you that you're going to be disappointed. There's nothing to justify your hopes. Good luck, all the same."

The nephew brought out a large platter, laying it down at the head of the table. "Ah, the Risotto a la Sbiraglia," said Bellardo, rubbing his hands at the sight of the savory chicken, veal and rice dish.

Ambrosio suddenly reached for the bread. That's when Marya noticed that he was wearing a gold ring embedded with a huge ruby the size of a grape, glinting in the candlelight.

Her eyes looked past Ambrosio's hand in the bread-basket across the table to Liam again. Their eyes locked on to each other's in the mellow candle light. Carlotta, of the Botticelli face, was eagerly talking to him. But in this instant Marya seemed to have his total attention.

Emilia set down several more delicious platters on the table, all eagerly awaited, and quickly cleared. In the meantime, Bellardo continued to pepper her with questions about the motives of her quest. She reminded Bellardo of the legends of Homer and how Schliemann successfully used them, against all odds, to locate the lost city of Troy in Turkey. As the evening wore on, the wine, the bread, and the aromatic sauces of each dish were so delicious to her that she almost didn't care any longer whether anyone believed in her mission or not.

She again found Liam looking at her and noticed his soft brown eyes, set off by the fair skin of his face, dark eyebrows and neatly trimmed sideburns. She wished that they had seated her next to him instead of next to Ambrosio who was too engrossed in his food to attempt a conversation with her. She felt even more relaxed, in spite of Giovanni's pessimistic and discouraging views of her research. Overall, the evening was turning out better than she expected simply knowing that she had Liam's attention.

Bellardo's rich baritone voice dispelled her dreamy mood. "Ah, Strangolapreti," he said, pleased with the appearance of a cake studded with nuts, raisins, walnuts, pine nuts and almonds. A pleasant aroma blended with those of the preceding courses. And to match the dessert, Bellardo introduced a bottle of Recioto, a sweet, sparkling red wine with a delicate bouquet. Then he dropped the bomb of the evening. "Would either of you feel comfortable in telling me what may have happened today to require your move here? Or am I too indiscreet in asking?"

Marya felt that the time for evasion was over. She wished such a discussion had taken place before her arrival. Bellardo was clearly informed of the subject of her research. But it seemed Liam had not even given him a hint of the dangerous encounter she had had. If she were to live at the Bellardo home while conducting her research, they should know something, at least, about the hoodlums who had tried to kidnap her. She took a sip of wine and looked directly at Bellardo. "There was an incident this morning when I went to the convent."

Liam interrupted before she could continue. "The staff at the hotel have been rude and unaccommodating. I suggested to Marya…"

"No, Liam. Let me continue. I think Giovanni should know." She took several minutes to explain the whole scene at the convent, the attempt to kidnap her, her dunking in the canal, the wreckage in her room and Liam's intervention. She told him that she would need only a day or two to finish her research before she would be on her way and hoped and prayed that her presence in the Bellardo home would not have any negative consequences. Bellardo appeared unruffled. "I see," he said, staring at Liam and then her in turn. "If you are truly intent on your research, you may remain here. I see no problem with that, but I do insist that when you go to the convent tomorrow, my two sons accompany you. No one will tangle with them. And you need not worry about them getting in your way. They can wait outside while you get on with your work." Bellardo's heavy-lidded eyes then turned to Liam. "We must have a word in private."

After dessert, Bellardo rose and directed everyone to the salon for an after-dinner Amaretto. Along the way, Bellardo asked to be excused for a while for a talk with Liam. Marya knew that the business the two would discuss would have everything to do with what she had just frankly admitted at the table. She felt it was unfair of Bellardo to pull Liam aside without her. As far as she was concerned, Bellardo was as shady as a banyan tree. She feared being left out of a decision that could affect her research. Whatever the outcome of their private talk, she decided nothing would obligate her to accept limits on how she conducted her research. Let them talk all they wanted, she thought, as Bellardo and Liam veered off into the study, closing the door behind them.

CHAPTER 21

Bellardo took a bottle of wine and two glasses with him and led Liam into his study. He closed the door with his right shoulder. With a tilt of his head he directed Liam to take a seat and poured out two glasses of wine. "Now, how the hell did you ever get involved with this woman, Liam?"

"You angry?"

"Yes. You should have told me first. You should know before anyone else that there should be honor among thieves, my friend." He took a sip of his wine and put the glass down. "But that was then; this is now. The question is where we go from here. I want a complete explanation. Tell me all you know about that woman and why she is in Venice."

Liam told him all, from how he had simply bumped into her aboard a flight from Boston to their arrival together out front. He believed she was a serious scholar with no personal gain, meaning money, in her research in Venice. "I want to help her, Giovanni. I think there is something to her search. This could turn out to be something big."

"You must be cracked."

"No, I'm not. I have a feeling that she does have a chance of finding the gold and she needs help."

"Rubbish. She should just give up. She'll never find anything new to support her case."

"If it's rubbish, why is someone else so desperate that they would attack her?"

"I still disagree."

"There's more, Giovanni."

"What do you mean?"

Liam had wanted to avoid all mention of how a pair of thugs had waylaid Marya's assistant, but now it, too, had to come out. "Marya isn't an isolated case. A pair of thugs attacked her assistant, too, just a few days ago."

"What's her name?"

"Vittoria something. I don't remember. Sounds like Rodney. Vittoria Rodney. No, that's not it."

"Rodoni? Was it Rodoni?"

"That's it! Rodoni. Why? You know her?"

Bellardo refilled their glasses. "Absolutely. She's a friend of Pietro. What happened to her?" he asked, looking stricken.

"She was attacked at night on her way home from the National Library. Her research papers were stolen and she was knocked unconscious. She's in the hospital right now. It's been in the news."

"My God," said Bellardo. "I'll need to call the Rodonis. Go on. Tell me more. Who did it?"

"Very likely the same thugs who tried to kidnap Marya."

"Jesus. How serious is her condition?"

"Very. She's not fully conscious, could have a cerebral hemorrhage."

"But why, for God's sake? Why did they harm that girl? You think these attacks are linked?"

"I do and so does Marya. They must have something to do with the research, the search for Polo's tablets. It looks like someone knows about the research they've been doing and wants to muscle in."

With his glass of wine in hand, Bellardo paced around the study looking very alarmed.

"What's the matter, Giovanni? This is not just about Vittoria, is it?"

"No, I'm afraid not. What did the assailants look like? Any description?"

"Marya told me the man who attacked her was a husky Asian type, a big guy with a crew-cut. The other guy was piloting a taxi-boat. She thought he was Italian but maybe he wasn't. She couldn't really tell."

"God Almighty. Your professor is in big trouble. We might all be in trouble, I'm afraid."

"What are you saying?"

"I'm saying that the professor is in way over her head and the rest of us—I mean you, me and the family—we may be in for some big trouble."

* * * * *

In the salon, Marya sat enjoying time with the Bellardo clan, though Liam's absence still annoyed her. "It's been a wonderful evening. It was a great dinner and I feel very at home with all of you. I'm simply jealous of the way you are all there for one another."

"It's not always this way," Carlotta said. She laughed and gave Ambrosio's left shoulder a hard slug. "It's awful living with two big oafs like my brothers."

"Don't listen to her," said Pietro. "She's spoiled rotten. No one can do enough to please her. She thinks she is the Queen of Sheba, but she's more like Lucretia Borgia. Pure poison."

Carlotta gave Pietro a slug on the arm, too, and he listed at an exaggerated angle.

"Honestly, I can see that you all care a lot for one another. It reminds me of my own family in California, the way things used to be." Marya said. "By the way, I *would* like to have some of your recipes, Francesca."

"Yes, before you leave, I'll write them out for you. But tell us some more about your family."

Marya lay back against a cushion on the sofa. "There's little left of it now. That's my problem. No one to go to anymore when things get tough. My mother was a high school teacher. I got my love of learning from her. She's the reason they call me Doctor Bradwell today. She died of cancer years ago when I was in high school."

"I'm sorry to hear that."

"There's not really all that much to talk about anymore as far as my family goes. My only sister moved to the South Pacific with her boyfriend and runs a scuba-diving shop.

"Any brothers?"

"No."

"What about your father?"

"My dad left for another woman when my mother was in the hospital. I haven't yet gotten over that. I think he still lives with her in Vancouver. Only my grandmother remained to help when my mom was dying. She passed away last year, too. Anyhow, on a more cheerful note, you all remind me of the way it used to be in better times."

"Isn't there anyone special your life, Marya?" Francesca asked.

She paused. Khalid had shown her many kindnesses in the last three years. They had authored scholarly papers together and presented their findings at conferences together. They had gone on dinner dates. He had kissed her several times, in fact. He had always given so much of himself to her when her emotional life was at an ebb or when she had to do battle with the gang of three in the department. He had even made her current trip to Venice possible when all her other resources were exhausted. But he seemed simply too engaged in his professional work in Central Asian politics for their relationship to truly blossom. "No, I can't really say there's anyone very special."

"What about *him*?" Francesca asked, pointing to the door of the study. "I've seen how he looked at you during dinner. He has eyes for you. Bedroom eyes. Yes. Haven't you noticed?" Carlotta and the boys laughed in unison at what their mother had said.

Marya smiled and shook her head. "No, that's ridiculous. He's not my type, Signora Bellardo."

"Come on, Marya. You must have some small feeling for him. After all, you left the hotel and came here together,"

Carlotta teased. "I heard from a friend who works there that you shared the same suite."

"Well, yes, no. That was only a temporary arrangement. Really, he's not my type at all." She began to blush and the Bellardos began to chuckle. "Really, you guys, there's nothing between him and me. We're poles apart. Besides, he's just helping me out. I swear." She crossed her heart with her index finger. Suddenly, she was on that flight from Boston again, feeling his arms around her. She blushed even more.

* * * * *

Liam drained his glass and set it aside. Bellardo asked if he could do anything more for him. "Didn't you tell me earlier that you had a favor to ask?

"Oh, yeah. I almost forgot. Look, I've got a plan for helping Marya and I do need a favor. I need to get some Catholic clerical garb. You know any place I could get outfitted?"

"Sure, but what the hell for?"

"I'm going to help her find the golden tablets, but I need to get into the Convent of Saint Lawrence to do that."

"Christ, you telling me you want to get dressed up as one of the Sisters of Perpetual Indulgence?"

"No! I'm talking about a priest's suit and collar. Jesus. Give me some credit. I want to get into the convent in disguise to get something for her in the library."

"She's got you hooked on those golden tablets, too? Liam, let me tell you, that's a very dangerous thing to get yourself into right now. You've got to talk her out of it and you have to stay out of it, too."

"What do you know about it?"

"I've got some suspicions about the pair that attacked Vittoria and your Dr. Bradwell. It's risky to go anywhere near that convent right now."

"Let me be the judge of that. Just help me out, all right?"

Bellardo raised both hands in frustration with Liam. "Just don't say I didn't warn you. Come this way," he said, leading Liam through a door that opened into a large walk-in closet. I happen to have what you're looking for."

Liam looked all around the closet and saw another dimension of the devious Bellardo that he had not been aware of before. Tradesmen's outfits, professional suits, and many types of technicians' uniforms ran the length of one wall in two sizes: extra large and triple extra large. "What have you here, Bellardo, some kind of department store?"

"We need disguises from time to time when we take certain shipments. I won't go into it right now—you don't need to know."

"Who wears this stuff?"

"My sons, of course, Ambrosio and Pietro. They do all the field work for me. Carlotta has a separate wardrobe."

"You have Carlotta working for you in the field, too?"

"Of course. And she's showing great promise."

Liam walked halfway into the closet and shoved bunches of uniforms back and forth along the rack, looking for a black serge Jesuit suit and collar. "I'm impressed. Looks like you have uniforms for every occasion—except the one I need."

Bellardo pushed him aside and fumbled with a few costumes along the rack. He took a cleric's suit on a hangar and held it up to Liam's chin. "You're not as large as Pietro but this is what you're looking for."

"Great. Instant Jesuit priest."

"Liam, listen to me. I should really be trying to talk you out of this crazy idea. I can't prove it right now, but I think she's going up against some nasty competition. I'm referring to that crowd I already told you about, the ones from Central Asia. Poor Vittoria is only the first victim."

"You actually believe that criminals from Central Asia are now terrorizing Venice? That's completely nuts. I don't believe it. It's gotta be someone local who's onto Marya's search for treasure."

"You don't know what I know. I'm telling you, it's a gang from Tajikistan that I'm worried about. I warn you, Liam. You may need all the help you can get, including help from the Man upstairs."

"So now it's Tajikistan? Really? You've got to be kidding!" Liam took the Jesuit suit and slipped into the jacket. He stretched his fists through the cuffs, pleased that it was only a little loose on him but it otherwise fit well.

"I see that nothing I'm telling you is getting through. I may as well just give you my blessing and hope for the best for you and your dear Marya. Kneel down." Bellardo lifted an arched bishop's miter with its deep crosswise cleft off an overhead shelf and placed it on his own head. He looked down solemnly at Liam and made the sign of the cross over him, pronouncing the ancient Latin blessing, "Benedicat vos omnipotens Deus, Pater, et Filius, et Spiritus Sanctus."

"Amen," Liam said, quickly getting off his knees. "You're too much, Bellardo. It's always a damned drama. Ambrosio's just like you." He removed the jacket and hung it back on the rack. "Why don't we get back to the others?"

"You mean, get back to Marya. Now, that's *amore.*"

He laughed. "No way. She doesn't mean a thing to me. I'm already taken, anyway. Then suddenly he recalled the embarrassing moment with her at the rear of the plane on the flight from Boston. He led the way out of the closet and back to the salon.

* * * * *

Marya turned around when she heard the door of the study open and smiled when she saw Liam, but the expression on Giovanni Bellardo's face right behind him troubled her. She had wanted to prolong the pleasure of the evening and the glowing feelings that had become so rare in her life lately. She just knew from the aura surrounding Giovanni, though, that the party was over. The fun just could not last. He came directly across the room and sat down beside her on the plush sofa. He took her left hand in his and patted it. "Liam just informed me that we have a mutual friend—Vittoria Rodoni."

CHAPTER 22

In the quiet of her bedroom, Marya settled down from the intensity of her conversation with Giovanni. He had expressed his sorrow at the news about Vittoria, as well as with the disclosure of the attack on her. There was urgency in his voice when he told her that he needed to talk with her in the morning. "I hope you enjoyed the evening with us, but I'll need to talk to you again in the morning about all of this," he told her. She pressed him for an explanation but he put her off. She wondered what could have changed his demeanor so much after his talk with Liam. In a little while, after a few pleasantries, there were rounds of good night kisses and then the group broke up and headed for bed.

Before settling in to sleep, she needed to do some reading to calm the foreboding feeling that Giovanni's words had aroused. Getting into her pajamas, she stacked the pillows against the back of the bed. She noted the time on the large pendulum clock in the corner of the room. It was nearly midnight as she reached for her copy of Marco Polo's travels and lay back against the layers of pillows. The stately rhythm of the ticking receded. She was back to reading the Prologue, the part that told of the Polos' arrival at the port of Hormuz on the Persian Gulf. A wedding party, followed by the Polos, was disembarking. The year was 1295 A.D. Crowds gawked at the towering masts of three Chinese junks offshore, and at the small group of passengers, the only survivors of the hundreds who had started out from China.

Our fleet of ships at Hormuz created an uproar among the people, for the Chinese ships are much more seaworthy than those of the Arab merchants which are made without nails and easily sink. The Khan's ships are much larger, too, and the four-masted sails are an astonishing sight to the people of the port. They come by the thousands to see and admire. Our ships anchored in the port numbered only three out of the thirteen that had left Quanzhou.

Coja led us through the city to the palace of the Regent. Crowds of merchants and lackeys lined the streets and alleys. We saw faces of men from all regions of the earth and heard many languages. Besides a few Venetians and Genoese, we encountered many Persians, Egyptians, Greeks, Jews, Hindus and Chinese.

Hormuz is a city of great wealth. Though its streets are dusty and putrid with garbage and offal, yet the city is overflowing with rare spices like cinnamon, cloves, pepper and nutmeg. Jewel merchants offer sapphires, rubies, emeralds, topazes, turquoises, pearls and rubies, all in abundance. Wagons are loaded with fine stuffs of Baghdad, damasks, Persian rugs, silks from China, a large variety of knives and steel swords from Arabia, porcelains and many more rarities, all to be had for gold.

In the marketplace we learned that Argun, the ruler of Persia, had died at the time our fleet had left China. Argun's brother, Kaikhatu, was acting as regent for the son of Argun. What was to become of the Princess Kukachin now that she was without a bridegroom? The regent sent a large escort to lead us into the palace. During the feast that followed, he proposed that we outfit a caravan and take the Princess with her ladies to the Khorasan frontier where we would find Kazan, the son of the late king. He deemed the beautiful Mongol Princess a suitable match for Kazan and he wished to fulfill the desires of the great Kublai Khan in sending the princess to Persia. Princess Kukachin blushed and looked down as she learned of this proposal through a series of translations. She accepted. Accordingly, we delivered Princess Kukachin to

Kazan and she was much enamored of him. They wedded happily.

Marya read on, but drifted off to sleep, waking again at 3:05 A.M. Almost unconsciously, she put her book aside and turned off the light. In her dreams, though, her mind continued to work ceaselessly on the task of tracking the Polo's progress home to Venice.

Moreover, I must tell you that into our care, the Khan had entrusted another princess, not of the Mongol clans, but of the imperial family that had fled to the South, a princess of the Sung rulers, a girl of nineteen years and fair to behold. My uncle Maffeo told me that Kublai Khan had chosen her for a special purpose to accompany the bridal party, without revealing that purpose to me. Weary and ill from the long journey from China to Hormuz, and having seen as much of the province as she could bear, she asked permission from Nicolo and Maffeo to be excused from the expedition to the frontier. She would await our return from the frontier and would accompany us to our destination in Venice. I was very surprised by this and asked both my father and my uncle why the Sung princess should not remain in Persia with Princess Kukachin, but they told me nothing.

So, after leaving Princess Kukachin with the son of the late king, we went to Tabriz to find the regent again. Here we passed time conducting more business. We traded heavy goods that we had brought from China for gems and waited for the health of the Sung princess to improve. We took care, furthermore, to prepare a caravan that would not draw the attention of thieves and bandits of the desert. After nine months, we left Tabriz relieved of heavy cargo. We cleverly secreted our most valuable jewels in bundles on the backs of camels and within our own worn clothing.

We were most grateful to lord Kaikhatu for his generos-

ity and good will to us and especially for four new golden tablets of command that he conferred upon us. These he granted in recognition of our service to the Khan and out of concern for our safe passage northward. He advised us of rebellious peoples in those regions who refused to submit to his rule. The golden tablets resembled those granted us by the Great Khan of Cambaluc. Two of them were engraved with gyrfalcons, one with a winged lion, and the fourth without any engraving. Moreover, I tell you that they bore a solemn command to his people to respect the name of the Khan and to spare no expense in men and horses for our safety, lest they suffer death and the confiscation of all their possessions.

Upon leaving Tabriz, we had learned of the hostilities of the Sultan of Egypt towards the Persians along the coast of Syria. We decided it was safer to take the northern caravan route to reach the Euxine and to pass east of Baghdad in order to avoid spies and thieves. Along this route can be seen the remains of ancient cities. Indeed, it happened that wherever we went in this country, which was twenty-five days' journey in extent, strong guards protected us and the people of those parts welcomed us into their homes. The Golden Tablets of Command, therefore, were of the greatest use to us.

We reached Trebizond, which is on a hill that overlooks the Euxine. It presented a fair sight, with large walls surrounding it and enclosing some hills within. Beyond the city are rich orchards and fields of grain. We had safely crossed through a dangerous region with our treasures and our lives and thanked God Almighty for our safe deliverance to more familiar lands. The spirits of our servants and the Sung Princess were uplifted at the sight of the city and this inland ocean. The princess daily grew fonder of me and I of her. She also showed herself determined to assist us in all ways to reach Venice with the vast treasure we had borne thus far.

At Trebizond, we took care to maintain the outward appearance of poverty among those of our caravan. We wore only the shabbiest of clothes and no adornment. But the officials of Trebizond took a heavy toll on our wealth. My father and my uncle cursed the memory of this place, for the price they paid was high to pass aboard a ship at the port. Still, we boarded ship with all of our gold and most of the jewels that we had brought from Tabriz.

Our journey from Trebizond to Constantinople by ship took but several days. In Constantinople, we likewise remained but a few days. It is a city of which my father and uncle were fond, for they had lived and traded in this city over 35 years before. We boarded ship for the final part of our journey with our treasure and many slaves. The Sung princess had comfortable quarters for herself and we ours, yet she and I had occasion to speak often during the voyage. We had left China in 1292 A.D. I had not seen my Venice, Queen of the Adriatic, since 1271 A.D. when I was a youth of 17 years.

CHAPTER 23

She awoke at 8:00 A.M. to the muffled gongs of the grandfather clock with images of the trek to the Black Sea lingering on her mind. It had been a very vivid dream in which she saw a bearded Marco Polo laughing and chatting with someone she could only identify as the Sung Princess . She knew with certainty from her study of Marco Polo's tale that there had never been any mention of such a person. It must have been the usual incongruous stuff of dreams, the bunching of familiar people who would never meet in the real world. To her knowledge there had never been a Chinese princess, in any historical source whatsoever that had made the overland trek from Tabriz to the Black Sea. And yet it seemed so real. She picked the book up from the bedside table and scanned the Prologue again to reassure herself. *No, just as I thought. No Princess. That was a realistic dream. I could almost stroke Marco's beard and see a princess sitting beside him.*

She lay for a while in bed reflecting on the dream then told herself to get her "skinny" body out of bed. No doubt Francesca would have a hearty field-hand breakfast ready for her. As for Bellardo, she remembered that he had specifically asked to meet with her in the morning about Vittoria. After bathing and dressing, she came to the kitchen and found Francesca bustling about with her apron, starting her sauces for the evening meal and setting out coffee and a simple tray of pastries. No heaping platters of sausages and eggs or plates of home fries and buttery muffins, thank God.

"Buon giorno, Marya. Come, sit over here with me. We need to talk." It was Bellardo, gathering a cup of coffee and a pastry for himself and gesturing towards the table.

Marya took a cup of coffee Francesca poured for her and joined him. He seemed as apprehensive now as he was the previous evening.

"Marya, I have to get right to the point. Tell me about the man who attacked you. He was Asian, wasn't he? What else?"

"He had short hair, like a crew cut. He wasn't very tall but he had broad shoulders and could have weighed over 250 pounds judging from how he rocked the taxi boat that I was in."

"Did he have a scar on the left side of his face? I have to know."

"Yes, he did. But now he has two."

"Why do you say that?"

"Because I slugged him really hard with a full thermos on the side of his face and I'm sure I left an impression."

"You're lucky you got away."

"Giovanni, like I said, I don't rely on luck. I believe in action. That creep was lucky to get away from *me*."

"Don't be so sure. It's one thing to stand up for your rights, but it's another to take crazy risks. For your own sake, and for those around you, I urge you to give this search of yours up. Polo's treasure has been lost or buried for seven hundred years. You are placing yourself and others in danger for no promise of reward." He munched on his pastry and took a mouthful of the strong, black coffee.

"I can't quit. I won't. I'm going to the convent this morning and that's that."

"No you won't," he almost shouted.

"Why not? Liam told me that I would be free to continue my research from here. He assured me you folks would not interfere at all."

"That was before I knew what I know now."

"I'm sorry. I wish Liam had been up front with you. I told him so. Well, if it's a problem for you, I can move out."

"I'm not asking you to do that. It would not be hospitable of me either. Signorina Bradwell, you are in very great danger whether you know it or not. You've got to suspend your research. Better yet, give it up."

"Never."

"Vittoria almost died because of that research!"

"We don't know that with one hundred percent certainty."

"I think you know better. Why were two different people with identical research goals targeted by the same thugs? Believe me, this was not a random mugging. They attempted to kidnap you and surely would have harmed you the way they did Vittoria, God forbid. What else do you need for proof? They still might track you down, even here! And we all might end up floating in the canal. Do you want that?" Bellardo frowned at her. "I have been in the antiquities business for almost my entire life. Don't you think I know anything about people in this trade? Just the scent of gold draws them like hyenas to a fresh kill. They are after you. You don't want to end up like Vittoria, do you?"

She picked up her coffee, but it slipped from her fingers. The hot coffee fanned out across the little table and dripped onto Bellardo's lap.

Bellardo instantly pushed away from the table and rose. "Francesca!"

Francesca came running and sopped up the mess, casting angry looks at her husband. "Leave this girl alone. She's been through a terrible situation. She needs your help, not your criticism!"

He swung around to Francesca and roared, "You be quiet! Just get me another towel!" He shook his head and groaned. "Women!"

Francesca brought two and flung them on the table. He mopped the hot coffee on his lap with one and wiped up the rest of the mess on the table with the other, leveling his eyes at Marya. "You will go nowhere in Venice without our protection. Any visit to the convent will be under escort. Also, I've spoken with the Rodonis and they tell me that Vittoria is responding. You will visit her this morning and Pietro will take you to see her. You are to go nowhere until you have done this first. Do you hear me? Do you?"

It wasn't the order to go see Vittoria that enraged her. She had wanted to see her as soon as possible. It was Bellardo's patriarchal tone that maddened her. She hated being treated like a child, told what to do and what not to do by a man used to giving orders and taking none.

"Take her a bunch of flowers for me and, if you see her parents, tell them how sorry I am." He turned and flung the towels across the kitchen into the sink.

She agreed to do as he said only because she loved Vittoria and empathized with the condition she was in, not out of obedience to this Italian Moses figure. As she left the kitchen, she was glad over the news that Vittoria was improving. As for her research, nothing Bellardo had said would get in the way of her plans. As soon as she could, she would take off for the convent and if Bellardo attempted to block her way, she would pack her bags and find a new place to stay where she could do as she pleased.

CHAPTER 24

An hour later, with a bouquet of daisies, carnations and baby's breath in hand, she arrived at the Ospidale Generale with Pietro as her newly-appointed bodyguard. The blond nurse at the desk informed her that Ms. Rodoni's condition was still critical and that she was sedated for pain. She advised the two visitors not to stay too long. "Just put the flowers in a vase and spend no more than a few minutes," she advised sternly. While Pietro remained outside in the hallway looking fidgety, Marya went into the room and found Vittoria alone, half-reclining. She was sitting up, both eyes open. Marya didn't like the yellowish-olive bruising and puffiness on the right side of her face, but was glad that the terrible swelling around her eye had gone down.

"Good morning, Vittoria. I came by to see you. I brought you some flowers." She presented the bouquet to Vittoria who smelled them and then let it rest on her lap.

"Oh, Dr. Bradwell. I'm so glad you came by to see me.

"Vittoria, we've worked together so long and we've been through so much…you don't need to call me Dr. Bradwell, okay? I'm Marya to you."

"Okay."

"You're looking more alert today, thank God."

"Yes, I feel better. Thank you for the flowers. You can put them in the empty vase there at the sink."

Marya went to the sink and filled the vase with water. "Vittoria, I am so sorry for this. If I had had any idea at all that this would happen, I would never have asked you to…"

"Please, Marya, really, you mustn't blame yourself. Have you been to the convent?"

Marya was reluctant to broach the topic because she did not want to tell her about the attempt to kidnap her. She paused before answering. "Yes, I did, but they didn't let me in. I was told that the sisters were in prayer and I should come back later. So, I had to postpone it."

"You've got to go back there right away. I'm sure what I saw was really the personal journal of Marco Polo. It's just incredible."

"Do you know what happened to your papers?"

"I remember taking them later to the Marciana Library. I found some help in translating them, and—I, I just can't remember the name of the gentleman who worked with me. Sorry."

"Don't worry. Did you have those papers and the translation with you the night of the attack?"

"Yes, but I haven't been able to think about them until now. I have no idea where they are. I think I also had photocopies of pages from the journal. Would the police have them? Did anyone pick them up?"

"Not that I know of. I think that's what the attackers were after."

"Seriously?"

"Yes."

"But why? And how would anyone know? I don't understand."

Marya wanted to detour the conversation because Vittoria was getting visibly agitated and she didn't have any sensible answers to her questions. "I wish I knew. Do you remember any of the content of those pages?"

"Yes. Generally, they were about Marco's family on the island of Korcula."

"He said that he had family there?"

"Yes, yes." In her excitement she widened her injured eye and winced. "He mentioned lots of relatives—cousins and uncles in various professions—people that his father and uncle had known well. You know, it confirms what I found in Giustiniani's letter, the one I sent you by e-mail."

Marya gave her a blank look. "Huh?"

"Didn't you read the transcript of Giovanni's letter that I attached to my last e-mail to you?"

The puzzlement on Marya's face told her she had not. "You must have seen it. It mentions that Polo wanted his private journal to be given to his daughter Moreta and he said some of the same things about Polo leaving a fortune on the island...in some church in Korcula, I think. Don't you remember getting that attachment?"

Marya was dumbfounded. She only recalled an email and must have overlooked the attachment. She felt like a dummy. "Yes, you're right. I'm sorry. I must have been distracted or something. I bet I saved it to a disk that's in my briefcase at Mr. Bellardo's. I'll check it out as soon as I get back." Her mind raced ahead to her room at the Bellardo's and her briefcase with files saved on CDs. The disturbing thought struck her that someone at Bellardo's might be tampering with her laptop and materials at this very moment. She had to get back.

"Well, Vittoria, the nurse at the desk told me to keep it brief. Sorry but I've got to go."

"I wish you could stay a little longer. I'm not as weak as they say."

Marya leaned over and gave Vittoria a kiss on the cheek and told her that she looked a whole lot better than she had the last time and that she had a little surprise out in the hallway. She went to the door and signaled Pietro to come in. As Pietro entered, she stepped out, waving good-bye, and blew a kiss. She was happy to see a radiant smile on Vittoria's bruised face when Pietro appeared in the doorway. She figured that old Bellardo must have wanted to kill two birds with one stone in sending Pietro with her to the hospital.

Pacing the hallway while Pietro had his turn to visit, she strained to recall the important email attachment about Marco's confessor. It was urgent that she get back and read that piece immediately. She sauntered back and forth several times from the nurses' station to Vittoria's room before she stopped outside the door to listen. She could hear soft whispering and murmuring between the couple. She looked back at the nurses' station and saw that no one was there. Then, she peeked in on the two love-birds and saw Pietro gently caressing Vittoria's hands. What was it that he had just vowed to her with such devotion in his voice? Whatever it was, she thought, she wished that someone would be as loving and passionate with her.

Marya could take no more. She stuck her head back in the door. "Pietro? I'm sorry but we've got to get going. The nurse out here is telling me our visiting time is finished."

CHAPTER 25

Porca vacca! Sister Villana muttered as she dashed down the cloistered arcade towards the front door. The insistent rapping on the door during the hour of prayer always brought out the worst in her. She made the sign of the cross to get her anger under control. Whoever was at the door had better have good reason for this unheard of behavior. No one in the neighborhood would have dared. She swung the heavy oak door open on creaking hinges just as the caller had his hand poised to rap once more. He let his hand drop.

"Yes? You are . . . ?"

"Father O'Rourke of Waterford, Sister."

She knew that he was a priest by his suit and collar, but he could have been a movie star. She tried to pronounce his name to welcome him to step inside but she twisted her mouth and tongue in such a way that he had to pronounce his surname again for her. "Of course. Father O'Rourke. Please come in," she said with honey in her voice. "Yes, please." She was only too delighted.

"You must be Sister Villana with whom I spoke on the phone."

"Yes," she said, half giggling. "You are here for research on the late medieval period, you say?"

Father O'Rourke rattled off the names of three popes, Blessed Benedict XI, Clement V, and John XXII of the 13th and 14th centuries as his focus of research. He told her how he needed to examine the convent library's highly reputed collection. She reacted with surprise, telling him how astonishing it was that several researchers had also shown up lately looking for materials on the same period and that seldom, if ever, had the library had more than a handful of researchers per month. Father O'Rourke's curiosity was really aroused when she said that a large, middle-aged man—from Japan, she thought—had just been in an hour earlier.

"A researcher from Japan studying late medieval papacies. Madre mia!" She led him down the hallway into the library.

"All the way from Japan, Sister?"

"Well, maybe from China. Asian, certainly. He looked like a criminal, not a scholar, at least not a Christian scholar."

"Is that so? Did he ask for anything in particular?"

"Sister Fortunata told me that he was asking for some kind of journal belonging to Marco Polo. I told him that he had come to the wrong library for such an item. We would certainly not have it. He wandered about the library looking lost and left ten minutes later. Can you imagine? Do you suppose he was trying to "case the joint" as they say in those American movies? We've had trouble like that before, I hate to tell you."

"I can't imagine how someone like that would come here looking for Marco Polo's journal, of all things. I don't think any such thing exists. What nonsense," he said unctuously. *That must have been the thug who tried to kidnap Marya. He came back to see if he could find the journal on his own. How would he have known about it?*

"Well, let me introduce you to our librarian, Sister Fortunata. Unfortunately she will not be able to help you much with her limited English. Do you speak Italian?"

"Not as well as I should. Just a few stock phrases."

"How long will you be here today?"

"Just long enough to survey the collection and make a list of what I think will be useful. My actual research will have to be for another day."

Sister Villana led Father O'Rourke through a labyrinth to the library and presented him to Sister Fortunata, sitting at her desk. A natural, permanently incised grimace creased the face of the library monitor as Sister Villana introduced the young priest to her. Her chair creaked loudly as she leaned sideways to open a drawer. She muttered something in Italian to Villana who promptly left with a nod to Father O'Rourke. Fortunata took a pair of white cotton gloves from a drawer and gave them to him. With a few gestures and some guttural sounds in English she indicated the general area where he should look for materials on the papacies of the 13th and 14th centuries and a table he could work at. She resumed reading a religious tract sitting flat on the desk but Father O'Rourke sensed that she would be keeping a very close eye on his every move.

A notorious attempt to relieve the library of valuable illuminated manuscripts had taught the nuns a harsh lesson. One year earlier, a clever French college student-turned-thief was finally caught. He had learned of the existence of a secret passage to the library from an article in an obscure periodical. Over a four-month period, he stole some of the most valuable and ancient manuscripts in the collection, using the secret passage that ran from the library to an unused workshop in the neighborhood.

The nuns were completely mystified and grew alarmed as the manuscripts disappeared week by week with unbroken regularity. Since they could find no explanation for these terrible losses, they finally consulted the police. The police installed a hidden surveillance camera in the library and captured the culprit *in flagrante delicto* one evening as he hustled three precious volumes into the secret passage. He was arrested and after that the police returned all of the priceless stolen manuscripts to the library. Since the arrest of the thief, the nuns had not let down their guard for one minute.

Father O'Rourke entered the gloomy stacks and began checking the titles on many of the bound volumes. He opened a few with reverent care for their antiquity. He marveled at the good quality of the vellum, the intricate lettering by scribes who had used brilliant colors, still vivid after one thousand years. Row upon row of priceless pieces, bound in the finest leather sat, seldom seen, in the neglected nine-hundred year old library. He ventured to think that some of his clients would pay hundreds of thousands of dollars for any one of these volumes in such pristine condition. *This could be interesting. Some other time,* he thought. He had no use for the precious manuscripts today. He was looking for something more modest. And, within a half hour, he found it, on one of the lower shelves, in a dark recess of the library, just about where Marya told him it would be. He inched the little book out from between two large volumes and carefully filled the gap on the shelf with his breviary.

His heart skipped a beat as he heard a click overhead, coming from the corner. He stood up slowly, expecting to confront someone with a gun pointed at him. Instead, what he saw made him freeze. A shiny black eye stared down at him. *Hey. What the hell? I'm on Candid Camera!* He remained perfectly motionless for a minute, half-expecting the pounding footsteps of the *carabinieri*, but they didn't come. He breathed with relief and clutched the ancient little volume to his chest the same way he held his breviary when he entered the library. He walked slowly to the end of the row and came into view of the guardian. She looked up. Her eyes were all over him.

He managed to put a smile on his face even though he was sweating under his collar. Fortunata's glare looked like it would pierce the door of a Swiss bank vault. He started for the desk to say a polite good-bye, maintaining as casual an expression as he could. She continued glowering at him, her eyes fixed on his prayer book. *She's going to demand that I place the breviary on the desk. She won't even have to open it to know that I've got something of theirs. She'll alert the police. They'll haul me to police headquarters in cuffs, hold me without bail and drag me into court. There will be cameras all over my American ass. The papers will go nuts with this for months. Fraudulent American priest tries to rip off nuns of St. Lawrence! Marya will never see the journal and I won't see the light of day for a long time. Shit, shit, shit. Why am I doing this?*

Approaching the desk, he continued to hold the journal over his heart, posing perfectly as a man of the cloth. Would the ruse work? Or...?

The face of stone cracked slightly. "Did you find what you were looking for, Father?"

He laughed good-naturedly. "Yes, I did, Sister. *Grazie.* I'll be back soon to begin my real work in earnest. Ciao." *Sure. Like hell I will.*

Once he was out of the library, he sighed with relief. He passed by a chapel on his right and poked his head in for a quick look. Jesus was in the full throes of his passion and suffering on the crucifix over the altar, flanked by the two thieves. One of them he recognized as Barabbas. The bad guy. The other was Damien, the good thief. Something inside him that went all the way back to his elementary parochial school days gave him a twinge of guilt at the thought of stealing from the nuns. The feeling passed. Heck, he thought, with what he now held in his very hands, he could retire a multimillionaire. A minute later, he was out the front door, in a triumphant mood, still holding the stolen journal against his black serge Jesuit suit.

His euphoria vanished completely, however, when he caught sight of two police officers hurrying in his direction. Damn it all to hell. This is it. He raised both arms in the air as they approached.

CHAPTER 26

As soon as the taxi boat had pulled up to the landing stairs, Marya jumped out and raced to the showroom. She dashed up to her bedroom, all the while angry with herself for having overlooked the letter of Giustiniani. How could she have made such a dumb mistake, she thought, opening her laptop case.

"Hi, Marya." It was the cheerful voice of Carlotta who had heard her entering the store. "Did you see Vittoria? How's she doing? Better I hope."

"Much better. She's alert, but they have her on heavy pain medication. I think she's going to recover quickly. Her parents will be so relieved." She kept fumbling around in her briefcase, not finding what she wanted. She turned to her big suitcase in haste, fishing around in umpteen zipped pockets both inside and out.

"My father would like to see you when you are free. He asked me to find out when he could talk with you."

"What for?" she asked with no effort to be tactful.

"Sorry. He didn't tell me. But I know he's been worried about your safety."

"Carlotta," she said with exasperation, "I'm busy now. I'm trying to find something important and I can't afford to be distracted. Will you just tell him that I might be able to see him this afternoon?" She continued rummaging around in her things without even looking at her.

"What are you looking for? Maybe I can help...?"

"Thanks, but only I can figure out what I've done with my disks." She closed her large suitcase and flung a smaller bag on her bed. She dug into it feverishly. "Oh, God in heaven above! Oh, thank God. Here it is. Found the little rascal." The disk was clearly labeled with the title, Correspondence-Vittoria.

She turned on the laptop and inserted the disk, her heart pounding. Carlotta peeked over her shoulder. "What's got you so excited?"

Marya was too focused on the task at hand to tell her. Irritated, she stopped tapping on the keyboard and looked directly at her for the first time. "Carlotta, would you mind closing the door on your way out? I really need to concentrate on this." A dark expression came across the young woman's face. She turned and started to leave. "Carlotta. I'm sorry. I don't mean to be rude."

"I understand."

"Thank you. By the way, those are the most attractive earrings."

"Thanks, they're pure gold," she said, feeling one between her index finger and her thumb. "A gift I got on my 18th birthday. I'm only supposed to wear them on special occasions, but I don't listen to papa, either."

Fifth century B. C., Scythian feline motif, at least $4,000 apiece, Marya thought, recalling an auction of a similar pair at Christie's a year ago. Bellardo's done well in this trade, obviously.

"We'll see you this evening, I hope," she said, closing the door after herself.

Marya got right to work on Giustiniani's letter. As she began, she knew that this letter would tell of a second session the padre had with Polo on his deathbed. Polo had already made his general confession in the morning, taking almost an hour before his strength gave out and he had to rest. In the evening, Polo was quickly approaching death and knew exactly what he wanted to say. Though in growing pain, he spoke with a clear mind to Giustiniani, his friend for the last thirty years. He wanted his wife, Donata, and his three daughters, Bellela, Fantini and Moreta to be the executrixes of his estate. He made various bequests to religious houses and fraternal orders to which he belonged. He cancelled the debt of his sister-in-law, paid his tithes, freed his Tartar servant, Peter, from bondage and ordered his three daughters to divide the property equally among them after reserving certain furnishings and money for their mother, Donata. Marya knew all of this by heart from her study of Polo's story.

But Giustiniani's letter was something else. Reading it, she felt as if she were present in a corner of Marco Polo's room only moments before he died. The bare words on the pages of the letter became a living scene, a vivid reenactment. Shadows flickered on the wall, the padre's robes rustled as he approached Polo's deathbed. Outside the bedroom, women wailed over the impending loss of "Il Milione."

CHAPTER 27

Giustiniani sat down and leaned forward to make sense of the hoarse and labored whisper of Polo.

"Padre Giustiniani, I have asked you to come back here one more time this evening for a matter that is to concern just you, my daughter Moreta and me."

"I have vellum and my writing implements and I'm at your disposal. What is it that you wish, my son?"

"I need to add to the instructions that I gave you this morning but you will not need to write anything. Just listen, Padre, for I do not have much time left. When I returned to Venice at last, after many years away from home, I thought that my father, my uncle and I would be well received and that it would not be difficult to carry out the wishes of the Khan. But for the rest of my life, though I tried, I failed repeatedly and suffered unbearable ridicule.

"When we left China, one of our missions was to deliver Princess Kukachin to the Khan of Persia. She was safely delivered to the Persian Kingdom. But the Khan of Khans had other more important plans for us besides that. The great Kublai gave my father and my uncle a plan to accomplish with the wealth he endowed on us. They were to work with him towards the building of a great confederation of all the lands between China and Europe. It was his intention through creating this confederation to build a road, a path that would endure forever, uniting the eastern and western terminals of the continent. He knew of the ancient Romans and their clashes with the armies of the Han Dynasty. Why couldn't contact between the two regions now be made to work for mankind, perhaps through continuous trade and through the teachings of wise men? The Khan wanted to create schools and encourage an exchange of scholars. That was his dream. My uncle and my father, sadly, were poor vehicles for this message and, alas, after their passing, so was I.

"The Khan had hoped to lure the interest of an important ruler to help accomplish this goal. For that reason he sent with us on our return to Venice a second princess, a princess of the Sung. He ordered us to return to the West, find a royal match for her with one of the powerful kings of Europe, instruct the Pope to send a large delegation of wise men to China and maintain open trade with his Empire. My father and my uncle failed in these tasks as did I."

Polo was in extreme pain and he strained to continue. The Padre felt pity for the man who had written an amazing tale of his travels across Asia. Personally, he did not believe much Polo wrote in the *Description of the World* and he believed even less what Polo had just told him, but he felt compelled to comfort his dying friend. "In time men will believe," he simply said and then asked what he could do for him in his hour of need.

"Padre, I have not told the half of what I saw in China and elsewhere for fear of even worse abuse. But there is something that I wish to confide so that…"

"Is this to be a solemn confession, my son?" the confessor asked. The priest leaned forward the better to hear his weak voice. But Polo had long since confessed his numerous sins with women of many nations over the course of his life. What disturbed Polo so much at this point, he wondered?

"No, Padre," he rasped. "I already confessed this morning. No… this is about a donation… that I have made to a church on the island of Korcula. I made that donation to preserve the treasure of the Khan for a future time, for the sake of mankind and, lastly, for the salvation of my soul. Listen. Padre," he choked. "Do not interrupt. In the years since my return I have increased my wealth trading along the coasts of the Adriatic Sea. Of all the places in the Adriatic, I am most fond of Korcula, my homeland and the homeland of my fathers...and of my other children."

The priest was incredulous, seeing that Polo's mind was rapidly failing before his very eyes. Why, he wondered, had Polo endowed a church in Korcula and not in Venice? Ridiculous. Incredible. It also surprised him to learn that Polo had other children. But, Polo anticipated his concern. "I have made a large donation to a church on that island, a donation not mentioned in the will I dictated to you this morning. It was too dangerous to leave the gold of the Khan and his great gems in Venice. Genoa had just defeated Venice on the Adriatic Sea. There was....unrest...in our city. And it was...too dangerous to leave the fortune to my wife and children. My two married daughters and their husbands fought...their husbands have spent my daughters' dowries in pleasure-seeking. But that is all in the past. It is of no use to talk of that any more. I have called you here, Padre, because it is urgent that my daughter in the convent, Moreta, receives my last bequest and that she understands what I have done and why."

The priest assured him that he would do everything in his power to carry out his requests to the letter. Polo seemed relieved with that. "In the chest, near the wall you will find a journal. It tells of all my travels and trading activities since my return to Venice. It tells of what I left behind in Korcula—a treasure that does not belong to the Polos, but to the Khan and to all the people of the world that he hoped to unite. Will you see that only Moreta receives this journal and no one else? She must know the secret and she must preserve the journal for a future generation. I leave it to her to find a way."

The priest promised that it would be done and that Moreta alone would receive the journal. He turned aside from Polo and did as he was told. There was, indeed, an ornate wooden chest against the wall, not far from the bed. He opened it and reached inside for the fine leather-bound journal from among a few personal articles. When he turned to face him with the journal, the priest was shocked to see that Polo's eyes already had no motion, no life, only the glazed stare of the deceased.

Padre Giustiniani ended his account of Polo's lasat moments saying that this was his last conversation with him before he died, reconciled with Holy Mother Church. After Polo's burial at the Convent of San Lorenzo, the padre delivered the journal, without reading it, to Moreta who was a nun at the convent. He felt that Polo's last words were as absurd and amazing as his book of travels and he had no idea what Sister Moreta would do with the journal.

CHAPTER 28

Marya sat with her shoulders slouched, staring at the pendulum clock in the corner, almost incapable of digesting what she had just read. She shook her head to clear her thinking. The letter of Giustiniani, she figured, must have been written to the city council, to satisfy questions of the city fathers who hoped that they could extract taxes from the deceased's estate or from his heirs. It seemed doubtful that the letter had led to anything but howling laughter at the man whose lies, tales and exaggerations had amused the Venetians for decades. But in trying to make sense of this piece of the puzzle, it began to dawn on her what it really meant.

First, of course, it corroborated the existence of a hitherto unknown journal belonging to Polo. The letter indicated that the journal had been delivered to Moreta at the convent of Saint Lawrence, as requested by Polo and just recently discovered by Vittoria Rodoni.

Second, and better yet, the letter hinted directly at a significant treasure of gold and gems that Kublai Khan himself had entrusted to the Polos and that had been given to one of the churches on the island of Korcula. Was this letter a map marked with an "x" or what?

Third, it spoke of something never known in the annals of Chinese history: that Kublai Khan was far more enlightened than suspected. His grandiose plans encompassed the linking of the two ends of the entire Eurasian landmass through the creation of a pivotally important central Asian confederation of some kind. This, if proven to be true, could cause world history to be re-written.

Fourth, and most curious of all, the letter described

a princess of the Sung Dynasty who had come with the Polos to the Adriatic. What had become of her? And then, it struck her like a thunderbolt! The DNA studies she had discussed with her students—they revealed the presence of East Asian genes in the population of Croatia about the time of Polo! She couldn't wait to go back to the convent, find that journal and read it from cover to cover!

Someone knocked on her door. "Marya, can I talk with you for a minute?" It was Bellardo's deep voice and she didn't feel like listening to him and his continuously discouraging blather anymore.

"What do you want?"

"Pietro told me all went well. I suppose you want to go to the library at the convent this afternoon, but..."

"But what? If you're here to tell me it's too dangerous, I don't want to hear any more." She paused for a second and heard him ask her to at least open the door. "Okay, but I won't guarantee that I'll agree with what you say." She opened the door and saw a genuinely disturbed Bellardo. "Come in. Just don't try to talk me out of my research. It's not going to happen, do you hear me?"

Bellardo entered and rested his bulky body on the chest in front of the bed.

"I'll keep this short, Marya. I've got reason to believe that we're both in trouble—you because of your search for Polo's treasure, and me because of my own,...ah, my personal trading activities."

"Giovanni, stop for a second. What did I just tell you? Don't you ever listen?"

"I know, but just hear me out and then...well, then we'll see."

"I honestly don't think I need to hear the rest of what you're going to say. We both know where we stand. You cannot prevent me from doing my work...I won't have you trying to slow me down."

"You must reconsider the whole project—this crazy treasure hunt of yours."

"I have reconsidered and you know what? I'm more convinced than ever that I stand a great chance of finding it and proving Polo's claims were true."

"What gives you such confidence?"

"This," she said, pointing to the document on the screen of her computer. "Vittoria found this letter written by Marco Polo's confessor and notary in the municipal archives. When Vittoria found this and summarized it on the phone for me, I sent her to the Convent of San Lorenzo where she made a bigger find."

"What's this all about?"

She summed it all up quickly for him including the letter's explicit reference to a journal written by Marco Polo and a substantial fortune in gold and gems on the island of Korcula.

"Are you all right?" he asked, getting up and barging past her on the way to the door. "Dear, for your own information, we've all heard that nonsense about Korcula being the true home of the Polos. Another fairy tale. Go on. Go ahead. Try to dig up something at the convent if you want, and in Korcula for all I care. Just be sure you are carrying a gun with you when you go out that door."

Marya turned off her laptop and closed its cover. She stood up and faced him. "Mr. Bellardo, will you get to the point? What are you telling me? That my project is just a joke or that I have to have your sons as bodyguards everywhere I go or all of the above? What is it? Because, you know, to tell you the honest truth, staying here is just not working for me. I appreciate the hospitality you and your family have shown me but I think I had better get packing."

"Leave? And go where? Are you out of your mind? You've got to quit this nonsense before you get yourself killed. I'm trying to tell you about the real dangers that you *and* I are facing right now as we speak."

"If you're talking about the risks you take in your line of work, I already know all about that and, for the record, I have no respect for your kind of business. Liam told me yesterday that you deal in gold artifacts that are taken directly from archaeological sites. I wasn't supposed to tell you that I know, but I do. Your problems with the police and the authorities are entirely different from mine. I also have a big problem with you butting in and ordering me about. I'm here to tell you that it's curtains for that, too. Would you just step out now and give me a few minutes to pack my things? I'm leaving."

"I can't permit you to..."

"Permit? You still don't get it, Giovanni. I'm not a little girl. I can handle whatever comes my way now. I'm in charge of my life and my work from now on, and nothing you tell me will change that fact," she said, ushering him out the door.

CHAPTER 29

Half an hour after leaving the convent, Liam strode victoriously into Bellardo's establishment with Polo's secret journal tucked firmly under his right arm. He decided he would not mention the gaffe he had made by raising his arms to the oncoming pair of *poliziotti*. They simply looked at him dumbfounded and dashed past him. He realized then that they had come not for him but to talk with someone at the convent, probably to follow up on an angle of Vittoria's case. When he got to the door of Marya's bedroom, he stopped in his tracks at the sight of her, packing her bags and Bellardo gesticulating and looking totally flummoxed. "What's going on here? What are you doing, Marya?"

"What do you think I'm doing? My laundry? And look at you all dressed up like a priest. What's that all about?"

"I hope you're not thinking of moving. Tell me you're not going to do something dumb like that."

Bellardo joined in. "That's right. See? Liam agrees with me. What have I been telling you all along? For you to be anywhere in public in Venice would be suicide."

"Would either of you gentlemen have the kindness to call a taxi-boat for me?"

Bellardo folded his arms across his chest. "No, not a chance. Liam, you've got to talk her out of this. I've tried."

"I will. Gladly." Liam stepped a bit closer to her and slipped the journal from under his arm. "Marya, I have one good reason that will make you change your mind."

"What?"

"This." He held the journal out to her but kept a firm grip on it. "This isn't a prayer book. It's what you came to Venice for."

"Polo's journal?" she asked hoarsely.

"I'll let you have a look at it if you cooperate and behave."

"Marco's journal? Give it to me, Liam!" She dropped a pair of slacks that she had been folding and made a lunge at him. Liam retreated a step and raised the journal high over his head.

Bellardo placed his hand on Liam's shoulder. "Liam, don't give it to her. She's been stubborn with me. I've tried to make her listen but she won't."

"You be quiet, Giovanni." She turned to Liam, pleading, "Can't you just give me the journal and let Bellardo iron out his own problems? Why does he have to be involved?"

Bellardo resented that. "I tell you, dear. It's not just my problems I'm concerned about. They're yours, too. If you would just let me prove it to you."

Liam was intrigued. "What proof? Proof of a conspiracy or something against Marya?"

With a weary groan, Bellardo simply gestured for them to follow.

* * * * *

At the door of his office he found Carlotta and asked her to go get Pietro to stand guard while he took Liam and Marya into his office for a very private consultation. Pietro soon arrived and Giovanni bolted the door from the inside. Looking around the office, Marya was overawed. Its fine furnishings each in its own way represented Venice's long and glorious reign over the Adriatic and the eastern Mediterranean. She circulated around the office, stopping at the fine walnut desk and fiddling with an assortment of paintbrushes she found sitting in a tray. She picked one up and examined it. Bellardo told her that the brushes had belonged to Tintoretto.

"Let's get this over with so I can get on with my

research," she snapped, placing the brushes back in their tray. "So, why are we here?"

"You're about to find out," my dear. He sat down behind his desk with a grunt and reached underneath to press an unseen device. Silently a four-foot wide section of the bookcase to his right swung forward into the office revealing a dim light above the entry.

"What the..." Liam blurted out. He had been in this office twice just yesterday and suspected nothing of a passageway.

Marya had a feeling of dread that what she was about to see would adversely affect her quest.

Bellardo rose from his desk and led them to the secret opening in the wall. "No one outside my family knows about this passage. I wouldn't show it to you if I didn't believe I absolutely had to. Follow me. Liam, keep your head down."

They entered, closed the false door behind them and came to a metal door at the other end of the faintly illuminated passage. Bellardo took out a key, unlocked the door, and gestured for her and Liam to enter. A velvet blackness enveloped them. No noises from the street penetrated into the chamber. The air in the room was utterly dead and she sniffed a faint, earthy mustiness.

"You have to see this to understand the point I was trying to make with you upstairs." Bellardo followed them into the unlit room and switched a light on. Marya's eyes blinked at a glittering array of gold artifacts that covered several large tables in the center of the chamber. Chills ran down her neck and fanned out in waves across her shoulders. She and Liam looked at each other, wide-eyed.

"I'll give you a minute or two to take a look around first and, then, let me know what you think."

Bellardo prompted them to move forward and walk around the tables in the center of the chamber. Before them lay an unsorted profusion of gold chalices, breastplates, scabbards, helmets, signet rings, stylized animals on pendants, hundreds of hammered gold squares that looked like large sequins and three human skulls with their insides lined with gold. The craftsmanship of every single artifact was of the highest quality. Liam carefully examined the motifs on some of the artifacts. "Every scene on these objects depicts some kind of violence."

Marya picked up one of the skulls. "There's a reason for that, Liam. The Scythians were great craftsmen with gold, obviously, but they were also a very violent people. You wouldn't want to make an enemy of one, believe me. He would scalp you, skin you out, and make a cup out of your skull. Occasionally you do find motifs that don't depict gory scenes." She put down the skull and picked up a comb with a scene of a young man milking a ewe into a pitcher. "Like this one, for example. But this is an exception. What would you expect of Scythian artisans when their warriors had the habit of mingling blood with wine and drinking the mixture in their rites of brotherhood?"

"It's probably how they invented Bloody Marys," Liam said in jest.

"Don't joke like that, Liam. The Scythians were a vicious, barbaric race."

She picked up a gold pail decorated with three friezes of horsemen, war chariots, an animal sacrifice and naked warriors. "Where did you get this?" she asked Bellardo.

"From the Ukraine. From a kurgan west of the Don River that was previously unknown to the authorities."

Liam turned to Marya. "What's a kurgan?"

"It's the site of a royal Scythian burial. Scythian burials were bloody, horrifying affairs. When the king died, the community strangled human victims and killed horses, and buried them in a pit with the king, along with gold, lots of gold.

"So, what do you think?" Bellardo asked Marya.

"I have to tell you, I'm overwhelmed. Do you realize that almost every one of these articles is of museum quality?"

"Of course. Is that a problem?" he asked with a dismissive shrug.

"Doesn't it bother you to know that an important burial site was probably ransacked and desecrated to bring these objects here? These objects are a legacy of all mankind. They belong in museums. You can't just deal in them like so many pieces of furniture... you must..."

"I must sell them, make a profit, and make these beautiful things available for enjoyment to those who can afford them! And I will!" he roared back at her. "Besides, there's practically an endless supply of them on the Asian steppes. They're everywhere, like MacDonald's restaurants. One of these days, museums will get in on the act, too."

Marya shook her head, bemoaning the loss to science. "That's just lousy profiteering. You haven't changed my mind at all about what you do for a living."

Liam stepped forward. "Hey, another thing, Giovanni. You've been holding out on me."

"Yes, but I did that for a reason. It's safer to release these beauties a few at a time. I don't need any more trouble than I have going for me now."

"What kind of trouble? And that reminds me, I still don't get why you had to bring us here," she said, looking at a large golden bowl with sculptures of galloping Scythian horsemen.

Before answering her question he asked them to pull up a few chairs and have a seat. His explanation would take some time. He told them how his sons had gone to Croatia a couple of weeks earlier to pick up this collection and pay off the Ukrainian official, a man named Shevchenko, who had contacted him. At a warehouse where they made the exchange, the official had spoken of a bloody clash between the Ukrainian members of his team and about two dozen or more Tajiks who claimed that they were archaeologists acting on behalf of an unnamed head of state. As the last of the loot was hauled out of the pit at the dig site in the Ukraine, the Tajiks staged an armed attack but the official and his men blazed away and shot a bunch of them. The rest fled on foot. The official warned Bellardo's boys that the Tajiks were fanatics and had threatened revenge. He told the boys that their threat was serious and that the Tajiks would probably be back sooner or later.

"You mean they might come back and try to recover this treasure? Two dozen guys?"

"He could have been exaggerating, but there's very likely some truth to the warning. That's why I brought you down here. And I'm warning you that you do not know who you are dealing with. You need protection. I'm very worried about your personal safety. There are people who kill just for what you are looking for."

"I fail to see the connection, Signore. My search has nothing at all to do with the kind of looting that you are into. Nothing. And if that's all you have to tell me, I see no reason to waste any more time here. Let me tell you again, you will not slow down my work and you won't get your hands on Polo's golden tablets using these wild scare tactics."

Bellardo rolled his eyes. "Nothing could be more untrue. You and I do have something in common. This gang, this outfit, this organization or whatever from Tajikistan. They are here in Venice. They're the ones who put our friend Vittoria Rodoni in the hospital."

Marya reeled, speechless.

"The description you gave of one of the men who attacked you matches a picture I have of him."

"You want to show it to me?"

He handed Marya a mailing envelope. "Go ahead

and open it. Tell me if you recognize any of the men in the photo. It comes from the surveillance camera that is always running in my showroom. Your assailant was here yesterday with two other thugs."

"I don't believe you."

"Open it."

She slid a glossy, enlarged photo that was taken of the showroom at an angle from a corner near the entrance. The photo showed the three men, including the large, scar-faced brute with the crew cut.

"That's him. One of the men who attacked me outside the convent. My God! You're right. But why did they attack Vittoria and me?"

Bellardo told her that he wasn't absolutely sure but he had a theory. The Tajiks seemed to be after gold artifacts—and not just any gold artifacts—they clearly wanted gold that had royal provenance. The gold articles from the Scythian burial pit had one thing in common with the golden tablets she was looking for: they had somehow been touched by powerful, aristocratic figures. "Do you see where I'm going with this, Signorina Bradwell? As far as aristocracy goes, there's no one higher up in all of Asia than Kublai Khan. Remember. Kublai Khan himself commissioned the casting of the Golden Tablets of Command that he gave to the Polos. The Tajiks seem to want them, too, for their leader or their chief."

"I see. So, for them the tablets would be like the Holy Grail, the True Cross and the head of John the Baptist, with a finger bone of the Lord Buddha thrown in for good measure."

"Do you think the Tajiks have already traced this Scythian treasure?" Liam asked.

"No one knows this treasure is here but my family and you two. I'm sure when those bastards came here the last time, they were just fishing around. They've probably poked into other businesses like mine up and down the Adriatic coastline. But I'm not taking any chances. The boys and I are taking steps."

Marya picked up another skull on the table and peered inside. The interior was covered with a thick layer of polished gold while on the outside, every tooth of its smile seemed to mock her.

"Do you really get what I'm saying now?" Bellardo asked her. "Do you realize what precautions we all need to take from now on?"

"I get it, I do," she said, running her index finger along the teeth of the skull.

"Okay, Liam, give her the journal."

CHAPTER 30

A messenger was sent ahead of the Khan to the palace workshop to announce his arrival. But the imported Han Chinese artisans, five of them, had little time to prepare for the living divinity. They had worked hard all morning, sanding and polishing the enormous ivory frame now sitting in the middle of the long workbench. As soon as they received the news, they dropped what they were doing and set to work tidying up the work site for the Khan's inspection. Two of them quickly grabbed brooms and swept up bits of chipped ivory and the whitish dust that coated the floor around the workbench so that his highness would not dirty his jewel-encrusted slippers. Another craftsman put away tools and straightened the portrait of the exalted ruler that hung in the workroom. It was identical to the portraits of the Khan that hung in over a score of other rooms and halls in the palace. The other two artisans dusted and polished the frame and the finely sculpted dragons that adorned its whole height and width.

The Khan entered, preceded by another official who made the formal announcement of the visit. The Chinese artisans bowed low and retreated to a far corner of the room in recognition of their inferior status. The Khan ducked as he entered the door of the workshop. He was as large as a champion Mongolian wrestler and was magnificently clothed, as always. He walked to the bench, paying scant attention to the workers who had created a miracle in ivory that would eventually be placed above and behind his throne. After skimming his manicured hand lightly along the serpentine, scaly backs of one of the dragons, he held out his hand so the official could wipe ivory dust from his fingertips with a silk cloth.

The fierce dragon heads with their bulging eyes, flaring ears and fine whiskers were technical wonders, as were the curved claw feet. He visualized the golden tablets fitting vertically into seven slots with Mongolian lettering above and Chinese characters beneath proclaiming the Khan's majesty to the world. How his ancestor, Kublai Khan, would have approved.

The wall opposite the Khan's portrait was half-covered with a floor-to-ceiling mirror that the Chinese artisans had used to check the symmetry of their work periodically. The Khan, turning to leave, caught sight of his reflection, not without some pleasure, and stopped to admire himself, face first. The mustache that he wore amounted to little more than a few droopy strands, but he smoothed them left and right with loving care. He had his official remove the ochre-colored turban from his head so that he could pat back his thick, black hair. He angled his face to the right to examine a mole beneath his left ear and to tweak two long strands of hair that grew from its center. The all-powerful ruler knew with certainty that Kublai Khan would have envied him, his achievements, his physical beauty and his growing influence in the world.

He straightened the long brocaded scarf that hung about his neck and paunch, and stood staring at himself, thinking of Khadafy of Libya and his pathetic attempts to cut the figure of an oriental potentate. He was convinced that Khadafy would never measure up to his standards and taste. The best Italian designer of men's clothing and the most skilled tailors could not hope to match the Khan's wardrobe. It was not rare for him to change costumes many times in one day, depending on the kind of audiences he had to attend and the advice of his necromancers.

All was as it should be. *Very auspicious.* Soon, the artists would be finished with their work and he would be finished with them. The workroom would be renovated to make way for a crew of portrait artists who would do nothing but make more copies of his official portrait to be hung in his other palaces throughout the empire. He gathered the folds of his gold-hemmed robe and strode out of the workshop.

CHAPTER 31

Marya excused herself from Liam and Bellardo and hurried to her room with the littler leather volume. Her hands shook uncontrollably as she put on a pair of white gloves and sat down at the antique secretary. The startling revelations that had just taken place in Bellardo's secret vault were still fresh in her mind. How ignorant she had been to dismiss the antique dealer's warnings. As for Liam, how badly she had underestimated and distrusted him. How close she had come to walking out and missing the journal! What a blunder that would have been. She made a vow to herself to control her temper and her impetuous streak.

She trembled, knowing that she was now on the threshold of realizing her life's dreams. The precious object she now had before her would unlock the mysteries only hinted at in the letter of Giustiniani. It was in amazingly pristine condition, she could see immediately, except for the cracked leather binding that bore no lettering. The size of a psalm book, it would easily fit into a bag or under a coat. She imagined that Liam had tucked it under his shirt and walked out of the convent with it undetected. In her excitement in Bellardo's hidden vault, she forgot to ask him how he actually managed to spirit it away from the nuns. She would have to get the details of his coup from him, but that could wait. First things first. Study the book from cover to cover. Later, get it photocopied and return it to the unsuspecting nuns.

She looked at the pendulum clock and realized she had about six hours before someone would come banging on her door to come to dinner. Not enough time to read it all through, page by page, word by word. There were, it appeared, about two hundred pages of tightly written script. It would be better, she decided, to scan it through once, looking for any references to the location of the treasure mentioned in Giustiniani's letter. Secondly, search for clues to the identity of the Sung princess and her fate. And always keep in mind the authorship and authenticity of the artifact. She would need to bring to bear all that she had learned about Polo, ever.

She hefted the book and opened the cover slowly to check its fragility. She carefully turned the first two pages, which were blank, and came to the beginning of Marco's narrative—one that Vittoria had quickly seen and recognized as completely unlike his book of travels. Methodically, getting into a regular pace, she scanned each line of the first page, then the second and so on. Two and a half hours passed with the ticking of the pendulum clock in the corner the only sound she could hear in the house. She had found mention of the names of towns along both coastlines of the Adriatic Sea, names that she recognized as important trading ports under the domination of Venice at that time. But so far, not a word about Korcula. She wondered if perhaps her method had been all wrong. Had there been a different name for Korcula eight centuries ago? Was it spelled differently from the way it was now? What about the princess? She felt a growing pain running down her neck and halfway out to both shoulders. She shoved away from the desk in frustration, slipping a piece of paper into the page where she had left off. She paced around the room, rubbing her neck, wishing that she had a glass of wine to relax her nerves. She opened the door of her room to see if anyone was about, but only detected the aroma of good food in preparation. It must be Signora Bellardo, she thought, whipping up some culinary magic. If nothing were to come of this exercise with the journal, her hopes would be dashed but at least there would be a good meal and good company to console her. She went to the window to gaze out at the Grand Canal for a minute before tackling the journal again.

She returned to the desk, opened to where she had left off, turned a page and suddenly there it was. Korcula, written only once, and several pages further along, there it was again, along with names of various Polos. She stopped each time to check each one in context but there was nothing suggesting gold or gems. But her mood was now more buoyant. She turned two more pages when her eyes seemed automatically drawn to words she had seen before in Giustiniani's letter: *the Sung Princess.* It appeared again one, three and seven pages later, in one instance, together with the expression, *la Tatarica.* She retraced her steps and went back to read each of the pages on which the reference appeared and discovered that, indeed, the Polos had brought a second princess with them on their return voyage. The Sung Princess was clearly not to be confused with Princess Kukachin whom Kublai Khan had sent with the Polos to be joined in marriage with the Persian Mongol ruler. The Sung Princess had continued on with the Polo caravan overland from Persia, crossing to the Black Sea and ending up on a ship that would take them home to Venice, or perhaps to Korcula, in the Adriatic.

There had never been any mention of such a woman in Polo's book of travels, maybe because he wanted to avoid the notoriety, maybe because he wanted to spare himself more mockery. In fact, there was no record of this person anywhere, no mention of her unusual voyage in all the annals of European history. Why had the Polos brought her home to the Mediterranean all the way from China? Who was the woman, really? What was she like? And what had happened to her? This enigmatic creature, she felt, would somehow be the key to the quest for Polo's hidden treasure. *Cherchez la femme.*

Marya desperately needed more time to find the

answers to these questions and time was running out. She wished for once in her life that she could get some take-out—a burger, some fries and a milkshake at Burger King—if she could skip the coming banquet. She just wanted to plow ahead through the night with her reading. But that would be too rude. Signora Bellardo was undoubtedly slaving away all day in the kitchen making the evening meal. And she could not afford to snub either Bellardo or Liam after what they had done for her. Both of them had very possibly saved her from a foolhardy and fatal choice to go to the convent alone. She would look like the worst ingrate if she didn't come to dinner. Doggone it! She was tired of the interferences and the entanglements but she had better get used to them.

She settled for going as far with her reading in the ancient volume as she could and would quit the moment someone came knocking on her door. When she took up the story of Marco's private life again, his bold, cursive script told of a ship approaching the little fortified town of Korcula on the island of the same name.

I was nearly forty years old when we left the realm of Kublai Khan. My father and uncle were old and weary as we crossed the Southern Ocean, crossed Persia, and came by ship to the Adriatic.

During the voyage, I came to know the Sung Princess whom the Khan had sent with the wedding party of Princess Kukachin. But the Khan had a different goal in mind in sending this young lady of twenty years. He had never carnally known her, because he had hundreds of concubines on whom to bestow his affections. He entrusted her to our care, not to the three Persian envoys, so that we would see her betrothed to a king of one of the western lands, perhaps to an English or French prince. For this purpose, he provided a dowry, rich in jewels, fine products of Chinese craftsmanship and a written message explaining his wish to unite the lands of east and west in peace.

By the time our ship turned north from the Mediterranean Sea into the Adriatic, we had fallen deeply in love. Of all the women I have known in my travels, none approached the Sung Princess in beauty and skill. For many days, on the deck of our ship, we viewed distant coastlines and spoke to each other of our lives from the beginning to the present moment. She told of her childhood at the court of the defeated imperial family, driven to the Champa border in the south by the Khan's armies.

She had been a gift to the Khan in Beijing and was placed in the great harem. But she was of no value to him except as a gift to another ruler of a tributary state. He already had hundreds of concubines from whom to choose. She had been told that Kublai Khan also imagined that she would appeal more to a king of Europe with her Chinese refinements than would a Mongolian princess.

In great detail, she revealed to me the customs of the Han Chinese who are very different from those of the Mongol tribes now ruling the land. Her memories were of a refined China, a land of abundant food, spices, silks, pavilions, poetry and music. She recalled customs that we know not of, nor can imagine. The Chinese drink a beverage called tea made from leaves of a bush cultivated in the southern regions. She said that men and women may drink this at home ceremoniously or that men may drink it, entertained by women at designated public houses. She told me that many women of the wealthiest families have their daughters' feet kept as small as those of children. As they mature, they must walk in small, mincing steps and thereby become objects of attraction to men of Cathay.

She asked me to tell her about the victories of Genghis Khan who had begun the destruction of the Sung and about the Great Wall. The latter is a wall made of packed mud that stretches across the northern plains and hills, but lies in ruins in many places, so that it fails its purpose—to keep out those the Sung rulers used to call "barbarians."

The Princess asked me about our Venice, a city she deemed in her imagination to be a place of wonder and beauty. Alas, I told her that Venice did not compare with the excellence of Hangzhou or Suzhou, cities that are each far larger and superior in all ways to my poor Venice. The riches that pass through those cities, where I supervised the collection of taxes for the Khan, exceed those of Venice by far.

In talking of many such things, we passed entire days in wonderment at ourselves, at our past travels and at our present journey. I was in love with her and wished every minute to be with her. I promised that at the end of this voyage we would be inseparable.

Entering the Adriatic Sea in the year of our Lord, 1293, old Nicolo directed the pilot to bring us to Korcula to visit the large branch of the Polo family there and to regulate important business before sailing north to Venice. As we disembarked, the people of the village were amazed at our Tartar appearance. We presented ourselves at the home of one of Nicolo's uncles, but they refused to believe that we were relatives for they had believed us already dead for many years. Only when the oldest of the uncles appeared and when Nicolo recounted to him certain closely known matters, did they believe that we were truly the Polo merchants of Venice. The rejoicing at our arrival lasted for three days.

The Polos of Korcula were numerous and they were of many occupations: sail makers, boat builders, blacksmiths, fishermen and merchants. One was a bishop. Nicolo revived his connections with all of them, paid old debts and forgave others, earning the good will of the whole family there. He also won the respect of the community by contributing to the construction of the new bell tower of the church.

After a month, we made preparations to depart. On the

eve of our departure, at a banquet in our honor, I made a surprise announcement of my proposed marriage to the Princess. But woe to me! For, my father grew angry. He ordered me to be silent before all the guests. Later he summoned both the Sung princess and me to his presence and told me that she would remain in Korcula with trusted members of the family, while I continued with him and Maffeo to Venice.

Only then did he reveal the reason for the presence of the Sung princess on our journey home: she was intended for a royal match, not for me, a mere commoner. He also disclosed the nature of the dowry that the Khan had sent along with her—an immense quantity of jewels of stupendous size and quality, larger even than that of Princess Kukachin who married the Khan of Persia. I was to assist him in the tasks the Khan had set for him, including travel to the court of the Holy Roman Emperor.

What was the purpose of the match, I boldly asked, angry that I had not even been told of the plan. He replied that the Khan had written a letter to be delivered to the man whom the Princess would marry one day soon. I demanded to read it and he gladly produced it. It was written in four languages: Chinese, Mongolian, Turkish and Italian. The Italian version had been done with his assistance.

The Khan's vision for a new world was breathtaking but the Princess was only one small part of it—she would wed the Emperor of the Holy Roman Empire—and he would work with the Khan on a wide range of ideas. They would establish a system to exchange their best scholars and religious figures; found a school of geography to map the world; share their knowledge of shipbuilding, navigation, banking and currency, coal mining, construction, trade in silk and porcelain, create printing houses, build roads and bridges. The letter laid out the expectations of the Khan in providing the handsome dowry and required that the emperor and his heirs work perpetually towards a goal of unifying the entire known world, from China to Western Europe, so that peace might prevail for a thousand years. I was astounded at this. And I was crushed. The Princess would never be mine.

My father told us that he intended to initiate discussions in Venice for the one who would be my wife. In spite of our many years away from Venice, he had long coveted a connection with the powerful house of Badoèr. Thus, the Polo family of Korcula was charged with caring for the Princess until the time of her marriage and I, though once a counselor to the Lord Khan of Cathay, and now in my 41st year of life, was bound in obedience to my father to marry someone that I knew not. At that, the Sung princess and I looked at each other and wept.

On our last night together, I encouraged her with words that my father was feeble and would not live long. I encouraged her to believe that we would fail to procure a royal husband for her and that I would refuse to marry except for love. I promised to return to her in Korcula, but she feared it would not be so.

I left the island of Korcula, a paradise that had now become hell. Our parting was painful beyond belief. My last glimpse of her, before many years passed, was at the dock as I embarked with Nicolo and Maffeo for the last part of the longest journey any man had ever taken.

CHAPTER 32

The tragic separation of Polo from the Princess had so absorbed her concentration that she barely heard the knocking on her door. Carlotta had come to tell her that dinner was almost ready. "I'll be there, but I'll need a few minutes," Marya called back. More like an hour just to gather my wits, she thought. What she had just read staggered her. She struggled to grasp it all. How daring and visionary of Kublai Khan. How sad for Marco and the princess. And the treasure that was so clearly spoken of in the journal! She would have preferred to continue reading, taking all night and the next day, too, if necessary, but duty called. By the time dinner was finished she would be too tired to concentrate and would have to put the journal aside until tomorrow. "Why can't they just leave me alone?" she muttered, looking in her baggage for something to wear.

She chose a simple black satin Shantung silk sheath with spaghetti straps that accentuated all the graceful lines of her figure. Standing in front of the mirror, she gathered her hair in with a gold clasp and dabbed on some perfume.

As she entered the dining room, all faces turned in her direction. Francesca beckoned for her to come and sit between her and Liam. She winked and patted the seat twice. As soon as Marya sat down Liam commented on her perfume. A heavy silence settled over the group assembled at the table. Everyone there was obviously waiting for something. The tension around the table was like the instant before a summer lightning storm cracked and split the atmosphere.

"What," she asked, looking around at each of the eight people at the table. "What's going on? Do I have something on my nose?"

Liam was the first to answer. "Just tell us, quick. The suspense is killing us. Is it really his journal? What does it say? Come on, out with it."

She took a deep breath. "It's more than I expected to see in my lifetime and, yes, it looks like the real thing. Everything about the journal looks authentic, speaking of its physical condition. I can even say that another document I've come across recently corroborates what the journal tells me. It's from the right period. Its linguistic style looks correct. I don't think this is a forgery or hoax of any kind, but I still have to approach it with caution. My professional reputation is on the line, after all."

Bellardo whispered, "Well, go on. Tell us what you've learned about Polo." He helped himself to some wine from one of the three carafes on the table and his example was quickly followed by all the others. All eyes were still on Marya.

"I'm piecing together a picture of Marco Polo from a couple of sources—his secret journal, his book of travels and a letter written by his deathbed confessor. And from what I can determine, there was a great treasure that came back from China, but it didn't belong to the Polos and it probably never reached Venice."

"Then whose was it?" Carlotta asked.

"It belonged to Kublai Khan."

"Then what were the Polos doing with it?" Liam asked.

"The Khan gave Polo's father and uncle a special mission when he released them from virtual house arrest in the Forbidden City to return to Italy. Not only were they supposed to escort a bridal party to the Khan of Persia, but they were also expected to bring a princess of the Sung dynasty to Europe for a royal match. His reason for this was utterly fantastic and has never before been reported elsewhere as far as I know." She stopped for dramatic effect and took a sip of wine.

"Come o-o-on, Marya. You're killing us."

She smiled and put her glass down. "All right. This you won't believe..." She went on to tell them the details of the Khan's plan for a transcontinental empire through links of trade, education and missionary activity. The marriage between a princess of the Sung Dynasty and a member of some European dynasty supported by a great dowry was supposed to seal the deal.

"The treasure."

"Yes, the treasure. Whoever ultimately wedded the princess would bind himself and his nation's power to support the project over the long haul. And you know what that means. Centuries, not years." There was audible surprise around the table.

"It really isn't all that unusual when you consider traditional Chinese diplomatic methods. The emperors of China often used marriage and bribery to bring their neighbors to heel and to avoid war. But the scope of this plan is breathtaking. Kublai Khan's plan broke the mold."

"When you say 'bribery' being used by the Chinese, you're talking about the dowry?" Liam prodded.

"Yes. Bribery, dowry, whatever. And in this case, it seems like it was the mother of all dowries, gem stones of stupendous size. Polo spoke of large, uncut raw gems. Big ones that would probably be worth millions in today's money. Think about it, if the plan had succeeded, the consequences would have completely changed Western history and the history of the Far East as well."

"What happened to the treasure?" Liam asked.

"I can't tell you the answer to that—but I'm working on it. Believe me, I'm dying to know the same as you."

"Tell us more about the Chinese princess. Please, Marya. That's really interesting," Carlotta pleaded.

"I can't help you on that score right now. Sorry. I really don't know her exact identity and what she was like or what happened to her. I might know something tomorrow. By the way, everyone, please don't mention this to anyone. The journal is not yet authenticated and I worry about premature publicity."

"I promise you that no one at this table will ever utter a word about it before you permit it," said Bellardo. He eyed them all and got nods of agreement.

"I can tell you this much, though," Marya said. "If the journal is really Marco Polo's, then Polo indeed fell in love with the Chinese princess. No. Let me correct that. They were crazy in love all the way from Constantinople to the Adriatic Sea, if not sooner. Old Marco even announced his plan to marry the Princess in Korcula, but his father squashed that plan. It seems that Marco Polo returned to Venice, leaving the Princess behind on the island with the Polo relatives."

"Did they ever see each other again after he went to Venice?"

"I haven't read far enough to know the answer to that question, but it makes for interesting speculation, doesn't it?"

Carlotta looked very disappointed. "You have to read on and tell us as soon as you can."

Over a platter of fish done in the Adriatic style with wedges of lemon, the conversation turned to the town of Korcula. Marya asked if anyone at the table was familiar with the place because she would be heading there at the earliest opportunity. Bellardo wiped a bit of sauce from his lips and placed his napkin on the table. "We Venetians controlled Korcula beginning in the 13th century. It was a strategic point for war ships and merchant galleys en route to the Holy Lands and Egypt. You've probably heard that the people of Korcula claim that Polo was born there. But don't believe it. As I told you, it's rubbish. You can visit the home he was born in right here in Venice."

Carlotta objected. "No, Papa. The Korculans might have a better claim on him than we do. Their records are much better." She turned to Marya. "One of my professors says that the people of Croatia kept excellent records that go all the way back to the twelfth century." Only Carlotta could get away with contradicting her father in front of guests. Her demure smile and sweet expression charmed the old man every time.

"I should never have sent you to college." Bellardo went back to his meal, letting Carlotta take over.

"My history professor is from Croatia. The way he tells it is that the Polo family has a long and respected history in Korcula. They had many merchants, ship builders, priests, metal workers and stonemasons in the family. The people of Korcula are, to this day, proud of the place that the Polos played in their history. He also says that Columbus would never have made it to America without his Croatian crew of sailors. And he is also proud that Croatians can be found all over the world today, even in your California," she said with a nod to Marya.

"I know," said Marya. "I'm one of them. And yes, Giovanni, I, too, have heard that Polo was Croatian. The story goes way back in my family."

Platters of vegetables and veal scaloppini made their way around the table from one person to the next. As Liam passed one of the platters to Marya, their hands and their eyes met in a flash.

"So what's your next move, Marya?" Bellardo asked.

She deftly removed the platter from Liam's hands. "First of all, I'll read as much of the journal as I can and then get down to Korcula. I'm thinking I might even leave tomorrow morning by ferry and read it along the way. By the way, could any of you help me with ferry schedules?"

"You won't go to Korcula alone," Bellardo said, furrowing his brow.

"Excuse me?"

"I said, you're not going alone."

"I thought I heard that correctly. But I'm sorry. No one's coming with me to Korcula. I don't require babysitting. This is my project—it's been a lifelong dream. I won't put up with any meddling."

Bellardo roared back, "I thought you understood the dangers I spoke about this morning. Otherwise I would not have shown you the vault and Liam would not have agreed to let you see that journal. I repeat, for the third time, you are not going alone and I'm sure Liam agrees one-hundred percent with me on this."

"But Giovanni, Korcula is hundreds of miles away from Venice. There's no way..."

Liam turned to her angrily. "Marya, Giovanni's right. It doesn't matter whether you're here or in Outer Mongolia. These guys are killers. It's obvious to me that they'll do anything to track down the treasure and they're going to nail you in the process. Do you want Bluto with his arms around your neck in a choke hold? Have you lost your senses or what?"

"I'm sending my sons with you," Bellardo said. If you're worried about them getting in your way, don't. They can be subtle and low-key."

"Right. About as subtle as the running of the bulls of Pamplona. Sorry, Giovanni. Nice try."

Liam stepped up with an offer to go instead of the boys but Marya brushed his offer aside, too. He stood up and threw his napkin abruptly on the table to the surprise of everyone. He warned her to accept the offer or he would march right upstairs, take the journal and return it to the convent in the morning. He would also advise the nuns of the extremely valuable document in their possession, one that would undoubtedly fetch millions on the open market. It would be an eternity before she would see it again and by that time others would have extracted everything of use in it.

"You wouldn't do that, Liam. You can't."

"Try me," he said staring her down.

CHAPTER 33

The next morning, as she packed, she mulled over the solution to the impasse of the night before. It was settled. Liam would accompany her to Korcula and provide protection for the two or three days she estimated that she would need. She wasn't entirely happy with the plan but it was the better solution, considering the alternative of two very large men hovering about, tracking her everywhere on the island, attracting unwanted attention for sure. The evening had ended with the Bellardos offering to make arrangements to take them to the ferry early in the morning. After zipping her carry-on bag shut, she placed a call from her room to Khalid.

He picked up the receiver at the first ring. "Marya? Where are you?"

"I'm staying with friends in Venice right now, but I plan to leave here soon. Thought I'd just call and let you know how it's going here and find out what you're up to."

"I got that contract for consulting with the government of Kazakhstan and I'll probably head over there in another week. Gee, it's good to hear from you. I wish that you'd let me come over and give you a hand. I'd gladly set aside my plans to join you in Venice. No kidding."

Marya knew from earlier chats with him that he had not one, but several, lucrative contracts as an advisor to the newly independent republics of Central Asia and she was glad of that. It would keep him from dwelling on her absence. "I understand, but I really need to do this on my own, Khalid. It's a dream that I've cherished for years." She felt guilty for misleading him, blatantly omitting the fact that she had agreed to take Liam as a full-time bodyguard along with her to Korcula. "Anyway, I have great news for you. Vittoria was right—there is a Polo journal—and I've got it right here with me. It's just amazing."

"So, you found it at the convent. Congratulations, Marya. That is such good news. I had a feeling that you'd come across something important soon. Now you're really making me feel bad that I can't be there with you. Is it really his diary?"

"From all appearances, yes. I'd give it a better chance than even that it's the real thing. I'm cautious though. It's too soon to go public with it." She was beginning to feel sorry that she had called him, knowing that her successes only made him more miserable.

"Have you had a chance to go through it? Any mention of the Polo treasure?"

She didn't want to make him feel any worse than he already sounded so she decided on a white lie. "I haven't had a chance to go through the journal completely. One thing is certain, though, and that is Polo's repeated references to the island of Korcula. It seems that's where I need to concentrate my research. The journal reinforces what Giustiniani said in the letter that Vittoria found. I can hardly wait to read the whole thing."

"It sounds like congratulations are in order. Marya, I'm proud of you."

Something in the tone of his voice sounded flat and depressed. "Is something wrong, Khalid?" she asked.

"No, not at all. It's just the usual battle here with the Gang of Three. It's not the same here without you and I miss you. So, when are you leaving for Korcula?"

"This morning by ferry. I should get there early tomorrow." She knew it was not pleasant for him to hear that so she quickly changed the subject. "Tell me, what are my prospects there with the old boys? Do I still have a job to come back to?"

"Frankly, that's what has me in such a down mood. The news is not good at all. Lafferty has made his displeasure known to all. I've heard that he is recommending against your tenure and worse—I think he wants to have your contract terminated."

Marya knew that there were bad feelings between her and the old boys but it was still hard to accept what she heard. "After all my years of work there? And the popularity of my courses with the students? How can he do that? Six years of hard work down the drain."

"If you weren't so taken up with looking for the Polo treasure, I'd suggest that you come back and try to shore things up with him. It might make a difference. I don't want to lose another friend from the staff. I don't have many left. Besides, if you came back with the journal you could run it through some rigorous testing here. Sorry for running on like that, but I just want to help. Think about it, won't you?"

"Again, that's so kind of you, Khalid, but it's probably way too late for me to repair the damage with those guys. I simply will not kiss up to them. I've got to forge ahead here as fast as I can and see this research through to the finish, come what may. For me there is no turning back. I have crossed the Rubicon."

"I understand, and I'm sorry. Sounds like we'll be losing you. Well, it's good to hear from you. Just keep me posted from time to time. I should be here for a few days working on my pet project. If you should need anything, just feel free to call. I love you."

"I love you, too, Khalid. Take care. Bye." She put the receiver down gently.

She was relieved that he was still occupied with advisory work in Central Asia and that he had taken the news from her so well. It had gone better than she thought it would. Dear Khalid. Always so helpful and understanding. Someday, she would repay him.

After she hung up, she rolled her carry-on bag out to the kitchen and set it next to Liam's. He was already there chatting with Carlotta over their espressos. As soon as Marya came into the kitchen, Carlotta got up and went to the hallway, calling Ambrosio at the top of her lungs. He came into the kitchen at a full trot and gathered up the two bags while Marya questioned Carlotta about accommodations on Korcula. Carlotta was emphatic that she and Liam rent a private, romantic villa out of town and not take a *sobe* or flat, in town.

Marya laughed in embarrassment at the suggestion. "How would I get any work done in a secluded villa all alone with Liam?" she asked. It was the wrong thing to ask Carlotta.

"That's the point. You just work too hard. I can think of lots of things to do with a bodyguard at a romantic villa."

"No thanks, I'm sorry I asked. I'll just stick with the *sobe* in town and let Liam venture out to the countryside if he wants to." She blushed as she looked at Liam and thought he looked a bit disappointed.

CHAPTER 34

Ambrosio and Pietro delivered Marya and Liam to the ferry, stood on the dock for a few minutes to see them board and then headed back to their van. They had to deliver a shipment of antiques bound for Los Angeles to a ship docked at a loading zone a mile away. After unloading the shipment and signing batches of paperwork, they headed for home. Mounting the steps to the Bellardo showroom, they were puzzled to see the front door half-open as they entered. As far as they knew, only their parents and sister would be on the premises and they always kept the door closed as a regular practice. Their puzzlement turned to panic as they entered the showroom. Major pieces had been toppled, glass items smashed and the fabric of many pieces of furniture along the main aisle viciously slashed. They looked at each other and knew exactly who had been here in their absence. They both broke into a full run down the aisle, shoved the curtain aside, and charged down the back hallway, looking anxiously into each room. On the left, Pietro checked the office and spotted the top of Carlotta's head. She was on the floor, behind the old man's desk, trembling in stark terror.

"Hey, over here, Ambrosio. It's Carlotta!" he yelled. She made a muffled scream and in a second he was on his knees in front of her. She was staring back at him, bound and gagged, her eyes agog, with severe bruises on her face. He shoved Ambrosio back and yelled at him to go find their parents as he began removing the tightly bound cloth from Carlotta's mouth. He got it off.

"Pietro," she cried. "It was them. They know!" She trembled violently as he undid the ties around her wrists and ankles. Behind her, for the first time, he spotted something out of place on the wall. It looked like a large crimson letter "T." The paintbrush used to smear the letter on the wall had been left on her lap and was still fresh with what looked to him like blood.

Ambrosio didn't need to be told twice. He tore down the hallway, past the dining room, in a white-hot rage, shouting, "Bastardos. Cazzos! I'll get them." At last, he found his mother in the kitchen hunched over the table, holding her right hand against her head. Her scalp and forehead were bleeding and she was incoherent. He thought she was trying to tell him to find Carlotta, but he wasn't sure. She waved a hand in frustration and let it drop on her lap. He left her a moment to check on his dad who was doubled over on the floor, jerking in spasms. A knife wound on his shoulder, still gushing blood, soaked through his shirt, and dripped onto the floor, forming a thick, maroon puddle. He ran to the phone and called for an ambulance. When he hung up, he returned to his father and looked around the kitchen for a cloth to stanch his wound. As he checked the area on the kitchen counter near the sink, he found an artist's paintbrush from his dad's collection resting at an angle in a bowl of blood.

* * * * *

From the stern of the ferry, Marya and Liam stood side by side, looking back at Venice and its tall, slender Campanile tower already a half-mile away. She wore tan corduroy slacks and a matching turtleneck pullover under a blue windbreaker that matched her eyes. Seagulls circled above and behind the ferry, occasionally dipping to the sea for scraps tossed overboard by passengers. Her thoughts centered on the fact that she was now on her way to fulfilling her life's ambition thanks to the letter of Giustiniani and Marco Polo's secret diary, now traveling with her. She was thrilled and excited and feeling jubilant.

Almost. She had hoped fervently to be entirely on her

own in Korcula to pursue the clues without the hindrance of Liam or any of the Bellardos, but that was not to be. She had resented the way he used Polo's journal to leverage his way onto the trip to Korcula with her. And yet, somehow, she actually felt accepting of him. He had guided her through the calamities in Venice and knew that she would not be on her way to Korcula at this moment had it not been for his intervention. She stole a glance at him from his left side. The slightly aquiline shape of his nose gave him a kind of patrician Roman look. Quite attractive, she thought.

She recalled being mildly pleased when Francesca seated her next to Liam at last night's dinner. During the meal, her hands and eyes had met his more than once. She told herself it was accidental but the past four days had shown her that there was anything but random chance to what was happening between them. What lay ahead for them in Korcula, she wondered? How would she manage being with him over the next two or three days? And when she had found what she was looking for, would that be the end of it for them? Should it be the end? She still hardly knew him and what she did know of him and his thoroughly materialistic views on life was disturbing. Maybe it was best that Korcula be the end of the line for them. Still, she was grateful and she felt she should tell him so.

"You kept me from making a fatal mistake back there. I admit it."

"Bellardo and I were both afraid that something would happen to you."

"I'm sorry if I've been difficult. The fact is, I can't thank you enough for very likely saving my life. And thank you for getting the journal for me."

"Glad I could help."

"I feel like I'm taking you away from your work. You would be on your way back to Boston right now if it weren't for me, wouldn't you?"

"Not necessarily. I often leave a little slack in my schedule before I move on to new business."

"Still, it's generous of you."

"I've never been to this part of Croatia before—the islands I mean. I'm actually looking forward to seeing Korcula, besides the fact that I'll get to see it in the company of a very beautiful woman."

"That sounds like Irish blarney to me. Or is it Italian bologna?"

"No. Really. I mean that honestly and sincerely. You should learn to accept compliments. You're beautiful and there's an independent streak in you that I like."

"Thanks again, then," she said looking out at the white foamy currents churned up in the wake of the ship. "I'm too independent for my own good, I think. You know, before we left the Bellardos' place I called a colleague at the university, my good friend, Khalid Agarwal. From what he told me, when I get back to the university, I won't have a job any more. It's my own fault. This trip is a career-ender. Goodbye to tenure that I worked so hard for. The chairman and his pals never had much use for me and this Marco Polo research of mine anyhow."

"They're going to fire you? Who are these clowns anyhow? Don't they realize what they've got?" he asked indignantly.

"It's okay. I'll survive. You know, winning tenure at Harvard doesn't seem enough for me anymore, Liam." She took him by the arm. "Let's take a stroll."

He let her hook her arm through his. "What are you talking about? Your teaching, your research, the long years of training? You must be tops as a teacher and your project certainly deserves support. I wish I could have had someone like you as a teacher at BC, believe me."

"Well, let's just say that I feel like I'm turning a corner in my life. I'm looking for something new, something more in my life." She glanced back in the direction of Venice and saw that the Campanile had completely disappeared beneath the waters. A slight pitching of the ferry as it hit rougher waters altered her sense of balance. She skimmed her hand along the handrail, smiling, while Liam held her other hand. The breeze was stronger and she inhaled a more briny taste in the air. A thick odor of exhaust from the ship's smoke stack suddenly washed past.

"Don't be too discouraged about it all. Who knows? Things could change dramatically for you. I have a very strong hunch that you are going to hit it big in Korcula with the help of Polo's little journal. Your chairman and his buddies will keel over with envy."

"I'm pinning everything on that, Liam. It's all I've got going. It's my whole life. I've got to find what I'm looking for right there, or else."

The ship listed, causing her to stagger two steps. She didn't try to slip away as Liam put his arm around her waist to steady her. A heavy Italian fellow walked past them in the opposite direction, munching away on a big sandwich loaded with rich slices of cheese, prosciutto and hard salami, some of it showing in his open maw. She felt a bit of nausea at the sight so she stopped along the railing at the ship's midpoint and looked out to the horizon. Liam leaned with his arm on the rail and turned, facing her. She felt her cheeks redden and become almost unbearably warm as she looked into his dark blue eyes. The cool breeze of the sea gently lifted wisps of hair around her face but failed to do anything for the heat stirring within her or the lump she felt forming in her throat.

Liam took her chin in his hand and raised it gently. He looked down at her lips and slowly brought his mouth close to hers. She saw him close his blissful eyes in expectation of a long, passionate kiss. With the rising and plunging of the ship, her emotions seemed pulled now in one direction, now in another. As Liam drew her more tightly into his embrace, her knees buckled and she began to swoon. She realized she had to get away before something very embarrassing happened. She pressed both her hands against his chest and pushed him away.

"I'm sorry, but I've got to go," she said, covering her mouth with her right hand.

"Is it something I said or did? I'm sorry." He tried to draw her back.

"No, it's not. Please, just let me go." She slipped out of his embrace and ran for her room.

CHAPTER 35

It had been one of the worst nights of her life after she had gone to her room, leaving Liam alone topside. She got up from bed a dozen times with the dry heaves throughout the long night and managed to get only a couple of hours of sleep before she heard the blast of the ferry's horn. Morning light filtered into her room through a crack between the curtains and she realized she had better dress quickly and find Liam before the ship docked. She had no desire to eat anything at the breakfast bar and easily passed it by on her way to the upper deck where they had parted the night before. As she climbed the narrow staircase, she peeked down through an opening and saw that the ferry carried a full load of sedans, minivans and trucks in its belly with their drivers already at their wheels. Out on deck, scores of tourists lined the rails, all faces turned towards the medieval town a mile away, bathed in the brilliant morning sun. She was reassured by what she saw. The sea was as flat and placid as a millpond. Korcula was a long, heavily forested island. Its capital, the town of Korcula, had the shape of a rounded mass of honey-colored buildings on a peninsula, surrounded by medieval walls. Its reflection on the water cast a broad shimmering path of light towards the ferry.

She found Liam, wearing sunglasses, standing at the rail, admiring the view along with several hundred other passengers. Silently, she came up behind him and tapped him on the shoulder. "Good-morning."

He turned. "Hi. Sorry about last night? I should have realized. You still look a little pale."

"I feel a bit crappy, to be honest, but hey, it's a beautiful day. I'm so sorry about yesterday. Me and boats don't mix."

"No apologies necessary. Do you often get seasick?"

"I've only been out on the open ocean once before in my life. On a salmon-fishing trip out of Humboldt Bay in California with my dad. I turned green within a half-hour of leaving port. This time it was way worse. So, never again, cross my heart. I'll always and forever be a landlubber."

"How about your reading?"

"I just felt too miserable."

"I thought so."

Marya felt and heard the ferry's throbbing engines slowing down as they got closer to port. Besides the forest of pines that covered most of the island, she could now clearly see terraces for lemon and olive groves and vineyards. Walls of rock supported the countless terraces. She felt warm drafts of air flowing off the island bearing a blend of natural scents. It made her feel somehow like she was coming home. A loud blast of the ferry's horn startled her and a few other passengers.

Liam pulled out a tourist brochure that he had picked up below deck and gave her some details of the island's geography and history. The island measured forty kilometers east to west and six or seven north to south and was home to three thousand people. It had been settled in very early prehistoric times and had prospered and suffered from invasions down through the centuries. It was north of its famous neighbor, Dubrovnik, but south of Split, another big coastal city. Korcula produced a delicious local wine called Prosip and claimed to be the home of Marco Polo. Liam pointed to a photo of the Polo home in the brochure and she mentally put it on her list of important things to see in the town.

Above all else she wanted to know how many churches there were in the village. Giustiniani's letter had specifically mentioned a donation that the Polos made to one of them. Could it have been the treasure that was donated?

Liam searched the pamphlet and found five churches in and around the town but the most important one was the Cathedral of Saint Mark. He matched the picture of it with what was now coming into very clear view. He pointed out the cathedral, partly hidden by buildings in the foreground, and its bell tower crowned with a domed cupola, without a doubt the most interesting structure of the town.

"Incidentally, do you like swimming?" he asked, his eyes glued on the brochure. "Looks like they have some great little beaches nearby." The rumbling of the engine reverberated beneath their feet as the ferry drifted slowly.

"I love swimming. I was captain of my high school swim team."

"Really. Well, it says here that you can find a quiet cove not far from town and go for a naturist swim. What's that? Some environmental thing?"

Marya was taken aback. "You're kidding me, aren't you? Haven't you ever heard of naturist swimming?"

"No. It sounds healthy, though."

"It has nothing to do with health as far as I know. It's just fancy talk for skinny dipping." She giggled at him. "You're a riot."

"Oh." His eyes twinkled. "Well, maybe we should look into that," he said. "I hope you didn't bring your bathing suit."

"I didn't," she said laughing. "But that's because I'm going to be tied up with my work." The thought of a naturist swim with him didn't seem totally out of the question, however, provided she first found what she had come to Korcula for.

The ferry thudded gently against the dock, causing low reverberations and brief shudders throughout the vessel before coming to a complete stop. Passengers shuffled forward with mincing steps. Holding her bag and her briefcase securely, Marya moved along with them, with Liam right behind her. The beautiful stone work of the town's walls and fortifications awed her as she inched forward towards the passenger ramp. The treasure has got to be here, somewhere in this village, and nowhere else, she was certain. More than ever she was eager to get started.

Within five minutes of coming ashore, Marya negotiated a price for a *sobe* with a middle-aged couple, Mr. and Mrs. Zoran Sternich. Their home was on the main piazza, not far from the Cathedral. It took them only minutes to reach it, partly by taxi and the rest of the way on foot. Marya and Liam each settled into their separate rooms on the second floor. She spent a half hour, hanging up a few items and laying out her papers. The journal was a problem. What to do with it? She looked about the room and decided to just leave it on a bookshelf along with two dozen old paperbacks. With business taken care of, she changed quickly and quickly left her room.

Downstairs, she entered the kitchen and found Liam having a bite to eat. Mrs. Sternich had already laid out a platter of cubed cheese, salami, Italian-style bread and had a pot of soup simmering on the stove. "You hungry?" he asked.

"Not a chance. I can't even think of food right now. Move it, Liam. Let's get going." So as not to offend Mrs. Sternich, she interpreted what she had just told Liam. While Liam gulped his soup, she collected one hundred fifty kuna from her purse to give Mrs. Sternich and told Liam he would have to pony up the same amount for the two days' rent.

CHAPTER 36

The noon-day sun illuminated the majestic stone façade of the Cathedral to a dazzling white. Next to it, encased in a scaffold, the cathedral bell tower soared hundreds of feet into the cloudless blue sky. From the shady side of the piazza Marya studied the church. A combination of Romanesque and Gothic styles, she thought. Rounded arch over the main entrance flanked by two columns. Atop the columns two odd-looking lions, sculpted by an artist who had never seen one in real life, tried to look fierce. In reality, they simply looked like cats with long, human noses. Over the main door, a bishop wearing a mitered hat sat with a large book reposing on his lap. The book was closed, she noted, symbolizing that the city was at war when the artist had sculpted the figure. The façade had a modest rose window and a two-stepped roof of red tile. The Cathedral couldn't compare with the Renaissance beauty that was St. Mark's of Venice, but that didn't matter to her in the least. What was important was that the church had been renovated in the early 14th century, shortly after the return of the Polos from China. Of the town's five churches, it was probably the best candidate for the Polo donations, she figured.

Liam shaded his eyes with his right hand. "What's going on here, I wonder?" "Looks like they're doing some serious repairs on the tower. I hope it will still be open for tours." About a dozen levels of scaffolding wrapped around the four walls of the tower all the way up to the top of the cupola. Each level had two foot-wide planks of walkways and each level was linked by a ladder from one to the other, starting at the street level all the way to the large black cross that crowned the cupola. The sight of the scaffolding dismayed her.

He took her by the arm and led her from the shade of a palazzo into the sunlight. She felt a passing moment of delight, feeling their arms linked plus knowing she was on the verge of a discovery that could make history. Suddenly, a vision of herself in a bridal dress, coming out the main portal of Saint Mark's Cathedral with him, flashing a delirious smile, flashed through her mind. She laughed to herself and dismissed the outrageous thought. She was on her life's mission in Korcula and had better keep focused. Besides, the two days she had to accomplish her work left little time to plan nuptials with some guy who was her complete opposite.

At the main entrance of the Cathedral, they came upon a guide wrapping up a tour of Korcula's churches for a small group of elderly English tourists. Marya listened intently to what he was telling them and did not like what she heard. "Liam, he's got it all wrong about the Mongols."

"Oh, really? Why don't you just go over and point that out to him?"

"I can't do that, it would be too embarrassing. He'd lose face in front of all those people."

"Fine. So, what's his mistake?"

"Mistakes. Tons of them. Wrong century, wrong countries. The Mongols razed villages and cities and massacred whole populations all across Asia in the middle of the 13th century right down here to this very area on the Adriatic Coast. They could have knocked Europe back into the Stone Age if they wanted to."

"Why didn't they?"

"Guess."

"They were sorry for their crimes?"

"Wrong. They couldn't have been happier than when they were spilling blood and wiping out cities. It was their favorite passtime." She moved closer to Liam to tell him in a lowered voice. "The only reason Europe was spared was that in the nick of time, the Great Khan, Ogodei, died."

"And they needed a time out."

"You might say that. Their armies retreated to Southern Russia to elect a new Khan and they never came back to threaten Christendom again. This was in the middle of the 13th century, not long before Marco Polo was born. By the time he was a young man, the Mongols had cleared a bloody path from Europe all across the continent to China. That's how the Polos and a few other Europeans were able to go overland to Kublai Khan's court in Beijing. Polo senior and his brother made the overland journey twice."

Several tourists near them at the back of the group turned around to listen to Marya's version instead of the guide's. She noticed and stopped talking with Liam but decided to ask the guide a few questions of her own about the church. The guide confirmed for her that it was built in the early 14th century on top of a smaller cathedral on the same site and he informed her that the bell tower was off limits to visitors because it was undergoing earthquake retrofitting. Engineers were dealing with three major cracks in the masonry caused by a 1990 quake. Marya closed her eyes in disappointment because she felt she needed an unrestricted look at this church and its tower from top to bottom.

The guide then led the group through the big doorway into the cavernous church, Liam and Marya trailing them. The chattering group fell silent as they entered. Banks of red and blue votive candles lit the area in front of statues of the saints near the altar. Marya searched eagerly. She gazed at the Byzantine frescoes lining the dome and she listened as the guide intoned about the icon of the Virgin, the high altar piece, and the Annunciation by Tintoretto. She examined the carved wooden seats behind her, the tiled floor, the Stations of the Cross on the side walls and the stained glass windows. In her mind, she went over what Giustiniani and Polo had both said about the donation. It must be here, she repeated to herself. The other churches of Korcula were either built too late in time or were outside the walls of the town.

Discouraged, Marya took a seat in the front pew and ran her hands through her hair. Liam slid into the pew beside her, putting his right arm around her shoulders. She sat upright. "What are you thinking?" he asked.

"I'm thinking that I must be crazy. That's all."

"Crazy?"

"I mean, who am I to think I can pull into Korcula in the morning and before the day is out find a treasure that's been sitting right under everyone's noses for centuries."

"That *is* crazy, I agree. But hey, you're going about it the way I would. Look at it like this. You're just doing a reconnaissance flight right now. Taking a bird's eye view of the place. So, come on. Let's get out of here and hit the road. There's more to see before it gets dark."

CHAPTER 37

Lafferty sat at his desk, avidly reading a sheet he had taken from an interoffice folder that had just arrived. *Re: Dr. Marya Bradwell.* The Administration had acted on his evaluation of Bradwell, the select sample of student evaluations of her that he had provided, Bradwell's shortcomings in publishing and his report on her poor relations with peers. The memo stated that the Administration had no choice but to deny her tenure and further employment as well. "Ka-pow! Yes! One down, one to go," he said, punching the air with his right hand.

Within the hour, it was Khalid Agarwal's turn. He came into Lafferty's office forewarned by a source in Administration that Lafferty had already dumped Marya. He was furious. He expected nothing less for himself and he got it. Lafferty went over Agarwal's record, ticking off his deficiencies one by one. He raked him over the coals for what he termed ethically questionable advisory roles he was in with two Middle Eastern leaders. He denounced that employment, not only as damaging to his personal reputation, but also as an endangerment to the university. "What would the media do to us if your work with Khadafy and your involvement with the oil consortium were exposed on television?" He also lambasted Agarwal for his new consulting work with one of the Central Asian republics. "It's all very unsavory, Khalid, I hate to say, and you should have taken my advice and scaled back this business long ago. Your chickens have come home to roost, I'm afraid. To be frank with you, I'm recommending your termination." He leaned back in his chair and relished the moment.

"Lafferty, kiss my ass. You've always had it in for me,

the same as you had it in for Marya. I know what you did to get her removed." His piercing dark eyes bored straight through him.

Lafferty fiddled with the cap of his pen and cleared his throat. "Hmm. News travels fast."

Agarwal could afford to be off-handed with the prim little guy. His outside consulting work over the past few months was too profitable to worry about being let go at Harvard. There were plenty of other opportunities waiting for him elsewhere. What really bothered him was what Lafferty had done to Marya, the never-ending negativism, the constant road-blocks he had thrown in her way. The waste of four years of good teaching she had invested in the place. The University would be losing a valuable teacher, especially since Marya is on the verge of a mind-blowing discovery at this very moment. "You don't have a clue, Lafferty. You, Chen and Roache—you'll find out soon enough."

"Now hold on just a minute. She brought it all on herself. I had nothing to do with her dismissal. My hands are clean. And there's something you need to know about why you're being let go. The Administration has been after me for some time to close down the Center for Advanced Central Asian Studies. They've done the math. There's just not enough interest in the field to justify it any longer. It's not just what I think, bad enough as that is. It's the guys in Accounting and, simply put, the lack of warm bodies in your sections. There's no need for you or your esoteric expertise. Sorry. What can I say? I repeat. *No need*."

Agarwal's antennas had been up since he stepped into the office and he was in no mood to tolerate Lafferty's bull. A source who had told him how Lafferty maneuvered behind the scenes to oust Marya had warned him about what he could expect. "You say no need. I say, screw you."

He got up, knocking over his seat on purpose, and barged towards the door. He paused there and turned, throwing Lafferty a threatening look. "Go ahead and fill out your shitty paper work and then stick it up your ass. You'll come crying and bawling to have me back when I'm down at the Johns Hopkins Central Asia Institute bringing in the bucks. You're a goddam fool, Lafferty." He stormed out of the office and stomped down the hall.

Lafferty *was* foolish. The Central Asian states of Kazakhstan, Kyrgyzstan, Turkmenistan, Tajikistan and Uzbekistan, with Afghanistan thrown in for good measure, constituted the historical Eurasian corridor, the lands of the Old Silk Road of antiquity. Only in recent decades had they fallen on bad times. But it would not be long before they were on the path to glory and better. They were sitting on hundreds of billions of barrels of oil and trillions of cubic feet of proven reserves of natural gas. The untapped potential of their natural resources was phenomenal. Agarwal knew that within ten or fifteen years its hidden wealth in minerals would begin making the region into a powerhouse and a global player. Lafferty would have been wise to keep Agarwal and his special talents tied to the university and to his department.

The mineral wealth of the region had not escaped the notice of big-time players, either. The government of Russia was already trying to reassert its influence in the string of Islamic countries along its southern flank. The United States would try to establish a presence in the western region and militarize the corridor from the Caucasus all the way to China's western border. It might even find a pretext for war in one of the Central Asian countries, if need be, to protect a western oil consortium's investment there in expensive pipelines. In the meantime, China's hungry heavy industries would suck up ever-growing amounts of oil and its government would incite insurrections in the region to keep it weak and disunited. There was no end to the opportunities Agarwal could have as an advisor to those looking to shape the outcome for the region.

Lafferty *was* stupid not to retain him because he knew everything there was to know about the people, their history and their ethnic and sectarian relations. What the people of the region would do with their new-found freedom from Russian control was critical and Agarwal was one who knew. This was especially true of the Uyghurs over the next decade or so. They were the dominant minority in China's western province of Xinjiang and there were significant numbers of them in the Central Asian states. The territory they occupied was equal to one-third of what could one day become a politically unified bloc. Agarwal had written learned papers on the subject and even suggested names for a future mega-state between Russia and China. Among them: Greater Turkestan, the Union of Central Asian States, Turko-Mongolia, and informally, the New Khanate. As a vital source of cheaply exploitable oil and at the same time a main energy transport corridor, it held the key to world economic growth. The florescence of Central Asia was inevitable, if its key players had the right advice. Lafferty had indeed made a serious blunder in putting his personal agenda before professionalism and squandering Agarwal's expertise.

Agarwal was now a free agent. He could choose from among a number of options. A major post at an important American university or a job at an American think tank of any political persuasion. The U.N., the World Bank. But, in fact, he had already rejected offers from those folks, preferring a more hands-on role in the unfolding political experiments in Central Asia. He wanted a hand in the reshaping of destiny. He was in touch with up-and-coming, promising leaders in the region, one of whom had offered him a very sweet contract to come and work for his administration and he was ready to sign on. The world was his and Lafferty be damned.

In his office, Agarwal immediately began to pack his

books and remove his personal items. One of them was a framed photo of himself and Marya at the New England Aquarium. She was wearing an Irish knit sweater and he was wearing a leather jacket and Afghan-style traditional hat. He thought of that day and wished they had been lovers. Why hadn't he shown her how much he really loved her? They would have been such a dynamic pair and perfectly matched intellectually. Lafferty had seen fit to ruin her career just at the point when it was showing the most promise. She wouldn't be back. Too bad. Agarwal already missed her. But not for long, he hoped.

CHAPTER 38

The U.S. Embassy, Zagreb, Croatia

James Cage had come to Croatia, following a circuitous route from Duke University where he had been an outstanding football player. His marriage to the daughter of a wealthy Louisiana family of gas tycoons had ended in a bitter divorce. Fortunately, they had parted childless. He hit the road and went off to Cleveland and spent a year working with the Federal Reserve. Angry with trickle-down economics and paunchy plutocrats, he quit and moved on to Silicon Valley. Several times along the way, he politely declined offers of an interview with the CIA. In the end, though, he took a job with them.

After training, they posted him to the U.S. Embassy in Moscow. From there, they sent him undercover to each of the capitals of the Central Asian Republics as an economic attaché. Three years later, he landed a relatively cushy post in Zagreb, the capital of Croatia. His work on behalf of American corporate interests throughout those years was only peripheral, a mere cover for his specialty: monitoring and reporting on terrorist activity and its chief practitioners across Asia. In CIA circles he was the go-to guy on terrorism in Russia and its former satellites.

Cage looked the part. He was not the blond-haired, blue-eyed stereotype that foreigners generally had of Americans. His dark brown mustache and wiry hair, slightly graying already at the age of 37, gave him a pseudo-Central European look—a look that had been useful in conjunction with his fluency in Russian and other Slavic languages. He was also six feet five, putting him right up there with many southern Croats.

Cage ushered his CIA section chief, Ron Henderson, down the carpeted hallway to his office, offered him a seat and closed the door. He liked his office, liked the embassy and was beginning to like Zagreb. The city, he felt, was shaping up as a respite, a holiday of sorts, considering the grueling travel and lousy accommodations he had been accustomed to.

He didn't particularly like it that Henderson was here. At the back of his mind he had a gnawing feeling that Henderson's visit could be a signal that the party was over and his next assignment could be Outer Slobovia. Henderson had just arrived at the embassy after a long, overnight flight from Beijing to get a complete run-down from him on what he knew about a shadowy Tajik chieftain, Albasbai Kibchek.

Henderson sat down and unbuttoned his dark suit jacket. He loosened the knot of his tie and undid the top button of his shirt allowing the balloon-like pouch under his chin to fall to its natural level. "What have you got for me?"

Cage picked up a thick manila folder on his desk and held it vertically in front of himself. "I've got a lot on the guy. Do you want the whole story blow by blow or the quick and dirty version?"

"Just give me the salient points for now, Jim. I want your assessment of him. He's got our attention. All we know back in Langley is that someone's giving the Chinese all kinds of hell and this guy's name has come up. I figured that if anyone could fill in the details, it'd be you. We've got interests to protect in Central Asia and we need the goodwill of the Chinese or, at least, their acquiescence. The Chinese will eat out of our hands if we can give them any help."

Cage set the unopened file down. "I know this guy and I can tell you one thing—he's nothing but bad news. I met him once three years ago in Dushanbe and I figured then that I'd be hearing a lot more about him. Full name: Albasbai Kibchek. Father, Dolgat Kibchek, a Mongolian from Ulan Bator. Deceased. Mother, Nastasia Sadyk. Lives in Dushanbe, the capital of Tajikistan."

"What did you find out from Russian intelligence?"

"Plenty. They were only too happy to share what they had. The guy got his military training in the Red Army Academy—you know, the Ryazan Academy. Not exactly a playground. When he was at the academy, he got the highest scores as a sharp shooter they had ever seen. After graduating, he became a member of the airborne corps. He served the Russians with distinction for ten years in their Afghan war, killing lots of Mujaheddin. Towards the end of the war, he suffered a breakdown and went into treatment. A psychiatric report they had on him says he was paranoid delusional and sadistic in the extreme. He took great pleasure in personally torturing captives before executing them. Has a thing for lopping off heads and leaving notes of warning behind. But I'll spare you the details."

"Sounds like a piece of work. Got anything else?"

"Yes, but it's a little on the weird side."

Henderson looked very interested. "I don't care. Go on."

"He hoards gold."

"Hedging against inflation?"

"No, I mean, he collects ancient gold treasure. Has to be Asian gold, though. He's been picking up very pricey pieces from anywhere he can get it."

"How do you know that?"

"Found out from a double agent."

"May not mean anything. You never know, though. How about some coffee, Jim?"

"Sure. No problem." Cage picked up the phone and asked his secretary to bring them two black coffees. "Want a Danish with that, Ron?"

"No, I'm on a diet."

Yeah, right, Cage thought. "How's the chow in Beijing?"

"Loved the Peking Duck. Have you ever tried it?"

"No."

"Moo Goo Gai Pan?"

"Ditto. So, want me to continue?"

A secretary came in with a tray of Danishes and two cups of coffee. Henderson nodded to Cage as he lifted a Danish and his coffee from the tray. Cage resumed, telling the rest of what he had pieced together about Kibchek, how the Russians discharged him to return to a Tajik village, how he got into opium smuggling, how he became a local drug lord and how he expanded into shipping tons of heroine via Afghanistan, Tajikistan and Moscow to Western Europe. "Very lucrative. The guy has loads of money and he's bankrolling his military with it."

"What? He's got military capabilities?"

"A guerrilla army on steroids." Cage took a drink of his coffee. "Like I told you. He's not popular with the Russians. He's corrupted the whole 201st Division of the Russian Army. Big on car bombings and assassinations. His movement represents a growing threat to the southern flank of Russia. Get this—he's recruiting about five thousand volunteers annually and has a Praetorian guard numbering in the hundreds. He seems to be running a training academy of his own, using the sons of chieftains from hundreds of villages and communities. Naturally, the Russians want to see him laid to rest."

"Where's this training camp?"

"I never found it. Could be somewhere in the Tien Shan range."

Henderson pushed the last bit of flaky pastry into his mouth with his middle finger. "The Chinese will shit spring rolls if they learn about this. Do you have anything solid that could connect him with the trouble in Beijing? You've heard about the car bombings and mayhem there the other day, I assume."

"Yes, I've read about them but, no, I don't think he's

connected. Could be just local separatists strutting their stuff."

"I'm not so sure. We're talking about bold, well-coordinated bombings, arson and assassinations in Beijing. Seems to me it would take someone like a Kibchek to pull it off."

"That I don't doubt. And Kibchek has the potential to turn Asia upside down. He's got the charisma of the Dalai Lama and the ambition of Genghis Khan."

"Our contacts in the Chinese Foreign Ministry are worried about the unrest among the Uyghurs in Central Asia. If it isn't stamped out, they see a possibility of it spreading across the border into China's Xingjiang Province. Do you follow me? You can almost see what comes next. Another Chinese 'semi-autonomous' region that the U.S. will not abide."

"I'm there. I don't envy you the headache."

"Sorry to tell you this, Cage. You'd better stock up on aspirins"

Cage threw him a worried look.

"Langley's also sent me a report that a band of Tajik operatives has been in Venice for a week now and that a detachment has crossed from Italy into Croatia. From everything you've just told me I have a hunch these fellows could be connected to Kibchek."

Cage sat up. "I don't think so. His base is in Central Asia. I've never seen any indication of his involvment in Europe, aside from the drug connection."

"That's a good point. But I want this bunch tracked anyhow."

"Got anyone in particular in mind for that job?" Cage asked nibbling on his thumb nail.

"Yes. I'm looking at him."

CHAPTER 39

Marya remained sitting, impassive to Liam's suggestion to move along before it got dark. He reminded her that she still had a visit to Marco Polo's house on the agenda for the afternoon, but she simply shrugged. He suggested they at least go out and grab a bite to eat. It was almost six o'clock, the tourists had all left and he was getting hungry. She told him she needed a few more minutes to look around and asked if he minded checking out the menu at the restaurant across the square. He chose to remain.

Looking at the murals painted high up on the walls of the sanctuary she focused her attention on a panel to the right of the altar. Its main subject was the seated figure of the omnipotent Christ in majesty in a faux sky full of clouds. Her eyes wandered downward from Christ to an archangel painted with forceful lines, dark hair, solid chin and intense, dark eyes. The angel wore a bright vermilion-colored robe and appeared to point upwards at the enthroned Christ. There was something odd about the angel's manner, she thought, looking at its hand. It was pointing, not directly at Christ, but at someone or something else beyond. But what? She looked at a panel to the left of the altar and found a solemn collection of colossal figures, both saintly and secular. The two central figures also gestured with their right hands.

"Liam, look at those figures up there. What do you think? Are they pointing at someone or something, or are they raising their hands in blessing?"

"Seems to me they're pointing at something."

A masterful hand had painted the group. Angels hovered above the earth-bound figures. Reds, greens, and violets on a gold background gave the ensemble a sublimely spiritual aura.

"Almost done?"

"Not yet. I need another minute or two, that's all. Don't worry. I know you're hungry. I am, too."

She got up and walked towards the sanctuary not far from a bank of red votive candles. She examined the panel of the aristocratic figures on the left again. The whole scene portrayed the presentation of a gift. The two figures, one male, one female, in the center were attired in luxurious, worldly fabrics. *Husband and wife? King and Queen? Or just a prosperous bourgeois Korculan couple?* A dozen other figures, barefoot ascetics in plain robes, surrounded the noble couple.

"How about it, Marya? Let's get going."

She could not make up her mind about the panel. Both of the central figures appeared to have a message. "Wait up, Liam."

She hurried to the bank of red candles to the left of the main altar and lit one. "*Dragi Bog*. Dear God, give me a sign," she whispered. She made a small offering, turned and walked over to Liam. "We can go now."

"By the way, where's the Polo diary?"

"I left it in my room."

"Huh?"

"Don't worry. It's safe. I put it on the bookshelf with a bunch of paperbacks. No one would think of looking at it twice."

They walked down the central aisle and emerged into the late afternoon light on the steps in front of the Cathedral. The sun had disappeared behind a three-story residence opposite the church but it still cast enough light to turn the hand-hewn stones of the church a golden honey color.

"See anything in there?" Liam asked.

"I'm not sure. Maybe. There is something about that panel on the left I pointed out to you. Did you notice it?"

"Sorry, I didn't."

"I wish I knew what the event was that inspired it. I

need to find out who the central figures are. Maybe someone at the museum can help."

"You think it's an important clue?"

"It's a feeling. I think I see something in that panel but I can't figure out its message. I wish Jesus would descend on a cloud right now with a host of angels blowing their trumpets and scatter the darkness."

"Pretty disappointed, huh?"

"For sure. Okay, let's take a look at Marco Polo's house, for what it's worth and call it quits. As my mother used to say, 'Sufficient unto the day is the evil thereof.'"

* * * * *

Marya and Liam stood in the narrow lane lined with terra cotta pots of red geraniums and surfaced with flat granite pavers polished by centuries of foot traffic. They looked up at a tower three stories tall capped by a *loggia*. The tower rested upon an archway over the lane only two minute's walk from the Cathedral and just two lanes away from the ancient walls of the city. They turned right off the lane and took a short flight of stairs up to a door that led into a sparsely furnished room. A young girl seated behind a wooden table smiled at them and said *Dobro dan*. Good day. She asked them in English for the admission fee of two dollars per person and gave them a flier. In an alcove in the wall behind the young woman there was a portrait of Marco Polo and in front of the portrait a small bowl of flowers. They were the only visitors, judging by the absolute silence in the building. "Not exactly a tourist Mecca," Marya commented in a hushed voice.

It was just one more crummy disappointment for her. They took a narrow winding staircase up to the next level where there was another picture on a wall. It represented a naval battle that had taken place off the coast of Korcula—the battle in which Marco Polo had fought against the Genoese. The Genoese won that battle and took Polo captive. But Marya knew all this, she thought, as she read the caption beneath the picture. *Tell me something I don't know.* Aside from the place being only the approximate place where the home of Polo once stood, it looked like another tourist trap, a place that claimed to be what it was not. She saw nothing that remotely suggested the occupation of Polo. Nothing. Dispirited, she took the next spiral, stone staircase up to the loggia.

Through its slender columns and Romanesque arches she and Liam looked out upon the strait between the Peljesac peninsula and Korcula. Behind the mainland town of Orebic far off in the distance, a palisade hundreds of feet high reared into the sky, like some kind of tidal wave frozen in place. Peering into the adjacent, roofless structure, she saw two men, probably archaeologists, grubbing around in a chaotic jumble of stones and weedy plants at the bottom. She guessed that the long-abandoned building was more likely the former home of the Korcula clan of Polos and that the men working there were searching for clues to the identity of its former occupants.

She turned to her left and was surprised to see the bell tower of the cathedral looming large in front of her. She asked Liam to let her take a photo of it with his Nikon zoom lens camera. She scanned the upper portion of the tower, aiming the camera so as to catch the balustrade that surrounded the top of the square tower and the cupola with its own pillars supporting a dome surmounted by a massive cross. She snapped one photo while telling him how clearly she could see new supports that had been installed to support the dome. "I see some upright steel posts. Earthquake repairs. And on the wall of the tower I can see many iron bars in the shape of a 'T.' Old rusty ones." She was about to take another photo, but she fumbled and instead caught the alley below filled with a cluster of tourists.

"That's it, Liam. That's about all I can take for the day," she said, checking the two photos. Then, a wild idea struck her.

CHAPTER 40

Several doors up the lane, they spotted a gift shop and dropped in to have a look around. On a whim, she bought a twenty-dollar sketch of the Marco Polo building, laughing at the purchase. "A gag gift for myself in case nothing at all comes of this trip," she told Liam. Outside, she raised a trial balloon with Liam, suggesting that they go back to the bell tower before heading to the *sobe*.

"What's the use? It's getting late and I'm hungry."

"What's the harm? It'll only take a second. There's still some time to look around. Nothing says that Polo left his treasure *inside* a church."

"What are you thinking?"

"I had an idea."

"Why don't I like the sound of that?"

In a few minutes, they were in front of the tower again. The sun had just dropped below the horizon and the square was entirely in shadows. Marya stopped and grasped one of the posts of the scaffolding and said, "Liam, how about it?"

"How about what?"

"There's no one around."

"That's obvious. And we had better get going, too."

"Come on, Liam, let's get a look at the bell tower."

"Sure. Here it is. You're looking at it right now. Satisfied? Let's get going."

"No, silly. I mean, let's climb this ladder and use the scaffolding to see what's up there?

"What? Climb the scaffolding? To the top of the bell tower? It's getting dark. Are you nuts?"

She saw him go slack-jawed as he looked skyward. "Come on, why not? We've got time. No one's around."

"I'll tell you why not. You heard it straight from the guide's mouth this afternoon. The last big quake did severe damage to the bell tower. It's got serious structural damage. It's going to come down, guaranteed. You've even got picture proof of just how weak the tower is in the photo you just took. Good God, woman. Show some sense."

"If it's safe enough for workers to go up there, then it should be okay for us, too."

"Don't even think about it. You're not going up there, period." His hand locked on to her upper arm but Marya yanked herself free. She headed right for the ladder and took it up to the first level while he stood on the ground transfixed. She looked down at him and taunted him to try and catch her. She turned away and took the next ladder up to the second level and the third and fourth as if she had been a born mountaineer. Liam was incredulous. Looking about as if someone were watching, he grabbed the ladder and put his foot on the first rung. After that it was easier and he rose quickly up three more levels when he heard her calling out to him from above. "Didn't you tell me on the ferry that you admired my sense of independence?"

"Yeah," he hollered back. "But this is really pushing it, Marya. Just be careful." Marya stopped and waited for him to catch up. Gradually, as they rose to the level of the Cathedral's roof together, the homes and buildings around the square below seemed to shrink to the size of a Christmas toy village. Beyond, across a narrow gap of the sea, was the Dalmatian coast lit by a serpentine string of lights twinkling and reflecting on the water.

They came up to the level of the cupola that housed an immense bell. Marya was the first to step over the balustrade onto the masonry platform under the cupola and tripped over a bucket, but caught herself. The view was even more breathtaking. A refreshing gust of wind brushed her face and filled her nostrils. She reached out and gave him a steadying hand as he got his leg over the balustrade and onto the landing next to her.

"Why did we come all the way up here? Aside from the terrific view, that is."

"I'm not sure, Liam. It's just a hunch. A feeling I got when I looked at the tower from Marco Polo's house. I had to see the belltower—all of it—before quitting for the day. Besides, isn't it romantic?"

"Romantic, shmantic. This is plain crazy." Liam had not let go of her hand. The winds gusted through the arches of the cupola at his back, pushing him against her. Their faces were just inches apart. He looked at her lips. His arms slipped easily around her waist and she invited him to pull closer. They held each other without moving for a minute. She closed her eyes, feeling the wind whipping wildly through her hair. She sensed the touch of his lips on hers and wrapped her arms around his shoulders. He embraced her tightly and she surrendered, feeling his warmth and strength.

A slight tremor and a groan coming from somewhere within the dome caused Liam to pull back. "Did you feel that? Did you hear that noise? This tower... it isn't safe. I mean it. What in the world are we doing up here? Let's get down from this death trap. Fast."

She stalled, not wanting to give him up. "Kiss me," she said in a throaty whisper.

"Marya, we gotta get off this rickety tower. Now."

She let go of him and set her hands on her hips. "No. I won't. Who knows if we'll get another chance? We'll never get permission to come up here during the day."

"For good reason, too," he said, flustered. "Make it quick, then. I don't want to be here when this thing pancakes."

"Just stay right here. I'll only be a minute."

"What the... ? I thought you were just going to take a look at the underside of the dome."

"Just wait here. I'll be down in a sec." She turned to lift her left leg over the balustrade onto the scaffold.

"Are you daffy?" He took her by arm and blocked her way.

"It's now or never," she said breaking away from him.

He pulled her back: "Wait, I'll go. You just stay put. What am I supposed to be looking for up there, any way?"

"I told you, I don't know, Liam. Just look for a sign, any sign. There's a big treasure at stake and it's gotta be somewhere around this church. It's either in the church or in this belltower. I just know it."

He shook his head and grumbled something she didn't quite understand as he crawled out onto the scaffold. It could have been a nasty curse.

"What did you say?"

"I said I must be Daffy Duck." He climbed halfway up the ladder and turned his head. "This is crazy, what I'm doing. Look, if this gets us crushed to death under tons of stone and they send our mortal remains home in shoeboxes, I'll never forgive you for it."

"Be careful. Tell me when you find something."

"Right." He went out on the scaffolding and eased himself slowly onto an arched ladder running from the base of the dome to the foot of the cross on top. The wind was gusting at thirty or forty miles per hour and other than the flimsy curved ladder, there were no places on the metal sheeting covering the dome where his hands could gain purchase.

"What do you see up there?" she called to him, hanging out from the balcony.

"Not all that much. I'm looking at the cross. It's leaning at a bad angle. It looks wobbly."

She heard his feet scuffling overhead. "I'm coming up," she shouted through cupped hands.

"Oh, no you don't. You stay down there. Don't come

up. Wait until I come down first, dammit. I'm too young to die. And I don't have a will."

She waited, pacing. A minute later, he swung back onto the cupola with a grim look. "On second thought, you better not go up there. I'm telling you it's not safe. The cupola is cracked. It can't take too much more."

"Don't worry, Liam. I'll be careful. I'm lighter and I've got this," she said, taking a penlight from the pocket of her slacks.

He shook his head. "The cross isn't well anchored. It's tipping at an angle," he warned.

"I'm going up anyhow." Marya climbed up and hopped from the scaffold onto the dome but quickly clambered back down, her hands trembling. "You're right, it's in bad shape." She turned the penlight on the inside of the cupola's dome, instead. "Cracks. You're right. Better let it go."

"What did I tell you when we were safe down there at ground level? You should listen to me," he said peering over the edge at the square far below. "Come on, let's go home. In case you forgot, I'm still hungry."

"I'm sorry. How forgetful of me."

He gestured to the ladder to let her go first down the scaffolding. She nibbled her lower lip and almost began to cry.

"It'll be all right. It's not over yet. There's always tomorrow," he said encouragingly.

"I'm sorry. This was a dumb idea. Let's go."

Half a dozen levels down, at one point, she felt his warm hand wrap around hers on a vertical bar. She felt like lingering and taking him in her arms again, but he prodded her along, unaware of the turmoil and crushing disappointment she was feeling inside. Near the bottom of their descent, she looked up and saw his face dimly in the early evening light. She was glad that he was here with her, the only source of cheer in a cheerless day. She had found nothing inside the cathedral two hours earlier and climbing the belltower turned out to be harebrained and nonproductive. If it wasn't for his support, she knew she would now be blubbering.

"Liam, I'm sorry for the way I behaved up..." Her right foot touched the cobbled pavement of the square and in that moment a strong pair of hands seized her left shoulder and clamped down on her mouth. She screamed in panic but couldn't produce a sound. She writhed and twisted to get free before an accomplice grabbed her feet and quickly bound her ankles with duct tape. Seconds later she saw two more men loom out of the dark, tackling Liam on the ladder and dragging him off. She could see that they were having a hard time of it because of Liam's size and strength. One of his arms broke free and smacked one of the assailants across the face before the other kicked him in the ribs and knocked the wind out of him. He writhed in agony on the ground briefly before the first assailant raised his fist over Liam's face. She wasn't around long enough to see whether he struck Liam. The strongman hoisted her up and slung her over his shoulder, like a fifty pound sack of potatoes. He carried her away at a jog into a dark, narrow lane off the square. She realized that he was taking her towards the city walls. What was he going to do with her? Heave her onto the rocks to her death? Then, she heard the sound of a gunshot.

CHAPTER 41

As Liam pursued Marya quickly down the eight levels of scaffolding, he didn't know what to think of his new partnership. The woman was certainly unpredictable. So far, in the last three days, she had given him a surprise at every turn. He laughed, recalling the moment on the plane when she tumbled backwards into his arms. He pictured that other time when she entered the Gabrielli Sandworth Hotel with bedraggled hair and her clothes dripping wet. And now, this—this crazy adventure on a shaky scaffold far above the town square—in the dark. How different she was from Melissa, at home with her parents in cozy, comfortable, prosperous Newburyport. He was beginning to admit to himself that his already ailing relationship with Melissa was on life-support.

He wondered if Marya would ever find the clue to her quest here in Korcula. Probably not. What should he do if nothing turned up in a day or two? Go back to Boston and get on with his regular work? Try to make it with Melissa again? What about Marya? Would he see her again in Boston? Probably not, he thought. She was in the business of learning. He was in the business of business, making money. Different worlds. But, she did seem to enjoy his companionship.

He admired her agility and her swift, graceful moves descending the scaffolding. He didn't know how to assess her easy defiance of his warning not to climb the bell tower. But, all's well that ends well, he thought. He watched her moving quickly down the scaffolding one level below. A few lights shone in the windows of the homes and the palatial residences surrounding the square, but the rest of the square was dark and deserted. He decided that as soon as his feet hit the ground, he would take her in his arms and kiss her without holding back.

A cry from Marya pierced the darkness. "Liam!"

Two powerful men seized him and yanked him off the last ladder. He wrestled fiercely, kicked one of them in the abdomen and smacked the other with the back of a freed hand. They pounced on him together and shoved him to the ground, pinning him down while he thrashed wildly. Two more men ran past, leaped upon the scaffolding and climbed out of sight. His eyes returned to the figures holding him down. A raised fist above his face was all he could distinguish in the darkness. It was poised to smash his face into a bloody pulp.

He heard a muffled scream in the darkness and looked to his left. He saw a giant figure flip Marya over his shoulder and bundle her off in the darkness. He was powerless to do anything for her. "Marya!"

* * * * *

The minute that the Venetian detective had left his Papa's room at the hospital, Ambrosio took his place. The old man was weakened by his loss of blood and had already received two transfusions. Still, he was lucid enough to make some decisions. It was clear to him that his boys had to get to Korcula immediately to provide protection for Marya and Liam. Looking sternly at Ambrosio, he gave him the order to get going.

Within an hour, Ambrosio and Pietro flew out from Venice to Ploce. They got a rental car there and crossed by ferry to Korcula, pulling into town not knowing where Marya and Liam were staying. A few questions around town sent them to the Sternich *sobe.* They knocked. Mrs. Sternich appeared. She was at first suspicious of them but the desperation in their faces and a generous gift convinced her to tell them where the newly arrived couple had gone. "To the churches. Start at Saint Mark's," she told them. They took off running. Turning the corner into the square, they heard a commotion ahead. Sounds of violence. The muted scream of a woman. Men shouting. In the murky light of the square they made out a struggle in progress and dashed across the open space.

* * * * *

Pinned to the ground, Liam saw that one of the men over him was grinning, but in the next second, the grin suddenly turned to a panic-stricken grimace as he was jerked backwards by an invisible force. Then his partner was lifted away. The two men dangled above him, their gray faces and hands dimly visible, like marionettes suspended in the dark space immediately above him. The faces gasped, choked and sailed apart, and then flew together in a collision of flesh and bone that made a sickening thump. They dropped limply from the hands of a master puppeteer he could not see.

Ambrosio's face surged forward into view. "Are you all right, Signore?"

"Yes, fine." said Liam, though he was still reeling from the battering he had taken. Off in the distance he heard Pietro shouting Marya's name. Ambrosio helped Liam to his feet and led him about fifteen yards away where he sat him down and propped him against a wall. He noticed that a few lights went on in the windows of some homes around the square. He watched as Ambrosio left him and returned to the scaffolding. He saw the hulking man give the scaffolding a tentative shake at its front left corner. He shook it again. Then he got a hard grip of it in his meaty hands; his face contorted; he strained the way a weight lifter does with an impossible burden; then he rocked the scaffolding with the might of Samson.

The scaffold started to sway. The rocking motion gave off wrenching, grinding, metallic sounds. A few planks tumbled from above, banged resoundingly on the steps of the church and bounced onto the pavement of the square. Ambrosio strained again, veins throbbing on his forehead. The whole left side of the scaffold began to crumple, folding in a kind of slow-motion effect, and collapsed in a roar of crunching metal and wood. A human shriek pierced the air, followed by a crash into the debris. He saw the body of a man lying like a limp rag across one of the bars of the downed scaffolding. Then, the rest of it rocked and buckled, raining down tools, buckets, ropes and other construction material on the steps of the Cathedral. The entire scaffold came down like a poorly joined construction toy and settled in a chaotic jumble twenty feet high. After the din, Liam heard a weak plea for help from far above, coming from the lone man now marooned at the top of the bell tower.

Sitting where he was, propped up at the base of a stone wall, Liam heard the pan pon pan pon sounds of police cars. Three of them soon appeared in the square, circled around and screeched to a stop, their flashing lights casting weird shadows on the stucco walls of the palazzos and the Cathedral. Residents cautiously opened their doors and windows and peeked out at the scene in the square.

Ambrosio came back and patted him on the shoulder. "We thought you would need our help. Stay here. You're safe." Then, worried about a gun shot he heard echoing in a lower alley, he ran off to find Pietro.

CHAPTER 42

The police jumped out of their cars, looking wide-eyed at the spectacle. They took control at the scene of mayhem, hustling a clutch of onlookers back to their homes, tying off the area around the collapsed scaffolding and seeing to Liam's wounds. Ambrosio showed up a couple of minutes later supporting Pietro who was limping. One of the two who had taken Marya off had shot Pietro, hitting him in his right calf. The police relieved Ambrosio and took Pietro to the police van, sat him down and had him raise his leg for bandaging. While standing there watching the medics work on his brother, Ambrosio pulled out his cell phone and called his father in the hospital.

"Papa, there's been some trouble."

"Trouble? Are you all right?

"Yes, but Pietro's been wounded. Strangers have kidnapped signorina Bradwell."

Ambrosio told his father how he and Pietro came upon Marya and Liam in the midst of their being attacked in Saint Mark's Square. The sequence of events came pouring out of him. "You were right, Papa. The gang followed them to Korcula."

"Do the police know what happened to Marya?"

"No, only that she was taken off the island.

There was silence on the other end.

"I'm sorry, Papa, but there was nothing that could be done. What about you and Mama? Are you all right?"

"Never mind us. Your mother's home. They're going to release me from the hospital tomorrow. Emilia will take care of us and your cousins are running the operation out front. No problem. Stay and finish what you have to there. See that Liam is kept safe and look after Pietro."

"Yes, Papa."

"What about Liam? Where is he now?"

"Here. But he has to go back to his room to get his things."

"Watch his back and be sure he comes home alive with you. He must not go back to the United States yet. I need to see him. We have to talk about Marya and about revenge for all these things they've done to us."

"Papa, wait. I hear the police talking about him on the phone. They are saying that he must report to the U.S. embassy in Zagreb."

"Fine, but he still must come to Venice afterwards. Do you understand?"

"Yes. I'll do my best."

* * * * *

The U.S. Embassy, Zagreb, Croatia

Cage didn't know where to begin tracing the Tajiks who had just slipped into Croatia, but experience told him he wouldn't have to wait long for something to erupt that would lead him to them. When the phone rang at home at seven o'clock that night he had a premonition. The call came from a Croatian officer at the scene of a crime on the island of Korcula that the police were dealing with at that very moment. He described a scene of terrible wreckage in the square of Sveti Mrko, Saint Mark, in Korcula, involving two American victims, two Venetians and a band of gangsters. The Italians had rescued one of the Americans, a male in his twenties. He told Cage that the other American was a woman, a professor doing research on Marco Polo. She had been kidnapped. Her companion, an American man, had sustained moderate injuries. The officer said he did not have any information as to the nationality of the assailants. He gave Cage the names of the Americans, a Mr. Di Angelo and a Dr. Marya Bradwell, and went on to tell him that the kidnappers had escaped with the woman, probably by boat. He advised Cage that one of the Italians had taken a bullet in his leg. Medics at the scene were about ready to transfer the two Italians and the American to a hospital in Dubrovnik for examination and treatment.

Cage asked the officer to tell Mr. Di Angelo that the U.S. Embassy in Zagreb had now been informed of the event and that he should report to the embassy as soon as he could upon release from the hospital. The officer assured him that he would pass the message along to him. He ended by telling Cage that one of the assailants had died in a fall from a belltower while a partner survived. The survivor was in custody as well as two more of the assailants.

"Have they told you anything?" Cage asked.

"No one can understand a word they say. We've interrogated them in six languages but nothing seems to get through to them. None of us can even guess what language they speak," the officer replied.

* * * * *

Liam stood by in the glare of the whirling lights and within the range of staccato back-and-forth radio messages in Croatian between the local police and the police in Dubrovnik. He rubbed his neck and did some stretching to relieve the aches caused by the bad beating he had taken. He was thankful that Ambrosio had come along when he did. Otherwise, he figured, he would have had to undergo facial reconstruction. He felt sorry for Pietro taking a bullet in the leg and he was frantic about Marya. What were the authorities doing to speed up the search for Marya? Why were things moving so slowly? There seemed to be a lot of police milling around at the scene without any results. He moved over to the van to be with Pietro.

One of the medics was still working on Pietro's bandaging when an officer who towered over him approached and told him that he just got off the phone with the U. S. Embassy. He had given one of the officials there, Mr. Cage, a complete update of the incident. Mr. Cage was very interested in the situation and wanted Liam to report to the embassy as soon as he was cleared to leave the hospital.

Liam acknowledged the message but demanded they tell him what was being done to pursue the kidnappers. He told the officer that this was the second attempt to abduct Dr. Bradwell. When Liam told him that the attempts had something to do with her search for treasure hidden in one of Korcula's churches, he almost laughed in his face and simply told him to hurry and gather his belongings from the *sobe* he was staying at.

Liam felt his blood boiling. The officer obviously didn't believe a word he said about Marya's research. As he walked away from the scene, heading for the *sobe*, Ambrosio called out after him to wait up. He was coming along, too. "No, Ambrosio. Stay with Pietro."

"No, I'm under orders. I'm going with you."

"Whose orders ?"

"Papa's."

"Come on, then," Liam said. Together, they crossed the square and turned the corner into the Sternich's place. Upstairs, they found a solidly built young Croatian officer standing guard outside Marya's room and it reminded him that Polo's journal was still inside her room on a bookshelf. He had to get in to retrieve it. There was no way he would ever leave Korcula without it. It was too precious. It was the key to Marya's search.

The officer looked at them sternly from under the visor of his cap, clueless about the incredible object in the room that he was guarding. Liam opened the door to his room and pushed Ambrosio in ahead of him. He closed the door. "Shit, what the hell am I going to do?" he said, half to himself and half to Ambrosio.

"What's the matter?"

"I need to get something out of that room across the hall. The guard won't let me in there," Liam said, tossing his stuff together in his bag and zipping it shut.

"How do you know he won't let you in? You didn't even ask."

"Oh, is that so? Just ask, you say. Fine." He picked up his bag and opened the door. "Let's see what he says when we ask."

Liam stepped into the hallway and Ambrosio followed, closing the door. He looked up into the guard's stony face. "Say, do you speak English."

"Very little."

"There's something in the room that belongs to me. A book. I need it. Would you mind if I just stepped in for a second to get it?"

"No. No one is allowed in this room."

"I see," Liam said, turning around to Ambrosio. "I thought so."

Ambrosio placed his mitt on Liam's shoulder and nudged him aside, taking his place in front of the officer. "Do you understand Italian?" he asked.

"Very little."

Ambrosio gruffly said something in Italian and the officer's face registered shock. He reached for his sidearm but Ambrosio grabbed his wrist and crunched it in a vise-like grip, dropping the guard to his knees and holding him there. The guard winced in pain, begging to be let go. Ambrosio looked at Liam and told him that the officer said it was okay to go in and get what he needed from the room. It took only fifteen seconds before Liam was out again with the vellum-covered book.

"Thank you, sir." Liam put the diary in his bag. "Very kind of you."

Ambrosio relaxed his grip on the officer's wrist and

said something else in Italian that he didn't quite understand. Liam only knew from his limited, street-smart Italian that it had something to do with *cazzos.* And what he would do to them if he didn't cooperate.

The officer nodded, "Yes, yes. I understand."

Ambrosio extended a hand to the wary officer and helped him up from the floor.

"You got what you need?" he asked Liam.

"Got it."

"Let's go." Then he turned and said 'ciao' to the officer who stood there massaging his wrist and wearing a pained expression.

"Ciao," Liam repeated.

"Always remember the words of the Bible," Ambrosio told Liam as they went to the staircase.

"Which ones would those be?"

"Ask and ye shall receive."

CHAPTER 43

With the journal packed in his bag, Liam went back to the square with Ambrosio. Pietro's leg was bandaged and he was able to stand. He half-walked, half-hopped the length of the van to see what he was capable of. Then they all piled in and the driver took them to a larger piazza outside the gate of the town. He let them off near a helicopter waiting for them, its rotors already whirling. It took only minutes before they sped across the narrow body of water southeast to Dubrovnik fifteen kilometers away.

In his anxiety, Liam could only think of Marya. He hoped desperately that the police in Dubrovnik had turned up news about her kidnapping but was realistic enough to guess that the Croatian authorities were as much in the dark as he was. The helicopter unloaded them on a helipad on the roof of Dubrovnik's main hospital. Four policemen and two orderlies escorted them to the emergency room. One doctor got to work on Pietro, anesthetizing the area near his leg wound, cleaning it and closing the wound with forty-five stitches. In the meantime, another doctor finished examining bruises on Liam's ribcage and on his face, pronounced him in satisfactory condition and released him to the police.

Liam discovered that there was no point in talking with them. They had nothing of value to tell him. They had no news of Marya's fate. No group had yet claimed responsibility for the kidnapping or asked for a ransom. They were mystified because nothing like it had ever happened in Korcula. Tourists had always been safe in the area. They had no strategy to pursue because their leads came to a dead end in Ploce. Actually, they hoped that Liam had information they could use. He decided to tell them nothing. Above all, he avoided mention of the connection with the treasure of Marco Polo to avoid ridicule and delay. In the end, the police just shrugged their shoulders and gave him a look that he could not mistake—they had no idea what to do next besides keeping in touch with the U.S. Embassy in case something new turned up.

Liam was boiling mad. The whole exercise felt like a charade, a perfect waste of valuable time. In the meantime, the kidnappers were probably half a world away with Marya. When would the nonsense end? Pietro and Ambrosio came out of the emergency operating area and joined him. The last thing that a Croatian detective on the case told Liam before he left was to report to the U. S. Embassy in Zagreb.

"Yeah, sure. Right."

"Oh, and by the way, we know where the perpetrators come from. We gave them an atlas and used sign language to got them to show us where they were from. They pointed to Tajikistan."

"You sure of that? From Tajikistan?"

"I know. It seems crazy that a criminal gang would bother to come all that distance to kidnap an American academic. She wasn't into any shady deals in arms or drugs, was she?"

"You've got to be kidding. Dr. Bradwell? Not a chance."

"Then do you have any other idea as to motive?

"No, sir. None at all. Am I free to go now?"

* * * * *

After taking the call from Korcula, Cage picked up the phone and dialed Henderson at his hotel to tell him he had news about a suspicious event and was coming over immediately.

Ten minutes later, Cage sat opposite Henderson in his hotel room.

"What did you say the woman's name was? Bradsmith?"

"No, Bradwell. Marya Bradwell. Dr. Marya Bradwell."

"Who is she? What makes her important to these people?"

"All I got from the police is that she's a professor of history at Harvard and that her reason for coming to Croatia was to do research into the life of Marco Polo and some supposed golden treasure." Cage looked at Henderson and picked up a look of astonishment. "I know. That's what I think, too. What was I just telling you today? Bradwell had a companion, too. An American. I've asked that he come to the embassy."

"Okay, this is big. What's your take now on a possible connection with Kibchek himself?"

"Right now, I think there's a possible connection but I'm still not entirely convinced. I *am* getting a bad feeling, though. It's just that there's such a distance we're talking about here. The Adriatic is not his territory. He has no direct stake in drugs or guns here that I know of. We'll know soon enough, though."

"Why do you say that?" Henderson asked.

"I mean, if this Bradwell lady shows up decapitated..."

"Exactly. Well, sit back and listen to this, Jim. I got a report from Langley just before I left the office tonight. I intended to take it up with you first thing in the morning, but since you're here, I'll share it right now."

Cage leaned back. "What now?"

"A big bomb was set off outside the Ukrainian Ministry of the Interior in Kiev."

Since his assignment to Croatia, Cage hadn't given another thought to the former Soviet satellite he had made so many trips to. He was familiar with the building that housed the Ministry that Henderson was talking about. "How much damage?"

"Huge. Evidently terrorists left a parked car packed

with explosives in front of the main entrance early this morning and it blew the front of the building off up to four stories above street level."

"Anyone killed?"

"Only two security guards. It was before opening time, so no one was there except security. The group that did the bombing claimed responsibility for it in a phone call to a newspaper. They said that they had avenged a crime against their nation committed by an official of the MVS. And they left directions to a place in a forest where the police could find the official's body. The internal police and some units of the militia drove out and found a decapitated body with its head sitting on the victim's chest. He had been badly slashed before he was killed. He was one the higher-ups in the organization, a guy with a long history of corruption and brutality, a man named Shevchenko. You know him?"

"I heard of him. Never met him. Did they tell the newspaper where they were from?"

"Tajikistan."

CHAPTER 44

Liam talked with a pretty clerk in reception who helped him arrange for a taxi. Pietro came limping out of the emergency room leaning on Ambrosio and the three of them went out to the front entrance to wait for the taxi just as the first light of dawn crept over the mountains above the city. It had been a long night and the day ahead of them would be just as long. Dubrovnik, sitting at the southern tail of Croatia, was not a transportation hub.

At the bus station where the cab dropped them off, they waited an hour for the ticket office to open. They got their tickets and settled in for another wait for their bus. The Bellardos would accompany Liam as far as Zagreb and take another bus from there to Maestre across the lagoon from Venice, then board a *vaporetto* home. Liam felt sorry for Pietro. When the local anesthesia began to wear off in the bus station he was miserable, shifting around on the hard wooden bench trying to find a comfortable position for his outstretched leg. The young man would not be good for much physical work for some time to come.

But that wasn't as bad as the situation he imagined for Marya. The whole process of answering the questions of Croatian police authorities had sapped his morale and only made him more apprehensive about her fate. He pictured the long, slow ride ahead, stopping at every small town on the coast along the way. Time that could be used to find and rescue her. He wondered if going to the U. S. Embassy in Zagreb would prove any more fruitful than the hours he had spent with the Croatian police during the night. In a way, he was as frustrated and hobbled as Pietro.

They had to wait an agonizing one and a half more

hours before the earliest northbound bus appeared. Liam became aware that something was clearly bothering Ambrosio. He hadn't stopped pacing in an hour. He decided to probe and had Ambrosio sit down with him.

"Something wrong, Ambrosio?"

His face looked stricken.

"Out with it. What happened?"

"We have had some trouble. Some men came to our place after you left Venice..." His composure began to crumble.

"Did something happen to your parents or Carlotta? Tell me."

"A gang of criminals came to our place while Pietro and I took you two to the ferry...When we returned, we found our parents...badly beaten up. My mother was half conscious. Papa was slashed in the shoulder. He lost a lot of blood. He's in the hospital."

Liam slammed his hand on a bench. "And Carlotta?"

"We found her beaten and tied up on the floor of Papa's office."

"How is she? Okay, I hope."

"They beat her up and frightened her badly with a warning painted in blood on the wall...my dad's blood."

Liam was horror-struck. "Is she all right?"

"I can't say. We'll see when we get home."

Liam realized that Ambrosio was not telling the whole story about his parents and Carlotta. He was choked up, finding it hard to speak about the ordeal they had gone through. He decided not to push too far for details. In due course, he might learn. Or not. But he was still amazed at the boys' coming to Korcula rather than remaining in Venice.

"Why did you come to Korcula? How..." It dawned on him in that second before Ambrosio spoke, that Bellardo had been right about a gang of thugs nosing about his premises. He had taken extraordinary precautions to hide his loot and keep it under wraps for good reason. He had insisted all along that he would have trouble from Tajiks. The detective at the hospital confirmed, too, that Tajiks were involved.

"Papa knew that gang would come after you, too. He sent us to warn you and to give you help in case..."

"In case they showed up in Korcula, right?"

"Yes. You must promise that you'll come back to Venice after you finish at the embassy. Promise," he said, with his heavy right hand on Liam's shoulder.

"Of course, Ambrosio. You can tell your father I will definitely come back to Venice."

"Good. We will restore the honor of the family," he said with an unforgiving edge in his voice.

* * * * *

At eight o'clock the bus pulled into the station and they managed to get Pietro into a seat by himself. Ambrosio gave him a cup of coffee to help wash down a pain pill and then hunkered down in a seat by himself in front of Liam. Liam remembered that he had the journal in his possession. It was his first opportunity to examine the object at the heart of this whole dangerous episode. He slid it out of his bag and carefully opened it. The supple vellum pages rustled as he turned them and what he saw amazed him. The book was filled with a strong but fine handwriting in medieval Italian. The very words and private thoughts of western history's most renowned traveler. It was a privilege just to be able to touch the artifact. *Damn. I wish I learned Italian with Dad when I had the chance. God knows he tried hard enough to teach me. I was always too smart or too busy to give it a try.*

As he put the journal back into his bag and zipped it, he thought of Marya again and how hard she worked all her life to find it. He made a vow to himself that if there was one thing he would do, it would be to see that she had that journal in her hands again. The bus rolled along northward to Zagreb throughout the morning hours. About mid-afternoon, after more than a half-dozen stops, the bus pulled into the station in the capital city and they all got off. Pietro hung on to Ambrosio, leaning heavily on one crutch, and hobbled off to a bus bound for Maestre. Liam waved goodbye to the brothers and hailed a taxi for downtown.

CHAPTER 45

After leaving Henderson the previous night, Cage no longer harbored much doubt that Tajik agents were responsible for Dr. Bradwell's kidnapping and that Kibchek could be involved. By the time Henderson came to his office in the morning, Cage was ready to share a theory about the abduction.

"The word is that Bradwell was taken aboard a boat to the mainland and that there was a suspicious flight out of the small airport at Ploce shortly after the kidnapping. I'm leaning towards the idea that the Tajiks have captured her, for reasons I can't yet fathom. If that's the case and if she was aboard that plane, she could be heading to Tajikistan or be there right now."

"Sounds plausible. What's on your agenda today?"

"An interview with Bradwell's boyfriend or companion. I told you about him last night. He escaped the kidnappers with the help of two Italians who happened to be on the spot. I expect he'll be here sometime today."

"What's his name?"

"Liam Di Angelo."

"Weird name. You think he can tell us anything?"

"He's the only one right now who can give us any background. We'll see. I hope he's got something for us to go on."

"Fine. I'll hang around. Should be interesting. Let me know when he gets here."

* * * * *

Liam reached out to shake hands and introduce himself to Cage. Cage ushered him into a cramped, windowless room, furnished with a Formica-topped table and three chairs. He closed the door as he entered behind Liam. There was another man already present in the room, occupying a chair in the corner. He half-rose as Cage introduced him to Liam. "This is Mr. Henderson from the State Department. On special assignment here to help us."

"Call me Ron," he said affably, reaching out to shake Liam's hand. He sat down with a grunt and let Liam know that he would take notes on the meeting and forward his recommendations to the State Department in Washington. "This is a very serious matter, as you know, and we are giving it high priority. We expect that there will be big international repercussions and huge media interest. We're gonna treat this meeting confidentially and release only what is consistent with the safety of your friend."

Cage took it from there. "I agree with Ron completely, Mr. Di Angelo. I can't tell you how seriously we regard this whole tragic event and how concerned we are for Dr. Bradwell's safety. And we can only imagine the state you must be in."

"Thank you." Liam was heartened by the impression of efficiency and urgency that the two men gave. At last, he was talking with someone who would listen and take him seriously. "I'll tell you all I know. I'll do anything to help."

"Well, let's get started. We are counting on you because we've had so little to go on from the Croatian authorities. Thanks for coming today," Cage said, pressing a button under his desk to activate a recorder. "We're hoping that since you've been . . . ah . . . travelling with Dr. Bradwell, you can fill us in on the critical details. Anything."

"First, you've got to realize, there's nothing going on between us two. We're more or less just travelling together. We've literally just met. So . . . ."

"Fine. I hear what you're saying. Please go on. How do you happen to know Dr. Bradwell?"

Liam summarized the story of how they had met on the plane from Boston and crossed paths again in Venice. He gave them all the details on the violent encounter she had had with a pair of thugs and how he had intervened to help her hide from them at the Bellardos. Cage questioned him intensely about the nature of Ms. Bradwell's research and asked more about her quest for treasure connected with the Polos of Venice.

Liam was not sure how much he should say, given the ridicule he had experienced at the hands of the police in Korcula. He decided that it would be wise to tell what he knew, at least about the Golden Tablets of Command. "According to Marya...I mean the way Dr. Bradwell explained it to me, she was on a quest for seven gold tablets. Three given to the Polos by Kublai Khan and four given to them later by a Persian khan. This is her goal in life. I mean, finding the golden treasure of the Polos—these tablets—she wants to prove Marco Polo's story true. She really believes she has a chance of finding them."

"Anything else you can tell us about these tablets?"

"Yes. Kublai Khan had them engraved with warnings to the people of the empire. He wanted his subjects to provide aid and protection to the Polos anywhere they went, or he would punish them by death and strip their families of all their possessions. She described them to me as super passports that would get the Polos safely across the Empire and home to Italy. She said that today they could easily be worth tens of millions of dollars at auction."

Liam saw Cage's eyes shift to Henderson at the mention of the Golden Tablets of Command. Henderson got right up and asked Cage to continue the interview without him. He quickly left the room. Liam wondered about that but continued answering Cage's questions about his travels with Dr. Bradwell in Venice and Korcula.

"A minute ago, Mr. Di Angelo, you told us that Dr. Bradwell had barely escaped being kidnapped in Venice but that you didn't expect that trouble would follow you to Korcula."

Liam looked confused.

Cage repeated the statement in context. "You said you didn't expect violence, not in Korcula."

Liam paused. "Oh, right. Not in Korcula. Dr. Bradwell and her assistant had each been attacked in Venice. But when we got to Korcula, so far from Venice, I guess we were just... I don't know... just less worried, I suppose. We never really saw it coming."

"Go back to the events in Venice, will you, and tell me what else you recall about the attacks on Dr. Bradwell and that assistant of hers."

Liam related what he recalled and also mentioned what Ambrosio told him about the attack on his parents and sister.

"What did these guys look like?"

"I think they were Asian. One of them had a crew cut and a scar on his face. Big build. That's all I know."

Cage asked him if he knew of anyone else, besides these assailants, who might be considered a threat to Dr. Bradwell or her mission.

He hesitated. "Well, I wouldn't say that her mission was widely known. But certainly, her colleagues in the Department of History at Harvard would have known about her purpose in coming to Venice. Maybe some even knew that she was heading for Korcula as well. I don't know. She told me that some of them in her department strongly opposed her line of research and that she was on the outs with the department chair. She didn't expect to have a job when she got back to Boston."

"Why was that?"

"They didn't believe in her or the value of her research, I guess. It was the quest for the treasure, she said, that put her at odds with them. Personally, I think they are just jealous of her. The department chair has a long history of antagonism against her."

"You know his name?"

"She told me but I forget. Flannigan. Flaherty. Some Irish name like that."

"She was with the History Department?"

"Correct."

"Your turn now," Cage said.

Liam decided to plumb Cage for what, if anything, he suspected about the nationality of the kidnappers. He had a card to play with the information he had from Bellardo and the medic in Dubrovnik. "Mr. Cage, do you think she could have been kidnapped by a gang from Central Asia?"

"What makes you say that?"

"I'm an antiquities dealer. And I've noticed some odd things going on in terms of rare gold artifacts. Scythian pieces. Yuan Dynasty gold. Like the kind that I deal in. Like the Golden Tablets that Dr. Bradwell has been researching. Some Tajiks have been after a lot of this kind of stuff. I know what I'm talking about because it's my business to know." Liam left it hanging there, vague, hoping that Cage could tell him something the government knew.

Cage hunched forward over his desk and Liam sensed that Cage was slightly shaken. "Actually, that's a very good conjecture. Look, there's something I've got to tell you, Mr. Di Angelo... And it's not going to be pleasant news for you. We're on the alert for reports of activity such as this. I mean reports of treasure or golden artifacts."

"You are?"

Cage let his hands rest on the desk, palms up in a gesture of helplessness. "That's it. All I can tell you is that we're pursuing information involving numerous transfers of valuable items, like those you described, to some place in Central Asia, maybe one of the Central Asian Republics like Kirghizstan or Tajikistan, as you have mentioned, for instance. I can't be more specific than that with you at this time."

Alarms went off in Liam's head with mention of Tajikistan. He realized that Cage was playing a close hand but seemed to be aware of something. He felt encouraged that he was being taken seriously for the first time. "I want to do something to help rescue her. I would like to be part of any plan you have for bringing her back safely. Do you understand? If you're putting a team together, you've got to include me."

Cage shifted in his chair. "That just won't be possible right now, Mr. Di Angelo, believe me. And if we can make further use of your knowledge on her behalf, we'll certainly keep you in mind. But at this stage we need you to be patient. There are serious risks involved, you must understand."

"You can't keep me out of this."

"Mr. Di Angelo. Hold it right there, please. We don't understand yet exactly why but, somehow, Dr. Bradwell has got herself caught up in a dangerous traffic."

"What traffic are you talking about?"

"I mean this business with those golden…what did you call them?"

"Tablets of Command. She's a researcher, a Harvard professor. She's not trafficking in anything."

"That was a poor choice of words. Sorry. What I mean is that the Tablets of Command could very likely be what that gang is after. I know she's not dealing drugs or arms. But if Dr. Bradwell is in possession of such artifacts or knows something about them, her life is at risk. The guys I'm talking about will stop at nothing in dealing with her. They are murderous, brutal individuals and, to be very frank, it's possible she could be in their hands right now."

"What can I do if you won't bring me aboard?"

"Nothing, Mr. Di Angelo. Don't do a thing on your own. You must not interfere. These guys are like a pack of wild animals. I've seen their handiwork in person. It's too risky for civilians like you to get involved. You've got to realize—she's our top priority and we're putting a lot of agents on this. Stay out of it."

Liam was alarmed by what Cage had just said but he wasn't about to be put off. "How do I know you're telling me the whole truth? You know what? I'm sure you have an idea where she's been taken."

"We don't know for sure yet."

"I can help."

"You already *have* and if you remember anything else that might be important, we need to hear from you."

"That's all? Tell you what I know and leave the rest to you? Shit, that's not right. I won't be ignored and shut out. You and all the powers that be in the State Department can't stop me."

"Hold on a minute. We have people working on this. That's why Mr. Henderson's here. He's taking this to the top. Besides that, Dr. Bradwell is now my personal priority, too. I'm just not free to give you the specifics or bring you personally into the operation. It's just too dangerous. I'm sorry to have to urge patience on your part. Don't go off trying to locate and rescue her. I'm being as honest and clear as I can."

"Oh, you're being plenty clear. And you know what? I say the hell with you and your pal Henderson. If you guys happen to remember anything important, just get in touch with *me*." Liam pushed himself away from the table and stalked out of Cage's office.

Cage quickly followed him out. "Stay out of it, Mr. Di Angelo. For your own sake."

Liam didn't even bother looking back. He barged down the hallway, down the stairs and out onto the sidewalk to hail a taxi.

* * * * *

Cage went down the hallway and found Henderson in the communications office. "It's really bad, Ron."

"I know. I heard everything on the intercom."

"Bradwell's in the hands of the psychopath. That's for sure. Even Di Angelo knows and suspects something about Tajik involvement. But he hasn't got a clue about who he's up against. We've got to keep him out of it *and* keep him from getting in our way.

"I don't think your attempt to sandbag him worked."

CHAPTER 46

The burly guy who had hauled Marya out of the Square crowded her into a waiting Zodiac manned by three thugs. Within an hour, they landed her ashore on the mainland, north of Dubrovnik, and had driven to a small airfield at Ploce. A private jet sat on the runway with its engine running. They dragged her out of the car, up the steps and into the plane. It was night time and the airfield was far from anywhere. It was pointless to try to cry out for help. A veiled woman shoved her into a seat and used sign language telling her to buckle up for take-off. Marya wondered where in the world she was being taken. If she weren't so scared for her own life and for Liam, she thought it kind of flattering to know that people out there wanted her bad enough to kidnap her.

The jet wheeled around to head south, zoomed down the runway in the surrounding darkness and was airborne in a minute. It banked to the east. She could tell because of the lights of villages and cities below, not the black emptiness of the Adriatic Sea. It was about four hours before dawn showed faintly on the horizon. They flew over yet another large body of water, if not the Black Sea, she thought, then the Caspian.

The burkah-clad woman watching her without budging for hours finally tossed a small bag of pistachios at her and shoved a Coke under her nose. Obdurate silence met every question she asked. For the sake of hearing her own voice and simply to pass the time, she invented a little game. Marya asked her if she had attended Miss Porter's School for Girls in Connecticut. The woman threw her an evil eye and turned her surly gaze to the window. "Did you major in charm? Oh, you did? How marvelous. Magna cum laude? That's wonderful. Oh, I'm so pleased to know you and to be the lucky recipient of this lovely free trip," she persisted, not even waiting for a reply. "Your sweet mother must be proud of you, now that you're an airline stewardess. By the way, I have to go pee now. Would you be so kind as to show me the way? I bet it must be so inconvenient for you girls always tangling with those wretched black sheets every time you gotta go." The black-garbed woman turned to her and raised her thick eyebrows. "I told you once and I won't tell you again," Marya chided in a sing-song voice. "I have to do my wee wee." She pointed at herself and then pointed to the rear of the plane. The harpy understood her sign language and escorted her to the lavatory. When Marya didn't come out in five minutes, the woman began pounding on the door.

"What the heck do you think I'm doing in here anyway? Disabling the smoke alarm?" Marya screamed inside the lavatory. "It's against federal law, you know. Give me a break." As she slid the bolt of the lavatory door and came out, the black-veiled witch immediately seized her by the arm. She shrugged herself free of the woman's grasp and did the rumba back to her seat—anything to irk her keeper. Once she was buckled in, she was tired of her little game.

An hour later in the flight, the tallest mountains she had ever seen loomed in the distance. Her knowledge of the region's geography told her that they must be approaching the Pamirs. Nothing could surprise her now, not even the thought that she was close to the western border of China. Sheer fatigue and the brutal treatment they had given her had worn her down. Her traveling companion was completely devoid of personality. She had bruises on her arms and legs and she was exhausted from not sleeping all night. She heard a crack over the intercom followed by a brief instruction. The private jet began its descent.

The plane landed in barren territory bounded on the

north by tall mountains. Her captors led her out of the plane and into a waiting car. Dust clouds rolled out behind the car as it sped across a dirt road that circled north of a sizeable city. All the people she saw from the car windows were decked out in medieval garb: turbans, skullcaps, vests, ballooning pants, vests and head-to-toe robes. She thought of old movie versions of *The Tales of 1001 Arabian Nights* and wondered if she would manage to survive captivity as Scheherazade did.

They drove away from the city to a remote region that was empty except for boulders, mountainous sand dunes and occasional hardy shrubs, standing out against a backdrop of steep mountains and cloudless skies. The car pulled up before a non-descript, mud-plastered, weather-beaten compound, unremarkable except for its great size. Another matron led her through a front door of heavy rough-hewn planks to a windowless room deep within the building and locked her in. She slept and ate alone for the next two days.

Marya felt despondent and isolated, locked away in the recesses of a fortress that she knew was somewhere in the middle of the Asian landmass. Her dream had been snatched from her and, now, she faced an unknown foe. During those two days she cast about for a strategy she might use if anyone other than the tight-lipped servant with the trays of food should come calling. Should she resist, play dumb, lie, stall or assert her rights as an American citizen and demand to see the U.S. ambassador? She gave out a frightening laugh at the ridiculous thought and collapsed on her cot. This was not funny. Not at all. Who were these people, anyway? What did they want so badly from her?

She suddenly felt frightened by a creeping sense that she was losing control of her thinking. Her rationality and intelligence had always been a gift—one that she cherished and relied upon to carve out a successful life for herself. She felt it slipping away in her confinement. What did they want from her? When would they make up their minds and take her out of this brutal confinement? Was this all about the treasure? Well, she didn't have it. And she would likely never have it. Would her captors believe that? They could go see for themselves, if they didn't believe her. How long was this going to go on? She rose from the cot and banged on the door again and again. But no one came.

* * * * *

The same female guard who had brought her to her cell unlocked her door and yelled something unintelligible at her in a dialect that Marya knew was related to Turkic. *At last. Something different. They're going to let me out.* She rose from her cot, taking cues from the woman's gestures and shoves. After making her way through a labyrinth of hallways, she passed unexpectedly through a golden doorway into an opulent room decorated with an elaborate stucco ceiling and a row of crystal chandeliers. Forty paces directly ahead, at the far end of the hall, was a man sitting on a gilded throne. He was reading a large book that rested on his lap. He wore leather boots, pants that billowed out from them and a tunic fringed with wool. His dark eyes suggested oriental parentage and he wore his hair in a crew cut. His tanned, weathered skin gave evidence of a life that confronted extremes of climate. The downturn of his mouth at the corners alerted her to potential cruelty.

As she came within a few feet of him, she strained her head forward to see what he was reading and saw that he had been enjoying a collection of newspaper or magazine clippings mounted in an impressively sized album. She suspected that the clippings in some way or other were all about him.

"Dr. Bradwell. On your knees! Get down on your knees." The voice belonged to a studious-looking man in his twenties standing to the left of the throne. He looked neither Chinese nor Western, but some blend of both. And he was trembling slightly.

"Who are you? And why should I kneel?" she demanded, folding her arms across her chest.

A look of panic spread across the young fellow's face. His eyes shot from the throne to Marya. "You better use a civil tone, Miss. Otherwise, this will not go well for you."

She looked directly into the dark eyes of the man on the throne. "I am Dr. Bradwell, an American. And I . . . "

The seated man roared in what she thought was the same Turkic dialect the female guardian used with her, silencing her. The translator again warned her urgently. "He says shut up and kneel. He is close to losing his temper. When you are on your knees, place both hands flat on the floor and touch your head to the floor three times."

The *kowtow*, she thought, feeling utterly demeaned. The practice had been dropped over one hundred fifty years ago by the emperors of China. Pure anger and revolt coursed through her as she went down on her knees as she was told, touching the carpet with her forehead. If he was only close to losing his temper, she thought, she didn't want to see him go stark raving bananas. She quickly did two more kowtows.

The young man resumed translating, pacing the voice from the throne. "Your fate is hanging by a thread. So, listen well and speak the truth. We have brought you here for one reason—to recover our Golden Tablets of Command."

Marya was appalled, but focused. She stared up at him.

"Miss, don't look at the Khan. Look down. This is Temujin," the translator said in a low voice.

A second shock struck her. *Temujin! Good God. He thinks he is Genghis Khan.* This man was modeling himself after one of the most bloodthirsty individuals in all of human history, the man whose barbaric hordes swept out of Mongolia to engulf the world. Marya now knew that she was dealing with a very loose cannon, a delusional type. She weighed her chances of surviving captivity at this faraway, forbidding home for lunatics and found they didn't weigh very much at all.

"What do you want from me?" she asked, directing her words to the translator.

"You will tell us where the Golden Tablets are to be found. If you do, you will live," he said, word for word.

She heard the implied threat and was almost dumbstruck. Sizing up the man in front of her, she knew that he wasn't clowning. "What are you talking about? I have never heard of any such thing." She wondered if the Khan would think her response was lame, but it was all she could think of.

He did and then he pounded the armrests of the throne, this time with both fists clenched, and lashed out at her. "I am Temujin, the heir and successor, who has come down to earth, the brother of Jesus and Mohammed. The Golden Tablets that were given to Marco Polo—I want them." His hair seemed to bristle and his eyes hardened as they fastened upon her. He flung the large album from his lap and spewed out a long utterance that needed no translation. He was not one to play with.

The young translator was quaking as he translated for Marya. "He says that the Golden Tablets belong to the people of this land. He says that you are a well-known scholar of Asian History and that the object of your research is a matter of public knowledge. He and all the people of the steppes demand their return. He says that if you do not help him recover them, he will turn you over to the executioner."

Temujin waited, tapping the fingers of his right had on the gold armrest of his throne. He pointedly looked at his Rolex.

Marya was speechless. The man was demanding that she not simply hand over her research, but actually deliver the goods. She opened her mouth and stuttered, "But I don't know where they are. I don't have them."

Her words fell on deaf ears. His dark eyes bored into her like a relentless electric drill. He touched his Rolex. Her time was up. As he continued staring at her impassively, he clapped his hands once. Instantly, a door on her right opened, and her executioner entered the hall to lead her away.

CHAPTER 47

Liam almost did a one hundred eighty when he entered the Bellardos' living room and saw what a sorry state they were in. He was tempted to make a dash for Marco Polo Airport without looking back. It was his promise that made him show up but nothing said that he would have to stay long. What had he been thinking?

On the bus from Zagreb to Venice, he replayed the whole interview with Cage. The pencil-pushing bureaucrat had turned him off completely with his warnings to leave the search for Marya to the professionals. He knew that Cage knew much more than he revealed. The U.S. Government and its agencies had more information at its disposal about events around the world than anyone could imagine. He was impressed that Cage and his cohorts at the State Department had already pinpointed a criminal gang somewhere in Central Asia, specifically Tajikistan, but were not showing their hand. They were simply pumping him for more information and had no intention of accepting his offer of help. And that's what had enraged him.

Now he was here with the Bellardos. What did the old man have in mind? The family presented a very troubling sight. One look at Francesca, her arm in a sling, and he knew that the onslaught in the home must have been horrific. She sat in her chair, subdued, in some kind of semi-vegetative state. She was not the woman he had come to know—efficient housekeeper, superb chef, doting mother and loving wife. She managed a weak smile as he entered.

He went to Giovanni first and awkwardly shook his left hand. His right arm was in a sling and there must have been some thick bandaging on his shoulder, judging from the abnormal bulge under the shirt. The hospital had just released him that morning. His color was sickly and washed out. Yet, Liam thought he detected something defiant in his eyes. "Welcome back to Venice, Liam," he said, with a surprisingly strong grip.

"I know what you're going to say, Bellardo. I am like a son, right?" It brought a smile to the old man's face. More than ever before in his dealings with the clever old guy, he felt there was some truth to it.

It was different with Carlotta, as he turned to her. She was sitting in a large leather-upholstered arm chair. She greeted him without any expressiveness. She had bruises on her once-lovely face and an air of bitterness unnatural to her. The bruises would heal, he knew, but the emotional injury that the criminals had inflicted on her would take some time to recover from. What had they done to her? He would never probe the family in any way for details. On the bus from Dubrovnik to Zagreb, Ambrosio had mentioned several vague things about the assaults on his mother and father, but said almost nothing about his baby sister. Still, he saw something in Carlotta's look. And it was anything but resignation to fate.

"How're *you* doing?" he asked Pietro who sat quietly on the sofa, with one leg out straight and a crutch leaning on the arm of the sofa.

"I'll be all right. They told me to cool it for a while."

Only Ambrosio looked physically unscathed. How he felt inside, Liam had no idea. Overall, his review of the troops was discouraging. It looked hopeless to expect that Bellardo and he could talk and work out a plan to rescue Marya. Normally the family was a picture of energy, health and determination. Now, their world was upside down. Liam looked them over again, unable to shake a sense of responsibility for their present miserable condition. He had brought Marya to their home without sufficient warning beforehand. It was his doing that had set in motion events that brought the Bellardo family to this low point. He was amazed that Bellardo had enough generosity of spirit to send his sons to rescue him and Marya in Korcula.

Liam raised both hands imploringly. "I'm really sorry. So sorry. This is all my fault. I should never have brought Marya here in the first place. And I should have been more watchful in Korcula."

"You aren't to blame. That gang was prowling about here days before you ever arrived. This would have happened anyhow. We knew about them—I told you this before." Bellardo struggled with one arm to raise himself from his chair. "Ambrosio, get us some drinks. Welcome back to the family, Liam. Have a seat. Let's talk."

Liam watched as the old man got to his feet and ambled to a large highboy across the room. He stood with his back turned to everyone and pounded it hard with his left fist, rattling glasses and decanters. As Bellardo turned about, Liam saw him wince in pain and his free arm shoot to his shoulder. He couldn't believe the patriarch's next words.

"Damn it, Liam, we are going to counterattack!"

* * * * *

Over the past two months, Agarwal had been gradually clearing out all but the essentials from his office, knowing that the axe was going to fall sooner rather than later. In the wake of his blow-up with Lafferty, he was able to gather up and pack the rest of his stuff within a mere two hours. By mid-afternoon, his office was bare and the keys handed over to the department secretary, a gray-haired woman who wore a small gold cross on a chain. She had a fretful look on her face as she said good-bye to him and wished him all the luck in the world.

"Take care of yourself, Dr. Agarwal. And God love you."

"It's all right, Mrs. Taylor. I'll be fine. As you Christians are fond of saying, 'I am going to a better place.'"

"Heaven? Don't tell me you are leaving us because you're terminally ill. God forbid." She covered her mouth with both hands and looked stricken.

"No, no, no, no. Certainly not. I'm talking about a heaven here on earth for my people."

"Oh, I see," she said, but didn't.

He left the office, with a carton filled with CDs and papers. The rest of the afternoon, he placed several important calls to a destination on the other side of the globe. He closed two bank accounts at different locations, wiring the proceeds overseas. He prepaid the rent on his apartment for a year and saw to the maintenance of his Jaguar XJ while he was away. All the time, his thoughts were focused on the new position he had opted for as advisor to an obscure figure who would soon be creating waves on the international scene. That is, if his strategy played out as he expected. His position at Harvard had been very useful, he admitted to himself, in spite of having to work with a few dolts and buffoons in the department. His years at America's premier Ivy League school had enhanced his prestige and had given him time to work out the master plan he would soon put into place in the service of a charismatic ruler.

He wished he had had more time at Harvard to put the finishing touches on his chef d'oeuvre. And he also would have been overjoyed to be around to see Dr. Bradwell achieve her goal before he left to take up his new duties. After all, he had been her mentor for several years and their work had dovetailed so nicely. But being fired by idiots with power was one of those things that could not be helped. He was happy and thankful, at least, that Marya's work was coming to fruition. He looked forward to the day when she made the long-awaited discovery. It was bound to be a spectacular find. And she would deserve the honor that went with it.

CHAPTER 48

"Did I hear you right, Bellardo? Did you say counterattack?!" Liam was almost apoplectic as he took a glass of white wine from Ambrosio. "Who are you kidding? With this army of the living dead? Sorry. I didn't mean that. Hey, I came up here hoping to put our minds together on a few things. Work out something we could do to rescue Marya. But I never expected this. I had no idea. I'd like to support you, especially after what you've all been through, but, I mean, just take a look at yourselves..." he said, pointing to a large gilt mirror. "You need time out for convalescence, not another battle."

"We're going to rescue Marya and we will do it for honor and family!" Bellardo bristled.

"Settle down. Settle down. I'm one hundred percent with you but we can't take that gang on by ourselves. No way."

"Stop right there, Liam. Think about it. Do you want to do something to help Marya or do you want to turn tail and run off like a clucking chicken?"

"I'm not a chicken. You know me better. It's you and your family I'm worried about right now."

"Forget about us. We'll recover. Scars will heal. But as for Marya, well, that's another matter entirely. If you don't join us, what are you going to do? Tell me. Do you have anything at all in mind? Did you get any help in Korcula?"

"No."

"In Dubrovnik?"

"No."

"Anywhere in Croatia? Did your people at the U.S. Embassy help?"

"Not really, but..."

"But what?"

"They said they're working on it. They've already got men on the case. The U.S. State Department."

"And you believe that?"

"To be honest, yes, but I think they could do more."

Bellardo took a drink from Ambrosio and sat down next to Liam. "What did they ask of you?"

"Nothing. They want to keep me out of it. The official in charge of the case at the embassy warned me not to get involved."

Bellardo patted his arm. "I thought so. I know you well, son, and that's not what you are going to do."

The whole group jumped into a chaotic, rambling discussion, brainstorming and arguing vehemently through four bottles of wine. Signora Bellardo put up with as much as she could take and went to the kitchen to help Emilia. She had seen times like this before. The men would exhaust themselves in argument and shouting. A few hours later, they would charge into the kitchen, looking for food. She was expected to be prepared at all times to appease their appetites.

The Bellardos wanted to hear the entire conversation that Liam had had with Cage at the embassy. They went over what they knew of the vicious group that attacked them in Venice and Korcula. Several things were certain. The gang had come from Tajikistan looking for antique gold objects. They had kidnapped Marya who herself was in search of important gold artifacts. The gang, it was certain, was after not just any gold, but only gold artifacts that in some way reflected the history of the Asian Steppe. The more noble or imperial in origin, the better.

They discussed the golden treasure hidden away in Bellardo's secret vault. They talked money. They went over international travel and border restrictions. They considered hiring mercenaries and lobbying the U. S. Government to get aggressive. They argued heatedly about how much military force it would take to bring Marya out alive if the State Department's diplomatic efforts failed.

Carlotta remained with the men after her mother left, most of the time just listening. But her mind was engaged and after two hours of heated argument, she jumped into the fray. Bellardo, his sons and Liam sat stunned as the lovely young lady with the cherubic face laid out a Machiavellian plan that seemed all too simple. "We know all that we need to know about Marya's kidnappers. They want golden artifacts, articles that are symbols of national power, things once owned by ancient rulers. Don't you see? That's why they came here looking for the Scythian pieces, and that's why they have kidnapped Marya. And where have they taken her?" she asked, looking at each of them in turn for an answer.

"Go on," Liam said. "You seem to know it all."

"Where else? Tajikistan!"

"Yeah, okay. So, now what?" Liam asked with a tone of parental condescension.

"It's obvious, don't you see?" she asked, tilting her head slightly.

"No, forgive me. I don't." It irritated him that this bright young lady seemed to have it all figured out. It didn't help, either, that he was half in the bag after so many glasses of wine.

"What dummies you all are! We go to Tajikistan, of course, and we take along a selection of the finest pieces from Papa's collection. Come on, guys. Simple."

The men were dumbstruck.

She continued. "We lure Marya's kidnappers into the open by offering them the artifacts that they specifically want, of course. And we happen to have plenty of them just lying around in Papa's secret vault, right Papa? Ambrosio told me all about it."

Bellardo frowned. He did not like the direction that Carlotta was taking the discussion.

"Sure, it's as simple as that," Liam said smacking his forehead. "I should have known. Okay. All right. Let's follow this through," he said, still incapable of reconciling her sweet beauty with her sharp logic. "So, we take some of your dad's precious collection out to Tajikistan. We dangle the pieces in front of who? I'm not exactly sure what you have in mind here. And then, somehow, we lure them into the open. The bad guys rear their ugly heads. And then we call in the U. S. Marines? Or should we ask the Navy Seals if they can lend a hand? Or do you whip out your radio and call in some aerial drones? Help me out here."

Carlotta was offended by his sarcasm. "This will not involve big teams or hundreds of men with million-dollar technology. We are dealing with a conspiratorial bunch, not a great army. We have seen how they operate. Clandestinely, in small groups. And we can be effective, too, with small numbers."

"You're saying we do it ourselves? Oh, my God. *We're* supposed to take them on? Your dad, me, Ambrosio and Pietro. Just us? Right? Is this what you're suggesting? Get real, Carlotta."

Liam looked at Bellardo helplessly, waiting for him to object to Carlotta's plan. He looked at Pietro and Ambrosio for their response. What he saw shook him to his core. They were nodding in agreement with her plan to bring Marya back home from Tajikistan. *This can't be done. I'm outta here tomorrow.*

CHAPTER 49

Marya felt as if she had been struck in the abdomen with a large rock when Khalid Agarwal entered the throne room from the side door. Nothing in the world could have prepared her for the shock of seeing her friend from Boston suddenly appear right before her very eyes in one of the remotest wastelands in all of Asia. She got up from her feet slowly, blinking her eyes to make sure it was him. It *was* him.

"Oh, my God, Khalid. It's you. Thank goodness," she shouted. He smiled at her as he walked barefoot across the gleaming marble floor.

He reached out to her as she stumbled a few steps toward him and caught her by the shoulders. "Marya. Are you all right?"

"Yes, thank you. But I'm in bad trouble. I don't know why I'm being held here, except that that whacko on the throne there thinks he's Genghis Khan's reincarnation or something and he's demanding I give him the Golden Tablets of Command. I'm so confused now...what do I do to get out of here? And, what are you doing here?"

Agarwal darkened at her derogatory description of his new employer. "That's no goon, Marya, and you'd better get used to it. Just watch that you don't offend him or even appear to be offensive in the slightest way. That's important for your survival. I'll explain everything in a little while when we're alone." He let go of her, asking if she could remain standing on her own.

"I'm fine," she answered in a whisper.

"Good girl." Then he walked to the throne and stood before the seated ruler. He bowed to him from the waist and spoke in the same language Marya had heard earlier. After a minute, he returned to her.

"What did he say, Khalid?"

"He wants you to come with me and tell me where the Golden Tablets of Command are hidden."

"But, Khalid, I don't know. One minute I was at this church in Korcula with Liam and the next minute I'm imprisoned here. I don't know where they are. Believe me. And I think they shot Liam when they kidnapped me."

"Who's Liam?" he asked with a frown.

She remembered how she had told Khalid that she would only work on her cherished project alone and chose her words carefully. "Oh. Liam? He's a salesman. He came along for my protection in Korcula. I didn't want to have anyone with me, but I had to accept. They insisted."

"Who are *they*?"

"The Bellardos. And. . . ." She saw that her explanation was only getting her in deeper.

"Never mind that now. We can talk about that later. Right now I've got to get you out of here before anything goes wrong."

"Wait, tell me what this is all about. Are you with these insane people? You're not, are you? Tell me you're not."

Temujin snarled and barked out an order to Agarwal who bowed again and turned to Marya.

"What did he tell you?"

"He said that he wants me to get the golden tablets from you any way I can and that includes removing your skin inch by inch."

"Oh, my God. He's a monster."

"Don't worry. I'm sure you and I can figure some way out of this mess for you. Now stand by my side and we'll bow to him together."

"Oh, my God, you do work for him, don't you?"

Temujin roared once more before dismissing them.

"What did he say?" she whispered, feeling Khalid's hand on her upper back, ushering her to the side door.

"He said for me to take care of everything because he's got some explosive issues to handle with Beijing. It's a kind of inside joke."

* * * * *

Temujin used the rest of the morning productively. He visited the workshop of the Chinese artisans again and inspected the huge ivory frame that they had finished. He gave instructions that it was to be moved carefully to another holding room on the other side of the imperial headquarters. Then he instructed his aide to have the five artisans decapitated and their heads delivered to Beijing in separate wooden chests, the covers engraved in Chinese with the words "*Da dao gung fei di guo zhu yi!*" Down with Chinese Communist imperialism!" They would be placed on the ground in front of the Gate of Heavenly Peace, beneath the gigantic portrait of Mao Tse-tung at noontime when the crush of tourists would be heaviest. Simultaneously, a car painted to look like Chinese security, loaded with explosives, would be just yards away and be detonated by remote control to go off with the greatest possible loss of life. The message to the Chinese leadership would be unmistakable. Hands off the autonomous regions and their western neighbors.

* * * * *

Agarwal led her down a long corridor and into a room on the right. It was windowless, stifling and unfurnished, except for some cushions on the floor around a low table.

"Sit down, Marya, and we'll talk. I know you must have questions."

"Are you kidding? It's not just confusion I'm going through here. This band of loonies kidnapped me and have held me incommunicado for two days. I'm angry and I'm scared to death. And you haven't answered my question. Are you working for them?"

"I am your friend and I hope that it will always be that way." His words gave no hint of apology for what his employer had done to her.

"You haven't answered my question."

"Yes. I am now working for the Khan."

She flew at him in a rage and pounded his chest. "You bastard. You must have known!" An even worse realization dawned on her. "You're with those men in Venice, aren't you? The ones who kidnapped me...and...and...nearly clubbed Vittoria to death!" She kept pounding his chest and trying to slap his face.

He grabbed both her wrists tightly and forced her down onto a cushion. "Stop it, Marya. I'm your friend. You must believe me. Yes, I had a part in bringing you here, but only because our work overlaps in an important way. I never intended that the agents would be so clumsy and heartless. I apologize. Please listen."

She drew her knees up towards her face and clasped both hands together in front of them. Tears formed and she began to sob. "I won't. This is unforgivable. You should have seen what they did to Vittoria. Even if you never laid a hand on her personally, you share the blame for that." She recalled the gunshot that rang out in the square when she was bundled off in a Zodiac. Khalid must have had Liam killed. She threw him a defiant look. "You won't get anything more from me. I hate you!"

"I'm truly sorry you feel that way. I'll see to it that those agents are taught a lesson," he said without a trace of emotion.

"Is that all you can say? Get out of here, you liar!"

"Marya, I'll leave you alone for a little while to think about something. You may not love me. You may even resent me. Granted. But that makes no difference in what you face here and now. What matters is the Khan and what he wants. In a nutshell, he wants the Golden Tablets of Command. I think you do know where they are. You will help see to it that he gets them. I'd reconsider if I were you. The Khan will have no qualms about having you chopped up and fed to the buzzards. That's for sure. I'll be back soon to have your answer. Think about it."

CHAPTER 50

Ron Henderson finished reading a cable from CIA headquarters, and proceeded to his meeting with Cage in his office. Cage had a carafe of coffee, two cups, and a half-dozen glazed bear-claws on a paper plate set out on a side table.

Henderson didn't wait for any niceties. He poured himself a cup of coffee and took one of the bear-claws and a napkin. "Morning, Cage. There's been more trouble in Beijing. A police car exploded right near the Gate of Heavenly Peace. About ninety deaths and twice that number of injured rushed to various hospitals. A bloody, frigging mess. Body parts scattered all over. My opinion is that it's the work of Kibchek." He picked up his coffee, letting the startling information sink in.

"What do you know?"

"Our people happened to be taking a few U. S. Senators who were in town to the Forbidden City for a nice day out. Figured it would be a blast for them. It was, but not the kind they expected. But the kicker is what they saw right at the main entrance... You know, under the picture of Mao. They managed to penetrate a circle of Chinese tourists and guess what they saw. Five boxes each with a severed head inside. One of our people overheard locals talking about what was written on the lids of each box. 'Down with Chinese Imperialism.' Fortunately, our folks moved on just before the blast. None of them were hurt."

"Sounds like Kibchek's style," Cage said, shaking his head. "Decapitations, as I've noted, are his signature."

"You're right. Well, as you might have expected, Washington wants us to really beef up our work on this case. Do what it takes to pinpoint his location. Got any ideas? I need to get back to them this morning."

"Sure. The first thing I'd recommend is surveillance of Dushanbe, Tajikistan's capital. But I'd do it from the air. It's too dangerous for an American to go in on the ground right now. Any foreigner, in fact, would be insane to go there."

"Where do you think Kibchek is going with these bombings and severed heads and what not?"

"I think he's trying to stampede the Chinese into something rash."

"Like what?" Henderson asked, polishing off another pastry.

"I'd say....something like sending in a division or two of the Red Army into Xinjiang Province. Raising alert levels in Mongolia. Coming down hard on demonstrations among Uyghur people in Xinjiang and along their western border. A raid or two to show they've got muscle and can use it. Public executions. Stuff like that that would push the minorities to rebel and give Kibchek an opportunity to show himself as a leader standing up to Chinese oppression."

* * * * *

Liam hadn't slept too well when there was a knock on his door to come to breakfast. He got dressed and showed up in the kitchen without bothering to shave or to brush his unruly hair.

He had to admire the Bellardos gathered around the kitchen table. They were a plucky bunch, as his mother would say. They had suffered a knockout blow, but they were already back on their feet and looked eager for action.

Bellardo spoke first. "We need to know if you are with us as we press the attack on the enemy."

Liam sputtered into his coffee. "Press the attack. Oh, that's a good one. First, you've got to convince me that we have the manpower behind us to pull off the kind of operation Carlotta laid out last night."

Carlotta spoke up in defense of her plan. "Liam, listen. Too much manpower would harm the operation. It's got to be surgical. I propose a two-step approach. Flush the kidnappers out with an advertising campaign, offering Papa's Scythian gold artifacts for sale, as I explained last night. Then, when they surface and show interest in the gold, we offer them the prize, the journal of Marco Polo in exchange for Marya's safe return. That should be enough to close the deal with them. After all, that is what they need to find the golden tablets."

"But even Marya would not consent to that exchange. The journal is the key to her search. It would kill her spirit to lose her last chance at finding the answers she needs to locate the treasure. You know that, too."

"At least she'd be alive. Right now her very life is at risk, and she probably doesn't have long if something isn't done. We can't just sit on our hands here and do nothing. Or, do you want to leave it all to your State Department?"

"All right, let's suppose we do use the journal to bargain for Marya's freedom. It's still going to be very risky. Think about it. Just us against a criminal mob that's probably heavily armed, on their own ground—Tajikistan at that. I've heard it's a dangerous, war-torn, third world country, and that's being generous. We need numbers. Seriously."

Carlotta continued. "No. It has to be surgical."

"What does that mean, exactly?"

"It will only take four. A small, well-prepared team can do it. Four people. We don't need an army. In fact, it will be faster and more effective, the fewer of us that are involved."

"You mean, like your dad, Pietro, Ambrosio and me?

"No, Papa's doing enough by bankrolling the operation."

"Then who's the fourth?"

"Me, of course. Who else did you have in mind?"

"You?" Liam stood up and flung his arms in the air. He stomped around the kitchen. "Mother of God."

Bellardo calmed him down. "Look, Liam. Ambrosio is ready to take them on. Pietro wants revenge for the bullet he took. I will put up the money and the gold articles for the mission and supply transportation. And Carlotta will . . ."

"Stay home and bake biscotti," Liam said, his hair bristling, directing his temper at Bellardo. "There's no way that I'll be a part of this if Carlotta is in on it. It's too dangerous for a young woman out there. Women in Tajikistan cannot even show their faces in public. How could she be of any help to us whatsoever?" He looked at Carlotta. "Sorry, Carlotta, no offense."

Carlotta's eyes raged at him.

Bellardo sent Ambrosio to his office for something and then turned to Liam.

"Carlotta is essential to the plan. If she doesn't go, then it's off. You have to trust me on this, Liam. She's well-prepared. I've personally overseen her training."

Ambrosio returned with a fine walnut chest the size of a suitcase. Bellardo took it from him and opened it, revealing three magnificent gold articles. "Priceless Scythian artifacts. I'm putting these into play along with money for expenses. What do you say? Do you want to wait while they hold a knife to her throat or do you want to do something? If you're worried about Carlotta, don't. You do not know her. She has been on what I call trade missions for me before, in places you cannot imagine. You will all be safer with her present." He passed the chest of priceless Scythian art objects to Liam.

All eyes were on him as he looked at the exquisite gold pieces. Carlotta had made sense. A large military force could not move as nimbly as a well-trained crew and would be like using a sledge hammer to kill a flea. Trouble is, he had no experience in commando raids. How many times had he been called upon to rescue beautiful women from captivity in faraway places? None whatsoever. He looked around the room at the expectant faces. It seemed they had a plan. Not a plan he had great confidence in, but a plan. He made up his mind. "It's crazy. It's suicidal. But, what the heck. We gotta do something. Count me in."

CHAPTER 51

Marya sat on the floor in the corner opposite the door of her cell resting against a propped-up cushion. She sat up as soon as she heard someone with a key unlocking her door. It was Khalid. He had a small tray of food with some Turkish delights and other sweets and a cushion for himself.

"I won't tell you anything."

"You could be home safe in a few days if you cooperate."

"Do you think I believe that for one minute, after what you've gotten me into?"

A server came in behind Agarwal with a teapot and filled two cups for them.

"Marya, come sit with me. I won't bite your head off. Do come have a bite to eat and some tea. I'm afraid I was too harsh with you a while ago and I do apologize."

She had come to loathe the mélange of British English and his own brand of Indian English. She was hungry and the sight of food and the aroma of tea got her on her feet. She sat down reluctantly opposite him. She was still disoriented from her trip and the time difference. She had seen lunacy itself elevated to the imperial throne and she had learned only an hour earlier that Khalid, her best friend, had betrayed her. She felt isolated. No one could suspect the danger she was in, much less have any idea of how to get her out of it. No chance to get a ticket for a plane back to Boston. She could only sit and listen.

But with a few sips of tea, her composure improved somewhat and a degree of rational thinking was restored. Her mind had always served her well in the past. It was the only thing that might get her out of the mess she was in. "Just for the record, what kind of operation is this that you're involved in?"

"A great one. And you have a chance, too, not only to save yourself, but also to participate in one of the great unfolding dramas of our time. You're at the headquarters of a vast network that stretches from the Caspian Sea to Manchuria—across great stretches of the old empire of Genghis Khan."

She sipped her tea, listening and silently assessing his sanity. "What's the plan?"

"This land, including all five of the Central Asian Republics together with Mongolia, Tibet, Xinjiang Province and Manchuria, will one day be united under the firm leadership of Temujin. Where once the people of these lands suffered under Russian and Chinese oppression, there will be a new Empire of the Khan."

"A Khanate of Turkestan? I remember you once delivered a paper on that subject at Tufts."

"Good. Very good, dear. We are still casting about for a name for the empire. Temujin envisions a vast Asian superstate, not to include Russia or China, an empire of federated nations."

Marya looked directly into Agarwal's eyes and thought she detected a glint, a sign of fanaticism that she had never seen in all the years of their association at Harvard. She had long known that he greatly admired Genghis Khan and Tamerlane but it amazed her that she had not picked up a hint of latent fanaticism. She sipped her tea, thankful for having a moment to assess her chances of escaping. She knew, however, that Temujin and Agarwal held all the good cards and they were about to call.

"How will you get this operation rolling?"

"It's not an operation. It's a strategy I've had a leading hand in designing. It will bring about the end of outside dominance of this region by first handing China a devastating blow in Xinjiang Province. That will be the signal for our cells in Tibet, Mongolia, and the Central Asian

Republics to launch the revolt that will create a new empire spanning Central Asia and uniting people of Turkic, Mongolian, Persian and Tibetan stock wherever they are scattered, including those in certain parts of Russia and China." Agarwal rocked back and forth on his cushion, casting a blissful look past her.

My God, the Mother of All Restorations. The return of the Mongol Empire, she thought.

She felt she had no real stake in this conversation. The topic was too unreal, beyond the outer boundaries of fiction, and she reminded herself that her ultimate goal was to find a means of escape. She had no doubt that Khalid's master plan would fail and with a lot of bloodshed. But, she decided to engage him in further discussion. "Let me play the devil's advocate, Khalid. Yes, success in Xinjiang might spark revolts, but the Chinese will not give up Xinjiang without a struggle. With its huge oil reserves and nuclear testing facilities at Lop Nor, it's strategically important to China. They will go all out to defend it."

"We expect that. But that response will play right into our hands, as we see it. The differences between the Han Chinese on the one hand and the Turkic people, the Mongols and the Tibetans on the other will simply widen and the Chinese will be the losers the more they clamp down. The unrest among the people of this region is at maximum levels now."

"You are right. The Han Chinese have not been very sensitive to the aspirations of these minorities."

"Xinjiang Province has been the homeland of the Uyghurs for thousands of years. There are tens of millions of them across the continent. The Chinese have employed so many repressive measures against their young men, their mosques, their Islamic schools, including regulating Ramadan observances. They are trying to erase our culture."

She sensed a pleading in his voice, maybe hoping that

he could still enlist her in the cause for the downtrodden. "We need a powerful monarch to stop Chinese cultural imperialism," he said in an urgent tone.

"What's your role in all this, Khalid?"

"Temujin has hired experts in various fields, mine included. I'm responsible for political advice on establishing his legitimacy as the first ruler of his dynasty. I will recreate the historical past and help secure cultural artifacts important to getting him accepted as a ruler on par with Genghis Khan or his grandson, Kublai Khan. There are others besides me, well-known authorities, who advise him on economics, defense, telecommunications and other areas. We have specialists and technicians of all kinds working with us."

"What if the Chinese find this base, this palace or whatever you call it? It'll be curtains."

"The Chinese can't see us operating right under their very noses. Temujin has cells of activists and loyal paramilitary units scattered throughout the region. He is building an army that will be able to strike with lightning speed when they least expect it. The Chinese don't even know that I am here at this moment. I flew from Boston to Kazakhstan and crossed the border late the other night.

"But this must take oodles of money. Where does the money come from? It seems to me, as a government in hiding, which this is, you don't have any tax revenues to count on."

"The Khan has sufficient revenues."

"No doubt from something like selling opium and smuggling guns."

"That is unfortunately true, Marya, but it is a temporary compromise. Temujin will correct the problem as soon as the situation improves."

"How?"

"Temujin controls the transportation of all the opium

now coming out of Afghanistan. This monopoly provides a substantial income, although it's causing problems with heroin addiction in China's Xinjiang province. But most of our revenues come from Europe and North America. Billions of dollars. As I said, this will all change."

"And when will he get around to doing that?"

"When the empire is restored, Temujin will pull in all the revenue he needs from legitimate sources and do away with opium and its derivatives completely. If he has to use public executions to stamp out drug trafficking, he'll do it."

"What legitimate sources?"

"Xinjiang Province sits above huge oil reserves, for instance. The same is true at the western end of the region near the Caspian Sea. There are proven reserves of billions of barrels of oil and trillions of cubic feet of natural gas. In addition, international mining companies are in a gold rush to Mongolia as we speak. As mineral revenues increase, he will phase out and eventually suppress opium completely. I assure you, Marya, my plans for Temujin's new empire are well thought out. He will soon be the universal leader of the people of the steppes. First, Xinjiang Province will break away from China. Then, Inner and Outer Mongolia and Tibet will rise up to join us. They will be followed by Kazakhstan, Kirghizstan, Tajikistan, Afghanistan, Uzbekistan and Turkestan."

His rant was breathtaking. It reminded her of Hitler at his hysterical worst with his orations about the conquest of Europe. She realized that she must try to escape not only for her own sake but to warn the outside world of this monstrous plan to restore the empire of Genghis Khan.

He put his cup on the table and stood up, towering over her. "Come, I have something to show you. Something you will definitely appreciate. You'll see why I was such an ardent supporter of your research."

She gulped her tea and followed him, wondering what

marvel he had to show her. He led her through a confusing maze of corridors to another wing of the palace. She hoped at every turn to find some weakness, a cubbyhole to hide in or a doorway out. *How will I ever get out of here? Think!* They came to an ordinary door that might be the entrance to a closet or a storage room. He opened it with two keys and turned on the lights.

"Look for yourself."

She stepped in and stood frozen in place, speechless and unbelieving at the sight of an enormous store of golden treasures, porcelains, carpets, tableware and imperial robes. She gasped, thinking of the treasures in the Imperial Treasury of the Hapsburgs she had seen last year and the Crown Jewels of the British monarchy, the year before. They now seemed to her like tacky trinkets and junk that was sold in a one-dollar-buys-anything store.

He drew her attention to a wall on the opposite side. "Do you see that frame of ivory?"

"Yes. Gorgeous. Tang Dynasty."

"No. Twentieth century."

She was surprised at her mistake. "Really? But it's empty."

"Of course. Can you figure out why?"

Marya studied it and realized that there were seven vertical slots enclosed within the borders of the frame. Then, it dawned on her. "Are you telling me that this was created to display the Golden Tablets of Command?"

"That's right. You see, Marya, I've had confidence in you for quite some time now."

"Your confidence is misplaced, though. I don't even know where they are. Your men kidnapped me before I even had a chance to try to find them."

"Come now, Marya, be honest with me."

"Be honest? You want me to be honest?" She felt Agarwal putting the noose around her neck and regretted being so naïve, sharing her plans with him when she called him from Venice. "How can you stand there and talk to me like that, Khalid? You were my friend. You deceived me. How dare you talk to me about honesty?"

"Can it, Marya. I don't have time for a lover's quarrel. I'm engaged in serious work for a great leader who will change the map of Asia. This region has been the plaything of great nations for too, too long. You know that the Russians suppressed over 700 monasteries in Outer Mongolia, looted their precious art and killed over 700 monks. The Chinese killed hundreds of lamas and began a campaign to colonize the country with millions of Han Chinese. Today there's not a trace of nomadic culture there. That kind of thing is not going to happen again! Do you hear me? I'm working for the Khan to see that no outsiders have an opportunity to push us around. We will have our day in the sun under the rule of Temujin the Second. We need those treasures. You are going to work with us until we get them. Do you have that straight?"

She couldn't believe she was talking with the same Khalid Agarwal who had kissed her so passionately before she left Boston. He was a very different man and her response to him was changing by the minute. For the worse. "Face it, Khalid. The people here don't need you, Temujin, or any other reincarnation of Genghis Khan to take up their cause. They do deserve freedom from outside interference and the rights they've struggled for. But do I believe that you and Temujin will offer them that freedom? Not for one minute. And I doubt my life is worth a nickel to you. Temujin is nothing but a power-crazed, delusional warlord, and you are just his footstool. What has happened to you, Khalid?"

A dark look crossed his face. "Nothing has changed. I've always had the interests of my people at heart."

"Your so-called interest seems to have turned into fanaticism and I don't recognize you any more. I will not be a party to what's going on here. Never."

"Have it your way, but the golden tablets will be found and they will come back home where they belong—among the people of the steppes. You will cooperate."

"Did it ever occur to you that beating my assistant nearly to death, shooting my friend in Korcula, and kidnapping me to this remote desert is not exactly the way to my heart? If I even suspected where the golden tablets were concealed, I would never tell you now. Besides, I don't have the journal."

"You had it with you in Venice. You must have taken it with you when you went to Korcula. No doubt you left it at that boarding house. I've given our agents instructions already to get it for us."

She shuddered at the thought of what would happen to the Sternichs. She drew back from him. "I won't work with you or that mad man on the throne—ever.

Agarwal flew at her and belted her in the face. "You stupid, American bitch!" The blow knocked her to the floor, dazed. A trickle of blood oozed from a cut on her upper lip. Agarwal called in two guards at the door to haul her back to her room and left to report to the Khan.

CHAPTER 52

The white CL-600 that Bellardo rented from a private jet charter company for the team streaked into the sky from Marco Polo Airport and banked to the east. It soon reached its maximum speed of 529 miles per hour and would cover the distance from Venice to Dushanbe in seven hours, give or take a half hour. Canadian pilots, Scotty Wilson and Dave Borger, were old hands with the jet's features and capabilities and the galley was well stocked. Bellardo knew all too well what his son Ambrosio needed to function on these jaunts.

The whine of the jet engines rang in Liam's ears. When the jet leveled off, he undid his seatbelt and leaned to hear Carlotta better. She gave him more details of the transaction her father had concluded with Shevchenko to get the entire Scythian collection and how her brothers had gone down to Croatia to pick it up. She gave him all the information she had on Shevchenko and his warning about the dangerous Tajiks.

"So, you're convinced we're going to meet up with these folks and their leader in Tajikistan and somewhere along the line locate Marya."

"I'm almost certain. In any case, our most reasonable course of action is to start looking in the capital city."

"What's the name of the place again?"

"Dushanbe. If they are not in Dushanbe itself, they can't be too far from there. That's my best guess."

"We'll have to be careful anywhere we go in Tajikistan. From everything I heard about the civil war and drug battles there, it's still dangerous. It's probably worse for outsiders like us, too." He paused and scratched his head. "You know,

Carlotta, you really surprise me. I wouldn't have figured you for this role. Do you really grasp how dangerous this mission is going to be? If I were your father…"

She arched her eyebrow. "You can't imagine the situations I've been in working for my father. Don't worry. I've had lots of experience in Eastern Europe and Russia. This one might be a little more risky than the others, but I can handle it."

"How did your family get into this business in the first place?"

"It started almost by accident with the troubles in Russia. After the Soviet Union folded, valuable Russian religious icons became a staple in our acquisitions. From there we branched out. My father cashed in on it big time, at first taking my brothers along on buying trips. Pietro and Ambrosio are now old hands at that. Then, Papa broadened his search into other East European countries and the former states of the Soviet Union. He's had my brothers do countless jobs. I'm the last to join the team but I've had a lot of training. Now, not only can I hold up my end of the job but Papa also trusts me with the lead role. So, if you're nervous, don't be. I'm fully in charge of this operation."

Liam had badly underestimated Bellardo. And Carlotta. "I often suspected there was another side to the family business, but I had no idea. And not a clue about you. So, you're not just another pretty face!"

"I'm the team captain, you might say. Whenever we're on a mission, I plot out the moves and my brothers are the muscle. They pick up the goods, see to safety issues and take care of other tactical matters."

"Where do I fit in on this mission?"

"My dad says that he has a lot of respect for you but that you're a little green. He wants me to treat you as my equal, though."

That was a novel idea, Liam thought. *Me the equal*

of this pretty young thing. The Bellardos have something to learn about me, too.

Carlotta brushed some wayward curls back from her forehead and looked out at the vast expanse of the Black Sea. They would soon cross the Caspian Sea farther to the east. Then they would soar over the vast open spaces of Turkestan, and beyond Turkestan, towards the Pamirs and the Tien Shan range of western China. The airplane would descend there in the obscure little Republic of Tajikistan near night fall.

"Tell me more about this two-stage plan. Who's going to do what?" he asked. Carlotta gave him the rundown. Upon arrival in Dushanbe, she and Liam would be responsible for scouting the local bazaars and shops, displaying Bellardo's high- quality artifacts in an attempt to pique the interest of the people behind the attacks in Venice. Once they had a firm lead, it would be up to her and her alone to close the deal with a specific buyer, hopefully the head honcho or another top leader in the gang's structure. "Keep in mind, Liam, that when I'm dealing with that party, I don't want you or my brothers anywhere in sight. You might be recognized. I will make my presentation directly to the end buyer on his own ground. In his home or in his headquarters. Once I'm in, I'll look for a chance to find Marya. If she's there, I'll let you know and then I'll drop into the background. That's when phase two kicks in. You'd better be ready to take it from there and run with it. I've thought this over and I see no other way."

"What are our chances?"

"They're very good that we can raise interest in the articles that we show around. Fair that we can pinpoint the buyer. And dicey that we get out alive with Marya."

"Dicey?"

"No question. We're up against dangerous people in a very dangerous part of the world. It's certain we're going to experience violence somewhere along the line."

Liam looked at her and she appeared unfazed. "You seem cool with this."

"I am. And so are my brothers. They're satisfied with the plan. We want to restore the honor of the family. We want revenge, Liam. How about you?"

"I want Marya back."

Carlotta arched an eyebrow, "You *are* lovers, aren't you?"

"Not yet, we aren't..."

* * * * *

The plane landed in Dushanbe at 8:05 P.M. local time. The airport was small and the formalities for entering this remote land were perfunctory. The feeling about the place that Liam got was of some post-apocalyptic outpost of a dying civilization. As he pulled his luggage through the shabby airport, he half expected to see leather-clad, armed survivors straight out of a futuristic sci-fi movie like *Water World*.

The man helping them load their bags into a battered van turned out to be the cabbie, but was dressed like a camel driver. He wore a neat, stitched, white skullcap, voluminous trousers and a vest. "I take you to Dushanbe," he said. "Cheap, just one-hundred dollah." His was the only vehicle to be seen in the entire pick-up area.

"No," Pietro countered. "Fifty is enough just to go five miles."

The driver promptly removed one of their suitcases from the van and left it in the street.

"Who else can we get, Pietro?" Liam asked, looking around the abandoned airport entrance.

The driver took the remaining bags out and moved around to the front of the vehicle and opened the door. He looked determined to leave them at the sidewalk and take off.

Pietro was flustered. "Okay. Sixty dollars."

The driver only shrugged.

"Seventy. And that's final," said Pietro.

"Seventy-five and I take you."

Pietro accepted. "It's a deal. Seventy-five." He took out his wallet and peeled off the exact amount.

The driver reloaded all the bags from the sidewalk into the van.

It unnerved Liam to see how badly battered the vehicle was, as if it had been pressed into service in wartime. In fact, it had been. Six bullet holes pierced the front door on the driver's side. The right side of the windshield was almost caved in from some smashing force that left a web-like tracery. The unflappable Bellardos all piled nonchalantly into the back seat of the cab as if it were a Mercedes limo.

The first thing that Liam noticed when he got into the passenger seat in front was the Kalashnikov submachine gun lying on the floor at his feet, partially hidden under his seat. The driver had several spare clips in the console between them. Liam turned around to alert the Bellardos. "This guy has a machine gun."

Pietro leaned over to see. "You're right. It's a Kalashnikov. This one can kill at up to 1,350 meters."

"Is that right? Is that supposed to reassure me? I didn't know I was going to have to ride shot-gun."

Pietro went on. "It's probably standard issue here. Times are tough. Nice thing about it is it's real light. It only weighs three and a half kilos loaded. Nice to know you can get them here."

"You guys for real? You want to get one of these?"

Ambrosio patted Liam's right shoulder. "Relax, brother. If you want you can come back and sit with us. Carlotta will take your place up front." The two brothers burst out laughing together.

"We're lucky to have one of the best marksmen in all Italy riding with us," Pietro added.

"Huh?

"Carlotta. She has a ton of trophies in her room."

Liam did a one hundred eighty degree turn to look back at her. "Nice to know that," he said, mopping sweat from the back of his neck. She waved like Queen Elizabeth, with slight twists of her wrist.

While the Bellardos had their fun with Liam, the driver struggled to get the rickety van's engine going. With no warning, there was a loud blast and a cloud of bluish white smoke engulfed the front of the vehicle, making Liam duck and cover his head with his arms. His instincts told him that someone on the airport's roof had fired a Stingray missile at the van. "Watch out!" he screamed to the others.

He looked up and was surprised to see the van still in one piece. He saw Camel Driver turn the ignition key, making the van backfire again. Liam just gripped his thighs and felt stupid. The driver gave him an apologetic look. He heard the Bellardos chuckling and didn't dare turn around to look at them.

The van heaved and wobbled as it turned away from the curb and headed off in the direction of downtown Dushanbe. The play in the wheel was phenomenal but Liam tried to place things in perspective. He knew that the team was about to plunge into a society still reeling from the violence of civil war. Over fifty thousand had died in the violence since the end of the Soviet period. Top-ranking American officials were not welcome here and two western journalists were recently killed. What kind of welcome party would there be for him and the Bellardos in town?

As they pulled into town, reality hit home. In some sections of Dushanbe that they passed through, buildings were bombed out, leaving only parts of exterior walls standing, like charred fingers reaching skyward. Shelling had ripped off the corners of others. Missing doors and windows gave entry to scavengers and squatters. Carlotta pointed out bullet holes that riddled the walls on every other block.

The shuttle left them at the entrance to a hotel that turned out to be as shabby inside as it looked from the outside. Dushanbe's hotels at one time housed news teams from around the world covering the war in neighboring Afghanistan. The hotelkeepers had become used to easy money and still gouged foreigners at every opportunity. The reservation desk at this one charged one hundred fifty dollars per night per occupant, down from three-hundred twenty-five dollars per night during the worst trouble in Afghanistan.

The next morning at breakfast, they compared the conditions of their rooms. Dirty linens, broken air conditioners, toilets that didn't flush and lukewarm water in the showers seemed to be the norm. Liam made a mental note to cross Tajikistan off his personal list of tourist hotspots.

"Did you have bedbugs, too?" he asked them. They nodded in unison.

After breakfast, they split up, Pietro and Ambrosio heading off to check out the local bazaars and see if they could buy some clothes like the kind that Tajik men wore. Ambrosio also wanted to pick up "some hardware." Carlotta and Liam would try to show the special Scythian gold "merchandise" around the town.

As Liam and Carlotta watched them leave, he asked her why Ambrosio needed hardware. "That's just Ambrosio," she said with a shrug of the shoulders. "He's into tools and gadgets."

Liam didn't believe her for a minute. An AK-47 or a grenade launcher is more like it, he thought. He was learning quickly.

CHAPTER 53

After breakfast, they selected two of the best gold artifacts that Bellardo had contributed to the effort, wrapped them carefully and placed them in two ordinary canvas sacks. The others were put in safekeeping at the hotel. They headed for the main entrance of the hotel. Carlotta opened her purse to take out a silk scarf to cover her head. He whistled softly when he noticed a pistol in her purse.

They were off for their morning errands at the jewelry and goldsmith shops of Dushanbe. Using basic, telegraphic English and sign language they got the message out that they had high-quality gold treasures to trade and were looking for interested buyers. They spent the whole morning, showing the items to gray-bearded shopkeepers, leaving their hotel number with them and promising a bonus to anyone who could connect them with a serious buyer. By noontime, they had the routine of displaying the wares and leaving their contact information down pat. But there were no takers after more than a dozen stops, many of which were staffed by hostile, suspicious merchants. Two of the shopkeepers were so frightened at the sight of the two pieces in the possession of these foreigners that they hustled them out the door, locking it behind them.

"Do you think we've got the right country, Carlotta?"

"Let's give our advertising some time to do its magic. Be patient. We'll find the right buyer," she said.

Before returning to the hotel, they passed by the front of the Firdowsi Library where a beautiful poster was hung, inviting visitors in to see its new exhibit on Steppe Cultures of the Past. On a whim Liam suggested going in. They came upon the head librarian and curator of the artwork that was on display in the main hall, a Dr. Chandahar. He was busy making some last-minute adjustments to the featured piece, the gold crown of a Scythian king excavated at a dig only seventy miles away.

The dark-skinned man in his mid-thirties told them that he was Oxford-educated when Liam commented on his impeccable English. When Liam asked him what kind of market there was for Scythian artifacts such as the crown on display, he looked astonished. "There is no private market for such a masterpiece," he said. They are automatically turned over to the State. No one has a right to own such things. The idea that such a market could exist in Europe continually amazed him, he said. "Why do you ask?"

"Because we want to sell some," he said bluntly. "Here. Take a look." Liam opened the canvas sack and unfolded the cloth around the gold diadem he had carried all about this morning.

"I see," Chandahar said, choked up. "It's lovely. Exquisite. You must take care not to show this around."

"Too late. The word is out all over Dushanbe. Got any suggestions?"

"Leave at once. Go back to Europe....or... "

"Or what?"

"I shouldn't say. But if you are still hopeful of selling this piece, go to Kashgar. You're far more likely to find an interested buyer there. In Kashgar you will find a bazaar unlike any other on the face of the earth."

"Thanks for that suggestion, Dr. Chandahar. We will look into it," said Carlotta. "How far is it from the capital?"

"My friends, Kashgar is not close to the capital. The only safe way is by air."

"It's far away?"

"Come with me. I'll show you where it is in an atlas."

They followed him a few steps to the reference section. He slipped an over-sized book off a waist-high shelf and opened it for them. “Here we are in Dushanbe,” he said, pointing to a mountain-ringed dot in the southern part of Tajikistan. “And here is Kashgar.”

Liam and Carlotta leaned over to see its precise location and whether any roads connected it to Dushanbe. Liam looked up and stared at Chandahar in awe. “Kashgar is across the border in the Peoples’ Republic of China.”

“Yes, sir. Precisely. About four hundred miles to the east. Everything is for sale there. “To be rich is glorious. That’s the slogan they all live by in China these days.”

* * * * *

Outside the library, frustrated with the news that the curator had given them, they stopped to confer. “What do you think, Carlotta?”

“Kashgar is over four hundred miles from here and it’s in China, if you weren’t listening.”

“But there’s a market there for what we’re offering. We’ve got to give it a try. We’ve come all this distance. Three thousand miles, for God’s sake. What’s another four hundred?”

“I was sure that we’d track the gang to Dushanbe. I don’t know. I’ll have to talk it over with my brothers. You don’t just hop across the border into China the way Americans and Canadians just cross the border, you know.

“We have to be flexible. Marya’s kidnappers are going to be where the money and the gold are. And it ain’t here in this dirt-poor nation.”

“I just don’t understand. I was almost a hundred percent certain we’d find the buyer here in Tajikistan. I don’t think we should go to Kashgar. It doesn’t make sense.”

“You heard the man. We’re not going to find that buyer here. I’m for getting the hell out of here. Marya’s life is at stake. For me, it’s either take our chances in Kashgar or give up and go back to Venice.”

* * * * *

After leaving Liam and Carlotta, Ambrosio and Pietro trekked across town to Dushanbe's main bazaars, first the Barakat and, then, the Shamansur. At both bazaars they feasted royally on kebabs, rice and bread and bought some typical Tajik apparel: "jamas," knee-length jackets that tied at the waist. For three dollars and fifty cents they also bought skullcaps in a paisley design. Then they got some fine leather boots, paying a pittance for them. To a great deal of laughter by one wizened, toothless merchant, they also picked up two pale blue burkhas. Ducking into the vendors' tents, in a partitioned space, they changed immediately into new clothes and shed their western ones, cramming them into a travel bag.

On their way back to the hotel in the early afternoon, looking as if they had been born and raised in Dushanbe, they stopped at a *chaikhana*, a teahouse, and powered down more kebabs, bread, sweets and tea. They found their host convivial and accommodating. Indeed, the owner of the teahouse had never before seen the likes of men like Ambrosio and Pietro. Though they were infidels from the West, somehow they fit in like native sons. He and the other customers at the teahouse adopted them, singing together and eating lots of barbecued meat.

In fact, Pietro and Ambrosio got along so well with the locals at the teahouse that they even managed to make an important purchase. In a hush-hush backroom deal, Pietro handed over a large wad of euros for an AK-47 and stashed it away in the bag.

CHAPTER 54

Liam did a double take when he saw the Bellardo brothers entering the hotel. "What the heck are you guys up to? What have you got in those bags?" he asked them, but they just shrugged the Italian way and strode across the lobby to the elevator.

"Mr. Di Angelo, Mr. Di Angelo. You have a message," a teenaged desk clerk called to him across the lobby. He too, had wondered who the locals were and how they happened to know Liam and Carlotta. "There's a call for you from the operator of a jewelry shop here in Dushanbe."

"I'll take it here."

"No," said the clerk, "I can put the call through to your room."

He and Carlotta rushed to the elevator and caught up with the boys. All four of them barged into Liam's room. Liam picked up. "Hello? Yes? This is Mr. Di Angelo. Who am I speaking with? You have found a customer?"

There was a terrible pause. "How much?" Liam shouted. "You're crazy. We can't pay you that much just for finding a buyer. I offered you five thousand somoni morning. That's as far as I'll go."

Another pause ensued.

"Yes, yes, of course we are interested in talking with him." Liam held his hand over the receiver and told the Bellardos that one of the merchants they had visited in the morning had found a buyer. He said that the pieces we showed him were a perfect match for him. "That's the good news. The bad news is this merchant wants a piece of the action. Five-thousand somoni. That's a thousand dollars. He's off his rocker."

"Take it," Carlotta whispered. "I want that lead no matter what."

"All right. Five-thousand," he yelled into the phone

The Bellardos stood by mute, following every word.

"Fine. Okay. Yes. Come to my room at the Dushanbe Hotel. I'll have the cash for you. Yes, good-bye."

Liam hung up and turned to Carlotta. "It was that second goldsmith we visited this morning. Damn crook! He wants to make a killing."

A short while later, the goldsmith knocked. Carlotta went to the door and admitted the turbaned, hawk-nosed old man. He looked her up and down suspiciously and went straight to Liam.

"What have you got for us?" Liam demanded harshly.

The goldsmith handed him a slip of paper. "This. Now give me the money."

"Not so fast, pal. I need to see what you have here." Liam looked at the slip and almost cursed at the merchant. "What the hell is this? It's only a telephone number and some scribbling. And you want me to fork over five thousand somoni for this? Get the hell out of here before I have you strapped to a camel and dragged out to the desert."

"You don't need a name to do business with this man," the merchant said bitterly, baring yellowish-brown stumps for teeth. "No one knows his name."

"Do you know him personally, then?"

"Yes, quite well. A regular customer, but very demanding."

"What is that supposed to mean?"

"Just don't try to cheat him."

"We're the honest ones around here with money on the line."

The goldsmith's shifty eyes scanned the group. He made a grab for the money that Liam held in his hand but missed as Liam swiftly put his arm behind his back.

The evil-eyed merchant muttered something unintelligible. Liam stared him down. "Is there something wrong with this contact? Something you haven't told me? Out with it."

"Nothing. He'll do business with you if you don't anger him. If it turns out later that the price is too high for what he gets or if there's something wrong with the merchandise, he'll be angry."

"Naturally."

"Then he'll come after you and make an example of you to others," the old merchant hissed through his few remaining teeth. Some of my competitors are no longer with us, if you know what I mean."

Liam pocketed the slip and shoved the money at him. The goldsmith flew out the door holding on to his turban and disappeared.

Carlotta took the slip from Liam, read it and looked up at him with surprise written all over her face. "Did you see what's on this piece of paper, Liam? He's got a telephone number plus the name of a city. It's Kashgar."

* * * * *

Henderson had left for Washington not long after he heard the news of Bradwell's kidnapping, almost certainly by Kibchek' people. Cage thought that Henderson was more concerned about sharing intelligence with the Chinese to maintain good ties with them than with rescuing the hostage. Worse yet, if that intelligence were shared, it might lead to armed action that would put the hostage's life at risk. He preferred that the U. S. stay out of the mess, let the Chinese stew in their own juices and let national movements take their course in Central Asia. The U. S. simply could no longer afford to be the policeman on the beat for the whole world.

He knew that an army of lobbyists was mobilizing in

Washington to push for greater protections for American business interests and consortia doing business in western and central Asia. But he felt that Uncle Sam should let them bear the responsibility for their investment choices. All too often he had seen private enterprise come begging to Uncle Sam for help when times got tough. Celebrity CEOs had no problem with seeking help from Washington on the one hand while calling for downsizing big government on the other. It was a cozy relationship the government had with big business, whether the incumbent President was a Republican or Democrat. Many a government official quit to take a job or a cushy appointment to a corporate board or lobby firm, and vice versa. *The ever-spinning revolving door.* And money was what made it spin round and round, with the taxpayer shouldering the risks and private enterprise raking in the profits.

Now the lobbyists for oil fields in Asia were bellyaching about the exposure of their pipelines and refineries throughout the region. Some were even calling for the Defense Department to build military bases smack in the middle of the region. Cage was sick of the hypocrisy. Christ, he thought. It won't be long before they'll find an excuse to get us into a war in Afghanistan to clear the way for a pipeline to the Indian Ocean. Even though his work as an economic attaché was a mere cover for his real work with the CIA, he had seen a lot that disgusted him.

His phone rang. It was Henderson, wanting to know if he had anything new on Kibchek. The Chinese were frantically cleaning up after the bomb blast and sweeping the story of the decapitations under the rug. They had made overtures to the U.S. government to share knowledge with them about the possible perpetrators. Henderson told him that their suspicions centered on a mysterious figure operating somewhere in Central Asia but that he was as elusive as ever and they could not put a name tag on him yet. "It's a top priority issue for them. And the bigwigs above are putting pressure on me. What have you got for me? Anything?"

Cage was between a rock and a hard place. On the one hand, the terrorist attacks in China seemed to have the signature of Kibchek on them, judging from the man's history and the techniques he had seen him use against Russian and Chinese targets. But there was never any claim made owning up for the attacks and all that he had on Kibchek was circumstantial. Not enough to share with the Chinese as verifiable truth. Anyhow, he didn't necessarily want to help the Chinese in their predicament. He happened to have wholly different views from theirs about how to handle minority people in Central Asia, Tibet being one of his pet peeves.

"Wish I could help, Ron. I'm planning to make a trip to Tashkent in a couple of days. I might have more for you then. I do have a juicy tidbit for you, however. We have a fix on a foursome that just landed in Dushanbe from Italy. Three men and one woman. Antique dealers."

"Big deal. Is that all?"

"Well, guess who's with them."

"I give up. Who?"

"Our friend, Mr. Di Angelo."

CHAPTER 55

"If the buyer wants to do a deal with us, it's just impossible. The problem is we don't have the papers to get into China. And we don't have a rationale for working with someone so far from Tajikistan. I wish we knew this before leaving Venice. I didn't foresee this." Carlotta paced back and forth in the room. The boys said nothing yet.

"Well, what do you want to do? We can't just wait around here. I say we go for it—just fly into Kashgar and try our luck. Marya's life is at stake. Under the circumstances we have to improvise. You convinced me in Venice that the four of us could do this as a small, surgical team, Carlotta. That was supposed to be our advantage. Now it's me telling *you* that we've got to take that chance."

"Yes, yes. I know I did, but I've been thinking. What if the Chinese seize our plane? We don't have insurance coverage on it for this mission. We couldn't get any. And what if the Chinese lock us up for illegally entering the country? They can be tough bastards."

"Hey, come on. We know now that it's useless to remain here another day and we can't just turn tail and fly back to Italy empty-handed. Your father would be furious. I bet if he were here, he'd be willing to take his chances flying into Xinjiang province, with or without papers. We can deal with the officials when we get there. Maybe they can be bought off."

Carlotta stalled. She asked her brothers what they would do. She turned to Pietro who was lying down, one foot touching the floor and the other leg stretched out on the bed. "Do you agree with Liam and risk losing a million-dollar airplane for what might turn out to be a dead end?"

"Liam's right. We're here now and we've got a mission to accomplish. Father would want it no other way."

"And you, Ambrosio?"

He stopped the reps he was doing for his biceps with a Kalashnikov in each hand. "Let's go kick some butt. I'm ready for action."

"Hmmm. Not a very cogent argument but I hear you." Carlotta turned to Liam. She was anxious. "I don't like the choices, but I think you're right. We've got to take some action. Go ahead and give the buyer in Kashgar a call."

"Why don't I let you do that? You're still the team captain."

"It's a man's world out here. They don't deal with women."

Liam took the slip with the telephone number and dialed it. It rang four times before a suave voice with an educated English accent answered. "Who's calling?"

"I'm Ken Dalton, owner and CEO of DGE, Limited. That's Dalton Global Enterprises. A mutual friend gave me your number..." Adding to this lie, Liam went into a high-powered sales pitch about the artifacts that he was offering for sale. "I am told that you are interested in quality items like these."

The first thing out the target's mouth was, "Yes, we're very interested. I would like to see them."

"And you are....?"

There was a slight hesitation before the voice said, "Dr. Khalid Agarwal."

Liam was floored. He clearly remembered Marya telling him on the ferry from Venice that her closest colleague at Harvard was Khalid Agarwal. His saw the surprise on his own face in a mirror and struggled not to say anything that might tip the man off. He puzzled at how someone who had been so close to her could turn out as a prime suspect in her kidnapping. But he realized instantly that the team's efforts had paid off and they had smoked out a villain. He tried to remain focused on setting up a deal. "You said 'we,' Dr. Agarwal?"

"I am an agent…an adviser to…my client." Agarwal replied.

"My policy is to trade directly with the collector himself."

"But that will not be possible. Out of the question. I am authorized to make such purchases for him at my own discretion." Agarwal spoke with a tone of finality and Liam sweated over the right comeback. He had to push Agarwal to admit Carlotta into the heart of the organization, but not so hard that it would eliminate a deal. "I understand, Dr. Agarwal, but I've had bad experiences. It's my policy. My associate and I need to know who the actual customer we're dealing with is or there's no sale."

Agarwal paused before replying. "I will consider the possibility, but I make no promises. My client is a very busy man. He does not meet with salesmen. Why don't we meet in Kashgar and take matters from there?"

Liam wanted to reach through the line and throttle him. *The bastard. I bet he knows where Marya is right now. Slow down Di Angelo. Take it easy. We've got to get her out carefully.* Agarwal had stalled, but the door was slightly ajar. Liam suppressed his anger with a supreme effort and asked how he could contact him in Kashgar.

"Are you familiar with the city?" Agarwal asked.

"No. I've never been there."

"You can take a shuttle from the airport. Go to the hotel off the Id Kah Square, the Best Eastern."

Liam nodded at Carlotta and made the V sign with his fingers. "I have a problem, Dr. Agarwal. Right now we are in Tajikistan. We won't be able to enter China without papers. My associate and I had not planned on extending our visit from Dushanbe to Kashgar."

"You will have no trouble with the authorities at the airport. Call and let me know when you are settled in at the hotel."

Liam hung up and told the Bellardos what they were hoping to hear. "We've got our man, guys," he said triumphantly.

"Do you know that for sure?" Carlotta asked.

"Absolutely. This customer is a guy named Khalid Agarwal. I remember Marya talking about him. He's a colleague of hers at the university where she teaches."

"Then, you think that he is holding Marya captive in Kashgar."

"Yes, think about it. He works with her. He knows all about her research. In fact, Marya told me on the ferry to Korcula that she had spoken to him the morning we left Venice."

"Then, somehow he's the mastermind behind her kidnapping. It makes sense. He must have known about the golden tablets. Well, I may have been wrong about our destination but I was right about the strategy. "Yes, yes, yes. Whhoooeee." Carlotta kicked off her shoes and did a victory dance around the room before leaping upright on the bed, bouncing and punching the air with her right fist.

"One little problem, though, Carlotta."

That took the wind out of her sails. She stopped. "What?"

"He's only the agent. We don't yet have a promise from him to let you make that special sales pitch you wanted. I'll work on it, though."

She bounded off the bed and into his arms, throwing her legs around him, squeezing his buttocks. She kissed him on the lips, while Ambrosio and Pietro looked on disapprovingly. "Get me that invitation, Liam, and I'll find Marya for you. Then we can kick their butts."

* * * * *

They left Dushanbe the next morning. Bags packed, van loaded, they headed for the private jet revved up and ready for takeoff. They downed their coffee on the run. Soon after buckling up, they felt the jet turn to aim its sharp nose to the east and immediately accelerate, pushing them firmly back into their seats.

Liam felt his body urging the plane to pull up even more steeply. The jet rose at a sharp angle but still barely managed to clear the crests of the foothills. The snow-capped mountains rose all too quickly in their faces. The plane continued its steep trajectory, clawing for altitude. Sitting by the window, Liam looked down at the Pamirs, the Roof of the World, home of the yeti. Below, were the world's most dangerous roads. Burned out hulks of old trucks and cars, completely stripped, lay as rusting monuments to the chaos that followed the Soviet collapse.

His head throbbed with questions and worries. Why were the Golden Tablets so important that someone would go to the extreme of kidnapping? They had not even been located yet. Would it be as easy as Agarwal said for them to get through Chinese customs? Or would the authorities toss them all in a jail to rot? How did Marya go so wrong in trusting Agarwal? Who was Agarwal, really? What role did he play if any in kidnapping her? What about Marya? She must be going through hell. Could he pull off the deal? What if the plan failed and things turned ugly?

He wanted a gin and tonic but he feared that it would cloud his thinking, give him a headache or both. Instead, he leaned back in his seat and watched Ambrosio and Pietro. They seemed to be totally preoccupied with the packages of things they had bought in Dushanbe. They were a curious pair of young men. Inventive. Resourceful. He realized how much he was counting on them to pull the deal off and make up for his own glaring deficiencies in rescue ops.

He took another look at them. *What are they doing?*

By God, they're assembling Kalashnikovs. He decided it was not the time to nose around and ask dumb questions. As he watched, they stood up, each nonchalantly strapping on a Kalashnikov by a line connecting to a strong leather belt. The automatic weapons dangled between their legs and swung suggestively backwards and forwards as they walked about the cabin.

Pietro gathered up two long blue robes that looked like sheets or tents, one for himself and a much larger one for Ambrosio. Liam could not yet make up his mind what they were. All of a sudden Pietro slipped under the sheet and pulled it down so that its edges reached to the floor. *Burkhas!* He shimmied and loosened the robe, fluffing it out at the hips so that it sat loosely over his body. Pietro was now completely covered from head to toe, with only a small rectangular mesh where his eyes and nose would be. He instructed Ambrosio what to do to get himself rigged up the same way. Again they checked to see how the Kalashnikovs moved as they strolled down the aisle and turned about. On the surface of the robes, the butts of the guns seemed to leave a telltale bulge that they were not happy with.

Liam laughed. "You give new meaning to the term, 'hang loose,' guys. What are you up to?"

"Practicing. We'll get it right yet."

He did not have a clue as to what it exactly was they were practicing for, but their single-mindedness kept him distracted from his worries for over an hour.

* * * * *

Cage had met several times with Henderson over the Bradwell case and was deeply disturbed about it. He recalled his warning to Di Angelo to keep out of the way and let U.S. officials and agents do their work. Instead, Di Angelo was in Tajikistan. At least until now. What the hell for and where was he going this time, he wondered.

"Have you learned anything about team Di Angelo?" Henderson asked.

"I have a local guy on the payroll there who tells me Di Angelo skipped town

with the two men and the woman—took off this morning the way they arrived. In their own jet. That means that they won't be my concern any more. It's for our people in Beijing to handle."

"No way."

"Their plane was bound for Kashgar. I'd say by now that they've landed in the Peoples' Republic of China."

"Wonder why." Henderson mused, wiping some grains of sugar and strawberry jelly off his fingers.

"Damned if I know. But I'm glad for now, at least, that they're not in my jurisdiction."

CHAPTER 56

Two airport workers pushed a staircase on wheels up to the door of the jet. The door slid open, letting a large burkha-clad woman emerge first, followed by a smaller woman in the same kind of pale blue robe. The first woman swung a hulking leg on the staircase and descended slowly, ponderously, as if in pain and trying to be careful not to slip in the narrow, metal staircase. Carlotta was smartly dressed in western-style clothes and held a briefcase. Liam, in a dark blue business suit, carried a chest down the steps and paid just as much attention, mindful of the fragile diadem inside.

Liam tried to maintain his composure as the foursome lumbered across the tarmac from the plane to a severe, drab, gray-concrete building. He felt perspiration forming on his upper lip. If they made one trifling mistake passing through customs, he knew their plan would abort before it got started. The Chinese would haul his whole group off in shackles in spite of Agarwal's confident assurances on the phone. Officials would scream in their faces about violating Chinese air space and toss them into a cold, damp limbo for a few years. American and Italian embassy officials in Beijing would plead their cause, threaten sanctions, placate high ministers, but fail to win their freedom. They would waste away on a meager diet of rice and rancid, pickled vegetables. Marya's fate would also be sealed. He saw it all.

He entered the building trailing the three Bellardos. A no-nonsense Chinese official in a pea-green uniform bowed slightly and gestured with his hands to the section of the florescent-lit hall for foreign arrivals. As they approached a queue line marked off with black plastic poles and tapes, the slow pace of the group attracted three officers who came charging towards them, waving their hands and barking at them in Mandarin.

One of the officers, a slight man, looking like he weighed less than 120 pounds, was trying to make Ambrosio understand that he had to somehow reveal his face to compare with the passport photo. Ambrosio wailed in a high falsetto and waved his hands for the officers to back off. He was trying to make it clear that no inspector would sully the maidenly honor of an Afghan woman. It was an affront that would not be tolerated in any Islamic setting. "No, no, no!" he cried, backing up into Pietro. Pietro stumbled backwards but caught himself. Liam drew a deep gasp, just imagining what would have happened if he had fallen. One of the other officers started to tug at Ambrosio's head covering, searching for a way to open the facial mesh. But Ambrosio shoved him, letting out a high-pitched "Nooooo!" and sent him reeling backwards on the floor. The first officer drew his pistol and at the same time a piercing siren on a nearby wall began pealing out.

Carlotta turned to him, panic-stricken. "Quick, Liam. Do something. We've got to stop this. They're going to find the weapons. We're screwed."

He looked about the hall. Off to the left, on a second level, he spotted a glassed-in enclosure where three more officials stood looking down at the spectacle in horror. He waved to them. The door of the office opened and one of them came running down a flight of steps towards them, yelling at the customs men on the ground level. The brawl stopped immediately, with both sides in a glaring stand-off.

Liam was encouraged. He passed the chest to Carlotta and walked half-way towards the thirty-ish man from the office.

"May I see your passport?"

Liam handed it to him, impressed with the man's crisp

accent. He thought that like all other Asians who spoke good English, he must have attended UCLA.

"What seems to be the problem?"

"My business associate and I are here to trade a few articles. But it so happens that we also have two women in our party who have come to China for medical reasons. They have gynecological problems that—

"Excuse me. Guy problems? I do not understand."

"Female problems."

The man did not understand. Liam had to be more explicit. "Vagina. Ovaries. Tubes. Menstrual bleeding. Do you get it?" he asked, rubbing his abdomen.

"Maybe I should draw a picture for you."

"No need! No need! I see. Yes."

"They cannot be treated in their home country, for religious reasons. Male doctors are not allowed to examine or touch these women in those, uhhh, parts. The older lady is in great pain. She prevailed upon us to take them to China knowing they would receive good medical care. We had room. So, we decided to… "

"Be a good Samaritan." The official seemed proud of himself for knowing the biblical story and how to fit the word properly into English conversation.

"Yes, yes. That's right. The Bible tells us so. Look, we had no idea that it would be a problem in your glorious country."

"*Mei guanxi*."

"Beg your pardon?"

"It's no problem. It doesn't matter. I'll see to that." He snapped his fingers in the air and the three lower-ranking customs men came running. He rambled on loudly at them for two minutes and ended up with, "*Hun dan dongxi*! *Hun zhang wang ba dan*!" They reddened and lowered their faces. He barked out another order and a young, uniformed woman came hurrying over with an extra-wide wheel chair.

She looked at the gargantuan figure of the woman in blue, smiled and gestured to the wheel-chair. With the greatest caution, the blue whale settled into the chair and was wheeled off slowly through customs. Pietro, Carlotta and Liam passed through with no problems.

* * * * *

A shuttle van awaited them outside the front entrance of the airport. "The Best Eastern in Id Kah Square," Liam ordered. It bounced, shook and rattled across the rock-strewn dirt road from the airport to the fabled city on the Old Silk Road. Billowing clouds of dust followed them, as they whipped across the desert terrain.

In the back seat, the Bellardo brothers removed the burkhas and stashed them in a duffel bag. They were at the square in half an hour and checked into the hotel with no hitches.

Within minutes they met in Liam's room. The boys had stowed their weapons in such a way that room cleaners would never come across them. Carlotta had checked the chest to see if all was well and carried it into Liam's room.

"Whew. That was wild. I'm still in shock. We were lucky that the supervisor believed my story."

"Too lucky, if you ask me," Carlotta said. "Something's wrong. I can feel it. I'll feel so much better when this is over and done with." She put the chest on a table near one of the two windows that fronted on Id Kah Square.

"You think so? Well, if that scene at the airport was rigged for our benefit, someone in this country wants us badly and that's good."

"No, not so good, Liam." She was clearly still unnerved by the close call at the airport. "Where are the Kalashnikovs?" she asked her brothers.

"Safely hidden in our room," Pietro said.

"Good. Just don't go brandishing them around the square."

"Liam," she said. "Let's not waste time. Let's get to work. Call Agarwal."

Liam agreed. The sooner they were in and out of Kashgar the better. Hopefully with Marya in tow and all of them alive. He dialed and got Agarwal immediately. "Yes, who is this?"

"Ken Dalton. We're at the Best Eastern and we have the pieces here for your inspection. My associate, Miss Bellardo, will bring them to you. What's your address?"

"No. Wait there. I will come to your hotel room to inspect the goods. We'll see later about permission for you to bring them to my client. Will this afternoon be agreeable? "

"Fine. Miss Bellardo will be available to show you the items."

"But you are the owner of the business."

"My apologies, Dr. Agarwal, but I have already scheduled appointments with some other local merchants. I'll be out all afternoon. Miss Bellardo is quite competent to show you the articles. Come on over around 3:00 P.M."

"I'll be there. This had better be worth my trouble," he said and hung up.

Liam looked at the receiver. "Bastard. I don't like him. He's coming here this afternoon to see the goods. So, it's up to you. We'll be right next door in your brothers' room when he comes. Are you sure you can handle it on your own if he decides to let you see his so-called client?

"I'm sure."

Liam looked at her and again could not help being blown away by her innocent face. He hoped that she would do a good job presenting the articles to Agarwal and that she would get an address and an invitation from him, but the fear gripped him that if she succeeded she would be going straight into the lion's den. He drew a deep, anxious breath and said, "This had better work."

Hundreds of miles east of Tajikistan, in a border city of Xinjiang province in the People's Republic of China, Liam was beginning to feel like an astronaut at the end of a tether attached to an orbiting space station. How the hell did all this happen? He was supposed to be leaving Venice, heading back to Massachusetts and Melissa, a fat profit guaranteed for his latest deal with Bellardo. He had planned to pick up some bauble to pacify her. He no longer felt that way. His bank account seemed to matter less and less, and so did Melissa. She had all but vanished from his thoughts.

He watched Carlotta lift the glorious Scythian articles delicately out of the carved chest and he prayed that she would hook Agarwal on them and gain access to his boss. Marya's life depended it.

CHAPTER 57

Shortly before noon, Ambrosio and Pietro left the hotel and strolled across Id Kah Square towards an imposing yellow brick mosque. Its four minarets, one on each corner, flanked an enormous central dome. On the far right there was a tall gate tower, originally meant to accommodate the imam who called the faithful to prayer, but it was now equipped with loudspeakers.

They headed for the main entrance. On either side were round brick columns that rose 18 meters, half-embedded in the facade. Intricately designed blue tiles of intertwining floral patterns and Islamic prayers covered the walls of the entrance. Inside, the gardens and flowing fountains contrasted with the dust and noise of the square.

In the courtyard they came upon a small English-language sign provided for tourists: the largest mosque in all of China. 140 meters from north to south and 120 meters east to west, the mosque could easily accommodate ten thousand worshippers and could find room for up to twice that many if necessary. The mosque was now empty, except for a few elderly men sweeping the courtyard. Tomorrow would be a different matter. Thousands of men, arranged in long rows, facing west to Mecca, would come to pray under the leadership of the First Mullah.

They left the mosque, strolling in the direction of the bazaar. A few local merchants were already trickling into the square ahead of the tens of thousands expected early the next morning. Throngs would jam into the square coming from the surrounding countryside and faraway lands. This afternoon, it only remained for the Bellardo brothers to buy a truck they would park in one of the alleyways off the main square. Within two hours, they had finished the job and returned to the hotel to work out a strategic plan with Liam while Carlotta prepared for the meeting with Agarwal.

* * * * *

A call from the desk told her that her prospective customer had arrived. She told the clerk to send him up. She was at the door when he knocked. She thought he was attractive with his dark beard and mustache contrasting with his graying hair, but his wary eyes darting left and right behind rimless eyeglasses made her nervous. What was this Indian doing in the trackless wastes of China's west and who would he be working for, she wondered.

She was impeccably dressed for her performance and wore a cartload of rings and bracelets. She introduced herself as Mr. Dalton's business associate and directed him towards the table by the window. Agarwal brushed past her without a word. She had carefully arranged her father's precious artifacts on the table beneath black silk cloths and came alongside him to draw two of the cloths back quickly. "These come from a very important royal grave west of the Caspian Sea."

Agarwal's eyes gleamed at the sight and asked if he could handle them. Carlotta simply nodded.

He took the gold crested helmet decorated with inset precious stones in both hands and raised it towards the ceiling. "Gorgeous. Just gorgeous. The Khan will appreciate this," he mumbled.

Carlotta noted his use of the word "khan." It was the first inkling she had that Agarwal was buying for someone of noble rank. She gave him another minute to finish examining the helmet and then carefully passed him a gold fibula, an article used for fastening robes. Twelve inches in diameter and decorated with five winged lions, a great man like Julius Caesar could have worn it. "What do you think of it?"

He took it in his hands. "Remarkable. We have a place

for this as well. Why can't we conclude our business here? I find the pieces worthy of my client. Come, state your price."

"No. My business associate and I have had a policy for a long time. We do not sell without first seeing our client. I must present these articles to the customer in person."

Agarwal balked. "I am authorized by the Khan to make these purchases. He is too busy to handle such trivial matters."

"I understand, but that is not the point, Dr. Agarwal. Mr. Dalton discussed this matter with you already. It is our policy to deal with the collector of these antiquities directly. We need to be assured that this man, this khan of yours, is a bona fide collector. You can understand our position."

"No. Impossible. He's busy and he is a very private individual."

"Then, you are wasting our time as well as your own. This is really very annoying. Why did you lead Mr. Dalton to believe that we would deal directly with him?" She played the tune like a broken record while Agarwal vacillated, staring at the goods on the table. "We wouldn't have bothered to come all this way," she said with a frown.

"The Khan is a very busy man. He leaves it to my discretion to purchase what I see fit to build the collection. If only..."

"Sorry. I cannot proceed with the sale under these conditions." She drew the silk coverings over the two pieces she had shown him, shaking her head. Inwardly, she feared the sale was in jeopardy. Then, she reached for the silk veil covering the third item on the table. "It's a pity that your khan will not see these items, and especially this one. He would really have liked this last piece—definitely something for the most discriminating collector." She lifted the veil, revealing the last and most exquisite of the ancient gold artifacts.

Agarwal held his breath as Carlotta slowly raised

a gold diadem with both hands. Fine veins in the leaves revealed the consummate skill of the artisan. Each leaf was of perfect pinnate shape artfully placed on the crown to create an effect of majesty. She held it up in front of his face and he stood there marveling at it. Carlotta sized up Agarwal's response to it and sensed that she had him.

"Fit for an empress, Miss Bellardo. I am satisfied with what you have shown me. The Khan must have all three of these. Where's the phone? There might be a chance to get you in to see him for a very brief audience."

She showed him where the phone was in the entry way then turned away, crossing her fingers. He spoke quietly into the phone, but Carlotta still heard part of the exchange. He noticed her listening and his voice trailed off to a near whisper.

He hung up. "The Khan graciously permits you to come to his residence. He said that he will send a car with a driver to pick you up. Be ready to leave at eight o'clock tomorrow morning."

"Fine," said Carlotta, leading him to the door. "I'll be waiting."

She closed the door behind him, leaning her back against it, and let out a long sigh. She hammered on the wall with her fist three times and then went to the window. Agarwal's black Mercedes limousine blew out of the square, leaving dust in its wake. Liam and her brothers came racing in, asking how the show had gone.

"I'm in," she said, still a bit nervous. She sat down on the bed, fanning her face with her hand and told them how she had come close to losing his interest in the pieces.

They asked what he was like and she described him as an upper crust kind of guy, classy, well-educated. From India. But shifty. "I don't like him one iota. He's slimy and he gives me the creeps."

"Think you can pull this off, Carlotta?"

"I've got to. For Marya's sake."

"Any idea who his client is? Did he say who he's buying for?"

"Not directly, but he did say something like, 'this is for the Khan, the Khan would like that,' and so on, whoever the khan is."

"That's weird. He's buying for a khan? The khan of what? "

"I know. Can you believe that? Here in the People's Republic of China? I don't think the Chinese government would like the idea of sharing the country with a khan."

"Evidently, they're not aware of it. Would be interesting to see how they would handle him. So, how do you get to his place? If he's a khan, he must live in some kind of a palace."

"I don't know where it is exactly. He didn't say. He only told me that the Khan is sending a car to pick me up tomorrow at 8:00 A.M. You should have seen Agarwal's car. A high-end Mercedes. Looks like I'll be getting the royal deluxe treatment."

"This looks way too risky," said Ambrosio. "I'm not sure that Papa is okay with you going off to some unknown rendezvous alone. We've never had this kind of experience before—not being able to back you up."

"Bunch of psychos, if you ask me. I'm worried about this, too, Carlotta." Pietro folded his arms on his chest. "At the very least, we've got to be able to follow you to see where they're taking you."

"No, you can't do that. What if they take me somewhere outside the city? Look at this country. It's wide open. It's not like driving around Rome. If you tried to follow me, I'd end up dead. You guys, please, just stay out of sight. You'll have your chance soon enough, once my part is done."

* * * * *

Just before 8:00 A.M. the following morning, a large black Mercedes appeared at the front entrance of the Best Eastern Hotel of Kashgar. A driver came into the lobby. Carlotta rose from an overstuffed chair, waved to him and had him bring the chest to the car. Liam and the boys watched from his hotel window and saw her exchange a few words with the driver before they drove off.

"This is it," he said.

CHAPTER 58

The summer sun had risen to its highest point in the cloudless sky and temperatures in the high nineties were heating all the rooms of the mud compound like a brick oven, all except the Khan's throne room, private quarters and important conference rooms. In those rooms air conditioning was installed, powered by underground generators.

Lying on her cot in a corner of her cell, Marya sweltered and lay staring at the ceiling. She felt clammy, her whole body covered in sweat and her clothes sticking to her upper body. Her jailers had provided an enamel basin of water, a bar of soap and two washcloths but no change of clothes. The confinement of three days...or was it four?...had put an end to her fastidiousness and had nearly wiped out her usual patterns of thinking. She saw herself strolling on a northern California beach, with waves crashing and pelicans gliding smoothly over the waves. She saw sandpipers race across the sand, stopping here and there to probe the shoreline at the foot of towering cliffs. She let the cool misty fog roll in and soothe her.

A metallic click of a key working on the lock of her door startled her. It swung open and Agarwal appeared in the doorway. He stood silent for a moment in the doorway, observing her as an entomologist would look at a pinned butterfly. She returned the look and then went back to staring at the ceiling.

"Leave me alone."

"The Khan is asking about you."

"That's very kind of him."

"He's not concerned for your well-being. He wants to know if you want to keep your skin."

"You may as well take a knife to me and get it over with right now. I don't care any more what you do to me. Your so-called Khan is a very sick man and so are you."

"That attitude will only get you deeper in trouble."

She looked at him vacantly. "Doesn't matter. What do you call this? I don't exactly feel like I'm sitting on top of the world right now."

"We can make it worse."

"I know," she said, rubbing the sore on her lips where Agarwal had smacked her. She also knew that by keeping up with the right remarks she could probably provoke him into killing her in an instant.

"I have sent our agents to get the journal from your boarding house in Korcula."

"Want me to write you a thank you note for that?"

"When the journal gets here, I will give you a chance to redeem yourself. You know, it's not too late, Marya. You could still win your freedom. I'm sorry I was a little rough with you."

She looked at him, blinked and then lay back down. Then she rolled completely on her side to face the wall. She wanted him to go away. She wanted it all to end, even if it meant her death. This was not a life. It wasn't even an existence. There was no way to escape from this hell-hole and the insanity except by summoning cherished memories of the country she grew up in. And by concentrating on the face of Liam Di Angelo.

* * * * *

"Is this it ?" Carlotta asked the driver in English. He grunted in the affirmative. He motioned for her to get out while he went to the trunk and got the chest. She stepped out of the car in her stiletto heels in front of a low, mud and wattle building that was dun-colored like the sands and rocky detritus of the surrounding hills and canyons.

Her heart sank as she looked at the shabby exterior. She had been expecting a rambling mansion, if not a palace, for some kind of khan. Agarwal had lied to her, she thought. This dump was a place only a goatherd or camel driver would have inhabited and only seasonally, at that. She would have easily driven past it without a second look.

But there were two things odd about the structure. It was sprawling and the grounds about it were patrolled by men who were wearing turbans and toting machine guns. There must be something inside worth this kind of security, she figured. She was still doubtful. *Well, let's give it a go anyhow.*

She followed the driver along a rock-strewn path to the entrance, stumbled on the rough surface and barely avoided spraining her ankle just in front of the steps. The driver led her to a massive, weather-beaten front door and kicked at it twice. A uniformed soldier opened it and the driver stood aside letting her enter first. One peek inside at the foyer and she gasped. It was palatial, exquisite: tiled in black and white marble and lit by crystal wall sconces. Her spirits immediately rose. A male servant dressed in white linen was busy dusting a marble table above which hung a genuine Sung dynasty shan shui scroll painting. Life-sized sculptures lined a long, broad hallway that brought the eye to an illuminated alcove at the far end. Its recessed lighting illuminated the statue of a military figure wearing an ancient kind of armor. Altogether, the effect of the décor was very impressive and pleasant even though its theme celebrated a warrior class.

She must have been wrong about Agarwal. But why did this palatial residence have such an ugly, totally deceptive exterior? No self-respecting khan would put up with the impression of wretched, grinding poverty that it gave a visitor. It puzzled her that someone who could afford the treasures she came to sell could easily have thrown at least a few dollars into an effort to dress up the grounds in front. She heard a voice behind her telling the driver to give him the chest. She turned. It was Khalid Agarwal, dressed in a brocaded, Nehru-style jacket and dark slacks. "Follow me," he ordered.

"When do I get to see the Khan?"

"Not now. You'll have to wait. He's conferring with his military advisers. Come with me. I take it you brought the same pieces that I examined yesterday?"

"Yes."

"I'm going to verify."

"Whatever. What am I supposed to do in the meantime?"

"It should not be long. After I check the merchandise, I might take you on a tour, if you behave. Incidentally, during the audience with the Khan, you are to conduct yourself professionally and state your business as briefly as possible with him, do you understand?"

"Got it." She got the clear impression that he hadn't wanted her to come and that if it had to be, the visit should be as brief as possible.

"Also, you must address the Khan as 'Excellency.'"

"Anything else?"

"Yes. When you are first presented, bow down to him from the waist."

"What? You expect me to bow to him?"

Agarwal wheeled about suddenly and stood facing her. "I've had enough of you, Ms. Bellardo. It took some persuading to allow you to get in to see the Khan. You will agree to obey protocol or I'll march you right back to the car and send you back to Kashgar. Just go and try to peddle your trifles there and see where it gets you."

She nodded and followed him down the hallway, through several turns, deep into the heart of the compound, then down to another floor below ground level. Her apprehension grew as she saw more signs that this installation was more than a residence. It was a multi-storied armed camp in disguise, constructed at great cost. Along the way, they passed more armed men at every turn and workers moving loads of materiel into storerooms. What potentate lived here and why? Surely the Chinese authorities wouldn't tolerate such a violation of their territorial integrity.

She reminded herself that she should just keep her mouth shut and her eyes open. She was here first and foremost to try to pick up any clue she could about Marya. So far, she had seen nothing to suggest that she was on the premises.

As she followed Agarwal farther along an interminable corridor, she never before felt so alone on a mission. Pietro and Ambrosio were right. She had placed herself in danger and now there was no going back. With each step, it was like going farther and farther out on a high wire with no net.

CHAPTER 59

Her misgivings about her situation deepened as she followed Agarwal striding ahead so confidently along the dimly lit passageway. The rapid clicking of her high heels echoed off the stone-lined walls, making her feel more and more vulnerable. They passed two pairs of armed guards posted at different doorways and a fear crept upon her. If he wanted the pieces at this moment with no further trouble from her, he could easily order the guards to take her out and shoot her.

Suddenly he turned to his right into a kind of antechamber furnished with only a single table. He placed the chest on the table and without speaking to her, opened it and carefully inspected each of the articles. "Yes. Perfect. The Khan will be pleased. Come with me. We have some time left before the audience with the Khan in the throne room. There is something I want you to see." He crossed the antechamber, fiddled with his keys at a steel door and put his shoulders to it. "Take a look," he said, flipping a switch that lit up a huge hall.

The sight completely dazzled her. She felt as if she were stepping into a storybook cavern heaped with treasure. All about were piles of art objects and treasure representing all the major Asian traditions. Her attention went directly to a heavy gold collar with figures of a lion bringing down a stag. Its monstrously oversized rack of antlers was typical of the art of the Asian steppe, from the Caspian Sea to Mongolia.

"This is Scythian," she said, very impressed.

"Yes. You seem to be very familiar with the style."

"We do a brisk business in Scythian art. There's a growing demand for it lately."

"The Khan favors this style. The others, just so-so. We recently acquired two solid gold helmets and scabbards done by Scythian craftsmen in the 5th century B.C." He turned and waved a limp hand at the heaps of wealth almost carelessly piled about the room. "What you see in this hall is only a fraction of the total. The rest is off-site, for security purposes."

He crossed the hall with her and pointed out a pile of miscellaneous objects of vastly different styles. There seemed no end to the variety of wealth displayed in the hall. What fortune had the Khan conjured out of the desert sands to afford such a collection she wondered? Grandiose didn't begin to describe it. How sad that it was not available for multitudes to enjoy instead of being hoarded in a remote and scruffy wilderness.

Returning towards the door, she saw a platform upon which stood a life-sized figure of a Han dynasty army commander in full battle regalia, a warrior leader—maybe Qin Shi Huang Di, the founder of the first dynasty to unite all of China. Carlotta wondered what ambitions this Khan himself harbored. And why here, in this place that looked so ramshackle from the outside? She puzzled, too, over the cosmopolitan character of the collection. "Why are treasures of the Middle East here alongside Central and East Asian objects?" she asked.

"Don't you realize that the Middle East and parts of the Mediterranean were once part of the Mongol Empire along with Central and East Asia, my dear girl? There is nothing out of place in this collection. Who knows? Perhaps someday, all the nations from Turkey to the open plains of Mongolia and Manchuria may find common cause again. Look at this assemblage of fine Tang figurines from western China. Two grooms, a Turkish merchant and three Bactrian camels. You can see by his big nose that the merchant is Turkic. He's not Han Chinese. The camels look lifelike, don't you agree? The Bactrian camel is still common in Uyghurstan even today."

Years earlier she had seen a gorgeous group of figures just like it at the Ashmolean Museum in Oxford and had been transfixed by the bright yellow, green and brown glazes, in sharp contrast to the other ceramics of the collection. She had not known that Turkic people were so widely scattered across Asia. "I'm a bit puzzled. You mentioned Uyghurstan. I'm familiar with the people but not with the place."

"You soon will be. There are ten million Uyghurs living in this part of China today. They long to be reunited with their brothers in the Central Asian Republics and to be included in an independent homeland of their own."

"But this is Xinjiang Province, part of the People's Republic of China. Surely the Chinese will not allow that," she said disingenuously.

"True. The Chinese are now pouring into Xinjiang in large numbers. But, originally, this was—and still is—the homeland of the Uyghur people. The Chinese goal has been to make them a minority in their own land. The Khan has plans to reverse this intrusion."

"I see," she said without conviction, but deeply shocked.

They moved on to what she regarded as one of the most stunning and dramatic pieces she had yet seen: a bronze statuette of a flying horse, of the second century, one of its hooves resting on a bird in flight. She could almost hear the beast's finely cast hooves rhythmically striking the ground. The erect ears and the flourish of its tail gave the impression of rapid flight through the sky. "We have dozens of other bronzes such as this one stored at another location," Agarwal boasted.

She realized then that the collection that filled this vast chamber not only would do honor to the khan she was about to meet. It would also reduce the rest of the world's remaining royalty to groveling jealousy. Strolling amid the tables loaded with treasure, she had difficulty believing that this was only a minor part of the Khan's private wealth.

Agarwal looked at his wristwatch. "We must move along."

They headed for the door, but she halted before another dramatic piece. "What is this?" she asked, pointing to the wall.

She saw a faraway look in his eyes as he gazed at it. It was a stupendous frame sculpted in pure ivory with intertwining dragons soaring in flight.

"What are those indentations? What is this supposed to represent? It looks unfinished."

Agarwal crossed his arms. "You're right. It's incomplete. The spaces you see there are reserved for the crown jewels of the collection, so to speak. We expect to have our hands on them soon."

"Well, Dr. Agarwal, you've aroused my curiosity. Please tell me all about them," she said teasingly.

"In this frame," he said, raising his head, "we will display seven plaques of solid gold. They are tablets inscribed with commands of Kublai Khan himself—he gave them to the Polos, but we intend to get them back. We have a consultant working on it now, an American woman from...."

"Where?"

"From Bob Jones University," he answered after an awkward pause.

"Great. How marvelous," she said, struggling to control the incredible turmoil and excitement she felt inside. She saw through his ruse and realized in an instant that Agarwal had confirmed her suspicions. Marya was somewhere on the premises and very much alive. If she had her Glock with her she would have put him out of his misery on the spot. She wanted to call her brothers and... But she needed to remain disciplined and focused. "Why are the gold plaques so important to your Khan?" she asked.

"That should be obvious to an antiquities dealer like you. They were perfect symbols of the Khan's authority over the largest land empire that ever existed. As passports, they worked well for the Polos and, properly exhibited, they will be perfect symbols of the Khan's rising status. I'm not free to say more at this time. It's what I would call a matter of state."

As he rhapsodized about his khan, Carlotta almost heaved. She hated him for the greasy sycophant he was and what his gang had done to Marya, to her and to others in her family. *Wait until you get a taste of my status, too, you fool.*

CHAPTER 60

Liam found the Bellardo brothers lazing in their room. "Okay, gentlemen, let's go down to the square and run Carlotta's and your plan through its paces."

They were bored with being cooped up and very edgy since Carlotta had taken off in the morning. They eagerly took up his idea. Walking through the square, they came upon the first clusters of country folks bringing in their wares for the weekend bazaar. The truck that the Bellardo boys planned to use was still parked in the alley. It started up easily. They figured down to the second how much time it took to get from the expected point of exchange to the alleyway. They looked into several of the stalls on both corners of the alleyway for anything that might either become a problem or be put to good advantage in case things really started to go wrong. Considering Carlotta's description of Agarwal it was only common sense to expect some kind of ambush or doublecross from him.

Standing at the corner of the alley, looking across the Square at the huge mosque, Liam wondered where Carlotta was at this moment. He had agreed with the boys that she was putting her life on the line, going off alone with the driver to an undisclosed location. What was he thinking letting her go this morning? He glanced at his watch. By now, she should have made her presentation to the client and be on her way back. He felt sorry for the Bellardo brothers as he watched them scouting about this end of the Square. They had endured so much. He saw by the deadly serious expressions on their faces that they were deeply worried.

And what about Marya? His feelings towards her had changed immensely in little over a week. She had entered his life as an annoyance but somewhere along the line she had become the reason he had flown halfway around the world to Kashgar, ancient city of the old Silk Road. And he had changed, too, he was beginning to realize. From profiteering business man and underhanded dealer in antiquities to some mutant James Bond figure about to execute a very dangerous exchange for an imperiled hostage. How did this all happen? He shook his head in disbelief at how fast the changes had overtaken him.

Where is Carlotta? Will she have news about Marya? Good news?

* * * * *

An aide came to tell Dr. Agarwal that the Khan wanted them in the audience hall. Agarwal took the opportunity to lecture Carlotta on etiquette again as he closed and locked the door of the hall. "When I present you to the Khan, remember what I told you. You are fortunate that he has granted you permission to see him. Just keep it short and sweet."

Yeah, yeah, yeah. And you, Dr. Agarwal, will be fortunate if I don't kick your ass today. It galled her to have to listen to his prating when she knew that with her karate skills she could easily disable him. She felt that she had scored a victory, though, just learning that Marya was being held captive, probably not far from the treasure chamber that housed the magnificent ivory frame. And she would hopefully score one more victory before leaving today by delivering Agarwal and his ambitious Khan a big surprise. She kept silent and let Agarwal lead the way to the audience hall.

Armed guards in medieval costume straightened their long-handled pikes and let them pass into the reception hall. Her appearance at the door, one hundred feet from the throne had a visible effect on the khan. She saw him straighten up, swipe his hand across his crew cut hair and pull both sides of his sheepskin-lined leather vest across his middle-aged paunch. As she approached the throne by Agarwal's side, she knew that her choice of shoes, gold earrings and hair style were working on the khan. Agarwal stopped and made a restraining touch on her forearm. She stood still and took in the sight of the khan. He sat with his elbow on one armrest of a peacock throne studded with rubies, diamonds and sapphires, its stylized tail feathers flaring outward in a semi-circle radius of five feet. His wardrobe needed upgrading, she thought. He looked like he was trying to blend the look of some post-apocalyptic warlord with that of the current president of Afghanistan. Three traditionally garbed soldiers stood at attention on either side of the throne. A number of white bearded sages stood by gaping at her and a young man stepped forward on her left. "I will interpret for you," he whispered. "Be not afraid. You've been told what to do?"

"Yes. I'm to bow and all that nonsense."

"It's not nonsense. If you make a mistake, you will be punished."

Suddenly she heard Agarwal intone something in a guttural language she took to be some Turkic dialect. The translator whispered to her, "He said, 'By the power of Eternal Heaven, all respect to the name of the Khan, Temujin the Second.'"

"Step forward, Ms. Bellardo, and bow to the Khan."

She did as she was told. When her eyes moved from the khan's boots up to his chest and face she was startled. The pupils of the man's eyes were large and jet black. He was staring at her up and down. She felt him disrobing her with that look. Nervously, she looked away from him to Agarwal and to the translator but still felt his eyes all over her, making her feel icy within. His was the coldest stare and the cruelest mouth she had ever seen on a human face.

Agarwal spoke to the khan briefly. Then, he opened the chest that Carlotta had brought to the compound. Her moment had come: this was the outward reason for her visit to Agarwal's client—to make a direct sales pitch. She had yet to deliver the surprise which was at the heart of her strategy. She felt rattled and her mouth went dry but she screwed up her courage and bided her time. She let Agarwal remove the three precious articles from the chest to show to the khan.

First, Agarwal removed the Scythian gold helmet from the folds of cloth. The khan nodded his approval. Then, the pectoral. It impressed him even more. He actually rose from the throne, descended the three-tiered platform and strode to a floor-to-ceiling, gold-framed mirror, spending more than a minute pressing the pectoral against his chest. He strutted back and forth posing with it and returned to the throne spouting some gibberish back and forth with Agarwal. Carlotta knew that she had scored two hits. How would he react to the next item? When Agarwal revealed the gold diadem, the khan made a loud exclamation. Agarwal handed it to him and stepped backwards and down the three steps. The khan rose and his voice thundered. He pointed to Carlotta.

She was confused and looked to Agarwal for direction. "What does he want?"

"He says kneel on the second step." She obeyed, dumbfounded. The scene was not unfolding the way she had imagined. She wanted an opportunity to spring the surprise on them that she had carefully rehearsed. She wanted a chance to tell the khan how he could have something of far greater value than any of the objects that she had brought today: the secret diary of Marco Polo. It didn't look like she was going to get it.

The Khan gave her a piercing look. She hesitated but took a step forward. Two more steps and she was kneeling before him. She saw him raise the diadem and place it directly over her head. She felt it being gently lowered. The golden laurel leaf wreath fit perfectly about her brow and the pendants dangled about her cheeks and ears. Gold seemed to rain down all about her. She could not believe this was happening to her.

She felt transformed, as if the impromptu coronation had made her an empress of Rome or Constantinople. She had once seen a photo of a similar diadem on the head of a German archaeologist's wife and now she understood why the woman had begged her husband to let her model the ancient treasure.

Afraid to move, she heard the Khan bellow something to Agarwal. "What's he saying now?"

"He said that I am to prepare you for the harem, but first he wants you to take a seat beside him."

Her head swiveled to the Khan again and she saw the cruel twist of his mouth. This time, though, it rounded into a smile. Her mind went blank and she felt an icy fear in her entrails. Things had taken an ugly and totally unexpected turn. Becoming one of the khan's wives was not part of her carefully constructed plan.

CHAPTER 61

Over seven hours had passed since they watched Carlotta leave in the chauffeured Mercedes. They had finished scoping out the Square and rehearsing the scenario the way they wanted it to play out and then returned to Liam's room.

It was getting late. Where was she? Liam gazed out the window at the Id Kah mosque, aware of an increase in animal-drawn carts, cars and people. He hoped that the plans he and the Bellardo boys had developed would be foolproof. All depended on Carlotta's safe return and the information she brought back to them. If anything went wrong, they might never find Marya. He turned away from the window and joined the Bellardo boys at a table where they were poring over a hand-drawn map.

Ambrosio spoke first. "I'm worried about Carlotta."

"I am, too. But I know she's coming back. She's factored into everything we're planning. Are you satisfied that we're ready for the exchange tomorrow?"

"Yes. We've chosen the best spots to make the exchange and to escape from the Square." Ambrosio's thick finger jabbed a point on the map in the open square and another at a corner opposite the mosque. "I see no better place for a fast escape."

"Good. You happy with the truck?"

"Yes. It starts. And it runs."

"And you, Pietro? How's the leg? Are you okay with this?"

"No problem."

"Can we run through how it will all work, from the beginning, one more time?" Ambrosio asked.

Liam chalked the request up to compulsive behavior

on Ambrosio's part, a way of gaining some sense of empowerment over events that could easily spin out of control. Or maybe it was simply good practice, given the nature of their work with the shadowy underworld of dealing in antiquities. Then again, maybe Ambrosio just had to keep his mind off the danger his sister was in. Whatever it was, Liam was glad to go over the plan from the beginning with them again. He pointed out how he and Carlotta would leave the hotel together while the two boys took up their positions at the designated corner at the height of market activity. He would meet Agarwal and Marya in the open in the middle of the square, take Marya's hand and give Agarwal the journal. Then he and Marya would bolt to the alleyway and jump in the truck to head out to the airport. Carlotta would have already jumped into the rear of the truck and taken up her position while the boys had the truck revved up and ready to go, providing defensive coverage at any point necessary up to that point in time.

"We will hand over the journal here." Liam put his finger on a spot in the square about fifteen yards from where Ambrosio and Pietro had their positions. "But only if they bring her out into the open. With the crowds and the Chinese police circulating all around us, there's less chance of any monkey business."

"What's that, signore?"

"Monkey business. You know... trouble... other men with guns, working for Agarwal. That kind of thing. Once we make the exchange, we've got to get the hell out of there, with you two covering us. You gotta have the truck running and be ready to pull out right away, okay, Pietro?"

"Understood."

"Time to kick buttocks," Ambrosio said, appearing more satisfied. "Isn't that how you say it in English?"

"Close enough." Liam could not imagine he was orchestrating this scene. International intrigue had not been in his repertoire, not until now. Where was the CIA when you needed them? Why wasn't Cage or Henderson here instead of him? But he knew the answer to that already. Probably sitting on their thumbs or shuffling papers at their desks. He was doing this for Marya and he was grateful that he had the Bellardos with him. Their years of experience in the field gave him the nerve he needed to pull off this coup.

"I'm curious, you guys."

"Yes?" Pietro asked.

"Do you have a problem letting your little sister call the shots so much of the time?"

"No, not really. She has a talent for it. We have our own set of skills. We make a good team. How about you?"

Liam was taken aback. "Well, I guess, yes. I do....or did have a problem with her taking the lead. My image of her was different. I thought she would be more into perfume, makeup and romance—all the frilly stuff—and leave this macho business of rescuing Marya to us men."

"Not to worry."

"Huh?"

"When she gets back, that should be the end of the first phase of this operation. You're taking over from there and we're counting on you. You better have what it takes."

* * * * *

The Khan's words had shaken Carlotta to the core, but she realized instinctively that this was the moment to make her move. Time was running out. She ached for the chance to win Marya's release and get her revenge on these monsters.

But the first order of business was to keep her distance from the amorous Khan. That wouldn't be easy from the look on his face. He pointed to the smaller, winged throne one level lower than his. Marya asked Agarwal what to do and she caught a very worried look on his face. "He wants you to take a seat in that throne next to him. So, go on. You can play Queen for a Day, like all the others."

She sat down warily only halfway on the throne, keeping her eyes on the Khan. Slowly, she removed the diadem from her head and gently cradled it in her lap, hoping he would not go ballistic. She started to speak, but the khan silenced her with a dismissive wave of the hand and called Agarwal forward to translate what she just said.

Agarwal looked uneasily at the Khan as he translated. "She said, 'Khan, you do me a great honor, but I am not prepared for this. I must have time, Excellency. I have come here prepared only to sell you my humble wares.'"

"You will be my wife," Agarwal translated for the Khan.

"That would be so lovely," she said through a cheesy smile. She eased herself fully onto the winged throne. "I promise that I will someday be your wife. But I have something of great importance to tell you first. Your advisor, Dr. Agarwal, has spoken to me of your interest in the Golden Tablets of Command. I think I can help you."

The khan looked at Agarwal with a blank expression and caught him hesitating to translate. He immediately called for his young translator to stand by. Agarwal got the message immediately. If he distorted what Carlotta had to say in any manner, the khan would know of it and his head would be on the chopping block. As Agarwal translated accurately, the Khan's expression went from mild interest to outright rage. He looked at Carlotta, bewildered, then at Agarwal, furious. He shouted at Agarwal in his harsh tongue. Agarwal had been stupid to tell her about the plans for the golden tablets and, now, he saw her smirking at his predicament.

With hardly a second for her to defend herself, Agarwal came up and grabbed her by the arm to haul her out of the Khan's presence. He wrenched her to her feet, sending the diadem crashing on the steps. She lurched to avoid it, but with Agarwal throwing her off balance, her right foot came down on the crown, crushing the leaves and snagging the pendants with the high heel on her right foot. She was hobbled and could barely keep her balance. She staggered down two steps dragging the diadem. At the bottom she kicked off both her shoes and finally steadied herself.

The Khan stood up and roared at Agarwal. Red-faced, Agarwal whirled around, still holding tight to Carlotta. He addressed the Khan, making accusations that she could not understand but that, she was sure, were hostile. One thing she did understand was that she needed to make a bold move immediately or she would find herself locked up in a harem, spending the rest of her days playing tiddly winks and pinochle with bald-headed eunuchs. Not good. She threw off Agarwal's painful grip, pirouetted like lightning and gave him a vicious blow to the midsection with the heel of her left foot, drop-kicking him six feet back from the steps.

The Khan quickly summoned the young translator. Through him, he asked her about the journal of Marco Polo. Carlotta was brief. "I know how important it is that you have this journal to find the Golden Tablets of Command and I happen to know where it is right now."

Agarwal drew himself up from the floor, his eyes spitting fire at Carlotta. He jabbered some more, protesting Carlotta's statements and defending his own position. The Khan silenced him and continued to listen to her instead.

Carlotta made her closing remarks. "Your Excellency, we have Polo's journal. Right now, it is in the hands of my business associate at the Best Eastern Hotel and I urge you to have an expert make arrangements to examine it. If you so desire, you could have it in your hands by tomorrow."

"You have the journal?" Agarwal asked her, astonished. "It's here in Kashgar?"

"Yes," she said with another smirk, enjoying the

chance to torment him. Why don't you ask the Khan, too, if he would like to see it?"

Agarwal translated the question. The Khan took his seat again, giving Agarwal a long command.

"He says that he now understands the real purpose of your coming to his palace and that he admires your....your...ah...physical attributes. You are free to return to your man in Kashgar temporarily. He wants me to negotiate a purchase of two of the objects that you have brought today, but not the diadem. You are to be compensated for the damage just done to it. I am also ordered to contact your colleague to make arrangements to buy the journal at a fair price. At the same time he issues a warning to both of you not to try any trickery or he will flay you both alive." Agarwal failed to tell her that he would share the same fate if he failed to get the journal.

Pale and shaken, Agarwal escorted her from the audience hall to a room where she awaited payment for two of her Scythian pieces and partial payment for the damage done to the diadem. A servant appeared with the old case containing the crushed diadem. From there, Agarwal led her to the Mercedes waiting in front of the compound. As she took her seat in the rear, Agarwal looked in and passed her a sealed manila envelope. "If you have any notion that you will play any more games with me, you should first examine the photos I have collected for your enjoyment on your way back to Kashgar." He slammed the door in her face and knocked twice at the driver's window.

Two miles down the road, she opened the envelope and slipped out two photos. The first one was a black and white photo of Liam and her passing through customs, partly obscured by two large Afghan women in burkhas. One look at the other photo and she held both hands to her mouth in shock and let out a muffled scream.

CHAPTER 62

From his window, Liam saw the Mercedes pull up in front of the hotel, with Carlotta in the back seat. She got out and the driver handed the chest to her. She was back with the articles, he thought. No sale. Ambrosio and Pietro, already waiting in front of the hotel, dashed out to help her. They took the chest and escorted her into the lobby.

Liam joined all three of them in Carlotta's room. "Thank God, you're back. Looks like they didn't buy the goods."

"Wrong, Liam. They bought two of them. I had to bring the diadem back. It got trampled during some tough negotiations, you might say. I'll tell you about it another time."

"You don't look so good. Can we get you something?"

"Yes, please. Some water. I'm so thirsty. They weren't what you'd call hospitable out there."

Ambrosio went for some water and ice. Before sitting down on her bed, Carlotta took a look at herself in the mirror and winced.

"Where was this place anyhow? Near town?"

"No, it was way out, in the direction of that mountain range to the north. It took almost an hour and a half to get there. Good thing you didn't try to follow."

Liam couldn't wait to ask. "All right. Tell me. What did you find out about Marya, anything?"

"I sure did," she said. "We were right about following this lead here. I'm one hundred percent certain that Marya is there. I didn't see her, but I know they're holding her somewhere in that building."

Liam beamed. "What makes you so sure?" Ambrosio brought a glass of water for her as Liam pulled a desk chair across the room.

"She has to be there. And just take it easy, Liam. You're rushing me."

"Sorry. Take your time. But hurry."

Carlotta arched an eyebrow and got into telling the three about her experiences at the remote hideaway of the Khan in the order that she experienced them. She explained how deceptive the palace of the Khan was from the outside in contrast to its sumptuous interior, complete with throne room. The Khan was not a fiction, but a real man whom everyone addressed with respect and who had some incredible plans to conquer all of Central Asia.

"So the Khan is not some made-up story?"

"Not at all. He's a very real person. Incidentally, he wanted me to sign up for his harem. Fortunately I weaseled my way out of that," she said smiling. "I didn't like the neighborhood. Sorry, that was supposed to be a joke."

The three men hung on her every word. She explained how Agarwal had given her a tour of the treasure chamber while waiting their turn with the Khan in the throne room. She listed everything in it that she could remember. It was there that Agarwal gave her the first pieces of information that had any bearing on Marya. "He told me that they had an American woman working on a project. Guess what project that was?" she asked, taking a gulp of water. "Getting possession of the Golden Tablets of Command which they plan to set into a big ivory frame. It'll probably end up on the wall behind the Khan's peacock throne. If that doesn't tell you something, nothing will! She's there, guys. Marya is in that, that place. I just know it."

Liam felt his heart skip. "Go on."

"The stuff they have in storage is unbelievable. Treasures of all kinds heaped up on the floor, on tables, hanging from the walls—everywhere. Gold, ceramics, carpets, antiquities from all over Asis."

"What are they doing with it out there in the middle of nowhere?"

"It's part of a plan. The Chinese don't know anything about it, but Agarwal claims they soon will. The Khan is planning to unite all the minorities of Central Asia, including those in parts of Russia and China, into one big new empire."

"Holy shit." Liam jumped up and paced excitedly around the room.

Carlotta took another sip of water, letting the last remark sink in. "She's not on a Club Med vacation out there, you know. She's there only because she is of value to them. She knows everything there is to know about the Tablets of Command and the gems and they want to pick her brains clean."

She ended her debriefing telling them about the khan's original plans to get her into his harem, but how that idea went south after she tried her karate moves on Agarwal right in front of the khan. After that, dealing with the crazy khan was like dealing with a lamb. She finished telling them how Agarwal had been set up to come and purchase the journal of Marco Polo here at the hotel. "The plan is in place, men. The khan wants the journal. You have to lay out the price and the terms."

"Did you tell them that we want Marya in exchange for the journal?"

"No, that's for you to hammer out with Agarwal. And believe me, he won't be happy to hear it."

"Well, you've done your part. I'll take it from here." Liam leveled his eyes on Ambrosio and Pietro. They looked like two wild animals waiting to be unchained.

"There's something else you guys need to know, Liam."

"What?"

"The khan has an entire army of heavily armed men out there. They were everywhere—outside patrolling the grounds, in the hallways. It's a military base in disguise.

This is where I wish we *did* have an army backing us up. Also, Agarwal warned me when I was getting in the car that he'd get us if we tried any tricks. And then he gave me this to study on the way back." She handed him the manila envelope. "You'll need a strong stomach for this."

Liam opened the envelope and looked at the photos and gagged. "Poor devil, whoever he was. Looks like they skinned him out like a rattle snake. That's supposed to keep us on our good behavior, I suppose, while he does whatever he wants." He passed the photos to the Bellardo boys. "Their Khan has to be an animal. Thank God you're back here with us. Now we've got to see how we can get Marya out of there."

* * * * *

Liam wasted no time in getting Argawal on the phone. "We have the journal of Marco Polo. It's the real thing, Agarwal. And if you want it, you can have it for a very modest price."

"Who are you people?" Agarwal growled.

"I'm not Ken Dalton and I'm not a CEO of any company. I happen to be a personal friend of Dr. Bradwell. Does the name Di Angelo ring a bell?"

"Di Angelo. Yes. Marya mentioned your name once to me not long ago. So... I see. She hired you to work with her in Korcula. I knew she wasn't telling me the whole truth. Well, what about her?"

"We know that you and your crackpot leader have her there and we've come to take her home." Liam heard only a lingering silence.

"All right. She is here. She's working on a project for us and she'll be tied up for a while until it's finished. Can I take a message?"

"Cut the crap, Agarwal. You will bring her to us on our terms in exchange for the Polo journal."

"The journal is useless without someone who understands it."

"You know that she's already narrowed down the search for Polo's gold tablets to St. Mark's in Korcula. All you need is a translator to read the diary and go hunting on your own. That's as far as she got before you bastards got in on the act. Take this deal or leave it."

"Did Miss Bellardo share my warning with you?"

"You mean about being skinned alive? Listen to me Agarwal and get it straight. You and your idiot leader have no power over us."

"You're not in the United States anymore, Mr. Di Angelo. You are in the Khan's domain now. How do you think you passed through the airport so easily? We can take the journal from you whenever we decide to."

Liam hit him with a counterpunch. "Wake up, Agarwal. Last time I checked, this is still the People's Republic of China. You aren't exactly invited guests here, either. Miss Bellardo has done a thorough reconnaissance of your base out there. All we have to do is blow the whistle on you and you'll be vaporized in a nuclear test. Poof. Good-bye. Nice knowing you."

Agarwal backed off fast. "How do you want to do this?"

"Bring Marya to Id Kah Square tomorrow morning and follow the directions I give you."

"But I haven't cleared this yet with the Khan."

"Your problem, buddy. Not mine."

"I have to see the journal before I agree to the exchange."

"Then come and take a look at it in my room at 11 o'clock tomorrow morning, and no later. When you're satisfied, go back to the Id Kah Square. You'll find Miss Bellardo and me in the Square fifteen yards from the northeast corner. Deliver Marya Bradwell at that spot and I'll hand the journal over to you."

"I'll need some way to keep her under guard when I'm in your room inspecting the journal."

"I'll let you have two women to accompany her; but there will be no other escorts, no gorillas, no paramilitary...just Marya, yourself and the *two women*."

"But there will be thousands of people there tomorrow," he protested.

"That's the idea. And don't forget, the Chinese police will be hanging around, too. Did you get everything about the exchange or do I need to repeat it?"

"I got it. One more thing. I will need help to check the journal's authenticity."

Liam was flustered by Agarwal's obvious stalling and angling for an advantage. "Bring just one expert with you to my room but don't try to smuggle in one of your goon squad. We're armed and we'll take you on."

"Don't threaten me, Mr. Di Angelo. You forget that I hold your friend in custody. Do you want her back or don't you?"

Marya's face flashed into his mind. "I told you. You will deliver her to us safely. If you've harmed her... "

"Can it, Di Angelo. I'll be at your room at eleven." He hung up.

CHAPTER 63

Marya lay facing the wall when she heard the clatter of keys in the door. Someone entered her cell. The person put down a tray. She suspected that it was Agarwal again, standing there, just watching her. Slowly she ran the back of her hand across her dry lips and the taut skin of her cheeks. It had been two days since she had had anything to eat or drink. It was clear what he was doing. His story about the Khan's order to flay her if she didn't cooperate had failed to move her and now he was trying to play nice by bringing something to eat. It wouldn't work. "Just leave me alone," she moaned.

"It's not what you think. Here, have a bite to eat." He moved the small table beside her bed. "I've just been talking with a friend of yours."

She opened her eyes without turning to face him. "What friend? I don't have any."

"Your Italian boyfriend. You know, that nice Mr. Di Angelo whom you engaged for services in Korcula."

She bolted upright into a sitting position, facing Agarwal. "He's alive?" She took a second look at the tray. It was within reach, tempting her with incredible aromas. Water began to flow in her dry, cottony mouth.

"Yes, and he's at a hotel not far from here. In fact, just this morning we also had a visit from a Miss *Bordello*." He emphasized the name with a leer.

"Carlotta was here?"

"Yes. Pretty little thing."

"Why didn't you let her come see me?"

"You were asleep. I told her you had given us orders that you were not to be disturbed. Besides, you look like . . . Well, let's just say you look like you need a complete overhaul at the beauty salon."

"You liar!" she screamed at him. "Liam's dead. You had him murdered. I know it. Just go away and leave me alone! I don't believe anything that comes out of your mouth any more. And take the lousy tray of food with you."

He pulled a little wooden stool over to her cot and sat down. "Honest, Marya. Liam's alive and I have had a visit from the Bordello girl. It was clever of them to trace you here. I don't know how they did it or why they were so foolish. It won't do any of you much good. Not for long, anyway."

"Why?"

"First, go ahead and have something to eat, then I'll fill you in. Go ahead. Eat up. Have all you want. No strings attached."

She reached for the tray and placed it on the bed beside her, keeping to the side so that she didn't have to look at the serpent. She gulped the water first, and then she stuffed a flat pocket bread sandwich of mutton, vegetables, and a yogurt sauce into her mouth. She almost inhaled the rice pilaf. Once she began to eat, she was ravenous. A glimmer of optimism awakened in her and she suspected from Agarwal's behavior that something big was about to happen.

Agarwal resumed his taunts. "Your pals are offering something of substantial value in exchange for your freedom."

"Money?"

"No, Marya. Something much better."

She stopped chewing.

"Try the diary of Marco Polo"

"No. They wouldn't do that. It's just another one of your stupid lies. I'm not listening. Blab all you want."

"You're wrong—you'll see. Tomorrow morning, I have

an invitation to examine the journal in Mr. Di Angelo's hotel room. If it turns out to be genuine, then I will turn you over to him in the square. At least, that's how he thinks this deal will play out. I have a little surprise prepared for him and Miss *Bordello*, though."

"It's *Bellardo*. And you need to do something about your mental problem, Khalid." *He's nuts. Liam wouldn't do that. He knows how valuable that journal is.*

He got up to leave. "That's a good girl, Marya. Eat well and make yourself presentable for tomorrow. Why don't you do something about that hair?"

She threw half of her mutton sandwich and a bunch of grapes at him. "Get out!"

He threw his hands up to block the flying food. "Oh. I almost forgot, dear. Don't worry about your job in the history department."

"They're going to give me tenure?"

"No, the last time I was in Lafferty's office to turn in my resignation, he told me that they had terminated you."

* * * * *

Towards morning, Liam managed to fall asleep, but woke up two hours later, feeling haggard and drawn. All night he had tossed in bed, picturing Marya held for days in a dark cell. She appeared to him disheveled, famished, her eyes dark and sunken, her lips pleading for release from her torment. Over and over again, he had reviewed every aspect of the plan that would win her freedom this morning.

In the bathroom, he blinked at puffy eyes in the mirror. "The big day," he said to his reflection. After shaving, showering and dressing, he went to meet the other members of the team at the café on the first floor. Over a breakfast of hot rice gruel and Chinese deep-fried *you tiao*, he and the Bellardos reviewed their roles. Each had an important role to play in the crowded Id Kah Square shortly after eleven o'clock this morning. Right after breakfast, they split up, the boys heading to their room to change into local garb, Liam and Carlotta going to his room to await Agarwal and his expert.

When Agarwal arrived, Carlotta opened the door to let him in. He threw her a nasty, condescending look and barged past her into the room. A wizened little man with a bristling gray beard remained in the doorway, holding a briefcase. Behind him, in the hallway, Carlotta saw two large figures in flowing blue burkas hurry past. The gnomish old man turned his head to look at the astonishing pair and rubbed his chin. They were well over twice his size. "My goodness," he said with a trace of an Oxford accent. "What big women!"

"Hurry, come in," she said, ushering him into the room.

Agarwal introduced the scholar. "This is Amir Ibn Dihlavi. Dr. Dihlavi is a multilingual expert on European and Islamic medieval manuscripts and is a permanent member of the Khan's staff. His expertise is without peer in academic circles. Let him have a place to work, a good table with light," Agarwal demanded.

"Over here at this desk by the window, Dihlavi. Don't try to use any photographic equipment." Liam handed him the small journal. "You have to work fast—I'm giving you thirty minutes."

Dihlavi sat down and took out a thick binder and a dictionary and placed them on the desk. He produced photocopies of medieval Italian documents and laid them alongside the journal. He immediately set himself to task, beginning with an examination of the cracked leather cover. He quickly scanned the handwritten entries of the whole book and selected two pages in the middle on which to focus his efforts. Carlotta stood by him, looking over his shoulder as he worked.

"Move away," said Dihlavi, irritated by her obvious attempt to spy on him.

Agarwal paced while the little man concentrated on his task. Carlotta moved off to a corner of the room and got to work trying to undo the worst damage to the diadem, much to the irritation of Agarwal. Liam simply stood near the door with a view of the whole room, arms folded, watching the scene vigilantly.

Twenty minutes later, Dihlavi straightened up in his chair, drew a handkerchief from his pocket and blew his nose. He turned in his chair and removed his eyeglasses. "Jolly good. Finished!"

Agarwal rushed over to him. "What's your conclusion? Is it genuine?"

"Yes, I'm certain that this is a genuine manuscript dating from early 14th century Italy. It is, indeed, of Venetian origin. I can say that there is a good possibility that this is Polo's diary. The handwriting, the contents, the physical qualities are very convincing. Quite good, in fact. Still, I cannot, at this moment, say with absolute certainty that it *is* Polo's diary in his own hand." He wheezed and coughed at the end of his verdict.

"What?" Agarwal snapped. "You don't know for sure? You idiot." The gnome cowered and shrank from him, like a turtle drawing its head and limbs into its shell.

Liam moved from the side of the room and stood between them. He knew that this was the make-or-break moment and that he had to keep the deal from falling through. "This is Marco Polo's diary. Dr. Bradwell's own assistant located it at the Convent of St. Lawrence in Venice and I was the one who went in and got it for her. It's clearly seven centuries old, as your expert has said, and even if it does not lead to the treasure, it is worth untold millions of dollars on the market. A fair enough exchange for Marya. She was working with this diary in Korcula and it was only your brainless goons that kept her from finding the Golden Tablets. She was only this far from finding them," he said, holding his thumb and index finger an inch apart.

Agarwal wavered, then bore down on Dihlavi again, grabbing him by the collar and shaking him until his skull-cap fell off his head. "You heard that. What do *you* say?"

"I agree with him," the terrified little man said, choking out the words. "Yes, Yes. By all the virgins in heaven! And all the camels of the Sahara! I swear it. May they issue a fatwah on my head if I'm not telling the truth."

Agarwal loosened his grip. "Forget your virgins and the fatwah. You better be right or your carcass will end up feeding buzzards." He shoved him aside and went to look out the window.

Liam followed Agarwal and made a last attempt to close the deal. "If you want the seven Golden Tablets of Command, this is your last chance. You won't find them without this diary. Take it or leave it."

Agarwal swung around, clearly still angered by his expert. "All right. I'll take it. Bring it to me in the square and I'll hand Dr. Bradwell over to you." Agarwal flew out the door pushing the quaking old man ahead of him.

CHAPTER 64

Liam stood by the window looking down onto the Square, following Agarwal's moves. When Agarwal had reached the middle of the Square, he told Carlotta it was time to go. She grabbed a leather satchel containing the diadem and hurried out just ahead of him into the hallway, leaving everything else they owned behind. They swept across the lobby and stepped out the front door of the hotel into the largest open-air market in all of Central Asia. A northwesterly wind was blowing, kicking up swirls of dust in the bazaar. The din of thousands of voices and the panicky cries of animals merged in waves across the square. Sweet and pungent odors washed over the huge open space.

From all over Central Asia, Uyghurs, Afghans, Tajiks, Uzbeks, Tibetans, Pakistanis, Russians, Mongolians and Persians converged on the Square, having brought with them an overwhelming array of handicrafts, foods, furniture, fabrics and clothing for sale as far as one could see. Kashgar was open for business, as it had been every week for the last two thousand years, a bustling marketplace along the fabled Silk Road.

Leading Carlotta along, he barged his way past densely packed groups of people. They wound in and out among stalls, past piles of bagels, open sacks of coffee beans and tethered sheep and goats. Bleating animals lay on their sides, trussed up for inspection. Dismembered carcasses hung from wooden poles. Carlotta held her hand across her mouth as she passed the severed head of a goat on a metal hook, its strange, glassy eyes, seeming to follow hers. "Oh, my God, Liam."

Liam took her hand and moved on grimly. "Let's hope

we don't end up like him." Neither of them had ever seen such a variety of foods: large flat pans filled with tidbits of meat, stacks of mutton kebabs and meat pies, displays of vegetables—spinach, cabbages, onions and greens, heaps of melons, dates, fresh fruits, and candies. They threaded their way through incredible crowds of peasants and wide-eyed animals, bumping into them at every turn. They were surprised at the number of children and how many of them were actively engaged in selling goods. One of them, a little girl sitting in front of a sprawling pile of shoes, yanked on Carlotta's sleeve and held a pair of shoes up to get her attention. Carlotta tried to slow down, but Liam kept pulling her along by the hand. "Come on, Carlotta. Keep moving."

They plunged on through teeming numbers of humanity and countless stalls, simmering pots, traditional musicians, bicycles, donkeys, sacks of kindling, woven baskets, handicrafts, brightly colored fabrics, housewares, copper and brass pots, fine carpets. And overseeing the organized chaos, scattered here and there in the crowd, were keen-eyed, Chinese policemen.

Liam looked all about over a sea of heads for Marya, but saw no sign of her until Carlotta placed her hand on his shoulder and shouted while pointing in the direction of a low line of tiled buildings, "There she is, at the corner." Liam quickly spotted her and saw that two female guards were holding her tightly in their grip. It was not supposed to be this way. Agarwal should now be approaching him with Marya in tow. Something was wrong. Where was Agarwal?

Then he appeared, as if from nowhere, struggling through the crowds towards him and Carlotta—without Marya. It was what he feared and expected. Agarwal was not playing by the rules.

Carlotta had seen him too. "Time for plan B," she said.

* * * * *

Early in the morning, Marya was trundled out the front entrance of the palace and shoved into the back seat of the black Mercedes by one of the Khan's turbaned commandos. She sat between two chadoor-enshrouded women. Agarwal took the wheel and pulled out into the rutted rocky track that led in the direction of Kashgar. He looked at her again and again in the rear-view mirror while also keeping an eye on the two other cars in the caravan which were packed with troops.

"We're off to meet your Latin lover," he taunted her. But she didn't have the energy to waste on his stupidities. During the whole two-hour ride she said nothing to him. She only regretted that her life's work was going down the drain and that she was dragging her newfound friends along with it, all because she had not seen the dark side of the man at the wheel. How could she have been so blind, so naïve? She prayed that she would have a chance somehow to alert them to the danger they were in before they were caught in the web of Agarwal's plot. She feared what Agarwal's armed men would do to Liam, knowing that he was no more capable of overcoming heavily armed commandos than she was. She grieved over the loss of Polo's diary to this ruthless madman she had once believed to be her friend.

"It has been a pleasure having you as company chez Khan but you know what they say in America about fish and company after three days. They stink! Ha, ha, ha."

Marya tried to ignore his stupid flippancy and kept her eyes on the road ahead. More than once along the way, the car struck a rock, causing the rear to fishtail, but each time Agarwal maneuvered the car expertly back on track. As they pulled into the northern outskirts of Kashgar the three cars plowed through gaps in the crowds of people and beasts of burden, honking their way past endless shops and tented stalls. All three cars came to a quick halt just off of Id Kah Square.

Her two female escorts were not large, but they were tough and wiry, as if they had lived lives of constant physical drudgery. One of them grasped Marya's upper arm in a vise-like grip that she was sure left bruises. She banged her head as the witch yanked her out of the car. The two of them dragged her down an alley in the direction of a large white and yellow mosque that towered above the crowds across the Square. She saw the armed men from the other cars melt into the crowd under Agarwal's direction.

Agarwal looked back at her and her guardians and barked out an order to the women. Immediately, they both dug their claws into her arms. "You wait there and keep your mouth shut. Don't try anything or my girls will beat you to a bloody pulp, Mongolian-style." Then he moved out into the wild commotion of the crowd in the Square, directing his paratroopers.

What could she do? There wasn't much left in her after four days with hardly any food or water. She was at the end of her rope psychologically, with two painful bumps on her head. She knew the odds were stacked against her friends who at this moment were about to fall into Agarwal's trap. She knew that Agarwal had only kept her alive today for one purpose—to lure the others. He had no intention of a quid pro quo. He would take the precious diary from them and kill them all before the day was over. So, what did she have to lose? She made up her mind as she stood at the corner of the square in view of thousands of people that she would not go down without a fight.

* * * * *

Her female guards stood on either side of her, each gripping one of her arms. She strained to look above the heads of the crowd to see if she could see Liam and warn him somehow, but her struggles against the harpies were useless. She could see little but her own immediate surroundings—a long line of stalls stacked with household items, trinkets, boots, electronics and clothes and people coming and going, occasionally staring at her curiously. Two Afghan women sat on a blue tarp at her feet like a pair of beggar women with a meager assortment of clothing and beads spread out before them. Crinkly blue burkas covered them from head to toe.

These poor, down-trodden women, she thought. Trapped in their own way, too. Though she was powerless to do anything, she still had pity for them and wished that she had a coin or two to toss into the near-empty bowl that sat in front of them. It was crazy, but the old Chinese adage came to mind, *"ren shan ren hai"—people mountain, people sea*, and she thought that nothing short of millions of dollars would scarcely matter in such a vast ocean of poverty. Besides, she had problems of her own to deal with, like trying to signal Liam and Carlotta that Agarwal was out to kill them.

Standing on her toes, looking over the heads of the crowd, she suddenly spotted Liam, his head bobbing and looking all about for her. She craned her neck further and screamed his name once before one of the evil women dug her claws in more deeply and yanked her down. She struggled fiercely with both of the women and managed to free her arms. She elbowed one of her captors in the eye, while backhanding the other across the mouth. They reeled back but scrambled back up right away.

"Liam. It's a trap. He's is going to kill you." The din almost drowned out her voice, but she saw that he had at least seen her even if he had not heard her warning.

Agarwal's women quickly dragged her to the ground and smacked her in the face. She rolled her body and flung them off balance. With another supreme effort she got to her feet again, shaking off one of them with a smart punch delivered straight to the left eye and landed a punch on the other one's nose. Through the swirling dust in the square she saw Agarwal draw closer to Liam who had his hand in the air, holding the precious diary of Marco Polo! Agarwal made a lunge for it and accidentally sent it soaring into the air. It was unmistakable. The journal came apart in mid-air.

The two witches rose to their feet, clawing at her shoulders, trying to drag her to the ground again. She whacked one and rammed her right knee into the other's jaw. Then, off to the left, Agarwal's men charged through a thick crowd towards Liam and Carlotta. "Liam," she screamed, pointing towards Agarwal's men. "Watch out!" At the same moment, the pitiful Afghan women who had been sitting nearby scrambled to their feet. Marya marveled at the size of one of them.

Once they stood up to their full height, the women placed their large hands at the back of the harpies' necks and dropped them to their knees. They fell limply to the ground, faces in the dust. Marya gasped in shock. The large one seized one of her hands and dragged her off into the alleyway. Before rounding the corner, she screamed, "Nooooo. Liam. Over here. Help me!" She had one last glimpse of the square and pages of the journal floating in the wind, scattered like the feathers of a pigeon rammed in flight by a falcon. They fluttered across the square, drifting down over the heads of the peasant masses and fell to earth under the trampling hooves of goats, sheep and donkeys. The sight of it was like a knife wound, a mortal blow to her life's dream.

CHAPTER 65

In the background, Liam saw the commotion stirring around Marya when suddenly Agarwal appeared out of the crowd, his eyes fixed on the journal. "Give me that," Agarwal yelled, lunging at him.

Liam shoved him in the chest. "No. You know the deal." He raised the diary out of reach, over his head. "What the hell are you doing? Get Marya and bring her over here." He heard Marya scream out some kind of warning. Over Agarwal's shoulder, he saw a gang of armed men wearing turbans separate into two groups. One was heading back towards Marya and the other coming to back up Agarwal. He heard Marya scream again. Distracted for a second, he felt Agarwal punch his raised hand, sending the journal flying into the air.

"You thieving son of a bitch..." Liam clenched his right fist and sent it smashing into Agarwal's mouth. His two front teeth bent inward under the impact and he sagged to the ground in shock. Blood flowed heavily from his mouth onto his chin and his shirt. He scrambled to his knees and charged at Liam. But Liam swung and managed to get off another solid blow to Agarwal's face, this time to the nose, and dropped him for good.

Liam looked up to see the desert wind whip the diary's pages over a broad area of the marketplace. He knew there was no time to try picking them up. He had to get Carlotta out of harm's way and go get Marya. "Carlotta, quick, head for that alley. I'll do what I can to block Agarwal's men and get Marya."

While she sped off, Liam plunged into the crowd, keeping low to dodge the men chasing after him. He threaded his way through the throng towards the alley where he had last seen Marya and surprised two of Agarwal's turbaned men. He took the first one down with a well-aimed chop to the back of the neck. The other goon grazed his face with his pistol before Liam dumped a nearby pot of simmering meat on his head. He staggered backwards, screaming and holding his eyes. The vendor cursed at Liam and came after him with a hatchet, calling for help from others.

Three more turbaned commandos came after him. Liam immediately took them out of action by wrenching a wooden pole from a meat stand awning, raising it like a baseball bat and swinging it full force into their faces. He heard bones break and saw them drop their weapons.

The situation in the square was going from bad to worse. The tumult Liam had created drew the attention of swarms of men. Some of them came tearing after him, screaming and cursing, thinking he was an invading infidel. Liam looked at the useless wooden pole in his hands, threw it down and ran all out for the alley with the growing crowd in fast pursuit. Ahead of him by about forty paces was Ambrosio, already hauling Marya into the alley.

* * * * *

Marya broke into tears of anger. The loss of the journal meant the end of her life's work. It could never be resumed, reassembled or reinvented. It was her life's dream that was gone, borne away by the hot, dry winds of the Xinjiang desert. She struggled furiously to pull free of the woman in the blue robe. Her grasp was inescapable.

She heard a voice under the veil tell her, "Dr. Bradwell, take it easy."

She stopped thrashing. "Who are you?"

"It's me, Ambrosio. We're heading for that truck up ahead. Get ready for me to lift you in, fast."

* * * * *

Liam was only yards away from the opening to the alley. He saw the truck half way down, parked on the right in the shadows. Carlotta was racing for it, just ahead of Ambrosio and Marya. Carlotta sprinted to the pickup and clambered into the bed. Ambrosio pushed Marya towards the truck and turned to face the mob gaining ground on Liam. He planted his feet in the dirt next to the pickup truck and gathered up the hems of the blue burkah. A Kalashnikov swung free from underneath the robe. He aimed a loud burst of gunfire upwards. The shouts and the screaming stopped. The crowd halted in its tracks. Some turned and fled, pushing against those behind them. It gave Liam a desperately needed second of breathing room. Ambrosio lifted Marya into the bed of the truck as if she were a toy.

The crowd surged forward again, screaming and cursing. Liam knew that if they got their hands on him they would tear him to pieces. With a glance at the truck he saw Marya sitting safely beside Carlotta and ran with all he had in him.

* * * * *

"Hey, Pietro," Ambrosio shouted, "Did you get me my meat pie?" He climbed onto the rear bumper with his Kalashnikov, lowering the bed of the truck several inches.

Pietro stuck his head out the window of the driver's side. "Of course. Hurry, stupid. Get your fat ass in the truck. Move."

"Where did you get that?" Marya was aghast when she saw Ambrosio's machine gun.

"I picked it up in Tajikistan. Never mind that, though. Just get down!"

Then, Ambrosio ripped off his burkah, flung it away and lined up his weapon over the tailgate. "Okay, Pietro. Roll!" he shouted.

"No," Marya screamed. "Wait for Liam. He's coming!

Come on, Liam, hurry!" Marya was frantic as she eyed the crowd closing in on him just a few yards from the tailgate of the pickup.

Ambrosio let off another round of fire at the feet of the mob. Liam made a dash for the truck as market-goers continued racing down the alley after him. Pietro threw the truck into gear and started off. Liam reached for the tailgate. He stumbled and almost fell. He touched the ground with the tips of the fingers of his right hand and regained his footing. He had lost four or five feet but with another mad sprint he almost caught up.

Ambrosio let his weapon down for a second. "Hurry, Liam. Grab my hand." Their hands refused to connect.

The crowd shrieked and hurled what debris it could gather from the ground and the stalls all around. Cabbages, potatoes, boots, and CDs flew through the air, some striking Liam and some landing in the bed of the truck. Liam took his deepest breath and used his last burst of energy to make another grab for Ambrosio's outstretched hand.

Ambrosio leaned out as far as he could and got a firm hold of Liam's right hand. Carlotta rolled back and out of the way to make room as Liam seemed almost to levitate into the truck. Liam landed with a thud, smack in the middle of the truck bed. A loud backfire reverberated in the alley as Pietro put his foot to the metal. Ambrosio lifted his gun in the air and waved good-bye to the mob as the pick-up accelerated. "Go in peace," he cried out to the inflamed mob.

Marya pulled Liam to herself and threw her head on his shoulder, nearly hysterical. She may have lost her life's work back there in the Square, but she had found Liam again. His embrace tightened protectively around her.

Pietro had no use for brakes. He accelerated through alleyways, knocking aside stalls and scraping against mud walls. In the truck's wake, boiling clouds of dust rose and, in the distance, the sirens of Chinese police cars wailed.

Pietro held his head out the window and yelled, "Our Canadians better be there waiting for us."

Liam watched for the police. "Don't worry about that. Just get us there—fast."

They pulled out of Kashgar and hit the road to the airport south of town. The road was clear of traffic, as if the entire population of Xinjiang Province were concentrated back in Id Kah Square. Liam massaged his right shoulder, nearly wrenched out of its socket when Ambrosio had hoisted him aboard. Carlotta got busy with assembling parts of a rifle that Ambrosio had tossed to her. Within a minute, she had it sitting across her folded legs. Marya looked at her with her mouth wide open and then back at the fast-receding city of Kashgar. She was replaying the whole nightmare of the last six days, leaning against Liam, rocking with the motion of the truck, tears streaming down her face. Ambrosio peeked into the cabin and banged on the window. "Pass that pie out to me," he roared at his brother.

Two police vehicles appeared, at first far behind but now gaining on them. Liam gave orders. "Carlotta, slow those guys down. Ambrosio, get back behind us. Marya, you, too." He let go of her and she made herself as small as she could get. The Chinese were in hot pursuit. Soon they would be on their tail.

Carlotta took her place at the tailgate, raised the rifle to her shoulder and peered into its sights. "I'll do my best. If only Pietro would drive straight!" she yelled. Despite the potholes and the constant bouncing and swaying of the truck, she took aim and fired two good rounds. A tire burst on the first car, causing it to spiral off the road. The second bullet pierced the radiator of the other car, disabling it without injuring its occupants.

Pietro raced across the airport tarmac, headed for the far end and pulled the pickup up alongside their jet with screeching tires. The jet engines were already revving up.

The sky was clear, but strong winds out of the northwest buffeted the truck and the jet. Unloading their few items from the truck and piling aboard the plane took less than two minutes. In another three minutes, the plane was soaring above the desert floor on a non-stop flight to Venice. Mission accomplished.

CHAPTER 66

Marya sank into her seat, her heart pounding. Only yesterday she had given up all hope of ever leaving the Khan's place alive. "I could kiss you all," she said, barely recovered from the violent escape. Her lower lip quivered as she wiped tears away with the back of her hand. "I just don't know how to thank you. I can't believe I'm out of that awful place and that we're all alive." She glanced out the window. Some of the world's tallest mountains reared their summits against the dark blue dome of the sky. "I really thought we were dead."

Liam was holding her hand, patting it gently. "It's all right. We're together and safe, heading home."

"I used to think I was strong, you know, independent and all that. Now look at me, blubbering like a baby." She leaned to the right and put her head on his shoulder.

"Marya, it's okay. You *are* strong. You've been through a lot, but you made it." In truth, her gaunt appearance worried him. He thought she was dehydrated and made sure that there was a bottle of water at hand.

Carlotta got out of her seat and stood next to her. "Don't expect too much of yourself after what you've been through." She turned to Ambrosio and Pietro. "Hey, what about a little in-flight service, guys? Get Marya something to eat. And I don't mean a lousy bag of pretzels. She looks half-starved." Pietro headed back to the galley and rummaged around.

Liam looked up at Carlotta. "What a team! I don't know how to thank you and your brothers. Marya, these are three unbelievable professionals. They even brought out the best out in me! Wow!"

Looking up at Carlotta, Marya, too, had gratitude all over her face. "Thank God and thank *you*. I hope I'll never have to face men like them again."

Liam squeezed her hand gently. "Don't worry. You won't."

She smiled. "This all happened so fast. I still don't have any idea where I was."

"Try Kashgar in Xinjiang Province," Liam said.

"Kashgar? Really? China? All I knew after being kidnapped was that we headed east, somewhere beyond the Caspian Sea, towards the Pamirs. We flew all through the night and early morning. I did see a city at one point on the way to the compound but I couldn't place it. It seems like a miracle that you found me. By the way, how *did* you find me?"

"It was a bit of a trick," Carlotta said. "But we had a little information to go on from one of my father's connections."

Liam, Carlotta and Ambrosio took turns telling how they were drawn to Tajikistan, ended up in Kashgar and plotted the details of freeing her from the Khan's grasp. They talked about Carlotta's visit to the compound of Temujin, the fantastic treasure stored there, the bold plan of the khan to recreate Genghis Khan's old empire, the violence in Id Kah Square, the treachery of Agarwal, the gunmen he brought along and the hair-raising escape plan.

"Thank you. The four of you did all this? Without help? Talk about bravery! You're all my heroes." Tears welled up in her eyes again, but this time she was smiling through the tears. "But I'll never be able to forget the sight of those pages blowing away in the wind."

"Sorry about that," Liam said. "It was the only way we could bargain for your freedom. And I'd do it again. I'd gladly slug Agarwal in the mouth a few more times for you, too."

"Don't get me wrong. I'm thankful for all that. It's just that I had come so far in my search and I was right on the verge of deciphering the clues. I think we would have found the treasure there in Korcula. In fact, I'm quite sure of that. I still have this feeling that something was staring me right in the face and that I overlooked it."

"Hey, don't worry about it. We can always go back to Korcula and look again," Liam offered.

"Not without the journal and its clues. And now the journal's gone."

"Marya, you don't think that I gave Agarwal the real journal, do you? You should know I would never do that."

Marya looked blankly at him. "But I saw it flying apart in mid-air."

"That was only a fake. The boys bought some red leather at a bazaar and stitched together a cover for photocopied pages and that's what I waved around in the square."

"Where did you get the photocopying done in Kashgar?"

"Not in Kashgar, silly. In Venice. I brought the copy along. I thought it was a wise thing to do. I have the real thing right here," he said, patting his chest.

"Then you've really got the original?"

"Of course. After we let Agarwal's expert take a look at it, I kept it in the inside pocket of my jacket." He took it out and handed it to her.

Marya screamed. She got up, threw herself on Liam's lap, hugged him, kissed the journal and smothered him with kisses, too. "There's more where that came from," she said huskily.

Pietro returned from the galley with a decent meal and Marya ate ravenously. One hour into the flight, the adrenalin rush had settled down. The boys were snoring and Carlotta, lost in her thoughts, simply gazed out the window. Liam and Marya talked in hushed tones. "How did you get that cut on your face?" she asked, running her finger across Liam's cheek.

"Back in the square, I think, when one of Agarwal's

men grazed me with his gun. What about that nasty bump on your forehead?" He touched it gently with the tip of his index finger.

"That's from the hags who dragged me from Agarwal's car. I bumped my head getting out, thanks to them. And in the square, they held on to my arms viciously with a death grip." She took off her sweatshirt and rolled the sleeves of her blouse up to check out her arms. "I thought so. I'm all black and blue."

"Well, our injuries will heal. We're alive, thank God."

Marya described her shock when Agarwal first walked into the audience hall of the Khan and how stupid she felt about thinking that he was her best friend. She hoped it was the last time she ever laid eyes on him.

"I honestly don't think you'll have to worry about him anymore. He's going to be tied up with his orthodontist for a while, even if the Khan spares his life. He really screwed up big time. And speaking of the Khan, Carlotta wants revenge on him and won't be satisfied until she gets it. No doubt old Bellardo wants revenge, too." Liam told her about the violent attack on the Bellardos in their home after she and Liam had left for Korcula. "There was some vague talk about a letter 'T' that was painted in blood on a wall in her dad's office."

"My God, how horrible," Marya said.

"Carlotta now thinks that 'T' stands for Temujin, our crazy Khan of Kashgar.

"Given what I've seen, that's very believable. I can substantiate everything that Carlotta just said a little while ago about Khalid and the Khan. He called the Khan Temujin several times in front of me. And the treasure chamber—she's absolutely right. It contains gold beyond measure and all kinds of precious articles. But the kicker was this huge ivory frame designed to hold the Golden Tablets of Command."

"The breakthrough was that frame, you know. That's what convinced Carlotta that you were nearby," he said.

"Funny. The golden tablets got me into this mess and, by God, they got me out of it."

"That's one way of looking at it, I suppose. But what is driving those people to amass all that gold and to go to such lengths to get the tablets?"

"Liam, that's the heart of the matter. The Khan and Agarwal, and lots of other advisors in the wings, they're all serious about one thing."

"What's that?"

"Creating a super-state or empire in Central Asia to unite all the various ethnic groups from West Turkestan to East Turkestan that their big bullying neighbors are dominating."

"Like Russia and China?"

"Exactly," she said. "They have a master plan to federate the people scattered all across the steppes of Asia, from the Mongolians, Tibetans and Uyghurs now under the thumbs of the Chinese, to the Uzbeks, Tajiks, Kazakhs, and Kyrghiz people, and on to Iran."

"In a way, that would be like bringing back the old Mongol Empire of Genghis Khan. How does the art collection fit into the plan, though?" he asked.

"They constitute the trappings of royalty, great regalia that they planned to display to enhance the prestige and authority of the Khan. You know, it's purely a psychological play, like Louis XIV and Versailles, the Romanovs and the Hermitage, the Hapsburgs and the Hofburg Palace. Royalty needs to show off its baubles to impress and overawe the lower classes. And the center pieces of the Khan's collection are the Golden Tablets of Command. The Khan badly wanted to get his hands on those since they were originally commissioned by the Mongol khans."

"Back to business. Got any ideas how we might help the Bellardos get revenge?"

"I'd be glad to help in any way I can. The trick will be to hurt Temujin, Agarwal and their kind without opening the region to outside domination. Let me think about it a little. We might have to wait until we get back to Venice or to the U.S.

"So. Case closed. Almost. Why don't we get a little rest?"

Marya let her seat back and saw drowsiness in Liam's eyes. He fell silent, his hand still resting on hers. She watched as his eyelids drooped and heard him say one more thing. "Is life always this exciting with you?"

"No, not usually. My mother used to call me Calamity Jane, but my life has never been this. . ." She looked at him again and saw that his eyes had closed. She stopped talking and closed hers, too.

CHAPTER 67

Marya found that Liam's arm was resting on hers when she woke up and heard Ambrosio say, "Uh-oh." She looked across the aisle. Ambrosio was peering out the window and talking to Pietro. "Look, a MIG. I can see the pilot. He's signaling to us to descend."

Just then, they heard Scotty over the speaker system, telling them to buckle up. The jet plane that they saw pacing them only 50 yards off to their right belonged to Uzbekistan's Air Force and its pilot had radioed them to land their plane at Samarkand Airport by order of the government of Uzbekistan.

She shook Liam. "Come on, wake up. We're going to land."

"Huh? Why?"

"I don't know. It doesn't look good."

"I've got to find out what's going on." He rose from his seat. "Maybe we just didn't get all the proper clearances for an over flight. I'm going to ask the pilot. I'll be right back."

He walked down the aisle, opened the door to the cockpit and pushed his head in. "What's going on, Scotty?"

"I have no idea. Air traffic control gave me no reasons. Far as I know, all the flight information was properly filed and we were cleared for Venice. Borger agrees with me." He was at a loss to tell Liam what to expect.

Twenty minutes later, all five of them exited the jet under the cloudy skies of Samarkand and headed for the two-story terminal building with instructions from a lieutenant of Uzbekistan's army to leave their personal possessions aboard the plane. It appeared it was going to be a temporary interruption of their flight. Halfway to the terminal, Marya saw two men in business suits advancing to meet them.

"I recognize them," Liam said to Marya.

"You do? Who are they?"

"The one on the left is a guy named Cage. He's from the U. S. Embassy in Zagreb. Supposed to be with the State Department but I don't believe it. I think he's really CIA. He and I didn't see eye to eye about how I would fit in with their plans to rescue you. The other's a guy named Anderson or something like that. I really don't like him."

Cage reached them two paces ahead of Henderson. "Hello, Mr. Di Angelo. Good to see you. And very much alive, I see." He extended his hand for a handshake. Hello, Miss . . ."

"Dr. Bradwell," Liam said to him. "Marya, this is Mr. Cage of the U. S. State Department."

"Pleased to meet you. Personally, though, it's hard for me to believe you're alive and free. It's incredible."

"You know about me?" Marya asked.

"Of course. Practically half the U.S. government has been looking for you. The media have been in a total frenzy over your kidnapping. Honestly, we're very relieved. From what we know about your captors, we had grave doubts you'd come back alive."

"I don't know what to say about the media except that it just feels so good to be back with these folks. And I have them to thank for it," Marya said, pointing to Liam and the Bellardos.

Cage then introduced Henderson. After more rounds of handshaking and pleasantries, Henderson took over, shepherding the group across the tarmac, into the building and down a hallway where two American Marine guards stood posted outside a small room. As he led them into the sparsely furnished room, he stopped. "This is a matter of importance to U. S. policy in this region, and Washington is desperate for information. We just need to ask you a few questions about where you have been and what you and your friends have seen during the last few days. Please, take any seat."

He remained standing as he explained why the U.S. government had forced their landing. The Chinese government had lodged a serious protest with the U.S. over some terrible mayhem in Kashgar they believed was caused by unnamed American nationals. U.S. intelligence had also known for the last several days that Mr. Di Angelo and three Italians had infiltrated into Xinjiang Province and the assumption was that the Chinese complaint was centered on them. Marya acted as spokeswoman for the group and verified that the assumption was correct.

"We got into a little hot water, but so what? Whenever the Chinese lodge a protest, it's just for public consumption," Marya said. "I fail to see what the urgency is all about."

"I'd say you were not just in a little hot water. More like a boiling cauldron. The Chinese are not dumb. They have put two and two together and they know, or strongly suspect, that it's one of their worst enemies, a fellow named Albasbai Kibchek, who masterminded your kidnapping. They want to know what you know about him, specifically, the location of his base of operations. If you know anything about this, then I recommend you share it with us. We'll pass it along to them. Obviously, it's vital that they get the information right away while it's fresh."

Marya looked across the table at Carlotta. She seemed to be bursting to tell Henderson all she knew. Marya shook her head at her and then looked up at Henderson. "Kibchek? Don't think I ever had the pleasure."

"I believe you have. Temujin is his alias. Passes himself off as some kind of khan," Henderson retorted. "Ever hear that name? Look, Dr. Bradwell. I can't afford to sit here and play games. We've gotta know now. Mr. Cage and I have been working on this case non-stop, right, Cage?"

Cage nodded but avoided looking directly at Marya. He didn't seem to her to be on the same page as Henderson.

Henderson continued. "Let me fill you in. This is bigger than you can imagine. Here are the basics: the U.S. is heavily involved out here and our operations are growing. Several of the Central Asian Republics have concluded cooperative agreements with the United States to monitor and deter terrorists, arms dealers and drug lords. We're talking narcoterrorism and we've got to suppress it. The Russians and the Chinese are completely with us on this and we're doing what we can to cooperate with them. We also have huge investments in the oil delivery infrastructure in the western part of the region. Billions are at stake. So, wherever separatists and terrorists rear their ugly heads, we are here to cut them off. That's where Kibchek, alias the Khan, comes in. We, I mean the Chinese and us, almost have him in our crosshairs. Will you help us or not?"

Liam slammed his fist down on the table. "You were supposed to put all you had into finding and rescuing Marya. I even offered my help, but you rejected it. If you've been tracking our whereabouts so well, where the hell were you when we needed you the most? Look at us. A bunch of amateurs on a shoestring budget. Where were you folks? You're supposed to be the experts. What do you do with all those damned billions we give you?"

"I can tell you," Cage started to say.

"I'll handle that question," Henderson said. "I apologize that we weren't there for you. You definitely beat us to the punch and outwitted the Khan. We never expected you to make it back alive, any of you. I hope you don't think we were dragging our feet. Just the opposite. Washington has been wracking their brains trying to find a way to get you out. They just needed to find a way to do it without stepping on toes."

"Stepping on toes? You mean offending our strategic allies?" Marya shot back.

"Let's get back to the issue, Dr. Bradworth, I mean Bradwell. Time's flying. Where did they take you?"

Marya stood up from her seat and confronted him. "I don't like the way you frame the issue. Let me straighten you out on a few things. First of all, you've got separatists all bundled together with drug lords and arms dealers. Newly independent, struggling democracies with our megalomaniac friend Temujin. Oranges and apples. If you know your history, Mr. Henderson, that name is particularly significant in this part of the world. Temujin means 'Universal Ruler.' It's the personal name of Genghis Khan. I believe this guy sees himself as the re-incarnation of Genghis Khan, if not his direct descendant, and that has terrifying ramifications for all Central Asia. He's not your garden variety separatist."

"What was your business with him?"

The question really shocked Marya. "I had no business with him at all. I was kidnapped! Look, Temujin and my former colleague have well-articulated plans for a pan-Turkic empire stretching from the Caspian Sea to the Amur River. Temujin needs legitimacy. He needs an aura that will impress all the disaffected people of the region. That's why he took that specific name and that is why he needs powerful symbolic regalia. As far as he's concerned, he needs only a few pieces to complete his collection: the seven Golden Tablets of Command of Kublai Khan. He needs them to pump up his legitimacy. That's why I was abducted. My colleague, Agarwal, whom I never suspected, knew that I was close to possibly finding them."

"Okay, that's how you fit into the picture. I get it. I get that he wants to restore the Mongol Empire. Okay, so where is this animal? You must help us get rid of him. He's wreaking havoc everywhere in the region and taking innocent lives. He certainly would have killed the five of you without remorse. Case here can tell you what he likes to do to his enemies before he has them killed."

"Look, Mr. Henderson. I want to see Temujin or Kibchek or whoever he is put out of commission, just as you do. Temujin is not just any terrorist. He has hijacked the hopes and dreams of minorities and separatists across the region and subverted them for his own selfish cause. I'm talking especially about the Uighur people, but also the Mongolians, the Tibetans and other Central Asian peoples. These people have been pushed around for centuries by their big, bullying neighbors. Chinese control over this part of the world has never been as cruel and as repressive as it is now. For decades, the Russians have used the most ruthless methods to crush the locals and to wipe out their cultures. And now we have this guy who thinks he's Temujin or his descendant and he could turn out to be a worse nightmare for these people than the Russians and the Chinese ever were."

"We are in complete agreement. What is your point, Dr. Bradwell?" he asked, loosening his tie.

"The point is I want to see a surgical strike, one that cuts the head off without doing damage to the separatist cause of minorities in Chinese-controlled regions. I want a declaration from the highest level in the United States that stands behind the rights of minorities across the region. We must not do anything that threatens to destabilize the new democracies in Central Asia or set back the hopes of the people of Tibet and all of Mongolia. I will sign on if we just alert the Chinese to Temujin and his organization but insist that they respect human dignity in non-Han regions." Marya caught the trace of a smile on Cage's face.

But Henderson was no starry-eyed believer. "Dr. Bradwell, you're too much of an idealist. It can't happen. I say, turn the information you have about his headquarters over to the Russians and the Chinese and let them deal with Temujin any way they please. Our hands will be clean. And..." he said, raising the index finger of his right hand, "we protect American interests at the same time."

Marya shook her head. "Sorry, Mr. Henderson. No deal. May we leave?"

* * * * *

Aboard the jet, Marya had to face the scowls of the Bellardos. They had not seen fit to contradict her in the meeting with the American agents, but it was clear from their brooding silence towards her as they buckled up that they were not happy with her choice. Neither was Liam.

"Why didn't you simply tell him, or let Carlotta tell him, the location of the compound and be done with it? Two to one, they're already clearing the place and heading for the mountains. They'll certainly come back to haunt us."

"That's not the point, Liam. I know the Chinese can easily smack them down. But then there would be the aftermath. Russia and China would have a carte blanche to do as they wish to all those minority peoples. I want the U. S. on record as being opposed to that. That's all. You must understand. I don't want to be a party to setting back the cause of human rights there for another thirty years. If those CIA guys and the Washington establishment could have given us something, some promise of protection for minority rights, I'd be glad to tell them all I know."

Scotty's voice came across the intercom. "We have a radio communication from the tower, folks. Please stand by for a Mr. Cage and a Mr. Henderson. They seem to want permission to board."

The Bellardos let Marya decide the matter. She quickly unbuckled and went forward to talk to the pilot. "Tell them that we will delay takeoff to hear what they have to say."

Henderson's voice came over their radio. "Langley tells us to get this settled with you people if it takes all day."

"We don't have all day, Mr. Henderson. We're taking off now. What do you want? Say it now."

"What I'm asking is that you give us seats aboard this

flight so that we can hammer out our differences along the way."

"I've got stiff terms."

"We're ready to talk turkey."

Marya had them and the bureaucrats where she wanted and she knew it. "Good. I thought you would see the light of reason. Come aboard." She turned to the pilot with a broad smile. "They're coming along with us. When they come out to the plane, Scotty, beam them up."

CHAPTER 68

The chartered jet roared into the sky above Samarkand and banked to the west. Marya conferred with the Bellardos and Liam in a huddle before coming back to speak with the two agents. "I want Carlotta and Mr. Di Angelo in on this chat, gentlemen," Marya said to them.

"Agreed," Henderson said with a frown.

Marya, Carlotta, Liam and the two agents swiveled their seats to face each other for an on-board conference. Over the next hour, she clarified the position she had taken with them at the airport, explaining her core position that the U. S. must do no harm in the region. She handed a whole laundry list of concessions and agreements, like U.S. participation in a summit conference on Central Asia that she wanted from them. An International University and Cultural Center established at Tashkent, Uzbekistan that would serve the cities along the Old Silk Road. She pushed for a set-aside from oil revenues of the western international oil consortium to be used for strategic economic planning and development to undermine the region's dependence on opium farming and drug trafficking. She called for appointments to speak with bigwigs of the CIA and the State Department plus an opportunity to address the Senate Foreign Relations Committee on the matter of China's rising hegemony in East Asia.

"Is that all?" Henderson asked, clearly stunned.

"For now, yes. So, get started."

"What do you mean?"

"I mean, we have excellent communications on board that you can avail yourselves of. Get hopping. Talk with your people. You said they want you to settle this if it takes all day. It just may. See to it that we have an agreement before we land in Venice tonight."

After Cage and Henderson moved towards the rear of the plane, Marya detained Carlotta and took her hand. "Don't give up on me, please. This is going to work out. Once it does, I want you to be the one to tell Cage and Henderson about the Khan's fortress and its location."

Carlotta smiled and got up to report to her brothers.

* * * * *

Following the meeting, Marya buckled up and let her head fall back against the seat.

Liam took her hand. "Why don't you take a snooze? You're exhausted."

"No, I'm too jazzed. My mind is going like a whirligig."

"Then how about relaxing with some good reading?" he asked, handing her Polo's diary. "Take a look at it. Maybe old Marco has a few words of wisdom for you about the struggles of east versus west."

"That works for me." She opened it and looked for the last pages that she had read. It seemed like eons ago. It was a pleasure to feel the ancient journal in her own hands again and she said a silent prayer of thanks that it had survived the mayhem in Kashgar. How would she have explained its loss to the nuns of San Lorenzo if it had been destroyed? She felt a twinge of guilt for taking it, but the pang of conscience was soothed, knowing that it was Liam who had actually done the pilfering. Nevertheless, she vowed to see it returned to the convent when she was finished with it.

She found her place. Her last reading had brought her to the sad point when Marco Polo realized that his father had drastically different plans for his future than his marrying the Princess. Turning the precious pages, she pictured Polo holding her in one last embrace while his angry father tried to separate them. Marco Polo was heartbroken and the Princess was weeping.

The story of my travels to Cambaluc and back is known from my book. Shortly after our visit to Korcula, my father, my uncle and I arrived in Venice. Weeks and months passed. The excitement among my countrymen in Venice over our travels faded away. I undertook to restore the family business in Venice but my work came to a stop as the Genoese started a war with the Venetians. It was a naval battle off the coast of Korcula in which I participated. In the heat of the battle, I scanned the shoreline, knowing that the Princess was living there—my true love. I never saw her at that time and I knew there would be no chance for a meeting between us for a long time when the Genoese won that sea battle and I was captured and thrown in jail in Genoa. My companion in prison for three years, one named Rustichello, persuaded me to tell him my life story and from the tale, wrote my book, Le Devisement dou Monde.

Finally, after three years, I was freed and returned to Venice. Nicolo's strong will prevailed over mine in the choice of my marriage partner and I wed Donata, daughter of Vitale Badoèr. My father was pleased: her repromissa of personal and real property was huge. Donata became my wife, but I did not love her. It was only a marriage of convenience. I loved only the Sung Princess.

Donata and I had three children, all daughters: Bellela, Fantina and the youngest, Moreta. Shortly after my marriage, Nicolo died. In the following years, my relations with my wife worsened and I became nearly the enemy of her family. Even worse, two of my daughters married greedy husbands. Their dowries only whetted their appetites. Moreta, my favorite, remained loyal to me in my late years. She alone among the three was spared the infection of greed.

For years after returning to Venice from China, I was

unable to return to Korcula, as I have already said. All that time I was mindful of my princess and how I had failed her. In the year 1308 anno domini, at last, on a mission to Constantinople, I returned to Korcula. The Polos there came out to welcome me and told me where to find my princess, Mei Hua—and our son Marco, a boy of twelve years. Time had changed our positions but not our passion. I could not marry her, but I would never leave her or my son forever. I traveled to Korcula many more times and fathered another child, a beautiful daughter, Marija, who resembled her mother. I have lived to see my son an apprentice in Lumbardo, the shipbuilders' place, outside the walls of Korcula.

I have had ample time in my last years to contemplate how to dispose of my property and money. I granted the home in Venice and its furnishings to my wife, Donata. In addition, I set aside a sum of money for her. My daughters in Venice will divide the remainder of my estate equally. This will provide adequately for them and their children.

But the other wealth, a large collection of jewels and plates of gold from the court of the Khan—they shall not see. It is an exceptional royal treasure that was intended to be used as a dowry for the Princess in her marriage to a powerful European noble

The task that the Khan had given my father was to study the hundreds of kingdoms and duchies of Europe and their ruling families and to find one that could provide a match for her. The chosen one must be of stature, influence and capability to make the Khan's plans a success. There was only one family that met the qualifications, the Habsburgs of Germany, headed by Albert I who was the King of the Romans and Duke of Austria. Albert was chosen king at the Imperial City of Frankfurt and was crowned in Aachen in 1298. In 1303 Pope Boniface recognized Albert as King and future emperor. He was a wise man who was known as protector and friend of serfs and Jews. He wanted to play a great role among the rulers of the world and, most importantly for the plan of the Khan, Albert had a marriageable son. The prospect of his son's succeeding to the imperial throne after him made him our logical choice. We worked for years to promote the alliance, using some of the jewels of the Khan for bribery in the course of this effort. All our work was for naught when the King's son died in 1307 and when Albert died the following year. After that, no other prospective ruler could be found who would be a suitable partner for the Princess. The treasure of the Khan has, to this day, been kept a secret. My Venetian family knows nothing of it.

I turn now to the disposition of this unsurpassed treasure. Having failed to carry out the plan of the Khan and seeing no hope of it ever being used as intended, I worked with the Princess and relations in Korcula to preserve it for the future of mankind. It becomes the heritage of all people, East and West. May our work be pleasing in the sight of God Almighty.

She had scoffed at the idea of a nap, but now an undertow of fatigue tugged her away from her reading. She drifted into sleep as the jet sped across the Sea of Azov, over the Crimea, on its way to Venice's Marco Polo Airport.

CHAPTER 69

Agarwal's squad caught sight of dozens of uniformed Chinese police swarming into the square before he did. His men raced towards him, still on the ground, yards from the alley, hoping to get him out of the square before the Chinese police discovered him. They hauled him to his feet and helped him into the back seat of the Mercedes in one of the side streets as he kept mopping blood from around his mouth with a rag. "Goddam Di Angelo," he sputtered. Every now and then he looked at the bloody cloth and cursed. He touched his two upper front teeth and found that they had been pushed back at an angle into his mouth and that they were only loosely attached. The salty, acrid taste of his own blood on his tongue trickling down his throat made him choke.

"Go, go, go, you fool," he yelled at his driver. Finally he made himself understood by simply pointing ahead. The Mercedes took off in a roar, plowing through the back alleys, sending people running in all directions to get out of the way. The car pulled out onto the track that led north just as a contingent of the Peoples' Liberation Army entered the square to back up the police.

Agarwal knew that neither the police, nor the PLA would have mercy on him if they had found him. First, they would charge him with violation of the "three withouts:" without papers, without legal residence and without permanent income. Then they would loop a rope around his neck that dangled a placard on his chest stating his crime. After a few hours of parading him around in front of the crowds, they would take him for an enhanced interrogation. If he was lucky, he would end up working on the railway line from Beijing to Tibet, not something he relished.

He did not look forward to reporting in to the Khan, either. The fiasco that he had personally orchestrated was bound to anger Temujin. Would the Khan have him executed? He decided that between the Chinese and the Khan, he would take his chances with the Khan. Almost two hours later, he entered the gates of the compound. He ordered his squad to stay alert for any sign of the Chinese and sound the alarm if they appeared. Plans were in place for a quick evacuation. He hurried from the car into the palace compound and went directly to the Khan.

"What do you mean?" Temujin roared at him. "The Bellardo girl and the Bradwell woman are gone? How did that happen?"

Agarwal stammered and slurred his speech as he dabbed at his mouth with the bloody rag. "The Bellardo girl had many accomplices and the crowds kept blocking our way, Excellency." Stinging sweat rolled into his left eye. He wiped it away, leaving his eye and cheek smeared with blood. "We did our best, but...."

The Khan's face reddened. "Your best? You are full of camel turds. You are a complete fool. We needed that journal. You told me it would be a simple matter." The Khan realized the scope of the disaster that the American professor and the Italian temptress could create for him. "You invited two vipers into our midst and they have escaped. At this very moment, they will be telling the Chinese all they know about us. Idiot!" he screamed, ramming his fists into the armrests of the throne.

Agarwal wished that he were anywhere but standing before the Khan. "I am sorry, but I am sure I can undo the damage and secure the treasure for you, Excellency."

The Khan dismissed Agarwal with a threat. "Go get it. Kill the American professor, but bring the Italian woman back to me, or I'll have you disemboweled. Do you hear me, imbecile?"

Agarwal bowed and managed a hoarse whisper, "Yes, Excellency." He felt his bowels begin to loosen, but he got a grip just in time. As he left the throne room, he heard the Khan ordering the removal of everything in the whole complex. In his room, he found a handkerchief and stuffed it in his mouth while he set about packing what he needed. He knew that the jet that had landed at the Kashgar Airport yesterday had to be the aircraft that Bradwell and her rescuers used to escape from China. For the time being, nothing prevented her from returning to Korcula and resuming her search for the treasure there. Indeed, he thought, it could be an act of divine providence that she had escaped. He looked forward to seeing her again there. By the time he had finished packing, the dream of a rendezvous with Marya in Korcula had cheered him up. With any luck at all, upon his arrival, she would lead him directly to the last great pieces of the treasure of Kublai Khan. No cloud without a silver lining, he thought.

Leaving the compound by the main entrance, he looked north along the dirt track and saw that a motorcade of trucks and SUVs was already wending its way along the dirt track north for a secret location in the Tien Shan range. The Khan had left ahead of large numbers of his followers who were still working at emptying out the compound. Scores of paramilitary warriors and slaves were rolling out crates and boxes in a continuous stream and loading them onto truck beds. Tons of treasure and weaponry would soon be on its way to a far more opulent palace than this. Agarwal knew that the Khan's absence from his people in China would only be temporary. He laughed and climbed into the Mercedes with four hand-picked henchmen and headed to the concealed airstrip four miles west of the compound. When the Chinese got to the compound, as they surely would, they would find nothing but a shell.

CHAPTER 70

When Marya heard the pilot advise his passengers that they would arrive at Marco Polo Airport in half an hour, she decided that time was up for Henderson and Cage. They had been in radio communication with Langley for hours. "Well, gentlemen? What have you got for me?"

Henderson ignored her question and lumbered off to the lavatory looking all bent out of shape.

"What's with Happy?" Marya asked.

"We have our differences. I'm sure you can see. He's not a bad sort. Just has this blind misplaced trust in the power of the free market, Adam Smith, laissez-faire and all that jazz. Whatever. You know what I'm talking about."

"What does that have to do with anything?"

"We got commitments on everything you asked for except one."

"Which is...?"

"The use of some oil revenues in Central Asia to fund future economic diversification. We cannot get the private sector to go along with it, even though there's immense good will in it for them besides hundreds of billions in profits. And Henderson agrees with the CEOs. It reeks too much of socialism for his taste."

"I see. I suppose he's not against the taxpayer coughing up money to send our troops to guard their pipelines or giving oil corporations all kinds of other subsidies."

"Right. That's what free enterprise has come to mean these days, it seems. Anyhow, long story short, we have commitments on all your other terms. I'm actually amazed."

"But, that oil money for reversing the region's dependency on the opium poppy is critical. You've done well, but it's not enough. The farmers are the backbone of the economy out here and opium pays. We must create an alternative for them to end opium production."

"I won't argue with that. Just don't ask the oilmen to contribute. That's why I came up with something else you might accept in its place. It's a little off the wall, but what the heck," he said with a grin.

"What?"

"We got you ten minutes with the President in New York before his address to the United Nations. He's going to make a speech on the crisis, the one that you're at the very heart of, by the way. Would that work for you?"

Marya was pleased by the unexpected offer and she thought she saw the glimmer of a new idea. She jumped. "It's a deal."

Cage beamed. "So where are Temujin's headquarters?"

"Wait a second, Mr. Cage." She signaled to Carlotta to come over and sit down. "Mr. Cage would like you to give him the Khan's street address."

"I don't understand, Dr. Bradwell."

"Sorry. Will you be kind enough to tell Mr. Cage exactly how one can find the palace of the Khan? How far is it from Kashgar? In what direction, and so on?"

"I'd be very happy to."

"And when Carlotta is finished," she said, taking a sip of water, "I'll give you a complete description of the Khan and his chief advisor, Khalid Agarwal."

* * * * *

After landing at Marco Polo Airport, Ambrosio and Pietro went off to wrap up details on the lease of the jet. Cage shook Marya's and Liam's hands and then parted ways, heading to the concourse with Henderson to catch their flights to Croatia and D.C. The boys caught up with Marya, Carlotta and Liam at a café. They headed home together.

As their taxi-boat pulled up in front of the showroom, Giovanni and Francesca were already out front to meet them with open arms. Bellardo gave each of his children a big hug and followed up with hugs for Marya and Liam. "Home at last, alive and well, thank God."

Marya cringed when she first caught sight of his arm in a sling and Francesca's head bandaged. It revived the nightmare of the attack on Vittoria. She felt responsible for the evil that had befallen them at the hands of Agarwal's hirelings. "I'm so sorry, Signore and Signora Bellardo. I had no idea…" her voice trailed off. She felt she would cry.

Bellardo hugged her again. "It is not your fault, Marya. This was the work of evil men and, don't forget, we had trouble with these people even before you came to Venice. Don't worry, the Bellardos are back in business again." He told Francesca to arrange with Carlotta and Pietro to let them borrow some clothes.

By this time Marya felt like she had just crawled out of the infamous Black Hole of Calcutta. "Giovanni, I'm sorry, but just look at this," she said, flipping her limp, stringy hair. "I can't wait to take a long, hot bath."

"Go right up to your rooms and take all the time you want getting cleaned up. Francesca will arrange with Carlotta and Pietro to lend you some outfits until you have a chance to do some shopping. Francesca and I are hoping that you'll be able to spend some time with us, a week? A few days, at least?"

"That's so kind of you, Giovanni. I haven't worked out my plans quite yet. I'm hoping to get back to Korcula as soon as I can. I know you'll understand."

"Well, let's talk about that at the dinner table tonight. Off with you," he said, shooing them along.

* * * * *

Marya dipped her right foot into the steamy, hot water and felt one of the greatest delights of modern civilization.

Time alone to soak away the troubles of the past week in a deep bath brimming with bubbles. Perfect, she thought, slipping into the tub and resting her head back to gaze at the ornate stuccoed ceiling. She took a washcloth and soaked it, then gently wiped up and down her calves and thighs, her thoughts drifting to the Bellardos and how generous they had been with her. How lucky they were, too, to have one another.

The image of her mother's face came to mind. She lay in a hospital bed for two weeks before she died with only Marya by her side. Her father had disappeared with the excuse that it was too much for him. He took up with a floozy in Oregon and had nothing more to do with his daughter. Her only sister had fled to Tonga and opened a scuba-diving outfit. She had written Marya telling her she had no intention of coming home—ever. So, Marya did what a teenage girl could do in the circumstances. She visited her mother daily, holding her hand, adjusting her pillows, doing what the nurses had no time for. The doctor told her mother that she would be gone by the end of the month, but she took it in stride, as if there were all the time in the world.

Her mother told her that she would inherit the house and that she should sell it and bank the proceeds for her college education. She talked about her modest bank accounts and insurance benefits, Social Security. They watched some self-help shows on television, wrote letters, did crossword puzzles and even joked. In the end, she faltered and the cancer overwhelmed her.

Marya recalled the many good times that the family had spent together. The summer campfires in the redwoods. Swimming along the Eel River. Sun-bathing on flat, house-sized, granite boulders in the streams. The spicy aromas of pepperwood and madrone trees. The picnics were big affairs with the old aunts and uncles of the family hobbling about, setting up chairs, unloading the cars. In minutes they would have tables groaning with "snacks." Crusty French bread, salads, red wine, cheese, salami. The memories soothed her, yet left her with the gripping feeling of being alone in the world, a feeling that she had struggled to keep at bay in her college years and her professional life. She missed everything about her younger days, except for the disintegration of her family.

As she stepped out of the tub after a long soak, an image of Liam's face appeared with startling clarity. Her feelings towards him had changed completely. She was infinitely thankful for his strength and the way he had led the team through the horrible dangers of Kashgar, saving her life for, what was it? The second time? What about him, she mused? Did he have feelings for her? How did she feel towards him? Was it only gratitude that she felt for him? Were they just basically two very, very different people who had gone through a grueling ordeal together and bonded only temporarily?

CHAPTER 71

Francesca saw to it, once again, that Marya sat next to Liam at her table. Marya complimented her as before on the table's magnificent setting. Francesca told her that they would be having some Middle Eastern dishes this evening. Then she winked at her as Liam came into the dining room.

She was glad as the Bellardos all took their places and Liam sat down beside her. She took another look at everyone around the table and wished it were her family. They appeared totally different to her after the crises of the past week. Beautiful Carlotta had confounded her completely when she picked up the rifle in the back of the pick-up and blew out the tires of the pursuing Chinese police car. Ambrosio had surged up before her in a billowing blue burka to become her protector in the escape from Id Kah Square. She also saw the other side of quiet Pietro, in love with Vittoria. Liam, of course, had shown her that there was much more to him than just padding his bank account.

"A toast to your safe return," Bellardo said, hoisting his glass. Marya clinked her glass against his and turned to do the same with those near her. The old patriarch was beyond reach, but she toasted in his direction, too.

Emilia brought out bowls of rice pilaf and an eggplant dish that brought sounds of appreciation from everyone. As Marya looked around the table, it suddenly struck her that the Bellardos loved each other, good food and drink and good company. They were utterly relaxed at table—as if nothing in the past week had happened to disrupt the round of banquets and the gusto for every day life that they seemed to take for granted. Giovanni took the freshly baked Syrian bread and broke off a chunk for her.

"You must be so proud of your sons and your daughter, Giovanni."

"I am very pleased with them. I feel the family honor has been restored. So, tell me about your plans now that you are back."

"I've got to go back to Korcula immediately, to Saint Mark's Cathedral."

"Have you finished reading the entire the diary?"

"No, not yet, but I've read enough to know that he took the treasure of Kublai Khan and preserved it somehow for posterity in Korcula."

"You still believe he hid a fortune there. Ah, to be young again. Your story makes me want to join your expedition." Bellardo broke off more pieces of the Syrian bread for the others around the table. "Did they do well, Marya? Did they learn the lessons I taught them—to blend in with people of the east?"

"They were perfect. I have to tell you something. When Agarwal's people dragged me to Id Kah Square, I noticed this pitiful pair of Afghan women sitting at my feet. I felt so sorry for them I was wishing I had some coins to give them. Little did I realize that it was Ambrosio and Pietro right under my nose! They had me fooled! I should have known just by looking at their size. Who else could it have been?"

Ambrosio almost spilled his wine and the whole group broke out laughing.

"They did well, then."

"Very well. In fact, if I hadn't been in such terrible danger from Agarwal and the Khan, I would say that I had the time of my life. But back to my plans. I'm going back to Korcula and I have one favor to ask, Giovanni. I'm afraid to bring the original of Polo's journal with me, so I'm only taking a copy with me. Can I leave the original in your vault?"

"Of course. I'll put it away for you personally. Now, about your escort."

"My escort? Marya looked at Liam, unsure what Bellardo was hinting at. "Well, I don't know. Liam has his work. I've taken up too much of his time lately and he needs to get his life back."

"Hey, don't worry about that. I'm sticking with you to see this thing through. You're not going back to Korcula alone," Liam said. "And this time we'll rent a car, drive down the Dalmatian coast to Split and then take the ferry to Korcula from there."

"Ambrosio and I go, too," said Pietro.

"Hold on, just a second," said Marya, surprised at this development. "I think I'll be okay from now on. The situation is under control. The Chinese are hunting down the Khan and Agarwal. I'll be safe. Besides, I've imposed on you folks too much already. Just look at what's happened since my arrival in your household. I've turned your lives upside down. I can't ask anything more of you."

"There is no way that you're going to Korcula without me," Liam asserted sternly. "I don't care what my business plans called for. We've come this far together and I don't want to see anything happen to you."

Bellardo touched her arm. "I agree with Liam. You can't go to Korcula alone. You're being too starry-eyed. I don't think that we've seen the end of these fanatics. Even the Russians and the Chinese combined hadn't been able to eliminate them. There are bound to be some die-hard remnants, believe me."

Marya was at a loss as to how to handle these offers. She had to find a way to convince them that from now on she would be in no mortal danger. She needed a free hand to pursue her research in Korcula unimpeded and for however long it took. It just wouldn't work with a bunch of big bodyguards following her around in the confined spaces of the island town. "Thanks for all your help, but I'll need to think about it. I'll let you know tomorrow.

Excuse me, please," she said and abruptly left the table for her room.

* * * * *

Liam got up and followed her out of the dining room, leaving the Bellardos all bewildered. He caught up with her in the hallway.

"Marya, what is it? Did we offend you?"

"No, Liam. Just the opposite. I'm overcome with all the offers of help. It's just that…I guess I don't know how to deal with it. I feel like I've been a burden to all of you."

"Well, the offer still stands. And I'm sure the Bellardos are sincere. They will go all out for you. There's something about this project that has changed us all, you know. We have an emotional stake in it, too, now. Don't turn us away. Not now."

"But I'm also afraid for them, Liam. My project has caused a lot of strain. Look at the shape they're in. Right now they need Carlotta and the boys right here at home."

"The Bellardos *want* to help. I want to help. Can't you see? You've got to let us help in some way."

She lowered her face, feeling her objections eroding.

"And besides that, Marya," he drew closer to her, lifting her hands in his, "there's no way I will let you walk out of my life just like that. I can't just go back to Boston and business as usual. I've learned more about myself being with you than I have in all of my life."

Marya felt the Mediterranean world drawing her both to Liam and the Bellardos. She took his hands in hers and looked up into his dark eyes. "Then, I'll have you come with me to Korcula and if they must help, I'll tell them that we'll call them if we need to." She looked at Liam for a reaction to her idea. He drew her close and kissed her and then he took her by the hand and back to the table.

CHAPTER 72

In the morning, Marya and Carlotta went off on a round of errands for some new clothes and toiletries for her trip to Korcula. Before noon, she made a quick trip to the hospital to visit Vittoria. Entering her room, she saw that the severe bruising and swelling on her face had disappeared. She was now alert and looking perky.

"Vittoria, you look great," she said, handing her a bouquet of flowers. Vittoria took the bouquet and put it down on a rolling table that extended across her bed.

"I'm feeling much better. They're going to release me tomorrow. And look at you. You look wonderful, too, so happy. Where have you been? I was hoping to see you more often while you were here."

"I've been gone... all week... I've been away."

"What? Where were you?"

"In Tajikistan and China. I was kidnapped," she blurted out.

Vittoria couldn't quite grasp what she had said. It took Marya a few minutes to recount the ordeal and at many points in the story Vittoria simply held her hand to her mouth, shaking her head in disbelief. Marya summed everything up for her, from her betrayal by Agarwal to the terrible suffering she endured in the Khan's palace compound and her hair-raising rescue by Liam and the Bellardos.

"I hope you never see that Khan again, dear God." Vittoria said, with a quick sign of the cross.

Then, Marya returned to the subject of the diary. "You were totally correct about it and I'm convinced of what you said from the start—that Polo himself wrote it. It was in the convent library, right where you said it was. It is just remarkable."

"I know. I couldn't believe it myself. I remember holding it in my hands, kneeling on the floor. I was shocked."

"Liam, the fellow I just told you about, disguised himself as a priest and found a way to go into the convent and bring the journal out for me."

The two laughed hilariously but the laughing made Vittoria wince from the pain in her jaw. "Did it help you at all to find anything in Korcula?"

"I'm sure I was within inches of finding Polo's treasure in one of the churches there.

"But then . . . ?"

"But then, I was kidnapped and the rest you now know. Look,Vittoria, this afternoon Liam and I leave for Korcula to continue the search. Before I go, I want to ask you if you'd be willing to keep working for me here in Venice."

"I can't, Marya. My father forbids it. He's still very afraid for me."

"I understand, but the danger is over."

"Is it really?"

"Yes, I promise. Absolutely. It's over for good. At this very moment, the Khan is facing the wrath of the Chinese authorities. Either he has been captured or he has gone so far underground that he'll never surface again. And Liam gave Agarwal a beating he won't forget. He'll be tied up with an orthodontist for a long time if the Chinese police haven't already arrested him. We've told the CIA all they needed to know and they're sharing that information with the Chinese. So, personally, I don't see a problem from them anymore. Please talk to your father about it again."

"I'll try."

"If you can convince him, I'll put you to work on a translation of Polo's journal with historical commentary, to be published under both our names. After all, you were the one who discovered it at the convent. I want your name as well as mine on any book on Polo."

Vittoria brightened. "I'd like that. I'll see."

Marya told her she had to get going soon but took a few minutes to tell her about the usual splendid dinner she had at the Bellardos the night before. Vittoria's face lit up. She confessed her love for Pietro and told her that they were talking about marriage. "And what about you? You've had this dreamy-eyed look since the moment you came to see me. Are you and that Irishman an item?"

To her own surprise, she said, "You know what? I think I'm in love with him and it makes me feel good all over." She stood up and twirled around the room. She swiped the bouquet from Vittoria's table and with long strides she twirled around the hospital room, humming the wedding march.

Vittoria's laughing touched off an ache in her jaw and she held her hand to her face. "I've never seen this side of you before. He must be really special."

"Well, to tell you the truth, he is special but he's the opposite of the kind of man I thought I was looking for, and I think he might like me."

"Is that all you can say? He likes you? He probably likes raviolis, too. That's nothing to talk about."

"Maybe there's more to it. We'll see."

"I hope it's true."

It was time to leave. Vittoria pointed to a spot on her cheek where Marya could give her a kiss without making her hurt. "Good luck to you in Korcula. Now, go find that treasure!"

* * * * *

Liam saw an image reflected in the windows of the shops he passed in the narrow lane. It was his father's face staring back at him. He thought it ironic that he was in Venice, his father's hometown, about to spend the morning buying new clothes. His father wore the same thing day in and day out for years. Nothing about him changed. He had not lost his heavy accent, always went to the same neighborhood church and was still deep down, that "greasy guinea" that the Irish called new Italian immigrants. When Liam was in his teens, he grew tired of the North End. It reeked of garlic and salami, table wines, cheese, bread and, of course, pizza. It was so ethnic and so old country.

He hated Dean Martin's song about the moon hitting your eye like a "bigga pizza pie" and the other favorite, "Volare," that was on the radio at least once a day, it seemed. That was not what he wanted. These days, he was making it big with his own business and had a great lifestyle with travel and all the goodies money could buy.

He entered an upscale men's clothing shop, paneled in walnut, with recessed lighting, plush carpeting and spacious displays of well-tailored merchandise. Within half an hour he chose a pinstripe suit of fine, dark blue wool, along with a striped shirt and regimental tie. He bought another suit of linen that could be worn with a polo shirt or a gray cotton long-sleeve T-shirt, and black slacks by Giorgio Armani. He paid with his VISA card and left the store. On a whim, passing by a jewelry shop, he saw a fine heart-shaped locket of gold with a chain, draped around a gray velvet post shaped like a neck and he decided to buy it. He entered the shop and had a sales clerk get the locket from the window. It snapped open easily, revealing a place for two miniature photos or portraits. "Perfect," he said. "I'll take it."

CHAPTER 73

Before noon the Bellardos saw them off at Riva degli Schiavoni where a *vaporetto* would convey them to the mainland. "Don't be surprised if we come down for a visit to Korcula. And don't get yourself into any big trouble before we get there," Bellardo said, wagging his finger at Marya. "And Liam, the minute you suspect anything out of place, God forbid, be sure to call us. I'll have Ambrosio and Pietro down there as fast as I can get them there."

Marya laughed. "You worry too much, Giovanni."

It was good that they were leaving Venice. News of Marya's abduction from Korcula a week earlier had been picked up by wire services the day after her disappearance. It soon became front-page news not only in Italy and Croatia, but also across the rest of Europe and the United States. Television coverage was extensive and sensational. The Italian media were saturated with interviews and discussions among officials in Korcula, Zagreb and Washington, D. C. Bellardo had told Marya this morning that television crews had even visited her hometown of Eureka in Northern California. They showed scenes of the port and the high school she went to. They interviewed one of her teachers. "She said you were an excellent student. And the people there put yellow ribbons all around the city in hopes you would come home alive."

"They did that? I can't believe it."

"You're all over the news, Marya. I don't know how we were able to keep it a secret that you've been here with us." With a wag of his finger he again warned her to stay out of trouble.

"I will. I promise," she said, giving him and Francesca

hugs and kisses. After crossing the lagoon, they went to a car rental agency near Maestre Station and hired a luxury Mercedes for the drive from Venice to Split, where they planned to take a ferry across to Korcula. She hoped they would be settled in by evening.

As she climbed into the Mercedes with Liam at the wheel, she was happy they had given the Italian paparazzi the slip. She was stoked, too, about getting back to work on locating Polo's hidden treasure. As they drove through towards Trieste and Rijeka, she decided to give the car's advanced phone feature a try. After a few false starts, she figured it out. "Bingo, it works," she smiled to Liam. "It's ringing."

"Who you calling?"

She held her hand over the receiver. "Sam Lafferty. Dear old Sam. I know his home phone number by heart. Agarwal told me when I was imprisoned at the compound that Lafferty blocked my tenure and got me terminated. He probably did, but I want to know for sure."

"It's 1 A.M. in Boston."

"He's dying to hear from me."

"Yeah, right. Well, give him my best regards while you're at it," Liam said, raising the middle finger of his right hand.

"Liam, I'm shocked....Oh, hello. Sam? This is Marya. I'm in Italy...I..."

"Hello? Who is this?"

"Marya," she said louder.

"It's after midnight. You woke me up. Couldn't you have waited and called me at the office? "

"Actually, no. It's urgent." She looked at Liam and grinned. "I must know what the decision was on my tenure."

"Your contract was not renewed. We're already breaking in your replacement. Hagar Bland, a new Ph.D. from Salt Lake City."

"Somehow that doesn't surprise me. What have you done with my papers and books?"

"Everything is still in your office. Roache offered to pack them up for you. But, you're always particular about your things, so I told him not to. You'll need to get back here to clear your things out as soon as possible. By the way, have you found the golden tablets yet?"

"No," she said, rolling her eyes.

"I thought not. When do you think you'll be back to vacate your office?"

"Is that the best you can do, Sam? Not an ounce of the milk of human kindness in you. You are just heartless. You haven't even asked me how I'm doing or anything."

"Okay. So, how's it going?"

"As a matter of fact, I'm doing very well. I feel great. I haven't felt this good about myself in quite some time."

"Well, I'm glad to hear that."

"And it's all due to being far from you, Roache and Chen. But don't worry. I'll be by to pick up my things in about a week. Now go back to sleep."

Liam grinned back at her as she hung up.

* * * * *

It was getting on towards evening and they were only near the outskirts of Zadar, a coastal town not even a third of the way to their destination. "There's no way we're going to catch that ferry from Split tonight," Liam said. "No use trying. I've got a better idea." He pulled off the main highway and took a smaller, more winding road that led them through cypresses to a broad shelf of land overlooking the Adriatic. He drove up to a secluded hotel that was once the palazzo of an Italian family. It paralleled the coast rearing its long, classical facade to the setting sun and the glittering Adriatic. From the car, they had a view to a large island off the coast, pointing the way, like a knobby finger, to the south.

They entered the hotel through an ornate door at the center and from the vestibule they descended a marble staircase. At the foot of the staircase on either side were truncated marble columns in the Doric style—fluted columns with plain capitals. Potted palms flanked the staircase. A carpeted corridor stretched left and right of the reception desk. Overhead, a series of elegant three-tiered chandeliers hung from the ceiling of a carpeted hallway. A well-dressed, twentyish young woman greeted them and registered them quickly.

After registering, unpacking and freshening up, they went out for a look around the grounds. They strolled along a crushed gravel path bordered by precisely trimmed shrubs planted in a symmetrical pattern. A square red-tiled pavilion framed a view from the cliffside to the Adriatic. Standing with one hand shielding his eyes, Liam pointed out a marina full of pleasure craft on the left and on the right, a quaint villa surrounded by Lombard poplars perched on the side of the hill near sea level. A long, narrow seawall created a tranquil private lagoon where two boats were docked. "Can't you see yourself living there some day?" he asked.

"It's just beautiful. Have you been here before?"

"Twice. You like it?

"Love it."

"How about the hotel?"

"A bit extravagant, isn't it?"

"I've done well on this trip, so relax. It's on me. Come on, there's more to see." They continued down a side path past an outdoor pool, a squash court, eight tennis courts, a vineyard and an olive grove. They turned onto a path uphill and entered a grove of laurels and linden trees. Overarching branches shaded the path at the end of which was a classical pool with a statue of Neptune and two other lesser deities. Beyond the pool of Neptune stood an imposing ancient aqueduct that still carried water for the pools and the needs of the hotel. All about them was the sound of birdsong, filling the forest. Wooded hills rose above the hotel, rising like a natural barrier to protect the private paradise against the outside world. For the first time since returning from Asia, she felt able to banish her problems and let down her guard. She thanked him for taking the detour and told him that she could be happy here for a long time. His concern and protectiveness touched her and she realized that it was far more than gratitude that she felt for him. She let Liam take her hand and lead her back to the hotel by way of a different path.

"Hungry?" he asked.

"*Ista ka medvjed.*"

"Easter, what?"

"It means, hungry as a bear, in Croatian" she explained. "You try it."

"Easter kah medveed."

"Perfect. Did you say you were from Dubrovnik?" She looked at him as they entered the hotel lobby and knew at that moment that she loved him deeply. She felt hungry for him, to the point that 'hungry as a bear' was putting it mildly.

They went up to their rooms to shower and change for dinner. Liam put on the suit he bought in Venice with the linen shirt and silk tie and came across the hallway to knock at Marya's door. She opened the door and saw his undisguised admiration for her. She was stunning in a new black dress with full taffeta skirt and v-neck velvet bodice matched by a pair of black patent leather pumps that fit the ensemble perfectly.

His eyes went avidly from her hair to her feet clad in black leather pumps. "Wow."

She was pleased at the effect her outfit had on him.

"This is for you," he said, giving her a little wrapped present.

She took the package from him and sat down on her bed to open it. Her eyes widened in appreciation as she lifted out a gold locket. "It's just beautiful," she said, putting her hand to her mouth.

"As soon as I saw it, I knew it was perfect for you."

She sat on the bed and let him fasten the clasp. "It's... I'm speechless. You're not going to believe this but it looks exactly like the locket that I lost in Venice. I treasured it because I had two photos in it—one of my mother and the other of my grandmother. You can't imagine how much this means to me. Thank you, Liam." After he fastened the clasp, she stood up, whirled around and gave him a long, tender kiss.

They left her room and went downstairs, passing through the lobby to get to the restaurant. It was a magical place with its French doors, soft candlelight, fine tableware and the exotic aromas of the dishes coming from the kitchen. Most of all she enjoyed looking into Liam's dark eyes. Her dinner, however, was something else. She eyed the dish he ordered, then hers. His roast partridge finished with sour cream in a mushroom and tomato sauce looked delicious. Her squid ink risotto was not so appealing after she remembered that it was the dish she had that night at Carlo's in the North End with Khalid. She pushed the dark rice about her plate with indifference, waiting for Liam to finish and order the dessert.

"Oh, my God. No."

"What's the matter? Lost your appetite?"

She dropped her fork and it clattered loudly on the dish. A few people at nearby tables turned their heads. She had seen someone near the swinging doors of the kitchen.

"What's the matter? You can't be seasick again."

"Look behind you! That man."

Liam turned back to see who she was looking at but saw no one. "I don't see anyone. Where?"

"He was over there, by the kitchen doors, but he's gone. He disappeared the minute you turned around. I've seen him before. In Korcula or in Kashgar, I don't know which. But I know I've seen him before." She pushed her plate away and began wringing her napkin.

Liam got up fast and dashed to the kitchen doors where he ran into the maitre d'hôtel. Marya saw the maitre d' just shake his head. He had not seen the person Liam described and Liam returned to the table, shrugging his shoulders. Minutes later, he paid the bill and they left.

The omen had ruined the evening for both of them. They parted in the hallway outside their rooms after he gave her a warning not to open her door unless she heard his voice outside and to call his room if she suspected anything. Before turning out the light in her room, she considered reading but gave up the thought. She felt as if the forces of the Khan had reached across the vast Eurasian land mass to end her quest for the treasure of Marco Polo. This time, maybe for good.

CHAPTER 74

From his room Liam put a call through to Cage at the embassy the next morning. "Mr. Cage, this is Liam Di Angelo."

"Where are you?"

"At a hotel just north of Zadar. We're leaving this morning for Split to catch the ferry over to Korcula."

"You sound like there's been some trouble."

"Well, kind of. Last night at dinner, Marya, ah, Dr. Bradwell saw someone she recognized from either Korcula or Kashgar, she doesn't know which, but it scared the bejabbers out of her. Whoever it was just vanished. No one else saw him. I'm calling to let you know that we think it could have been one of the Khan's people."

"You might be right, so be careful. I really can't confirm that possibility now because we're mostly keeping an eye on the situation in Tajikistan and Western China. It's still very unresolved."

"What's going on over there? I need to know."

"Since you folks left, the Khan cleared out and the Chinese have gone on a rampage, putting down riots, closing mosques and religious schools and rounding up separatists. There have been nightly raids on the homes of the Uyghurs and even some public executions. There's been pressure on the President to come out with a strong condemnation of human rights abuses."

"So, I take it you don't have anything solid to tell me about the Khan or Khalid Agarwal."

"No, I don't. Sorry. By the way, have you been contacted by anybody in the media?"

"No, actually we're doing what we can to avoid it. The paparazzi would only make matters worse for us."

"You're doing the right thing. We're monitoring the situation over there in China. Call me back in a few hours. I might have an update on the situation both there and here in Croatia. Give Dr. Bradwell my best and tell her I'm working on details of her upcoming private chat with the President at the U. N."

"Okay, I'll get back to you before we board the ferry."

* * * * *

Liam loaded their bags into the car and they sped off. He kept the car at the speed limit, but Croatian drivers still passed him at much higher speeds, taking suicidal risks on hairpin turns. They didn't seem bothered by the thousand-foot drop off the unguarded shoulder of the coastal road. They passed Sibenik, another ancestral home of the Polos, while off shore the islands of Kornat and Zirje were clearly visible. The unfolding vistas along the coast were spectacular, but Marya's attention was focused only on the fastest route to Korcula.

Liam tried to distract her with some small talk. He asked about her parents and the city of Eureka, California where she grew up. She confided that her early childhood had been very happy and full of outdoor adventures. When Liam told her that he had never even once gone camping and had never hiked a trail, she was appalled. "Do you recognize any of the trees or flowers along the roadside?" she asked.

"Haven't got a clue."

When she pointed out a deer standing on the roadside, she tested him again on his general knowledge. "You know what that is?"

"An antelope?"

"No. Try again."

"An elk?"

"You've got to be kidding. It's a deer. Liam, that's just shameful. You have no appreciation for nature."

"Sorry. But, you know, there weren't any deer in the North End. So, what do you expect?"

"That's no excuse. By the way, talking about the North End, you'll have to take me there some day to meet your parents. I bet if they could see you now, they'd think you're way too uppity for their taste, with your fine suits, your Rolex watch, your home in Upper Newton, hob-knobbing and all with Boston's upper crust."

"It's weird you should mention them. Actually, I've been missing them a lot lately."

"Didn't your Dad come from Venice?"

"Yes and, sad to say, I've been trying all my life to get away from him and his Venetian ways."

"You ashamed of them, or something?"

"It's the North End, not so much my parents. Have you ever been there? It's a dreary, old neighborhood. Nothing to see, really. Lots of people hanging out, going nowhere. My folks love it. But I couldn't wait to get out of there."

"That's a mean thing to say."

"I can't stand the dump."

"But, still, your parents live there. It can't be all that bad. I'd still like to meet them. I bet they're great people. Don't you realize how lucky you are to have them both?"

"Okay. Enough. I get the point. I won't promise anything right now. I'll think about it when we get back."

The chatter turned to her years of distinguished academic performance and her teaching. He asked if she was going to miss it.

"It's not so important to me anymore after the last two weeks. It seems there's a lot more to life out there in Asia."

"You saying you don't want to be a school marm any more?" he asked with a weird nasal twang.

It sounded really funny to her—a Bostonian trying to talk like an Okie. It was doomed to failure. "Will you give it up with that fake western accent? You Bostonians really believe you're Brahmins, don't you?" she said, teasing him back.

Liam kept up the banter until they pulled into a parking lot outside the former ancient, Roman city at Split. The palace of the Roman emperor Diocletian was so large that an entire city fit within its walls. It was obvious from a glance that everyday people had turned the place into living quarters and had been calling it home for fifteen centuries. Liam pointed out television antennas that stuck up above the tops of the walls.

"I need to get to a phone and talk to Cage again. My cell won't work here. Excuse me." He jumped out of the car and ran for the Post Office, knowing there would be public phones available there. In the meantime, Marya hurried to get a newspaper and pick up a ferry schedule at a kiosk.

* * * * *

"I've got that update for you, Di Angelo," Cage said. "Our satellites have picked up signs of a large-scale retreat from the Khan's compound north of Kashgar. We think he's running for a safe haven in the hills, with the Chinese in hot pursuit. Our sources on the ground tell us that the palace was deserted when the Red Army got there. Also, we've learned that Agarwal and a handful of men escaped in a small aircraft. We have no idea what their destination is. I'd treat that with some concern, though, if I were you. They could be headed for Europe."

"Not good."

"I'd say the same. I suggest that you two abort your plans for Korcula and go into hiding until we get a fix on Agarwal and take him into custody. Could you get her to do that?"

"I doubt it. She's spooked over the thought that the Khan's people could still be after her but she's bound and determined to get to Korcula."

"Well, I wish you luck, and when you two do get to Korcula, I'd get those big guys from Venice called up on active duty again."

"What about the police?"

"You've already had experience with them. Need I say more?"

"Then how about you people giving us some protection?"

"We can't just go in and throw our weight around. This is a sovereign nation. They would lodge a protest."

Liam hung up, trying to figure out how much of the conversation with Cage he should share with Marya. He decided he'd only tell her that the Chinese were still in pursuit of Agarwal and the Khan. He met her back at the car and they both got in. She suggested it would be faster to drive south to Drvenik and take the ferry from there to Korcula. He took the wheel and drove hell-bent for the next ferry departure there. But, even at higher speeds, Croatian drivers took mad chances passing him. One slip-up and they could have flown off the cliff into the azure waters below.

While they sped along, Marya intermittently translated several newspaper articles aloud. Every one of them pointed to a kind of worldwide firestorm over events in Asia concerning the "the missing American college professor, Marya Bradwell." "I had no idea. What a hullaballoo. My face is in all the papers. Thank God no one has noticed us yet."

They zoomed down the scenic coastal highway to Makarska and caught glimpses of steep mountains plunging almost vertically into the sea. It made California's Big Sur look puny in comparison. 25 kilometers later, they were on the outskirts of the little fishing village of Drvenik. Its small population lived in an arc of homes lining a small bay of translucent blue waters. A blinding Mediterranean sun was high overhead. They had covered a distance of 260 kilometers by the time Liam pulled into the village.

"Hurry, Liam. Look. Over there. The ferry."

He sped along the crescent bay to the loading dock. "Shit," he cursed as a herd of goats crossed the road and held them up a minute. He hit the accelerator again and zipped into a three-lane loading zone. They came to a rapid, whiplashing halt only to see the ferry's loading ramp being drawn up after the last automobile had driven aboard.

"Oh, no. It's leaving already. We just missed it by one minute," Marya said, almost in tears. She clutched the map spread out on her lap. "What are we going to do now?"

Liam slumped forward, his forehead touching the steering wheel. He raised his head and pounded the steering wheel with a clenched fist. "Nothing. All we can do is sit here and wait for the next ferry this evening. At least we'll be first in line."

CHAPTER 75

At 7:00 P.M. the black and white Jadrolinja ferry powered out into the bay, rounded a promontory, turned and plowed south to Korcula. Marya and Liam left their car, climbed a metal staircase and headed for the bow. The stimulating sea breeze in their faces lifted their spirits. At the bow of the ship were two men. One was an older fellow and the other, a younger, studious-looking man. Marya saw the younger man nudge the older, who turned to look in their direction.

"I think I've been spotted," she said to Liam.

The older man flicked his cigarette over the side and said something to the younger. He nodded agreement and then both men sauntered over to them, sizing up Marya.

"Good evening," the older man said in Croatian.

She paused, her arm locked in Liam's. "Good evening to you."

"My associate tells me that you look familiar, young lady. I hope we haven't embarrassed you."

"Not at all," she said. "I'm returning to Korcula to do some historical research. I was here almost two weeks ago. Maybe that's why you think I look familiar."

"I see. How interesting. Well, let me introduce myself. I'm Dr. Paul Vicich and this is my assistant, Mr. Viskovich." He held out his hand to shake hers and Liam's. "Maybe I can help you—I'm the curator of the Gabrielli Palace Museum."

"Pleased to meet you. I'm Dr. Marya Bradwell and this is Liam Di Angelo."

"We have a fine collection of historical artifacts and important historical documents. Have you visited the Gabrielli yet?"

"No. But this is really fortunate." She opened her purse and dug around for a few seconds. "Here's my card."

Dr. Vicich lit a cigarette as he squinted at the card. "What is it that interests you in Korcula?"

"I'm looking into Marco Polo's origins and his personal ties with the island," she said, trying to be brief.

He threw his head back to exhale a long trail of smoke. Marya was grateful for the sea breeze that wafted it away from her. "Many people of the island are convinced that the Polo family was from Korcula, not Venice," he said.

"I'm aware of that and I tend to agree with them on the basis of research I've done on him."

Vicich laughed. "It's only a legend. We've found no proof of it yet but you're entitled to your views." Dr. Vicich exhaled, flicked his cigarette and missed dropping the ash and some live embers on her, but the smoke found its way directly to her nose in spite of the brisk wind. She coughed and took out a handkerchief to hold to her face. It brought to mind Lafferty's stuffy office and how stifled she felt working with the old boys.

Marya ignored his remarks and decided to see if she could learn anything useful from the old expert. "Is there any archaeological work going on at the Cathedral lately? I mean the recent earthquake damage to the church seems to present a great opportunity to stop and evaluate thoroughly before beginning restoration work."

"As a matter of fact, the State Ministry of the Interior did order an inspection, but the report was confined to matters of structural damage. You're referring to a different kind of evaluation, I suppose?"

"Yes. I'm thinking of its art. The murals in the sanctuary, primarily. The Cathedral is such a gem. It truly deserves a complete, updated study."

"I happen to have some jurisdiction over historical structures in Korcula and as far as I know, nothing like that is being planned. The murals are ancient, but they're in good condition. It's almost a miracle that they haven't needed any restoration for hundreds of years. I've never come across anything in the museum's archives that relates to repairs performed on them. Incredible, eh?"

"Yes, that's miraculous."

Then, his face lit up in recognition as the ship rolled and he tilted towards her, attempting to balance himself on the deck. He took another look at her business card. "Aha! You're Dr. Bradwell, the American. I *do* remember you, or at least your name. You were involved in the murder and mayhem in our square last week, weren't you?" He turned to Mr. Viskovich and said, "You were right."

His gross accusation irked her. "I was kidnapped, Dr. Vicich. It's true that there was a disturbance and a death, yes, but I'm not at fault for that."

His eyes and his voice accused her. "You were trespassing on the belltower." Vicich turned to Liam. "And this is the American man also reported to be bumbling around on the belltower with you?" He squinted as he blew more smoke in the air.

"We weren't bumbling around on the belltower; we were doing an inspection," she countered.

"Whatever for?" he demanded indignantly.

Marya was suddenly caught in an embarrassing situation. "I wanted to know... that was my only chance... I had to see the belltower because..."

Dr. Vicich held up his hands to silence her. "Never mind. You two are just another pair of Americans nosing around where you have no business. Listen, Dr. Bradwell, do you realize what it cost us when that scaffolding came down? I'll tell you. Lots of time and money that we Croatians just don't have."

"I'm sorry, but..." She wanted to express her real regret. Her presence on the belltower that night was, indeed, a disaster. She was not prepared, though, for Vicich's sharp, insulting tone.

"You can spare us your apologies. From now on, visit the Cathedral like all the other tourists and don't go near the tower. Visit only during the regular hours. If you do not take this warning seriously, you will find yourself on a plane back to the U. S. I mean it." At that, Vicich lit another cigarette and walked off with his associate.

"I didn't get a word of that, but it doesn't look good for treasure hunting, from what I could tell," said Liam.

"It's a bummer."

"You can't blame him for feeling that way. Ambrosio made a junk heap out of the scaffolding around the tower."

"Well, I don't really care how he feels. I have to see everything in that church and the belltower, too. And I will."

CHAPTER 76

Liam got behind the wheel again and drove the Mercedes off the ferry. At Split he had called ahead to alert the Sternichs of their arrival and, sure enough, as they pulled into the parking area just outside the walled city, Zoran was there to greet them. He took their bags in hand and led them to the *sobe* within five minutes. Mrs. Sternich fixed them a modest meal and the two went up to the same rooms they had on their last visit.

He saw that Marya was simply dragging bottom from the ordeals of the day. The long, hectic drive from Zadar, racing on a dangerous road with madcap Croatians; learning that Agarwal had so far eluded the Chinese police; missing the ferry at Drvenik; being insulted and then warned by that old curator, Vicich. She was worn out and on the ragged edge. He wanted to spare her from anything else that might set her off.

After seeing her to her room and getting her settled in, he made a pretense of going to his own room by shutting his door firmly. Then he tiptoed downstairs again to ask Zoran if he could use the phone. Zoran pointed it out to him in a niche near the foyer. He dialed Bellardo and asked him in a hushed voice if he could put Ambrosio and Pietro on alert.

"You two are all right, aren't you?"

"For now, yes. I just want the boys to get ready in case something comes up. It's not urgent right now."

"What's wrong?"

"I'm not one hundred percent sure." He quickly told Bellardo how Marya had been frightened by a face she had seen at the restaurant in Zadar and how it had ruined the evening for her. But he had not seen the character himself nor had the maitre d' standing nearby. Maybe it was a case of the nerves, he told Bellardo. But, the bad news from Cage in Zagreb was that Agarwal was alive, had escaped capture by the Chinese and had reportedly flown out of Kashgar. Those were facts and they were not encouraging.

"Then lay low until my boys get there. I'm sending both of them right away."

"No, Bellardo. It's the middle of the night and…"

"And what?"

"There's no need yet. I'm not sure Agarwal is actually coming after us."

"When you are sure, Liam, it will be too late. I told you, lay low and wait until we get there."

"What's with this we?"

"I want to see how my boys and my daughter perform under pressure and I want to be there, too, to give this goddam bunch what for."

"No, Bellardo. Please. You're taking this too far. Right now there's no real need to…"

"We're coming and that's that. Sit tight until we get there. If that bunch shows up again, it will be for their own requiem."

Bellardo hung up leaving Liam confounded. "Christ, I shouldn't have called him," he muttered. He could almost see them now, packing the car with weapons and disguises, gearing up for an all-night ride to Split or Drvenik. They'd be here in the morning, spooking Marya half out of her wits. "Shit, just what she needs." Damn, he thought, I'll have to get her up for an early start in the morning before the Bellardo circus comes to town.

Zoran stopped him at the stairs. "You look like you need a drink."

"I do."

"How about a slug of Slivovitz? They use Slivovitz to launch Russian satellites and space station modules."

"Fine. Anything high octane will be perfect."

* * * * *

Marya slept as if in a coma. She awoke in the morning to someone tapping on her door.

"Marya, you up?"

"No, but I feel my eyelids fluttering and I think I can count to six or seven."

"That's progress."

"Seriously, Liam. I need another hour or two. Why don't you go for a walk or a naturist swim?"

"No, we've got to get going."

"But why? I'm so tired. Is there any reason I have to get up now? It's only 6."

"Wrong. It's almost 8 and it's a beautiful morning. The sun's up. The birds are singing. This is your day."

"Come on, Liam. Please. I'm not awake yet and I don't care about the birds."

"I'm not going to let you be a slug-abed. It's Sunday. You've got to get ready for Mass at the Cathedral."

Something in what he said began to click. It *was* her big day and she had suffered through incredible deprivations to get to this place at this time. What on earth was she doing, hanging on to her pillow? 'Get up!' a voice screamed at her.

"Give me a few minutes to get ready, okay? I'll see you downstairs."

Liam left her to shower and dress for the day ahead. She ran the comb through her hair, grabbed her copy of Polo's diary and went downstairs to the dining room where she found Liam already engrossed in his breakfast. From a table in the corner of the dining room, she took a large wedge of povitica, a hearty pastry, poured a cup of coffee and joined him at the table.

"Oh, Lord," she said, stuffing the lightly glazed pastry in her mouth. "This is so good."

"Zoran taught me the word for this pastry. It's called po-vee-teet-sa. The accent is on 'teet.' His daughter made it especially for us."

"I know all about povitica. My grandmother used to make this every Easter. It's made with chopped walnuts and apples, cinnamon and loads of butter." She took another bite of it with some coffee. Closing her eyes, she saw her grandmother peeking out her kitchen window waving to her.

Zoran came over to the table. He stood by them as they ate the pastry and waited for some sign of approval from Marya. Her smile said it all. She licked her fingers after the last morsel entered her mouth and made a circle with her index finger and her thumb. "Dragi Bog. Ovo je dobro."

Liam asked, "What did you tell him?"

"Oh, I told him it was great and I liked it."

Zoran was pleased. Then he pointed out the window. Peering over his glasses he said, "It's time you left for church." They looked out and saw clusters of people walking across the square to the cathedral. In the morning sun, the light reflecting off the honey- colored stone blocks of the cathedral's façade was nearly blinding.

"Right. We better get going if we want to find a seat at Mass."

"Do you have your prayer book?" Liam asked her.

"Got the little puppy right here." She patted her woven straw purse. "Ready? Let's go."

* * * * *

Arm in arm they strolled across the square to the cathedral. "Look, Liam. They've put the scaffolding back up again. They seem to be in one heck of a hurry to repair the tower."

"I hope you don't get any more wild ideas. If you do, I'll tell Dr. Vicich on you."

"You wouldn't dare."

They entered the church, dipped their fingers into the cold water of the marble font and crossed themselves. An usher at the front of the church raised his hand, motioning for them to come forward.

"Come on. The usher has seats for us up front," Liam said.

"Front row seats. Perfect. Just what I need for a good view of the sanctuary." Organ music reverberated on the massive stone walls and columns. Before the statues of the Virgin Mary and the Holy Family on either side of the main altar, banks of votive candles flickered. The distinct scent of the beeswax candles reminded her of old churches she had visited in many parts of the world.

Holy Mass began with a small procession from the heavily sculpted front portal to the altar. The priest followed two altar boys, one swinging a brass censer emitting clouds of incense, the other solemnly carrying a crucifix mounted on a mahogany staff.

The choir sang the Kyrie and the Gloria. Marya felt a nudge from Liam's elbow, distracting her from her concentration on Polo's diary.

"Look up there to the left, Marya."

"What are you looking at?"

"That woman. Do you see that noble figure?" he whispered.

"Yes, of course. I've been looking at her, too."

"She looks just like you, I swear. With dark braids, a few pearls, a gold crown, and robes, she's your spitting image. She's beautiful."

"Shhh!" She resumed her reading, occasionally glancing at the murals around the altar. A column of incense rose in the sanctuary. The ancient chants, the benevolent gaze of the saints and the sunlight pouring through windows far above the altar drew her back to another era. She had the sensation that Polo himself had arrived in Korcula after an absence of many years. She half expected him to stride down the aisle and tap her on the shoulder. He would speak to her personally and reveal his deepest secret to her. She looked again at his handwriting in the journal and she waited for something to come to her.

CHAPTER 77

I turn now to the disposition of this unsurpassed treasure. Having failed to carry out the plan of the Khan and, seeing no hope of it ever being used as intended, I worked with the Princess and my relatives in Korcula to preserve it for the future of mankind. May the offering of this treasure be pleasing in the sight of God Almighty and may it symbolize the true unity of mankind, East and West. Peace among men is what our Heavenly Father intends for us.

The treasure of the Khan consists of seven great golden tablets and more than three hundred large rubies, emeralds and sapphires. It was with the help of the Korcula branch of my family that we were able to mount the entire treasure for display in and above the Cathedral of St. Mark. I was fortunate to have at my disposal an array of talent in the family. We had goldsmiths, jewelers, artists and clergymen, one of these a bishop. Together with them, the Sung Princess and I conceived of a plan to display the gold of the Khan and yet conceal it from future robbers and plunderers.

The gold of the Khan has been mounted in a most clever contrivance that proclaims two messages—the power of the Heavenly Father above and the power of the Khan below on earth, displayed for all to see, yet hidden from the eyes of pirates, infidels and the perfidious Genoese who infest these waters of the Adriatic. Let all behold, and yet not see, the golden treasure that proclaims the unity of mankind from east to west. May God Almighty grant us eternal peace.

Working in the utmost secrecy, my cousins did likewise to mount the sapphires, rubies, emeralds and diamonds that Kublai Khan gave for Princess Mei Hua's dowry. Through their artistry the gems are visible to the faithful but appear only as painted ornaments in the murals of Saint Mark's sanctuary. The craftsmanship is so good that we had no need of the master muralists of Venice.

The Polos of Korcula in the name of God accomplished all this in the greatest secrecy. When the work was completed both on the top of the bell tower and inside the sanctuary, His Excellency, Antonio Polo, the Bishop of Korcula consecrated the donations at the church on June 12, 1321.

May God forgive me my sins. May the routes to the court of the Khan forever remain open. May the world know that I have told the truth. In the unity of east and west lies our great treasure. I have not long to live and entrust this diary to you, dearest Moreta. Blessings upon you, my faithful daughter.

* * * * *

A series of chimes rang out. Marya's eyes rose to the panels on the walls surrounding the main altar. In one of the panels was Tintoretto's *Annunciation*. In another, *The Virgin with Child*, wearing a robe of cerulean blue, with a fringe of gold, the Christ child in her arms looking up into her face. To the right of the altar was the Christ, seated on a throne, his left shoulder covered by a blue cloak that revealed a brown tunic underneath. He held a large leather-bound volume in his left arm clasped to his chest. His dark beard and his eyes, set wide open, magnified his authority.

Her view rose to the dome above the altar. It was ringed with arched windows that permitted sunlight to illuminate the entire space around the altar. She counted altogether sixteen figures of saints painted on the dome's surface. The saints seemed suspended in air with their sandaled feet protruding from the bottom of their long robes. Large, rounded, dark eyes in each figure in the assemblage evoked solemnity and distance from this world below. Haloes graced the heads of three of the saints. The three gray-haired men had their right arms raised to the level of their shoulders, the first two fingers of their hand raised, the last two fingers touching the bottom of the thumb in the conventional manner of blessing. The figures stood out dramatically against a background of gold and ochre.

To Marya, all seemed right and proper. She had seen similar depictions in many other churches all over the Mediterranean from Constantinople to Spain. There was a certain blending of east and west, a style that merged the new three-dimensional Italian artistry with the more hieratic style of the east, creating a sublime and mystical effect.

Within the panels, angels with highly stylized wings hovered in the air above the earth-bound human figures. The panels themselves were outlined in repeating, geometrical shapes and arabesques, intertwining branches and rosettes. Marya focused on the important panel to the left of the altar, the one that Liam had just spoken of, noting the woman's resemblance to her. Marya scrutinized this figure carefully. She had dark braids that hung from beneath a royal crown to her waist. The crown itself bore a representation of a large upright rectangular ruby at the center and sapphires on either side. Around her throat was an elaborate collar, again with a huge ruby painted at the center and sapphires painted on either side. The high collar, its top and bottom lined with pearls, rose up to her chin, giving her a regal bearing. She was smiling, too.

Lavish pearl decorations extended to her rich, maroon robes. In her left hand, the woman held a scroll tied at the center with a neat bow. Her right hand was raised in blessing. Marya imagined generations of worshipers looking at the beautiful woman, as she was now.

The figure was obviously someone of great stature in Korculan society. It would have required the explicit permission of the bishop of Korcula to depict this scene near the altar. Strangely, the pose of the figure and the crumpled folds of the gown at her feet reminded her of Guan Yin, the Buddhist goddess of mercy.

During the reading of the gospel, her attention was momentarily drawn away from the murals to the priest, high in the pulpit, reading from the letter of Saint Paul to the Ephesians: "...There is one body and one Spirit, just as you were called to the one hope that belongs to your call, one Lord, one faith, one baptism, one God and Father of us all, who is above all and through all and in all..."

After the sermon, the faithful shuffled to the altar for the Eucharist and returned to their pews. Standings, sittings, kneelings. "In the name of the Father and of the Son and of the Holy Spirit." The priest raised his hands and blessed the congregation. One of the altar boys lifted the cross on the staff from its resting place and began the march down the central aisle towards the main entrance of the cathedral. As the small procession passed by, the faithful knelt and crossed themselves. Marya and Liam stood solemnly.

Marya took one last look at the panel. Shafts of morning sunlight slanted down through the little arched windows of the dome onto the mural, making the figures appear in stunning clarity. There was something familiar in the face of the woman. *My God, Liam is right. She looks like me! The smile, the cheekbones, the eyes.*

Her eyes fastened upon a line in the journal still open in her hands. '*In the unity of east and west lies our great treasure.*' *What does that mean?*

Marya looked up again at the panel and began an examination of the male figure standing next to the lady. Her command of history told her that the Orthodox and Latin schism had split the Christian church, east and west, asunder. The pope had no authority over the church in the eastern Mediterranean. Marco Polo, she thought, probably had in mind this deep and lasting division of the two branches of Christianity with his repeated mention of east and west.

She focused on his costume. He was wearing a rich cloak of alizarin red. On his head he wore a crown of gold with inset pearls and a large ruby embedded in the center. A string of pearls descended on each side of the crown to a point below his ears. Each string terminated in a gold cross enclosed in a ring. His left hand was extended and gripped a large cloth sack bulging with unseen valuables. Its top was tied off and protruded above his grasp. The trompe l'oeil technique was so realistically applied to the sack that it really appeared to bulge with solid objects. *No doubt he was somebody in society.* She reminded herself to take advantage of the invitation she had at the Gabrielli archives to find out who this fellow was. The pair looked like husband and wife. They must have been wealthy donors who made substantial donations to the building of this cathedral. Suddenly, she had a thought. *An interracial couple! And she's pregnant! They've got to be Marco Polo himself and the Sung Princess, Mei Hua.*

The eternal gaze in their eyes and their happiness with the gift they were making to the church stood out more clearly. Polo's right hand was raised in the typical stylized manner of blessing, the index finger pointing upwards to the sky, the other three folded down against the palm of the hand and the thumb.

The mystery was tantalizing. Everything about the panel proclaimed worldly wealth. And the diary on her lap spoke of a treasure *in* the sanctuary as well as something concealed on the tower. Then it struck her that something was wrong with the way the blessing was portrayed. Normally, the first two fingers were raised, while the fourth and fifth fingers bent towards the palm. These figures had only one finger, the index finger raised, as if pointing to something.

Which is it? Are they pointing? If so, to what? To other figures around the altar? To the dome? To the cross mounted above the dome? To the sky? What are you pointing at, Marco? Tell me!

The mystery was tantalizing. She needed an answer and knew that this panel contained the vital clue. She looked at the expressions on their faces. They were smiling but their eyes held the same blank and timeless gaze as the eyes of colossal sculptures of Egypt.

CHAPTER 78

Agarwal arrived in Venice at night with four of the Khan's heavily-armed, best-trained men and made contact with the remnants of the band that had been searching for a lost Ukrainian treasure trove. A total of nine thugs under his direction headed for Trieste and the highway south along the Dalmatian coast. Agarwal's goal was clear. He suspected that Marya already arrived in Korcula and that she may even have deciphered clues in the diary. If the treasure were as large as he believed, she would need time to evaluate its scope and alert the Croatian authorities. And being the sweet, naïve Bo Peep that she had always been, she would do that. Even then, however, nothing significant towards removing the treasure could be done for at least a week and, very likely, for a much longer time frame, if the job were to be done properly.

His goal was clear. He would let her lead him to the seven Golden Tablets of Command and the hoard of jewels and then kill her. If her Italian boyfriend, Di Angelo, was still with her, so much the better. He relished the thought of inflicting pain on Di Angelo and seeing the terror on his face before he killed him, too. He played with a number of scenarios, each involving the slow killing of one before the other, using devilishly painful methods.

The team brought everything they would conceivably need for the assault and the plundering. His commandos were equipped to scale interior and exterior walls, drill holes in masonry, set off controlled explosions, keep squads of police at bay and haul off up to two tons of material by helicopter. They would drop in out of the blue and seize the treasure from under the noses of any Croatian authorities on the scene. It would take only minutes. He had studied the plan of the church and had calculated everything for speed and precision. The experience of the Venice-based cell that had kidnapped Marya would also be valuable, even though they had lost two men in that operation.

The sad thing was that he had to do away with Marya. What a waste, he thought. She was a beautiful woman. They had collaborated on well-received articles in scholarly publications for four years, though he had had his ulterior motives for that. Lately, she had seemed to warm to him, responding to his kisses. Why hadn't their relationship bumped up to the next level? Why had she refused his incredible offer to join him in his work for the Khan? He had thought that she understood his dedication to the cause of Greater Turkestan and its need for a charismatic ruler on a par with the 14th century Mongol khans. He had even dreamed of their marriage, one day, and being rewarded with his own khanate within the new Mongol empire.

But, he had somehow miscalculated with her. It was too late for that thinking now and too late for her to undo her grave mistake. The Khan had ordered her execution and she must die. Once she and Di Angelo were out of the way and the great treasure was in hand, he would also track down the Bellardo girl and bring her back to become one of the Khan's many concubines.

* * * * *

Bellardo and his wife had a long history of making family outings enjoyable. This would be yet another one, though slightly unconventional. Giovanni and Francesca put together a cooler full of food that they could eat en route to avoid having to stop along the way. They jumped into the back seat with Carlotta while Pietro drove with help from Ambrosio as co-pilot. The boys had packed their clothes and all other necessaries and stowed a rifle and a Glock in a false compartment of the car just in case Carlotta's extra special skills were needed. They left in the middle of the night and would be in Korcula by late morning if all went well along the way. Bellardo had posted a sign in the front window of the showroom that the showroom was closed and would re-open in one week. He left five nephews on the premises to guard the place against intruders and take care of Papa. He swore under his breath that if the gang that had kidnapped Marya was foolish enough to come back and try their luck again, they would pay for it.

* * * * *

Marya remained seated after Mass ended, more frustrated than ever at not being able to penetrate the mystery. What exactly is the message Marco and Mei Hua are giving me in that mural? After the procession passed by, the parishioners left the pews. Soon she and Liam were the only ones in the church except for a handful of women lighting candles.

She tried everything she could to interpret the mysterious portrayals of Marco and Mei Hua, using the critical portion of Polo's journal that spoke of the sanctuary. *The clues are here in plain view, but what do they mean?*

By now, she was alone in the cathedral with Liam. Laughter echoed into the church from the front entrance. Greetings among parishioners and snatches of conversation intruded into her thinking.

"This is so frustrating," she said to Liam.

"Got any insights?"

"Lots of them, but that's the problem. I just can't seem to figure out which interpretation of the symbolism is the right one."

"What've you figured out so far?"

"I know who that woman is up there. The one you pointed out to me. Guess who that is?"

"I haven't got the foggiest."

"That woman, Liam, is a princess of the defeated Sung imperial family, the one that Polo brought back to the West, and the guy next to her is Marco Polo himself, holding a sack of treasure. The whole mural is done very well."

Liam only had one word for her revelation, "Incredible."

"It's not as incredible as you think. Polo talks about a Chinese princess in his private journal here. He even gives her name—Mei Hua."

"But why? What are they doing together here?"

"She was intended to be a wife for a European king. Actually, Kublai Khan was angling for a better deal—getting her married off to someone who was his equal, someone like the Hapsburg king of the Holy Roman Empire. Kublai hoped to build strong ties with Europe to ensure growing trade and cultural contact between China and Europe forever. But the Polos failed because the king they put all their chips on died. This was after years of trying to pull off a betrothal and marriage. So, Marco grew discouraged with that idea and he and Mei Hua became lovers. Maybe that's what he had really wanted all along, anyhow. The journal doesn't say that in so many words, but I'm thinking those two had a kind of love that doesn't come along every day."

"I don't know how you figured all that out."

"I'm still unable to see the solution, though. Where's the treasure?"

"Haven't you got a single clue?"

"Just one. It's the way they are holding their hands in blessing."

"What's so different about that? All the saints up there are doing the same thing," Liam said, pointing out the line of apostles.

"No, they're not, if you look closely at them. Marco and Mei Hua seem to be pointing, see?" she asked.

Liam agreed. "It's a start."

As they walked out of the church together, Marya realized that for seven hundred years generations of villagers had looked at the richly painted scenes above the altar, but had not seen anything unusual or strange. Yet, she knew that Marco and Mei Hua were signaling the presence of an earthly treasure of immense value somewhere on the grounds of the church. On the front steps, something told her that she had to unravel the mystery and do it quickly.

CHAPTER 79

Bellardo knocked at the door of the *sobe.* When Zoran opened it, Bellardo asked if he had a Dr. Bradwell and a Liam Di Angelo as guests. Zoran looked at him and the other Bellardos behind him suspiciously and asked who he was and why he wanted to know. As soon as he heard the name, Bellardo, he asked them to step in.

"We'll need rooms, too, but first I must talk with Mr. Di Angelo."

"I've got vacancies. But Mr. Di Angelo and Dr. Bradwell aren't here. They left for the early Mass across the piazza," he said, pointing through a lace-curtained window.

"I see. Well, how quickly can you have our rooms ready? We'll need three."

"No problem. Just take your bags up now."

"They're at Mass? When does it end?"

"In ten minutes. You might meet up with them as they come out, but you've got to get going now to do that."

"Grazie, Signore. Here is my credit card." He turned to Ambrosio and Pietro and had them bring the bags upstairs quickly and get changed. Zoran took the card, looking at the two Bellardo boys dubiously as they barreled up the stairs.

* * * * *

Ambrosio and Pietro removed two nun's habits from their suitcases and spread them out on their beds. They quickly stripped to their underwear and then climbed into the voluminous black garb of the order of Notre Dame. Ambrosio crossed the room to check himself out in a walnut-framed oval mirror. "Does this make me look too heavy?" he asked Pietro, straightening the semi-circular white wimple on his chest.

Pietro came over and stood behind him, looking over his shoulder into the mirror. "You look like an orca," he said. He gave him a swift kick in the butt. "Come on, let's get going."

Ambrosio came charging after him, but Pietro was already out the door. He bumped into Carlotta coming from her room where she had spent a few minutes on her makeup and checking her handgun.

"Careful, Ambrosio. You almost knocked me down. Why are you running?"

"Pietro said I looked like a whale."

"You do not. Don't listen to him," she said, scowling at Pietro. "Wait, let me fix you up." She straightened the crooked wimple, cinched up the rosary beads around his waist and tucked his curly hair under the white band on his forehead. "There, you look as cute as Julie Andrews in *The Sound of Music.* Come on. Papa wants us downstairs fast."

"Where's Mama?"

"She's got a headache. She's saying her prayers and resting. Let's not bother her."

* * * * *

Marya and Liam walked out into the middle of the square. She placed her hand on his arm to halt for a minute. She wanted to get a good look at the façade of the church and its tall belltower. They were barely far enough away from the tower to get a complete view of the large cross anchored at the top of the cupola. As she studied it, she thought there was something odd about the way the cross was positioned. It faced east and west. *The cross should be aligned with the square, north and south.* It came to her all of a sudden as she recalled the figures in the mural.

"No, it can't be, can it?"

"What?"

"Do you suppose they would have done something like that?"

"What the heck are you talking about, Marya?"

"The Polos of Korcula devised some way to display the gold treasure without attracting the attention of pirates and raiders. No, they simply wouldn't have."

"Wouldn't have what? Stop talking in riddles.

"You'll laugh at me. I know you will."

"Come on, for Pete's sake. You're driving me nuts."

"Promise you won't get upset."

"Don't be silly. How could I get upset?"

"It's the cross, Liam. The tablets are hidden inside the cross!"

"What? No way!"

"The treasure is up there, I'm telling you. I felt it all along."

"Oh, come on, Marya, you're not back to that old idea, are you? We tried that once before and, I hate to remind you, but our last trip to the belfry turned into a long detour to Kashgar. Let's not go there again."

"I knew you wouldn't like it." She pulled away from him and started walking back towards the cathedral.

"Where are you going?" he asked.

She didn't answer, but he knew from the look that she shot him what the answer was.

"Wait, Marya. You're not really going up there again, are you?" he asked, scrambling to catch up with her.

"Guess again."

"Now?"

"It's now or never."

"Here, in front of all these people, in broad daylight?"

She turned around to face him. "How do I make you see it? It's there," she said, jabbing three times in the direction of the cross."

"How can you be so sure?"

"Marco Polo and Mei Hua told me."

"You're hearing voices now?"

She shrugged and shook her head. "You saw them in the mural. What were they doing? They were pointing upwards at the cross on the belltower. They were telling us where the golden tablets are hidden. I'm sure of it this time."

"Okay, now wait a minute." He looked around, stalling, trying to find a way to keep her from climbing the scaffolding in full daylight and in front of the church crowd. "Let's say you're right. Can't we go check it out after we get approval? You heard Vicich."

Her bland expression told him that waiting for permission was not an option.

"All right. All right. All right," he said in exasperation." Marya was headstrong. Like a horse with the bit in its teeth, there was no stopping her.

The area around the front of the church was still crowded with churchgoers who had attended the last Mass and others who were arriving for the next one. The priest, Father Sestanovich, stood near the doorway chatting with the new arrivals and waving good-bye to departing parishioners.

Passing by them on their way to the scaffolding, Marya greeted them like old friends, "Good morning, Father. Good morning, everyone." But neither she nor Liam had time to hang around for chit chat. They plowed ahead and clambered up the ground-level ladder without stopping. Three levels up, she heard two parishioners call out to them to come back down immediately but she ignored them. This might be her last chance ever to inspect the belltower and she intended to go straight to the top.

From half way up, about one hundred feet above the square, the shouting faded. She looked down and saw people waving to them, obviously unhappy with her trespassing. "Too late now," she mumbled to herself. Some of the women in the crowd took up rosary beads and kept crossing themselves. She continued climbing steadfastly, her hair now flying about her face. Liam was just below her, moving up steadily, also ignoring the cries coming from below.

As the sounds made by the parishioners faded, a different noise took its place, the blending of high winds and the beat of a helicopter's rotors slicing the air. "We're almost there," she shouted to Liam. Looking down at the square, she saw the crowd below coalesce near the base of the scaffolding, some of the people still waving, the vast majority simply spellbound at the sight.

They arrived at the platform at the base of the cupola out of breath. They stepped onto a narrow walkway with a low balustrade that ran along all four sides of the cupola. The view of the long coastline and of islands in the distant north, the sunlight flashing on the Adriatic, the wind gusting in her face, all caused a slight disorientation and the feeling that her feet were not solidly planted. She leaned back to look up at the dome looming above her and realized that she was within three or four yards of the huge black cross.

Liam cautioned her. "I think we better take a look at it one at a time. The dome might not hold up under our combined weight."

"Let me go first this time," she said with her hand on his arm.

The rhythmic thumping of the rotors of a black helicopter, circling above the square, grew louder. She drew a deep breath before placing her foot on the ladder that curved from the walkway to the top of the dome. Then she climbed the ladder, monitoring her grip on each rung. She paused near the top of the cupola, just two feet below the cross and watched as the helicopter swooped in front of the cathedral and lowered itself into the heart of the square. The crowds scattered as it touched down. The loud whine of its engine began to fade.

The police, she thought. The priest or a parishioner, maybe even that busybody, Vicich called them. Well, they're too late. She was still determined to follow her hunch about the cross.

"You coming down? Looks like the police are here," Liam shouted.

"You kidding? They can't do anything to stop me now. I've got a few minutes at least to take a look and that's what I'm going to do."

"Okay, but be careful, for God's sake. There are cracks in this structure and the cross might not hold if you grab it. Just be careful."

"I will. I can see that. It won't take long," she replied. She inched up the last few rungs of the ladder that followed the arc of the dome and got into position right underneath the black iron cross. She reached out and placed her hand on its base, her fingers barely reaching around one corner of it. She spotted a crevice in the black cross but realized she could not get close to it without getting off the ladder and onto the eastern side of the dome itself. Holding on to the cross, she shimmied over to the crack. A nearby hammer carelessly left sitting on the crest of the dome by a worker gave her the idea of testing the cross for sound. As she shifted her weight to reach for it, she heard creaking within the structure. She waited before moving again. Then she took the hammer and rapped on the cross three times.

"It sounds hollow, Liam. It's not one solid piece," she shouted above the rush of the wind.

"Stop it! Don't hit it again! You should see what's happening underneath the dome. Bits of masonry are sifting down. Be careful and get off that dome as soon as you can. And don't shift your weight too suddenly."

"There's a slight crack in the cross, if only I can get close enough to see what's inside.

"Be careful, Marya, but hurry. The police are on their way."

"I will. I'm trying. Just....I'm real close now... Uuugh." She pulled herself up to the peak of the dome and straddled the base of the cross with her legs. It put her precisely where she needed to be able to peer into the crevice. She angled her right eye only two inches from the cross. "Gold," she screamed. "Liam, I see gold. There is gold inside the cross. I was right. It's gold. I know I'm not imagining it."

"Holy Mother! Fantastic. You've found the treasure!" He almost lost his balance as he leaned out from the walkway and looked up. But she was completely out of sight. He heard her, though.

Marya whooped with joy. "Whhoooooeeeeee! Hold on. I'm coming down. Wow! We've got proof! I knew it. I'm coming down so you can take a look."

Marya drew her legs back up, placed them behind and below her, lay flat on the dome and sidled back to the ladder. Coming down one careful step at a time, she swung over the balustrade onto the platform under the dome and embraced Liam in sheer joy.

"Marya, I can't believe you've found it. You were right all along. How sweet! You've done it." He hugged her tightly and planted a long kiss on her lips.

She drew back a little. "Of course. What did I tell you? Let me catch my breath. Whew!" She waved her hand in front of her face as if the wind whistling through the cupola were not enough. "Liam, there's more than just the gold."

"What else did you see up there?"

"Not up there. Inside the church. I realize now what I was looking at in the sanctuary."

"Oh, oh. Now what?"

"There's a huge fortune of gemstones inside the cathedral, too."

"Tell me about it later," he said. "This is enough for one day."

"I could just scream with joy. The gold of the Khan. We found it!" She whooped again and threw herself back into Liam's arms. "Whoopee! Go up and look for yourself, Liam."

Liam was about to go up when they both heard a familiar voice behind them. "Did you say gold?"

They wheeled around. Marya blinked twice to check her vision. Liam's jaw dropped.

"Thank you from the bottom of my heart, Marya. I knew you would take me to the treasure." It was Agarwal, his face rising up before them like something from a bad dream. He spoke with a lisp through a wide gap in his front teeth and he had a pistol aimed at them.

CHAPTER 80

Liam clenched his jaw. "You asshole."

"Now, let's not hear any of that offensive language, Lover Boy. After all, it's Sunday and we're on the belltower of a cathedral. Remember your Sunday School lessons." He wagged the gun. "Get up there. I want the two of you where I can see you while I inspect the cross."

"Are you crazy? There's no way that dome will support the three of us. The structure is weak. It'll collapse. It can't even support Marya's weight. What do you think they're doing all this reconstruction work for?"

"Get up there. Now."

They didn't budge.

"You don't want to go? Fine, I'll just shoot you. Don't play games with me." He wagged the gun. "You, too, dear."

Marya knew instantly that they were dealing with someone who had gone completely around the bend. Agarwal looked as if he had gone berserk, even worse than he was in Kashgar. He wouldn't hesitate to shoot her and Liam and shove their bodies over the balustrade. She didn't see any alternative but to get out on the scaffolding and climb back up on the dome. "Come on, Liam. We better do it."

As Agarwal followed them, the cupola groaned and cracked. Underneath their weight, something came apart. A heavy chunk of plaster or rock had fallen under the dome. The cross tilted a few degrees more. At its new angle, Agarwal had a clear view of the opening Marya had just inspected. "You two, get around on the other side while I have a peek." He kept the gun trained on them while he placed an eye close to the crevice. "Yes, yes. Very good, Marya. Once more, I thank you. The Khan will be glad to know that we have found the tablets. I'll have this cross removed in no time at all." He glanced briefly below at the square and waved with the hand that held the gun.

Liam and Marya followed his glance and saw a scene of calm below that belied the actual mayhem that was taking place. The crowd's gestures and shouting had stopped. A helicopter sat in the middle of the square. At strategic points, a team of men had taken up positions with bipod-mounted submachine guns.

Leaning against the dome, she heard only the rush of wind in her ears. Then, a hawk circling far above the cupola let out a long screech, sending shivers down her spine. She wondered how Agarwal had any chance at all of taking the gold from the cross. *The helicopter. They'll try to wrench it out of the dome by force and take it to the airport at Ploce.*

"Now, Marya, it's time for payback. The Khan ordered me to see that you died a slow, nasty death and it is my pleasure to carry that order out to the letter." Agarwal laughed like a hyena and raised his arm to whip her in the face with his gun. She reeled back instinctively, throwing her body out of reach. The dome shuddered and settled an inch. But with the sudden move, she slid down the dome out of control, rolled onto the scaffold, and flew over the side under her own momentum. She reached for a brace and gripped it with one hand, then two. "Liam," she screamed, her feet and legs dangling in space over the square. People below hid their faces. Far out beyond her, riding warm updrafts, tracing leisurely circles, the lone hawk shrieked again. Would she scream the same way when she let go and dropped two hundred feet to the square?

Agarwal turned his attention to Liam. He held onto the cross with one arm, while lashing out at Liam, anger carved into his features. He struck at Liam and bloodied his face. Liam scrambled to regain his foothold on the dome and raised his arm against further blows.

"Liam, help me. I can't hold on. Please!" She kicked to get her feet onto something that would support her weight but it only made her hands ache worse.

Liam threw a split-second look at her. He rounded the dome and slid lower on it, planting his foot against a wobbling scaffold. He made a grab for Agarwal's left ankle and yanked it, but Agarwal held on to the cross and the priceless treasure concealed within. The dome groaned heavily and settled. The cross bent to a forty-five degree angle, grinding away at its foundation in the cupola.

"Help, Liam! Help." Her legs and feet thrashed in space, unable to gain purchase on the scaffolding. The tendons of her hands were straining to maintain a grip on the bars but it would not be for long.

Liam desperately pulled again at Agarwal's ankle even as the deranged man flailed madly at his skull with the gun. A bad gash opened on his scalp and blood rushed down his forehead into his eyes. He tasted blood seeping into his mouth. Agarwal could have blown his brains out, but he seemed fixated on thrashing Liam and keeping his grip on the cross.

Agarwal tried to kick free from Liam's lock on his ankle and knock him off the cupola. But Liam held on with an even tighter grip. Lying as far back on the scaffold as he could, he planted his feet against the dome, giving his all to break Agarwal's grip on the cross. The mortal struggling of the two men set off loud cracking and splitting sounds. With a strident, metallic wrenching and scraping, the huge black cross tilted at an even steeper angle, but Agarwal refused to loosen his hold on it. Finally, a portion of the top of the cupola caved in and the cross came completely free from its base. It toppled over, bouncing at the halfway point of the dome, onto the planks of the scaffolding, shearing off an upright pole. Liam let go of Agarwal's leg and got out of the way. Agarwal still held on to it with an insane grip, sliding down the dome, gaining speed as he flew out into space. He somersaulted over the cross, screaming all the way down to the cobblestone square two hundred feet below.

Marya nearly let go when she heard the clanging sound of the cross crashing in front of the Cathedral. She saw that Agarwal's last blow had stunned Liam into a state of semi-consciousness. His eyes rolled back into his head and blood gushed from his head wound.

"Liam, please! Help me!"

She saw him wipe blood from his eyes with the back of his hand. He struggled to sit up and find the strength to reach out to her. He swung his legs to his left and lay down on his right side, his right arm extended towards her. Their fingers touched. Her hand grasped his wrist solidly. Quickly she maneuvered her right leg up to the scaffolding. With his left arm, he caught her leg behind the knee and pulled with all he had left in him.

"Liam," she screamed again. But there was nothing more he could do for her. He fell back against the dome. His head lolled forward and he blacked out.

CHAPTER 81

Bellardo and Carlotta got to the square minutes after Ambrosio and Pietro and just in time to see the unfolding of a bizarre scene. There was the usual collection of tourists present: American men in aloha shirts with their wives in short, halter-tops and sandals; fashionable Italians, stodgy-looking English, beefy Germans and camera-toting Japanese. A large group of nuns was also on hand for the celebration of a local saint's holiday. But, as he and Carlotta drew closer to the cathedral, they noticed that something was terribly awry. The people were all shielding their eyes, enthralled by something going on at the top of the belltower. Some were waving and calling out to two people moving about up there.

"What's going on, Carlotta?"

She gasped. "There's a man and a woman up there. I guess they don't belong up there. Some of the parishioners look really angry."

"Do you see Liam or Marya anywhere?" he asked, looking around.

"No, I haven't seen them yet. Mass just got out, so they must be here somewhere. She paused and put her hand to her mouth. "You don't suppose that those two people up there are our Liam and Marya, do you?"

"Can't be. What on earth would they be doing up there? Are you all right, Carlotta?"

A deafening roar came from the other side of the cathedral. A helicopter rose menacingly over the high peaked roof of the cathedral and moved out into the space above the square, looking as if its pilot might want to land it in front of the church. Screams rose from the crowd and people began to scatter. Powerful blasts of wind whipped up by the helicopter's blades drove all the groups from the center of the square, shouting, tripping and fleeing for the perimeter of the square.

Bellardo pushed Carlotta towards the Gabrielli museum. "Hurry. Move! Get over there in the doorway." He followed her, huffing.

"It can't land here in the square," Carlotta said, huddled against the façade of the museum, sheltering her eyes from the powerful gusts of wind. "Can it?"

"They're doing it. Who the hell are these people? The police wouldn't pull a crazy stunt like this."

The helicopter touched down nimbly in the middle of the square and disgorged a team of black-clad terrorist types with submachine guns. They fanned out quickly and took up positions around the square in pairs. One of them dashed for the scaffolding and began a very fast climb. Bellardo saw that the man had a gun holster on his hip.

Carlotta reached into her bag. "Those are the Khan's men. That's gotta be Liam and Marya up there." She took out a pair of binoculars and aimed them. "I was right." She put the binoculars away and felt in her bag for her Glock.

"Keep that out of sight. They're heavily armed."

"Just checking," she said.

Soon the climber was at the top of the tower and a struggle had broken out between him and Liam. The cross was tipping at a precarious angle and looked as if it would soon topple over. Marya had slipped off the side of the scaffolding and was dangling hundreds of feet above them. Then, the armed man slid down the dome towards the edge of the scaffolding and flew out into mid-air, hanging on to the cross. It seemed to hover an instant before hurtling down, pulling the man along with it. Over the sound of the helicopter's rotors, he heard the man's hideous scream, followed by a terrible clang when the cross landed on his body and the church steps.

Around the square, visitors and locals alike reacted in horror to the spectacle. People crossed themselves or turned their faces away. Some kept their eyes glued on the grisly sight. Carlotta saw a priest and his flock kneel down to pray. The gunmen drew in from their positions looking about warily, the barrels of their guns aimed at the clusters of people pressed up against the nearby buildings. Very cautiously they approached their motionless leader not far from a small cluster of nuns huddled against the wall of the church treasury. Carlotta watched nervously as two of the nuns left the group and moved towards the gunmen. They seemed to be offering help.

The gunmen shouted a warning to them, but it looked like they didn't understand the strange language. They raised their hands as if entreating them for permission to help the fallen man. One of the gunmen shouted at them and brandished his AK-47. He must have been confused at the loss of their leader and the inexplicable approach of the nuns. He fired a burst of gunfire at the pavement. One of the nuns staggered backwards. Had a ricocheting bullet struck her? Carlotta clutched her father's arm.

The nun regained her footing and reached within the voluminous folds of her left sleeve. She pulled out a seven-pound paving stone and hurled it at the head of the gunner. Thwack! It was a perfect hit! Bloodied and dazed, the masked commando flopped to the ground, sending his weapon clattering along the pavement. He writhed and held his head, shouting to his comrades for help. The crowds around the square remained frozen in shock.

The larger of the two nuns, a woman of prodigious size, moved with the force and speed of a professional American football player. In an instant, she was on top of the pistol-wielding backup to the injured man. She tackled him and brought him down as he fired once in desperation. The random shot spared the people in the square but miraculously struck the bell in the cupola above. A wave of parishioners and tourists fell to their knees crossing themselves, heads bowed in urgent prayer. The Japanese tourists bowed from the waist three times.

At the same time, the smaller nun blocked the arrival of another pair of commandos rushing to the rescue of their comrades. She gathered up her robe, demurely stuck out her black-stockinged leg and tripped one of them who had been madly waving his AK-47. She smartly spun about on her black-heeled shoes and gave the other a hard kick to the mid-section, sending him reeling backwards. Then she launched herself through the air and fell foursquare upon him like a TV wrestler. At that point, Marya pulled out her Glock and raced across the square. She held her gun aimed at the guy with the AK-47 and signaled him to move away from it slowly and raise his hands. She bent her knees, keeping her gun steadily trained on the man while she picked up the automatic weapon. In the meantime, Pietro had given his opponent a knock-out punch and whipped off his black veil and wimple.

The larger nun continued thrashing about on the ground with the commando, creating a spellbinding scene. Tourists and local men quickly gathered around her to watch the struggle. They began cheering the large nun on. The on-going match kept the crowd glued to the scene. Pietro approached, quickly wrenched a camera from the hands of one of the Japanese tourists and took a long series of shots to capture the special moment of his brother, the nun, taking out a Tajik foe.

At last, the struggle ended with a victory for Sister Ambrosio. His garb, his wimple, and his face were covered with dirt and dust as he jumped up, thrust his fist in the air and gave a victorious whoop. The crowd burst into applause. Giovanni Bellardo looked on approvingly. In minutes, the Bellardo team had the commandos lined up and handcuffed.

"Well done. Well done. Now get up there fast," Bellardo ordered his sons.

CHAPTER 82

Marya found Liam in his hospital room, his head heavily bandaged. He woke up as she entered the room. "You're looking a lot better," she said as she got to his bedside.

He turned his face towards her and smiled tepidly. "You came, Marya."

"Actually, I was with you when they brought you over here in the helicopter. You were out of it, completely."

"How long have I been here?"

"Well, they took you into the emergency room before 3. It's now 5:30."

"Really?

She touched his chin. "I'd kiss you but I probably shouldn't. I really hated to leave you all that time but I had to meet with the police. I came up as soon as I could."

"I hope you're not in a hurry to leave."

"No. I can stay a while. They offered to take me back there after we've had a chance to visit. They'll want to talk to you, too, but from the looks of it, they'll have to wait."

"We're in Dubrovnik, right?"

"Yes, and by now you should be familiar with this place. This is your second visit to this hospital. You've got to cut this out."

He laughed weakly. "You can say that again. So, help me remember what happened. I recall a few snatches of fighting with Agarwal on the steeple."

"You mean the cupola. That was a nightmare. You saved my life, for a third time, you know."

"I did? You've got to stop throwing yourself in harm's way," he said with a chuckle. "I do remember trying to pull you up onto the scaffolding, but not very clearly."

"It was in the nick of time. One more second and I would have been gone."

"What happened to Agarwal? He really whaled the tar out of me up there. I felt myself losing it." Liam touched the bandaging on his forehead gingerly.

"He fell to his death."

"No great loss." He paused, trying to remember something. "What about the Bellardos. Did they come?"

"Giovanni, the boys and Carlotta. They all came to the rescue. I hear Francesca stayed at the *sobe* just saying her prayers. It's always too much for her when they go out on one of their missions."

"I remember a helicopter landing and a bunch of police... or something."

"I thought it was the police, too, at first. That turned out to be Agarwal and his brigade. The Bellardos took care of them, though. In fact, let me show you something I brought." She held out a newspaper. "Look at the photo on the front page. Do you recognize the flying nun?"

"Either Pietro or Ambrosio, I gather."

"You've got it. It's Ambrosio. Pietro borrowed a camera and caught him tackling one of our Tajik guys."

"I'm not surprised. They have the world's best collection of disguises and the nerve to pull off any stunt they want. What about the cross? Have you had a good look at what was inside of it?"

"I'm getting to that. The cross came down and landed on top of Agarwal. It was gross. The crowd moved in to get a good look, but the Croatian authorities finally arrived and quickly roped off the area. I've been told that the metal sheath broke open and the gold cross inside was partly exposed. I've briefed Vicich fully on the golden tablets. Everything has been moved into the museum and is under round-the-clock security. You and I are invited to an exclusive unveiling of it in the museum. I want you to get well quick and be there with me when they do it. Liam, I've waited for this all my life. I can't stand the suspense. I just want to inspect those golden tablets and run my fingers over the inscriptions in Chinese characters and Mongolian lettering."

"What about the jewels inside the church? When we were up on the tower, didn't you tell me that you thought there was more treasure inside the church?"

"There is. But I haven't said a word about that to anyone yet. I'm scheduled to see Dr. Vicich tomorrow afternoon at the museum. I'll drop the bomb on him then."

"Is the treasure as great as you thought?"

"Bigger. You remember the mural in the sanctuary, on the left side? The one that shows Marco Polo and his Sung Princess literally plastered in jewels? Well, those jewels, my dear, are real!"

"Good Lord."

"They're huge, jumbo rubies, emeralds and sapphires and there are dozens of them, adorning both Marco and Mei Hua. Polo's diary says that they concealed the treasures of Kublai Khan while keeping them in plain view at the Church of Saint Mark. They sure did a masterful job of it."

"How the hell did they manage that? I mean it's been on exhibit for seven hundred years, after all."

"I'll tell you how. They left the gems unpolished and dull. They look like nothing more than ordinary colored glass or paste. It was a perfect ruse. Almost. They intended it as a message to mankind, a symbol of peace and unity, a treasure to be put to use sometime in the future."

"And it worked."

"Until now."

"Wow, think of all the people of this island who have worshiped there and never had a clue."

"Fantastic, isn't it? Marco realized late in life that he would never be able to put the Khan's plan into effect in his lifetime and that unification probably wouldn't happen for a very long time, far into the future either. I think he wanted Moreta to take his diary and see that it was well-protected until the right time. And she did that. It was like tossing a message in a bottle into the ocean, hoping some day that it would be cast upon a hospitable shore."

"And you're the one who found that bottle. Marya, this is going to be a bomb shell. You do, realize that, don't you? Now, what I still want to know is how much all that stuff is worth, the whole lot of it?"

Liam's question took her aback. "Their value simply as gemstones is not as important as their historical value, Liam. What have I been telling you all along?"

"Yeah, I know, but still... what can you get for them? Bottom line."

She let out a sigh of frustration. "Okay. Best guess, Mr. Bottom Line. The gems, the Golden Tablets of Command and Marco's journal, the whole ensemble, could be upwards of a hundred million dollars."

"Sweet. And what's our take? What do we get out of it?" he asked in a deadpan voice.

"Not a cent," she said indignantly. "Why should we?"

"What? After all we've been through and we don't collect a farthing?"

"How could you think such a thing, Liam?"

"Oh, I don't know. Gosh." He gave her a mischievous look. "You'd think that there would be something in it for us, some little compensation for all our troubles. You know, something to sweeten the deal a little. Couldn't we just keep the diary and sell it for a coupla million?"

Then she realized she had been had and they both laughed together. Afterwards, they chatted for a while about their immediate plans, hers to check into her family tree, clean out her office and take a break in California and his to reconnect with his family.

"So that's it, huh? Is that all?"

"Yeah, that's about it. Gotta get going now. My helicopter is waiting." She put her hand gently on his cheek, keeping it clear of the bandaging. "Oh, I almost forgot. One more thing."

He looked at her expectantly.

"Do you recall the first time we came to Korcula on the ferry?"

"Sure I do."

She was a little uneasy with the next question. "Remember that little brochure of yours that told about the island's lovely attractions?"

He wasn't sure where the conversation was heading. "I think so. All that stuff about the orchards, the churches, the beaches et cetera. Yeah, I remember vaguely."

"And remember how I had to correct your understanding of the word, naturist?

"What are you getting at? That I'm some kind of dummy?"

"No." She hesitated to go on. "I was just going to suggest that, before we leave Korcula, you and I go for that naturist swim after all." Whew! There, she got it out.

Liam tried to raise himself from the bed, succeeding only a little before falling back. He gaped. His mouth went dry. "Ah. Well. That would be very nice, very nice. Yes, I think I could handle that."

"I know just the place. I've found a cute little villa on the north shore of the island with its own secluded cove and a little beach for swimming just a few steps down from the patio. It would be perfect for your recovery. I'm thinking of booking it for three or four days."

He managed to reach up and pull her towards him. "You picked a fine time to tell me about a naturist swim."

She leaned in closer and kissed him lightly on the lips, trying not to send him into a paroxysm of pain. "Just hurry up and get well." She straightened up and left his room, looking back at him with a smile.

CHAPTER 83

Monday morning, she found the Bellardos at the *sobe* packing and preparing to leave for Venice. All of them gathered by the car across the piazza from the main gate of the city. They planned to take the ferry across to Drvenik in the afternoon. "Grazie, Giovanni. Grazie, Francesca. I'm going to miss you," she said, hugging them. Tears came to her eyes.

Francesca took her in her arms. "Don't cry. This isn't the last time we will ever see you, you know."

"Of course. I just can't help it. You've been like my own family to me. After all that we've been through…"

"You *are* part of our family and you'll come back to Venice some day, I know," she said giving her a wink. "You'll come back with Signore Di Angelo again and you can stay with us as long as you want."

Marya smiled. "Grazie. Yes, that could happen, I suppose."

"You made a believer out of me, Marya," Giovanni added. "I thought you were insane to think you'd find any treasure belonging to the Polos. I had no faith in you. To tell you the truth, it's we who are indebted to you. When we get back to Venice, there will be lots of changes to make."

Marya knew what Bellardo was really telling her—there would be no further trading in treasures looted from archaeological sites. She had also heard that Pietro and Vittoria were planning on getting married and that Carlotta was going to finish her degree in art history and look for work as a curator. No more gun-slinging for her. And no more cross-dressing for Ambrosio. She hugged them all, had a round of laughs, and hugged them again.

Suddenly Carlotta shrieked. "Hurry, let's get going. Marya, run! Get out of here. Get to the *sobe*." A mob of news reporters, photographers and cameramen came charging across the piazza straight at them. The Bellardos piled into the car and slammed the doors, waving goodbye. Marya fled to the *sobe.*

* * * * *

That afternoon, Marya went to see Dr. Vicich at the Gabrielli Museum. She was not aware of a phone call from the Ministry of Culture in Zagreb that he had just received. The important caller put Dr. Vicich on the defensive demanding that he meet with the bishop of the diocese to work out arrangements for securing the valuable cross that had fallen from the cupola. "What were those Americans doing up there and why did I have to learn about it in the newspapers?" the voice screamed at him. "Are you some kind of incompetent?" The voice also threatened him with eternal damnation if any harm came to the treasure. "We're sending down a team of experts right away. Have accommodations ready for them." The last words rang in his ear as the caller slammed the phone down.

In his office she found Vicich red-faced and subdued. She told him she had come to do a little genealogical research while her companion was recuperating from his injuries. She wondered if he was going to give her a stern lecture on breaking rules and scaling the belltower but he didn't. "My apologies. You did well. I'm sorry I insulted you so badly on the ferry," he said sheepishly.

"That's behind us now. But there's something else you should know, Dr. Vicich. There's more to the Polo fortune than just the golden tablets. I believe you'll also find a trove of precious gems in the church sanctuary."

His face went white.

"Why don't we go look at them together. Genealogy can wait."

Vicich was not one to make the same mistake twice.

He told his staff that he would be out for a while. He walked with Marya across the piazza to the cathedral and went straight to the sanctuary.

"Up there, Dr. Vicich. Do you see those two figures? That's Marco Polo there and a Chinese princess known as Mei Hua next to him. I believe the jewels in their costumes are real."

He didn't really believe her but he got a ladder from the caretaker anyway and climbed up to within inches of the faces of the royal figures. He reached out and touched the crown of Marco Polo, gasped, and slowly withdrew his hand. The figures of Marco and the princess were studded with oversized gems. Sapphires, rubies, and emeralds seemed to smother them and dot the whole mural. A sack of coins Marco held in one hand also had a suspicious quality to it, as if its painted stucco surface might actually be hiding other jewels. Elsewhere in the sanctuary other figures of important townsfolk were bedecked in heavy rings and collars.

Marya conferred with him for a while before heading on to meet withVicich's assistant in the archives. Vicich headed to a phone right away and called the bishop, further advising him to lock the doors of the cathedral and post a sign, closing it for repairs. Fearing another tongue-lashing from the Ministry of Culture, he also placed a permanent guard on the premises before making a call about the spectacular, new discovery.

* * * * *

"Dr. Bradwell, you're just in time," Vicich's young, long-haired assistant said, as he emerged from a wire-caged section of the basement holding a box full of documents. He put it down with a thud on a wide oak desk.

"Looks like you've been busy, Mr. Viskovich."

"I sure have. No one's been into these records in

decades, I can assure you. In fact, I don't think anyone around here realizes what we have in these cartons. Come around this side. I have something to show you."

Marya went around the desk as Viskovich pulled a box closer. "This is what we have on Saint Mark's murals. If this is not enough, I have other boxes of stuff from five other churches in and around Korcula. You're welcome to go through those, too."

"This bunch is all I need, thank you. And what about baptismal records?"

"You'll find what you need in these cartons. They're the baptismal records of the parish of Korcula from the 13th century on." He pointed to the cartons containing bound volumes of varying age and thickness. "Please be careful with them. They haven't been microfilmed yet. That's my next project."

"Have you found any references to Polos in the 19th and early 20th centuries?"

"Yes. These volumes here contain a few references to the Pilichs."

"Pilich? That was my grandmother's maiden name."

"I thought you'd be interested in that surname—it's the Croatian equivalent of Polo. There used to be many Pilichs both here and up the coast in Sibenik. You realize, of course, that many Korculans emigrated to the U.S., especially to California about a hundred years ago."

"I thought my grandmother might have come from this island, but I wasn't sure."

"I asked around and I learned that quite a few left here for San Francisco and

other points along the northern California coast. It's possible your grandmother and her parents were part of that migration."

Viskovich left her alone, poring over volume after volume of baptismal records, here and there taking notes whenever the Pilich name appeared. Centuries of records fell away under her steady concentration and note-taking. She only stopped to relieve the tension growing in her neck muscles and to take one potty break, but she returned quickly to the task.

By late afternoon, as she closed in on the first quarter of the 14th century, she was getting both hungry and tired. She turned one more page in a very fragile volume, determined to quit and get something to eat at Zoran's, when suddenly her eyes were drawn to the notation of a baptism for Mrko Pilich, illegitimate son of Mrko Pilich and Lijpa Ružica, "the Tatarica."

"Found it!" She pushed away from the table and jumped up, clenching her fists and hitting the air with them. "Yes!" She couldn't believe her good fortune. She sat down again, forcing herself to proceed calmly, and examined the entry again. *1299 A.D. Father, Mrko Pilich—Marco Polo in Croatian, Mother, Lijpa Ružica, Beautiful Flower—a simple and direct translation of her Chinese name, Mei Hua. The locals called her the Tatarica—it must have been a catch-all designation for any Asian woman.*

She took notes furiously and then moved ahead to find records of other offspring. Two years later in the same volume, she found a daughter, also illegitimate, spelled Marija with the 'j' pronounced as a 'y.' "Bingo." She sat back, sighed, and let her shoulders slump both from exhaustion and joy over her discovery. As she took careful notes on this second entry, she realized that what she had just found might actually be proof of her grandmother's story. This would have staggering implications for her personally and for history in general. Her results showed that Polo did indeed have surviving children and that there was an unbroken succession of generations of Pilichs on this quiet Dalmatian island down to the modern period. She was a direct descendant of Marco Polo and Mei Hua.

She fiddled with the gold locket that Liam had given her and pondered over her findings. *I have the baptismal records of Marco and Mei Hua's children. I have portraits of Marco and Mei Hua themselves in the sanctuary. And I have objective proof of Marco's travels to the Far East in the form of a great treasure that's been staring people in the face for seven hundred years. By golly, I think I may have outdone Heinrich Schliemann.*

She gathered up her notes, put them into her briefcase and snapped it shut. Another bombshell of publicity was about to burst over the quiet village of Korcula. The Pilich clan had been a large one in the early centuries, but had diminished, eventually disappearing altogether by the twentieth century, with the last of them immigrating to the United States. As Viskovich had suggested, her great grandparents were among them. These findings together with the treasures revealed at the cathedral added up to an overwhelming personal victory and a major contribution to understanding the historical figure of 'Il Milione' himself. She had thoroughly validated his claims of traveling to China with his father and uncle and returning with a fortune of astonishing value. How would she manage the inevitable publicity? *Headlines in the New York Times: Descendant of Marco Polo discovers amazing proof of medieval travels from Venice to China.*

On her way out, she stopped to thank Viskovich.

"Think nothing of it. By the way, there's something else I came across among the old volumes." You should take a look at it. I'm told you can read some Chinese."

She was curious. What would Chinese language material be doing in the archive, she wondered?

He handed her several individual sheets of thick rice paper that had been folded in three. As she opened the flap on the right side of the first sheet, she saw what looked like an original petition to a Chinese emperor. A cursory look told her that it dated from the reign of Kublai Khan and concerned the question of permission for the Polos to return to the West. She reached out to grab the back of a chair to steady herself.

"Are you feeling all right?" he asked. "You look a little pale. Can I bring you a glass of water?"

"Yes, please. It's been quite a day." She sat down and took a deep breath before opening the second sheet. The document was in Mongolian and she was unable to decipher it. She set it aside. She got the shock of her life as she read the third one.

CHAPTER 84

There was a near riot in progress outside Sternich's *sobe* when Marya returned from the Gabrielli Museum. A throng of TV reporters and cameramen jostled and surrounded her, making it impossible for her to get to the doorway. Television crews from around the world clamored to get pictures of her and a piece of the sensational story of her kidnapping. Rumors of some kind of treasure discovered at the Cathedral and the role she played in the exciting clash atop the belltower only added fuel to the fire. The little fortress village of Korcula was now the focus of worldwide attention. News men and women begged her to give them a few minutes.

"Could we have a few words with you, Dr. Bradwell?" Katie Couric pleaded as she shoved a microphone under her nose.

For fifteen minutes they peppered her with questions about her abduction to far-away Kashgar. "What was the Khan like? How did he treat you? Are you planning to write a book? When would it be published? When will you give an extended interview? Where did the inspiration to research Polo come from? How did you deal with naysayers? She replied directly to some questions, evasively to others, and didn't dare mention her latest discoveries at the archive. She tried to leave. "Dr. Bradwell, how are you connected to reports of gold treasure discovered at the Cathedral?" a reporter persisted. She held a hand up to end the interview. "That'll be all... I've got to go. Thank you. I'll have more for you another time. Bye."

Zoran cracked the door open briefly, let her in and closed it fast. He told her right away that the phone had been ringing all afternoon for her but that he had not understood a word of what the callers said. He hoped that she would stay around long enough to handle all the calls herself.

She went to her room to reflect on the rush of events that were overtaking her. She made a few key decisions. She would have that date with Liam before anything else. After that, she would return to the U.S., grant one carefully chosen interview on her own terms, prepare for her ten-minute session with the U.S. in New York and then go up to Boston to clean out her office. In the meantime, Liam would return the diary of Marco Polo to the nuns at the Convent of San Lorenzo and rendezvous with her in the Boston area while keeping out of reach of prying reporters and their cameras.

* * * * *

Before noon on Tuesday, Liam placed a call from the hospital in Dubrovnik and got through to Marya after repeated busy signals.

"Liam, thank God, it's you. Are you all right?"

"Yes, fine, but you sound frazzled."

"It's been hectic. I don't want to go into it. When are you coming up to Korcula?"

"That's what I called to tell you. I'm doing fine. The doctors have checked me out and given me clearance to leave, so I'm taking the ferry up today."

"Wonderful. I can't wait."

"I'm really looking forward to our little getaway."

Marya hesitated. "…Ah, Liam. We've got a new problem."

"I don't want to hear it."

"We might have a little trouble with reporters and paparazzi."

"Is that all? That's nothing."

"It is if you still want to go for that naturist swim with

me. I don't know how you feel, but I don't want to have my *derriere* emblazoned on every scandal sheet in Europe and America."

"Are you kidding me?"

"I'm serious. I'm practically under house arrest here at the Sternich's place. There's a mob out there right now. If I so much as poke my nose through the curtains in the front window, there's a near riot. If the paparazzi catch us together, we'll never shake them."

"Well, the hell with them."

"But Liam, that doesn't help the problem."

"Get Zoran to run your errands and tonight we will slip out of Korcula like thieves in the night. No problem. I'll see you this afternoon."

* * * * *

Liam's words boosted her confidence. She took care of booking the villa, rented a car and planned the meals. She commissioned Zoran to do the shopping for her. He came back from his rounds that afternoon with a fine selection of local white and red wines, excellent cheeses and the fixings for some superb dinners.

Liam arrived in the late afternoon and got through the cordon of reporters out front with less trouble than she had earlier in the day. They waited until after 9 P.M. to make their getaway when there were only a handful of media people lingering about. Zoran had the car loaded and ready. They made a dash for it past the reporters, running down an alley off the piazza, along the outer wall in a great circle and ducked behind parked cars until they got to theirs. They hopped in and headed for the hills above the town. Ater a number of hairpin turns on a road through a dark pine forest they saw no auto lights behind them. An hour later, Liam quietly pulled the car into the driveway of the villa by the sea.

Scrub pines and dense shrubs covered the view of the villa from the road. A grove of olive trees on both sides of the villa further secured their privacy. Marya went through all the rooms, opening the windows to admit the sea breeze. It was breathlessly warm, but cool breezes soon made the villa comfortable.

Liam made trips back and forth from the car to the house with all her baggage, his backpack and the piles of food that they had brought along. He placed the last bag of groceries on the table and began to put the perishables into the refrigerator when Marya came into the kitchen. She looked into his eyes and gently closed the refrigerator door.

"That can wait," she said, tugging at Liam's belt. "You get into your birthday suit and I'll go get the towels." He stripped quickly as she dimmed the kitchen lights and went to the bathroom. She returned to the kitchen with towels for each of them and handed him one. Then she removed her top, let her skirt settle about her feet and stepped out of her clothes. In the dim light she could make out Liam's trim torso. She let him take her hand and lead her out through the open French doors onto the flagstone patio. Her vision sharpened under the brilliant light of the moon and she took a moment to appreciate his masculinity.

The full moon was high over the hills as they stepped out naked to the edge of the veranda. They stood on a gentle slope, only yards from the shore. The light of the moon created a sparkling path across the cove and waves of spice-scented, warm air wafted upwards from the slope before them. "Are you ready?" She suddenly tossed her towel on the patio, reached around and pinched his firm butt.

"Oooww. Hey, I'll get you."

She was already off and running down the path to the water.

Liam flew after her and when he caught up, he took his towel and flicked it, barely nicking her on the left hip.

He threw it behind him and, in a flash, seized her hand and pulled her into the water. He took her by the waist and drew her into his embrace. They wheeled around, ducked under water and came up laughing. Then, silent, kissing, embracing greedily, they let the salty tang pour down from their hair and seep between their lips.

Marya bathed in the glow of the shimmering waters, in the pure clarity of the moonlight, in the coaxing tenderness of Liam's arms. They rocked with the gentle motions of the waves that rhythmically rose and fell in the cove. She had a sense of being home, in the land of her ancestors, with the man she wanted. She had not anticipated this closeness, this passion, this sense of fullness that Liam brought her.

She learned that he could be exciting and serious, gentle and strong, and she trusted him, loved him deliriously, and wanted to be with him forever. The seduction of the Mediterranean was complete and she surrendered herself into his arms, holding him tight, hoping the moment would never end.

Liam picked her up and carried her to the water's edge where he found the towels and draped them over her shoulders and his. The warm updrafts of the low hills gave off a sweet, resinous aroma as they toweled off. They came up to the veranda and dropped onto a plush sofa, staring at the inky blackness of the western sky and the vast glow of the moonlight in the east. All about them only the sounds of countless crickets and the lapping waters of the little cove could be heard. It was a long time before they pulled themselves away from the evening outdoors to go to bed.

CHAPTER 85

Her time together with Liam was glorious and she believed Liam felt as she did. They explored. They laughed. They swam. They had candle-lit dinners, sipped wine on the patio and walked the hills and orchards all about the cove. And they talked. They joked. They thrilled to each other's stories.

"I never thought you'd really invite me to go skinny-dipping," Liam said, sitting with her one evening under the grape arbor overlooking the cove.

"Excuse me. Around here, the correct term is naturist swimming. And I'm surprised that we actually got out of town without a legion of photographers barging in on us. What if they caught us in the buff? I can just see the reaction of your father and mother back in Boston. No one followed us, though, I'm quite sure."

Marya broached the topic of going back home. She wondered if they would see much of each other after they got back to Massachusetts. Would their plans for the future cross? Or would they drift apart geographically and emotionally? She was still curious about his parents and his brothers and sisters. He had seemed reluctant to discuss his family as they drove down the Dalmatian coast and he never made a definite offer to introduce her to them since then.

But this time he appeared to open up to the suggestion. "My parents? Really? You still want to meet them?"

"Of course. I'd love to meet the fine souls that raised such a good man."

"Well, since you put it that way, I think I can arrange a special introduction, but only if you behave. I'll even give you the grand tour of the North End."

"The North End. I've only been there once." The recollection of the dinner with Agarwal soured her mood a little but she decided to say nothing about it.

"You'll have to reciprocate, though. I'd like you to show me northern California, those beaches you brag about all the time and the redwoods."

"Gladly. I'd go anywhere with you."

"Here's what we do: we spend half the year in Massachusetts, half the year in California and the other half here on the Dalmatian coast."

"You're math's a little wacky, but it's a great idea."

He pulled her close and kissed her. "This has got to end," he said teasing her.

"It will, and all too soon. It's going to be hectic when we go back."

"What's first on your agenda?'

"I have to fly to New York. I've agreed to do a televised interview with *National Geographic*. Then I'm going to chat up the President at the U.N. on the topic of Central Asia. I think he can use better advice than he's getting. After that, I take the train to Boston and clean out my office. I hope I don't have to see Lafferty, that's all."

"Aren't you forgetting something?"

"No, I think that covers it."

"What about Marco Polo's journal?"

She stood up. "Oh, I forgot. I've been enjoying your company and the villa so much."

"Why don't you let me have it? I'll take it back to the poor sisters."

"It's worth millions. Can I trust you with it?" she asked in jest.

"Moi? Of course, you can. You don't think I'd go and hawk it somewhere, do you?"

"No, silly. Can't you tell I'm just teasing?" She felt a little uneasy about the way he protested. "Where's that Irish humor?"

His face grew serious. "I'll take it back to them and may God strike me down dead if I'm lying."

"I believe, you, Liam. Don't take me so seriously."

"Fine. No problem."

She passed her hand through his damp, curly hair and looked into his blue eyes. "Good, and when I get back to Boston, the first thing I want to do is see you again."

He got up abruptly from the seat, snatched a cluster of grapes from the vine overhead and handed her a few. "Talk about going back to civilization, why don't we take a look at what's happening on T.V. I think we both need to brace ourselves for what's coming."

They went inside. Liam turned on the TV. Greenish images of a scene filmed with grainy, night-vision filtering appeared on the screen. The Croatian announcer spoke with animation and ended the news segment with a chuckle. Marya's face froze.

"Did you hear that?" she asked, forgetting that Liam didn't understand the language of the announcer. "Look, Liam. Oh, my God, no. They were here. They found us. That's us on TV. He gave our names."

Liam saw two pale green extraterrestrial-looking figures on the screen, dashing into the water, romping about and splashing. "Never thought I'd see my ass on a TV news program."

"With my luck, it will be the shot seen around the world," she said, holding a hand cupped over her mouth.

They looked at each other and both broke out laughing. It didn't really matter now. Nothing about their relationship could embarrass her.

Before they went to bed, she dug into her suitcase and found the diary. She gave it to Liam with no misgivings about entrusting it to him and watched as he put it in his backpack.

"There will be overdue charges. It's been over two weeks," he said sternly.

"I know. It's my fault."

"But the nuns at that run-down convent can use the money. Come to think of it, if they sell the journal, they could afford to turn that dump into a palace."

* * * * *

The unveiling of the Golden Tablets of Command was to take place under tight security in the basement of the Gabrielli Museum. Dignitaries from Zagreb and Dubrovnik filed into the museum besieged by mobs of gawkers and media people. The scene bordered on pandemonium. Television reporters babbled in front of the cameras in a dozen different languages. One of them, using the Cathedral as a backdrop, shouted news of the very latest discovery—a huge, unsuspected cache of jewels that had been on display for centuries in the sanctuary. He ordered his cameraman to pan across the square to show the overflowing crowds. Korcula, he emphasized, was now the hottest place in the universe, with Dr. Bradwell's imminent arrival for the unveiling expected to make it even hotter.

She and Liam, under police escort, were the last to run the gauntlet in front of the museum and enter the basement room just in time for the official unveiling. The Croatian Minister of Culture, Anton Antunovich, was on hand. Also present were the Bishop of Dubrovnik, Dr. Vicich, several archaeologists and a clutch of security men talking into electronic devices. Antunovich and the Bishop declared jointly that these treasures now placed the Cathedral in the front ranks of World Heritage sites. They announced plans for sending some of the treasures on a world tour, first throughout Croatia and other recently war-torn Balkan countries, then Western Europe, North America, Central Asia and the rest of the world. "Dr. Bradwell deserves credit for their discovery and for the idea of sharing them with the world," Antunovich said.

The pompous Minister delivered a long speech on the little-known contributions of Croatia to world civilization. Her seamen were responsible for the success of Columbus' voyages to the Americas and her farmers pioneered the development of a world-acclaimed wine. He also boasted that Korcula was the proven birthplace of the world's greatest explorer, Marco Polo.

Antunovich gave himself the honor of unveiling the golden tablets. As he closed his speech, he whipped the sheet off with a flourish. The hush in the room was a welcome relief from his pompous noises. The deeply engraved commands of the Khan on the tablets drew admiring stares. "What do the words say?" the Bishop asked.

Marya stepped forward and looked down at the tablets, each one engraved with the same command. She let her fingers slip into the sensuous strokes of the characters. The graceful calligraphy in gold transported her to the other side of the world and seven hundred years back in time. "Eternal Heaven, bless the name of the Khan. Let him who does not respect him be put to death."

"What were these things for?" the Bishop asked.

"They were the ultimate passports," she explained. "They were issued to the Polos to insure that all three of them got home safely to Italy with their wealth. Without them, they could never have made it alive across the khanates and home to Italy. Let's see the reverse side."

Marya held her breath as she flipped one of the tablets over. The Mongol script on the other side issued the same command, she imagined, but she could not read it. Liam leaned close to her and whispered that the market value of the objects had just multiplied one hundred fold. She shook her head. "They are priceless. They are the patrimony of mankind." Marya realized that Polo and Mei Hua had conspired in love to safeguard the incredible treasure from Kublai Khan's Beijing.

Antunovich turned to Vicich. "We need the utmost security placed on these objects."

After the unveiling ceremony, the exclusive group dispersed quickly. Liam and Marya went upstairs. He shifted the backpack that he already had on his back and retrieved a suitcase that he had left at the admission desk.

"I love you, Liam."

"I love you, too."

"Take care of that diary. Tell the sisters to get some good advice before they do anything with it."

"I will. Not to worry." He took her in his arms and gave her a kiss. "See you in Boston. Ciao!" Then he was off. She watched him as he was about to disappear around the corner of the Gabrielli. He turned and waved good-bye to her and she waved back, already feeling his absence. Then, she fled the square and teams of cameramen and reporters chasing after her.

CHAPTER 86

Marya arrived in New York for her interview with Elaine Brown, the middle-aged British host of the popular television journal, *National Geographic.* The cameras moved in for a close-up of the two women in the glass-paneled ground-floor studio. Outside on the sidewalk bunches of visitors to the city waved and performed antics for the benefit of the folks back home. "Tell me Marya, how did you first become interested in the treasure of Marco Polo?" she asked in her deep accent.

"My grandmother and my mother both were my inspiration," she explained, detailing the stories about her ancestry and the encouragement she recalled from her childhood days.

"What exactly were your feelings at the moment the officials unveiled the Golden Tablets of Command in the Gabrielli Palace museum?"

"I was thrilled. It was the high point of my life as a historian." She elaborated on the unveiling of the treasure in the basement of the museum and the sense of contact with the past that the treasure gave her.

Elaine turned to more controversial questions: "You must be aware of the uproar your discoveries have made. I'm referring to the squabbling among so many parties—like Croatia, Italy, China, and the Central Asian Republics—over the proper place for both the golden tablets and the jewels that have come to light. What's your take on the issue?"

Here she chose her words carefully to explain what she believed were the intentions of Marco and Mei Hua in disguising the jewels and the golden tablets the way they did.

"Their purpose was to provide a symbol of the essential brotherhood of all mankind. It is a message of peace that they are proclaiming from the sanctuary of Saint Mark's. I believe that when the treasures are exhibited around the world, they will have a pacifying effect. You can't fail to appreciate the message when you see them."

"What do you suggest be done with them, then?"

"I'm all for sharing the treasure, having it travel around the world as an exhibit that would remind nations of the oneness of mankind. I suggested this plan to the Minister of Culture of Croatia and he has endorsed the idea. Surely, Marco Polo himself and the Princess Mei Hua would have wanted something like that."

"We've all heard of Kublai Khan in our school days, Marya. Did you discover anything that helps us understand him any better as an important historical figure?"

"I'll have a lot more to say about that at a later date. For the sake of viewers, I'll just say that Kublai Khan was a great leader and thinker. Certainly his personality and the role he played in Asian history will have to be completely revised with all the new material that has surfaced. No question."

"You're referring to the secret diary of Polo, aren't you?"

"Yes, and some other, extraordinary documents from the Korculan archive."

"Are there any lessons in all of this for our world leaders today?"

"Yes. Definitely. I'd go so far as to say that leaders today would do well to implement some of the great ideas of Kublai Khan. If he were alive today, he would be considered a world class statesman. In the U.S. we use the word, 'presidential.'

"I understand that today President Hutchinson is going to deliver an important policy speech at the U. N. that relates to the U. S. role in Central Asia. We have learned that you will be talking to him just before he gives that speech. Do you care to let us in on what you're going to tell the President when you see him this afternoon?"

"I'll pass on that, thank you." Marya had thought deeply about the upcoming private time she would have with Hutchinson. If he listened to what she had to say, she would have a chance to influence the course of events. She did not want to be the one to steal his thunder in advance of the speech, if there were going to be any changes made in the direction of U. S foreign policy on Central Asia.

The interview concluded with a personal chat about Marya's plans for the future. "I have some very engaging business to take care of in Boston and after that I plan some quiet time in northern California with friends and family. I also have an urge to return to Croatia for some unfinished research." She was hoping that Liam was watching.

"Finally, Marya, would you care to comment on that widely circulated video that purports to show you and a significant other bathing in the nude in the waters of Korcula?"

"Oh that? Yes. I was afraid that would happen, I mean, I was worried that the paparazzis would catch us."

"Would you do it again?"

"Of course. The man in that video saved my life—twice. Excuse me. Three times. The first time in Venice. Another time in Kashgar and, then, he pulled me to safety on the belltower of St. Mark's in Korcula."

"Three times is a charm," Elaine Brown commented.

She hadn't thought of it that way and was at a loss for words.

Miss Brown quickly picked up the slack in the interview and brought it to a close. "Thank you, Dr. Bradwell. I'm glad you chose to do this interview with *National Geographic*. Your quest has truly taken us all on an extraordinary voyage of discovery and the lessons of your findings will surely have a great impact." The taping ended. Off camera, Ms. Brown told her, "I would give anything to have had the adventure you had with that Mr. Di Angelo."

* * * * *

A female security guard let Marya pass from the foyer into the spacious, well-appointed living room of a suite on the 14th floor of the U. N. building. The apartment was reserved for dignitaries and had a panoramic view of the Hudson River that drew her to the floor-to-ceiling windows. Because she was nervous, she declined an invitation from an aide to sit. How many opportunities would she have to talk to the President? How many opportunities would any expert on Central Asian affairs have at such a critical time in history? Her stomach was in knots with fear that she would fail to find the words to convince him that there needed to be a drastic turnaround in American foreign policy in the region before it was too late.

If she failed, she foresaw the growth from the present small infusion of 'military advisers' in Kazakhstan and Uzbekistan into a full-scale, all-out campaign requiring tens of thousands of U. S. soldiers. Would the NATO allies join us? She doubted it. Would conventional forces, no matter how well-equipped with the latest technology, be a match for a force like the Khan's? Possibly, but it would be costly and bound to take years, in any event, given the hyper-nationalism he was whipping up across the continent. Surely there had to be an alternative to the dead-end track the administration was on. She looked at the yellowed rice-paper document written in Chinese that she held in her hands. Kublai Khan would have approached the situation differently than a modern technocrat, she thought.

Hutchinson strode into the room. "Good day, Dr. Bradwell. So, you're the little woman who created the storm over Asia."

She turned but remained near the window as he

walked across the room, his hand reaching out to hers. His sculpted features and mane of silver-gray hair made him the equal of any Hollywood actor playing the role of president. Gregory Peck came to mind. "Mr. President, it's a pleasure and a privilege to be here."

He invited her to take a seat opposite him. A low table decorated with an arrangement of anthuriums sat between them. A picture of the beloved U Thant looked down upon them from above a false mantle. He looked at his watch. "Well, shall we begin, Dr. Bradwell? What do you have there, a crib sheet?"

"Well, I never quite thought of it that way, Sir. But, you're right in a sense. What I have, Sir, is a message worth sharing with you from another great world leader."

"Oh, who's it from?"

"Kublai Khan, Sir. It may be eight centuries old, but it's a perfect fit for the situation the U. S. faces in the region today." She took only seven minutes, but in that time she detailed the Khan's plan and pushed it as the most sensible set of ideas for the region that Hutchinson was scheduled to speak about in half an hour. She told him that it was the actual imperial commission given to Marco Polo's father and uncle. It summarized what they were to accomplish. Its scope was as grandiose as the geographical region it was meant to cover. If the world body were to adopt its proposals in education, religious tolerance, trade, economic reform and road-building, it could lead to important breakthroughs.

"What about our partners, the Chinese?"

"It would give them reason not to be so heavy-handed in their treatment of minority peoples under their control or to be tempted to intrude into Central Asia. This could also give hope to fledgling states in the region and keep the U. S. from stumbling into a disastrous adventure that could cost us lives and billions of dollars. I've prepared a translation of the document for you. I'll leave that with you, as well as a copy of the original for your Asia experts to pore over."

Hutchinson leaned forward and took the two sheets from her. "How does this address the problem of the Khan, though? He's still on the loose. The Chinese are pounding the hell out of the mountains he fled into. I don't see that doing any good."

"Study this paper, Sir. That's all I ask. If this program is implemented, the Khan is finished. He can stay holed up in the mountains forever, but he won't be able to block the progress of the people in the region." She saw the President glance at someone behind her and to her right.

"Thank you, Dr. Bradwell. My chief of staff is telling me I've got to move on. We'll take a look at it, but I make no promises. Anything else, young lady?"

"While we're at it, yes. Funding to support a world tour of the treasures of the Khan."

Hutchinson slapped his knees with both hands and stood up. "I'll look into it."

CHAPTER 87

At Grand Central Station, Marya went to a phone bank and dialed Liam to tell him all about her interview with the President. His phone rang and rang but no one answered. With time on her hands, she stopped at a newsstand and scanned the headlines of the newspapers carrying news about her and the Polo treasures. Most of the articles ranged from lurid to sensational.

The *Miami Enquirer* carried a story under the banner, "Professor Finds Treasure on Nudist Beaches of Dalmatia." Her hand flew to her mouth as she saw herself parading across the front page in the fuzzy green haze of the photo. She quickly put the paper back on the rack. The *National Tattler*, using a computer program to create an illusion, pasted her face over one belonging to a buxom concubine in a medieval, oriental harem. The accompanying article was headlined *The King and I* and its subtitle ran, "Mongolian emperor tutors female professor in the art of love, a shocking tale of unbridled sex in the palace of Kashgar," a completely fake story of an American woman's romantic dalliance with the mysterious figure of Temujin. She felt like wadding the paper up and throwing it in a trash can nearby.

She was less embarrassed by other coverage of her phenomenal adventure. The *New York Tribune* ran a story on the Bellardo brothers and their daring acts in Korcula. A photo embedded in the article showed a gigantic nun rolling on the ground with a tough-looking commando. She flipped through *T.V. Guide*'s news of a new prime time TV show in the survivor-reality genre. Its first contest was scheduled to take place in the Gobi and it promised to push the contestants to extremes never attempted before.

She went back to the phone bank and tried to call Liam again but still there was no answer. Disappointed, she went to the newsstand and bought the latest issue of *Newsweek* magazine. It had her face on the cover and ran a feature article six pages long. It seemed to promise a more serious treatment of her story.

She boarded the train for Boston and took her seat. After settling in, she avidly opened the magazine and began to speed-read the lead story. As the train moved out of the station, she found mention of a very recent interview of her arch-rival, Dr. Elizabeth McManus of Edinburgh University. She was jubilant as she learned that McManus actually had words of congratulations for her work. As far as McManus was concerned, she told the reporter, Bradwell's discoveries had put to rest any questions she ever had about the authenticity of Polo's *Description of the World* and she finished by saying that she had "...nothing but admiration for Dr. Bradwell." Flying along the rails to Boston, Marya put the magazine on the seat, closed her eyes and savored those last words.

A nagging sense that something was still missing flitted through her thoughts, though, and she realized that it was Liam's absence from her side that troubled her. Her happiness would have been complete even if she could only have shared some small talk with him on the phone. Why hadn't she been able to reach him?

CHAPTER 88

At home in Cambridge, Marya found a flood of messages on her answering machine and an endless number of e-mails, all congratulatory and admiring. Not one word from Liam, though. She decided to deal with the messages soon, but first she absolutely had to get in touch with him. She dialed the number at his home in Newton that he had given her, but got only a jarring ring and a message that the number had been disconnected. Puzzled, she checked the number and dialed again, but with the same result. She would have run to the computer to email him but she had no email address for him. He must have known she was home by now. Why hadn't he gotten in touch with her? She slipped into her pajamas and opened a can of soup. Sipping it from a cup at her kitchen table, she felt real worry overcome her. He should be at home, somewhere in the Boston area, certainly, but maybe he had had a problem en route? Was he injured or sick somewhere, unable to reach her?

* * * * *

She didn't sleep worrying about him all through the night. In the morning she took breakfast at a nearby café and headed for her office at the University, knowing that it would be the last time she did so. All that remained for her to do was to clean out her office and cut her ties with the department and the university. She was determined to finish as quickly and as quietly as possible, and hopefully without having words with Lafferty. Walking across the university commons, she bumped into students and colleagues who stopped her for a chat and even an autograph.

She entered her old, brick classroom building and

went upstairs. Her office was three doors down the hall from Lafferty's and unfortunately, Lafferty's door was open. As she neared it, she heard men's voices in an intense argument. She thanked God she would no longer have to put up with the creepy gang. She strode past the open door without looking in. The voices suddenly ceased. She heard the sound of chairs scraping across the floor and Lafferty's grating call behind her, "Hey, wait up, Marya. You're back! Come on back here. Come in," he said loudly from the doorway.

She stopped and turned around. "Yes. I'm back. So what?"

"What do you think you're doing, just walking by like that without a word, my dear?"

"I have nothing to talk about with you and that's the way I like it."

Ignoring her, he turned back to the others in the office and told them to arrange a seat for Marya. He rushed up to her all a-twitter and uncharacteristically took her hand. "You've got to come and have a talk with us. There's so much to tell you." She pulled her hand away but followed him back to his office, thinking she may as well get it over with.

The boys all rose when she walked in. Roache. Chen. And a new fellow, probably the Ph. D. from Brigham Young, she surmised. Lafferty surprised her as he offered her a chair, smiling. He also introduced the new recruit. "Sit, sit, sit. Marya, it's so good to see you again, back from your conquest of Europe. You have really made quite a splash." He gave a wink to the gents and they responded with grins. "We've had complete coverage or, a complete exposé on T.V., if you will, of your adventure, and I mean complete."

Marya knew immediately that he was referring to her naked escapade with Liam but she was not about to put up with his abuse and their leers. She stood up to leave. She had done nothing to feel ashamed of and every reason to be proud. "Is that why you asked me in? To ridicule me? This party's over, you clowns. I'm only here to clean out my office and get out of here, period."

Her sharp reaction brought Lafferty to his senses. "Sorry. I didn't mean to offend. Please sit down. I have a few serious things to discuss with you and, oh, congratulations on your extraordinary finds."

She sat down slowly and perched on the edge of her seat, ready to bolt at the next sign of ignorance.

"Marya, we have made some important decisions in your absence. You will be given a new contract and you will be granted tenure, of course. In addition to that, we have decided to reduce your teaching load in order for you to concentrate more on your *forte*. The department is also going to make substantial sums available for your field work to be used at your own discretion."

"Thank you, Dr. Lafferty, gentlemen," she said looking around at the others. "But, your offer comes a little too late. I've made up my mind. I would never consider working with you again. Period." She stood up. "Is that all? Don't you have any papers for me to sign? Do you have my mail?"

"Let's not talk like that, Marya. I wish you would reconsider. We want you back."

"I don't need to reconsider. I've had enough of you to last a lifetime. Sorry. Not interested. You've got to excuse me. Again, where's my mail?"

"On your desk, but..."

She turned and walked out.

CHAPTER 89

She had packed all her papers and books into her car, except for one cardboard carton full of files and a plastic bag bulging with mail. She sat at her desk for a moment to rest and gaze out the window at the commons for the last time. She would have to go through the mail soon but had little heart for the task as she thought about her departure from Harvard. She felt a surge of emptiness and she dreaded the thought of clearing out her apartment and leaving for California. Still no sign of Liam. Where could he be?

An important-looking letter from the Archaeology Department of the University of Pennsylvania slid from the bag onto the desk. She tore it open carelessly. An offer for a teaching contract and a position on a team working summers on a dig not far from Tillya Tepe in northwestern Afghanistan. She re-read it more slowly. She was familiar with the discoveries made there by a Russian archaeologist. Tillya Tepe, The Mound of Gold, a collection of burials with over 20,000 valuable artifacts, mostly gold and turquoise Bactrian-style jewelry. Tempting. I could do that, she thought. But what about us? What about Liam and me? What would he say if I asked him to come with me? The letter imposed a deadline for a response that was just three days away.

The more rational side of her mind argued against the offer. She needed time to recover from the events of the last few weeks. And why worry about what Liam would say anyhow? He was nowhere to be found. Obviously, he wasn't emotionally involved enough or didn't have the decency to get in touch with her. Worse yet, she realized he was supposed to have delivered the journal of Marco Polo to the nuns at St. Lawrence. Had he? She had trusted him enough to handle the priceless artifact and yet still had no word from him.

Suddenly she was startled by a knock behind her at her open door. "Liam!" she cried, jumping up and turning around. She felt crestfallen when she saw that it was a young lady with strawberry blonde hair and freckles. "Hello, Dr. Bradwell." She held out and shook hand with Marya. "I'm Ellen McColm, the student body president. I've come to ask you for a favor on behalf of the students. They've asked me to invite you to an impromptu ceremony and a going-away dinner in your honor. We hope you'll accept? The students are really all fired up."

Marya hesitated. "When?"

"Tomorrow night. Seven o'clock."

"That is so kind. I'd love to attend but I can't. Will you tell them for me? I have an engagement tomorrow evening."

"Whoever it is will also be welcome, I'm sure. Please, Dr. Bradwell. It would mean so much to all of us. Please. You can't leave without doing this. You mustn't."

Marya noticed a half-dozen students in the hallway behind Ellen. Her thoughts and hopes had been to get together with Liam tonight or tomorrow, not of spending the evening at some beery pub over fish and chips with a bunch of undergrads. Where the heck was Liam, though?

"I'll drive," Ellen persisted. "The food's gonna be great. Promise."

She wavered under the earnest stares of the students. What of Liam? There had been no communication from him but why should that affect her ties with her students? She couldn't do anything about that. Besides, she did not have any urgent need to rush off to California. There was no one from her family waiting for her there except for a few old school mates from long ago. She backtracked. "On second thought, Ellen, I'd be happy to accept the invitation."

At home that evening, she placed a call to Venice to learn whether Liam had visited the Convent of St. Lawrence and delivered the journal. Sister Villana answered her questions. No, no one looking like Liam had shown up at the convent recently. No, Father O'Rourke had not made any more visits to the library. No, no one had delivered a special book to them. No, they had not received any ancient journal in the mail. Nothing. *Niente.* Marya thanked the Sister and hung up. She began to cry, softly, and then in great waves.

CHAPTER 90

After a rough night, she resolved in the morning to spend the day, if necessary, tracking down Liam before going to the authorities to report a crime. The heist of the century, at least in antiquities circles, she thought. But there must be some trace of him at his home, his office or at his parents' residence. He had talked about them to her, however reluctantly and briefly, on the way down the Dalmatian Coast. Was it all a pack of lies? How could she have misjudged him? She felt stupid and blamed herself for giving in to him and trusting him with the journal. If she should see him again anywhere, she would immediately give it to him both barrels plus call the police, or both.

She started by locating his home in Newton. She found his address in a Cambridge Public Library phone book and drove over. Half an hour later, she pulled up in front of a mansion on a long, broad street lined with maples. Each of the homes in the buttoned-down neighborhood had to be worth a million, minimum, she thought. Big lawns, gardeners swarming all over the place. She got out of her car, walked up the path and rang. And rang. "No one's home," she heard a creaky voice call out from over a hedge of yews.

"Oh, hello," she replied. She saw a white-haired, bespectacled little man struggling to keep his head above the level of the hedge. "I'm looking for Mr. Di Angelo. Liam Di Angelo."

"Like I said, Miss. No one's home. The house is for sale. They left yesterday."

His words hit her like a rock. "For sale?"

"Yup."

"How do you know?"

"Word gets around. I know the realtor. He's coming over this afternoon to put up the sign."

"You said, 'they?'"

"Ayup. He left with his wife and their two kids."

Oh my God, she thought. She had been having an affair with a married man. She felt a searing pain flash through her head. "You wouldn't have any idea where they've gone, I suppose?"

"Sorry, Miss. He was a quiet one. Hardly ever had anything to do with us neighbors. Didn't fit in, I guess."

She ran to her car depressed and feeling more stupid and down on herself than the night before. She drove to the Newton Public Library and got the Boston Directory off the shelf. It was loaded with Di Angelos. She narrowed her search to four of them in the North End and quickly jotted their numbers down. In a phone booth at a nearby gas station, she stood and called each one of them. Three of them told her that she had a wrong number. No, they did not know of "a Liam Di Angelo." On the third call, a coarse man asked, "What the f…kind of name is that?" She was a bit shaken by his profanity but she dialed the last number and this time a child answered. There was a lot of noise and clatter in the background with what sounded like dishes rattling and loud orders being shouted. She could barely hear the child. A boy, maybe four or five years old. "May I speak with your mother, please, little boy?"

"She's working. She can't talk with you."

"It's important. Please call her to the phone." Then she heard a loud voice scream, "Luigi, stop that. Put that phone down and don't let me catch you playing with it again!" The connection went dead.

Exhausted, she returned to her apartment and concentrated on getting her nerves under control and herself ready for the evening with her former students. The thought of it, at this moment, just sank her deeper into depression. How could she have been so dumb? *I thought I knew him.*

CHAPTER 91

Ellen McColm skillfully maneuvered through the Back Bay traffic and into the warren of back streets of the North End. Familiar aromas greeted Marya. "Where are we having dinner?"

"Caffé Carlo. Terrific food." Ellen found a slot for her Honda Civic across the street from their destination.

Marya caught the aroma of a delicious sauce. "I think I've been here before. It was just a few weeks ago." When she saw the slightly gaudy entrance with classical pillars painted in faux marble, she remembered it well. It had been clean, cozy and unpretentious. In the main dining room there were faded mural scenes of Venice, some brick work, Venetian plaster and, oddly, wood paneling. The tables were covered with an assortment of textiles, mostly red-checkered.

"Yes, I've definitely been here before." As she entered, following Ellen, she saw the table against a sponge-painted stucco wall where she and Agarwal had last dined. The spacious dining room, with red-leather booths and many tables surrounded by padded chairs, could accommodate possibly a hundred or more on a busy night. The waiters were busy bringing appetizers, filling water glasses and carrying dishes off to the kitchen located at the far end behind two swinging doors with small circular windows. Recessed lights in the drop-tiled ceiling gave a hint of intimacy and romance to the basic working-class North End décor.

Standing near the reception desk, she even recalled details of the meal with Agarwal that night, the olive tray served with crusty bread and oil, two large home-made meatballs for appetizers, finely dressed Caesar salad, the cappuccinos, the pleasant waiters. It was nice. The owners obviously had something going for them to have lasted so long. Good authentic Italian food at a moderate price and a pleasant, if somewhat bizarre, décor that could use a makeover. Too bad her last meal here was with Agarwal. Too bad Liam had skipped out on her, she mused. Too bad this. Too bad that. She brushed a few wisps of hair from her forehead. Why was she so unlucky in love?

The place was already full of Italian families, talking loudly, toasting, waving their arms, wiping the faces of little children. To her left, were her students, about thirty of them, at several tables. They rose or waved as they caught sight of Ellen and her standing at the reception desk.

The same silver-haired, middle-aged waitress who had served her and Agarwal the last time led her to the head table of the group. Ellen followed her and claimed a seat beside her. It was elaborately decorated with flowers and a finer grade of table service than she spied on other tables.

Without sitting down, Ellen took to the podium and announced the simple program for the evening. Eat hearty and during the meal students would have a chance to say a few words about the guest of honor. Marya set her purse down and removed a shawl. She was pleasantly surprised by the group. Their smiles and laughter lifted her spirits. She was glad in the end that she had accepted the invitation. It distracted her from the ugly surprises she had had earlier in the day. She scanned the stained, worn menu. Caffé Carlo. Who was Carlo, she wondered. Looking over the entrees, she singled out Chicken Marco Polo. Why not? She place her order with the waitress.

Appetizers came and went. Wine was decanted. Student after student came to the podium to deliver straightforward praise or to needle her with some gentle humor. She laughed, at times, almost to the point of tears. During the meal, her eyes kept meeting those of the owner who wandered through the restaurant for a few moments every hour, greeting the customers. She recognized Carlo. He raised his index finger to signal that he'd soon be coming over to her table. Funny, she thought, he looked startlingly like a mature version of Liam. Were her eyes fooling her? Was she simply seeing what she wanted to see?

He came to the table, smiling broadly. "Dr. Bradwell. I knew that you would come back. Welcome to my restaurant again. This evening, I promise you the best-a meal you've ever eaten. Strictly Venetian style."

"You remembered my name. Now I truly am impressed."

"It's an honor to have such a famous celebrity grace my humble restaurant. How was-a Venice?" he asked with an endearing accent.

She sighed. "Oh, I just adored him."

"Excuse me? You met-a someone nice over there?"

"I mean I loved *it*. I loved Venice." She was flustered by his question and by the chuckles of those at her table as she tried to correct what she had said.

"After dinner, I want to show you around-a my restaurant." Carlo snapped his finger at a waiter who promptly brought a bottle of champagne and an ice bucket. "Enjoy. Compliments of-a the house." He left with a wave and went back to the kitchen.

Ellen leaned towards Marya and whispered, "Was it Liam Di Angelo?"

"What?" She was shocked by the girl's impertinence.

"It's not a secret, really. Your story is everywhere lately. So, you fell in love with him?"

"It doesn't matter how I feel about him, Ellen. He's not a part of my life any more. In fact, I could just kill him."

"Oh. Sorry." Ellen looked very disturbed at what she had heard and didn't dare ask anything more before she returned to the podium half an hour later.

While Ellen addressed the group, Marya's thoughts

roamed. She recalled her arrival in Boston in her early twenties. Winning a Woodrow Wilson Fellowship and a Fulbright scholarship to complete work on her doctorate; her field work in China, Turkey and Italy; the courses she taught; the lives she affected; the battles with her colleagues. And now, it was all over. In a blur, she accepted applause from the group, a bouquet of roses and many congratulations and good lucks as students filed past her on their way out. Ellen reminded her that she would wait for her at the table and not to hurry while Chef Carlo gave her the tour.

In the calm that followed, Carlo came over to her table and looked at her expectantly. "Well?"

"The best. Simply the best. Five stars," she said. "You were right. From the Chicken Marco Polo to the tiramisu, everything was great."

"Grazie. Now, please let me show you around." He extended his hand and led her towards the kitchen past a number of family groups who turned to look her up and down closely. "They are not being rude, Dr. Bradwell. They are my family and, if you come here again, you will get to know them all eventually," he said, gesturing at over forty smiling individuals. He roared at them, "How about a-welcoming Dr. Bradwell!"

A cry of *benvenuto* arose while some raised their glasses and shouted "*Salute*!"

As Marya looked at them, she sensed that they knew a lot more about her than she knew about them and that was, no doubt, the fault of the media. Anyhow, it was unlikely that she'd ever see them again, she thought. She smiled and made a slight bow. "I'm so happy to meet you. I can't believe that Carlo can do all this himself and still have time to socialize."

"He doesn't do this all by himself. He's got a new cook to help him," she heard one man in front of her mutter.

CHAPTER 92

Carlo gestured towards the kitchen, talking as he led her through the swinging doors. "Come, I want you to meet-a my new sous-chef. My son, Liam. I'm-a so proud of him. He's got a big-a job but he's giving it up to run-a da family business. Eh, Liam. Come-a meet this great important lady, Dr. Bradwell." He turned to Marya. "He's-a the one who cook-a da chicken Marco Polo. Tell him how much-a you enjoyed it, please."

Marya was floored when she heard Carlo mention the name. Could it be? How many times would one come across a Liam in an Italian restaurant in the North End? She had to check. "I'm sorry, Carlo. I didn't get your last name when I was here several weeks ago."

"It's Di Angelo. I'm-a Carlo Di Angelo."

She almost fainted and had to grasp his arm. She looked around the kitchen. There were three waitresses, a waiter and two dishwashers making a terrible clatter that echoed off the walls. Had this somehow been the place that she called to from the gas station in Newton? She spied a chef wearing a toque, his back to the central aisle of the kitchen, his head partly concealed behind large pots and pans dangling from overhead hooks, studying two new orders that had just come in.

"Liam!" Carlo shouted again over the din. He pointed to the cook behind the stainless steel counter. "Thatsa my son. Liam!"

When Liam turned around and spotted her with his father, he flashed a big smile and tore off his apron.

"Liam," she said, her mouth dry. She looked at Carlo. "I'm sorry. I don't want to talk to him. I'm out of here." She turned and headed for the swinging doors.

She heard Carlo call out to her with panic in his voice. Something about the swinging doors. She ignored Carlo and pushed the left swinging door just as a busboy entered, holding a large tray of water glasses above his head. Her push sent the busboy reeling backwards. He tried to keep his balance but the tray tipped and crashed to the floor with an explosion that made all heads in the restaurant turn.

She tried the door on the right and flew through it into the dining room with all eyes on her.

The busboy got up off the floor, dazed and hurried to pick up what he could with his hands while a waiter ran for a broom and a mop. Some customers actually came over from their tables to assist the busboy and to ask if Marya was all right. She pulled away and tried to signal to Ellen. Ellen waved back.

By this time, Liam appeared behind one of the doors, peered through and slowly pushed it open. He caught up with Marya and took her hand. She shook free of him. "Leave me alone. Where have you been? Why didn't you call me? You're just a scoundrel."

Carlo stood by Liam and objected. "He's not a scoundrel. He's-a my son. A good boy. He's a-done this all-a for you."

She confronted both father and son. "Oh really? A good son? Did he tell you that he has stolen a valuable artifact? Did he tell you that he has no regard for his wife and two children and has been playing me for a fool? He's a married man but he sure doesn't act like it! Can you imagine how I felt when I found out? Everywhere I gò, people will be pointing at me like I'm some kind of scarlet strumpet!"

Carlo looked puzzled. He turned to Liam, "What does-a she mean trumpet? Whatsa this all about?" Then he turned to Marya. "You talk-a crazy now. Liam has-a no family. He's not-a married. I wish he was a-married. Instead, he's-a selling his house in Newton to live-a here with us in the North End!"

Marya still had her doubts. She was confused and terribly embarrassed under the gaze of the huge Di Angelo family who were still looking her up and down. He hadn't contacted her in two whole days since her return and had not come clean with her. She knew that he had violated her trust, too, when he failed to return Polo's journal to the convent. He was obviously selling out and skipping town and she felt he had betrayed her outrageously. "Why don't you just give me the journal?" she said, jabbing his chest with her index finger. "A good son, my foot!"

"The journal? Sure. No problem." Liam signaled to a waitress who was standing by, holding a package. He took it from her and handed it over to Marya. "I kept it because I wanted to let two experts I always use authenticate it. They say it's the real deal. I did it because I realized you wouldn't likely have another chance with it." He tried to place his arm over her shoulder but she shrugged it off.

"What about your wife and kids?" she asked, backing away from the circle of customers and staff near the swinging doors. "Try to deny that! You've disgraced me and you should feel ashamed of yourself!"

"What wife? I'm not married and never have been. And I sure as heck don't have any kids. My dad just told you. Don't you believe us?"

"No. I don't. Your neighbor told me all about her yesterday. He had just seen you and her together the day before with your two kids."

"That wasn't my wife. That was my sister, Angel, and her two boys, little Luigi and Pasquale. They're over there with her right now," he said, pointing to a table near the back wall. He waved them over. "Luigi is five and Pasquale is seven. Here they are. And this is my sister and her husband, Nick. This was supposed to be a surprise for you. I've been working like a slave for two days, closing down the house in Newton and working on this banquet for you with my dad. Oh, shoot. What a mess I've made of it. I'm sorry, Marya."

She stood there trying to sort out what Liam said as

the young couple and their children waited, looking up at her. Her heart began to melt when little Luigi tugged at her sleeve.

Liam knelt down in front of Luigi. He took both Marya's hand and Luigi's. "Please don't be angry, Marya. I did this all for you. This is what you wanted, right? Didn't you ask me for a proper introduction to the Di Angelo family?"

Her heart was about to break at the sight. A smile formed on her lips.

Liam got up and drew her into his arms. He tossed his toque to little Luigi. "Hold this little fella, will you?"

Luigi took it and put it on his head. It slid down, covering his eyes. He marched about with arms outstretched, groping, playing Blind Man's Bluff. He found Liam and Marya and tugged at their hands. "Kiss her! Kiss her," the little boy taunted.

Liam gave her a tight hug and a long kiss. Then he whispered in her ear that he would love for them to return to Venice together. "Let's both take the journal back to the nuns. I'm sure they could use the money right now."

Marya whispered back that she would love to and added that after Venice, they should just keep going."

"Keep going? Where to?"

"Afghanistan."

"Afghanistan?"

"Yes. Why not? It's a beautiful, romantic country. You'd love it."

"I'm not so sure. Weren't the Russians horribly defeated in a war there just a few years back? You think it's safe?"

"Of course, silly. Trust me," she said with an affectionate nibble on his ear. Still in his embrace, she looked at all the beaming faces of Liam's extended family and gave them a wink while the whole Di Angelo clan rose and broke into applause.

AFTERWORD

The inspiration for *Gold of the Khan* came to me when one simple image appeared in my mind out of the blue in the summer of 2002. From it grew all the rest of the story. It was an image of a young couple in a European plaza, turning around and looking at the tall belltower of a church. In *Gold of the Khan*, that scene is found in Chapter 79, as Marya and Liam walk out of a cathedral onto a square. I don't know why such a scene came to mind but I do know that it caused me to take up the pen and write a novel for the first time. Eventually, I located that square in the real town of Korcula, on the island by the same name along the coast of Croatia.

Gold of the Khan blends medieval and ancient history with the fictional adventure of the heroine, Marya Bradwell, in the 1990s. I would like to take the opportunity here to distinguish between fact and fiction as used in this story in some of the more important areas.

In the Prologue, tomb raiders break into a burial mound in the Ukraine. In fact, ancient Scythian burials, called kurgans, have been found in that region and the human remains in them are often associated with elaborate gold artifacts. The 20th century events that took place there in the Prologue are entirely made up, however.

All the characters of the story are fictional. The character of the heroine was inspired by my wife whose grandparents were from Croatia.

The main elements of the treasure, the Golden Tablets of Command, were real and they did serve as passports across the vast Mongol Empire. I believe that a few of these *pai tzu*, as they are called in Chinese, are still in existence, one of them in the Hermitage Museum in Russia. None have been found in Croatia. If the tablets were, indeed, a cubit in length, then the gold alone in them would be worth millions.

There is no personal journal of Marco Polo, as far as we know. Polo's influential book of travels covers such broad territory in such great detail, however, that it is almost inconceivable that he did not keep a journal or diary of some sort. Marya's readings in his journal are, therefore, completely fictitious. Her readings in Polo's book of travels are only loosely based on the general itinerary of Polo, his father and his uncle.

It may well be believed that Polo returned to Europe via the Strait of Hormuz on a large, Chinese four-masted junk. Cheng Ho's voyages during the Ming Dynasty, which followed the Mongol Yuan Dynasty, are historically true and Chinese naval capabilities were impressive. They would have created a sensation and changed history dramatically had Cheng Ho taken his fleet around Africa's Cape of Good Hope to Europe.

Polo's stopover in Sumatra, Indonesia is briefly mentioned in the story. I have recently seen bold banners there that advertise commercial products under the name of Marco Polo. The locals seem to believe that there is some basis for believing that Marco passed that way long ago.

The British Museum has a small collection of gold Scythian artifacts exhibited in Plexiglas-protected cases. The Gabrielli Sandwirth in Venice is a real hotel but employees and events I've portrayed at that locale are products of my imagination.

There is no emporium in Venice run by the Bellardos. There is no Convent of San Lorenzo in Venice today, though there may have been one in medieval times.

Boston's Italian North End has many restaurants but

Carlo's Caffe is not one of them. It is a fictitious composite of restaurants.

A French student actually did find a secret passage into a European convent library and managed to make off with some valuable ancient tomes. After the nuns had a surveillance camera installed, he was caught making another attempt to steal from their collection. He was arrested and the nuns recovered their precious books.

The very last meeting between Padre Giustiniani with Polo was true in only a few details. Padre Giustiniani's letter in this story is fictitious.

The gold artifacts, including the gold-lined skull that Bellardo showed Liam and Marya, are based on descriptions of authentic Scythian gold pieces.

At the time of writing, (2002-2003) the U.S. State Department had issued travel advisories against travel in Tajikistan.

Some scholars question whether Marco Polo ever went to the Orient and they cite several missing items that should have appeared in his book but did not: tea, foot-binding and the Great Wall. Therefore, they question whether he really went to the Orient at all.

The Cathedral of St. Mark in Korcula is real and is an impressive church, but I have modified the architecture, the décor and its setting in a plaza for the purposes of this story. I enlarged the square in front of St. Mark's. Korcula is a medieval town crowded onto a little peninsula. There is little open space to be found in its confines like the plaza I describe in *Gold of the Khan*. Korcula is well worth visiting. A gem of the Adriatic, it is a compact version of Dubrovnik, but less crowded with tourists and all the more to be appreciated.

The people of Korcula claim Marco Polo as a native son. So do the people of Venice. I am inclined to think that Marco Polo was originally from Korcula. There is a quaint lane in this town that features the home of Marco Polo or, rather, the space where it used to be. You can climb a tower to the loggia and from that scenic vantage point, look out on the straits that separate the island from the mainland. You can also look directly into the belltower of St. Mark's practically next door and see steel supports under the cupola that help keep it from collapsing.

Mei Hua is a purely fictitious character. So is the Khan and his unique plan to restore the old Mongol Empire, capturing parts of China such as Xinjiang Province and Mongolia, and using Chinese oil resources to finance his central Asian empire. Given the heavy-handed way China rules these semi-autonomous regions, such a plan would be suicidal.

The Khan's compound/palace four hours out of Kashgar is a complete fiction. I personally decorated it, right down to the bronze horse. Id Kah square in Kashgar is real and so is its long-lived bazaar.

The unhealthy dependence of Afghanistan's economy on poppy farming for the export of opium is a fact; so is America's dependence on its derivatives.

The Chinese expression, kowtow, literally means 'knock head' and refers to the requirement of those invited into the emperor's presence to kneel three times and bump one's head on the floor three times with each kneeling. That was SOP even for the Mongols who adopted Chinese customs. It was always a sore point between the Chinese and foreigners before the 1911 revolution that destroyed the 2,000 year old imperial system.

The Croatians are a remarkable people in many ways. They had traditionally been great navigators and seamen. They have created some great wines. As mentioned earlier, many believe that the Polos came from the Croatian island of Korcula. People of Croatian descent are scattered around the world and can now be found in such remote locations as the southern tip of South America and, of course,

Eureka, California, where my wife's grandparents ended up. Croatia's Minister of Culture had reason to crow about his people the way he did in the story. In fact, all of the former territories that once made up Yugoslavia are incredibly rich in cultural and historical treasures.

By the way, try to see if you can make povitica, the apple and cinnamon pastry that Liam first tasted in Korcula. I should add that the Slovenians, Croatia's neighbors, also make a similar, delicious pastry called potica that, likewise, should be on everyone's bucket list of good desserts to try.

Little Luigi is a real person. He and his generation will someday soon inherit the world we pass on to him—one in which China becomes an increasingly important player on the international scene.

Made in the USA
Middletown, DE
11 January 2025